Midnight Requisition 2
Amateur Night

Holly Copella

To Avery Ortiz—
For unknowingly shaping my characters

ACKNOWLEDGMENTS

Copella Books: First Paperback Edition 2019
Cover Artist: Daniela Owergoor
Dani-owergoor.deviantart.com
Cover Model: ASDF_MEDIA
Stock Photography by NeoStock www.neo-stock.com
Printed by KDP, an Amazon.com Company

PUBLISHER'S NOTE

Chapter 1

Thursday, June 19th. The abandoned casino and hotel was located in the middle of nowhere, which was just north of Cripple Creek, Colorado. The building seemed structurally sound on the outside, although the old driveway was mostly grown over and the property lacked any sign of landscaping. When plans for the highly anticipated factory were scrapped, the highway was diverted away from the nearby town, and the owner's plans for the casino fell apart along with it. A small farm was oddly placed not far from the casino. Had the casino been finished, the farm would have been sitting on the edge of what should have been the parking lot.

The enormous, empty casino floor seemed to have barely survived a war of some kind. The war-torn room consisted of over thirty demolished table games that had once circled the center of the room. Above the large area where the table games were once located, a cathedral ceiling with a glass skylight allowed sunlight in and brightened the room. There were rows and rows of slot machines on both sides of the casino floor. Most of the machines along the aisle were riddled with bullet holes. The bank of slot machines in the center was completely torn apart as if a bomb had gone off and ripped them to shreds. The boarded up back door and tall windows were reduced to glassless, metal frames. The abandoned casino floor was left in ruins with massive, dried bloodstains covering a large portion of the gaudy carpeting.

A handsome man barely over the legal drinking age was tied with duct tape to a slot machine. The chair was bolted to the floor in front of the video poker machine on the end. The young man, Kane Wayland, had an almost steampunk sort of appeal about him. His brown hair was kept short although moderately spiky on top, and his neatly trimmed beard looked more like a five o'clock shadow. He was slightly shorter than average, being a tick over five-foot-eight. Kane wasn't built very muscular and his moderately worn clothes kept in theme with his whole steampunk look. Two men stood over Kane where he was tied. He stared at the men through innocent blue eyes. The corner of Kane's bottom lip was swollen and bleeding, and his cheek was red, indicating he'd been roughed up by one or both of the men.

"Quid pro quo," Kane announced while seeming unusually calm. He crossed his right ankle over his left knee and attempted to get comfortable for his interrogation from the man holding him captive. "I answered all of your questions. How about you answer some of mine?"

"Not how this game works, kid," the first man announced while flexing his sore hand. His knuckles were already scraped and bruised.

"You should probably put some ice on that," Kane informed the man then shifted his attention to the second man. "Look. Just tell me what I want to know, and neither of you will get hurt."

The men exchanged humored looks of disbelief then returned their attention to the man securely duct taped to the chair.

"Kid, you're tied up," the second man informed him. "How do you expect to put a hurting on either of us?"

Kane removed his ankle from its propped position over his knee and attempted to shift in the chair. The duct tape around his shoulders attaching him to the back of the chair easily hindered his movement.

"Well," Kane casually announced. "Firstly, I never said I would be the one hurting you. Secondly, you know, you didn't do a very good job at binding me."

Kane swiftly spun the swivel chair to the left and kicked the first man in the knee. He immediately spun the chair to the right and kicked the second man in the ribs before he could react. Both men gasped with surprise and some agony before jumping back and out of his reach.

"And on a swivel chair," Kane reported while shaking his head with disgrace. "I honestly don't know what you were thinking."

"You're going to pay for that," the first man snarled and lunged for him.

Kane whirled the chair around and kicked the man in the groin. As the first man went down the second man pulled a gun from his hidden shoulder holster and aimed it at Kane. Kane was now motionless as he stared at the gun.

"You guys really don't fight fair," he scoffed and shook his head. "I can kick your collective asses with both hands *literally* tied behind my back, so now you have to pull a weapon on me just to make the fight even less fair."

"Life isn't fair," the man scoffed. "Sorry, kid, we've wasted enough time with you already. It's time we parted company."

Kane groaned with annoyance and shook his head. "Typical dime store cowboys," he muttered. "I'm tired of playing games with you two momma's boys." He stared at the first man, who finally straightened after recovering from his groin shot. "Can we end this now?"

"Gladly," the first man snarled and was about to remove his own gun.

Kane met the man's gaze with a serious look and raised his brow. "I wasn't talking to *you*," he scoffed.

The man looked over his shoulder. An attractive, dark-haired woman in her mid-thirties stood directly behind the man. She spun into a high, roundhouse kick and nailed him in the face. He struck the side of the video poker machine and sank to the floor.

Kane chuckled with humor at the fallen man. "Ha, made you look," he cried out.

The woman threw an aggressive kick just past Kane's face and knocked the gun from the second man's hand. She grabbed onto the back of Kane's chair and put her weight on it as she kicked the man with both feet, nailing him in the chest. He flew backward into the nearby machine, striking it hard with his backside. She removed a switchblade knife from her pocket, flicked it open with one hand, and sliced the duct tape binding Kane's wrists and the layered tape holding his arms immobile against the chair. She flicked the switchblade shut as Kane freed himself and sprang to his feet.

"What took you so long?" Kane demanded while casting several glares at his partner.

"I had to avoid being seen by their two friends," the woman snarled back.

Macbeth, or Mac as she preferred to be called, wore her long, dark hair pulled back into a neat ponytail with a stray lock falling across her face. Her athletic build indicated she worked out extensively. Although her fresh face and sporty frame suggested she was a high maintenance, classy woman, the truth was less flattering. Kane had another nickname for her.

"I could have used your help about ten minutes ago, badger," Kane snapped. "They don't have any information. They don't even work for Sal Romano."

"No kidding," she snarled while searching the first man's pockets. "We walked in on someone's drug dealing operation."

"I didn't find any evidence that suggests Sal Romano deals in drugs," Kane informed her.

Mac glared up at Kane from where she crouched alongside the unconscious man. "That's because he doesn't," she insisted. "They aren't Sal's men. Listen to me; you'll live longer."

She found what she was looking for and removed the roll of duct tape from the man's jacket pocket. Kane marveled at how swiftly Mac bound the unconscious man's wrists behind his back. She seemed a little too skilled for comfort.

"Sal Romano is a dead end," Mac scoffed without looking at Kane.

She tossed Kane the roll of duct tape, which he immediately used to bind the second man, who was quite possibly dead.

"He knows something," Kane insisted while casting stray looks of disappointment at her. "If you hadn't burned your bridges with Sal Romano, I'm sure he would have told you something. You wouldn't even try to talk to the guy."

"Excuse me for not gracefully accepting my termination from my employers," she snapped back then straightened and glared at him. "Give up your little quest for Zack Kinsley. I told you; the guy is probably dead. He's used up all of his nine lives." She shook her head with annoyance. "I don't understand your obsession with him."

"You don't need to understand it," Kane informed her and straightened. He raked his fingers through his hair and sighed. "Just another dead end. I'll take a break if it makes you happy."

"Yes, that would make me happy," Mac remarked while glaring at him. "We need jobs that actually pay the rent."

"Fine," he reluctantly announced. "Let's get out of here before something else happens."

They headed across the casino floor for the open door that led into the hotel lobby and stopped when they saw several men with automatic weapons heading their way. Kane shut the door and turned to face Mac with little emotion.

"Uh, hide."

Both bolted away from the interior door and ran across the war-torn casino floor.

Chapter 2

Outside Cripple Creek, Colorado. The small motel just on the edge of town looked like a throwback from an Alfred Hitchcock film. The black rental SUV parked in front of the small motel office, which was at the end of ten cabins lined in an "L" shape. Three men and one woman got out of the SUV. The woman in her early twenties paused to assess the small, downtrodden motel.

"I'm not sure if this is nostalgic or just creepy," the young woman announced to her three travel companions.

The young woman, Scorpio Wayland, was mature looking despite being only twenty-two years old. Her long, dark hair was French braided to give her an added look of maturity, although her black leather jacket and black boots made her look mildly menacing. She was moderately petite barely making five-foot-four, but she was excessively toned, indicating the young woman was fairly athletic. The oldest of the three men, possibly in his early thirties, approached her and took in the surrounding area.

"This was the last place your brother used the credit card under his assumed identity," the man announced. "He checked in just two days ago."

Although undeniably handsome, Rayner Roderick had a nerdish genius sort of look about him. His light brown hair was cut short, and his face was clean-shaven to the point of meticulous. Despite that his travel companions were casually dressed; Rayner wore moderately expensive clothes. He attempted to look less professional by wearing an expensive leather jacket rather than a suit jacket, but he couldn't hide his obviously wealthy appearance. The remaining two men in their group, Ben Stone and Blake Maverick, stood on the opposite side of the SUV and stared at their travel companions over the roof of the vehicle.

"Well," Maverick announced to them. "Are we booking a room at the Bates Motel or what?"

Blake Maverick was in his mid to late twenties and stood just a tick over six-foot. Maverick was devilishly handsome with flowing dark brown hair in a short, businessman cut. Although not as tall and strapping as his friend standing alongside him, he had a solid, athletic build. Even dressed casually in faded jeans and a white button shirt, Maverick still looked like a hitman for the mob.

Rayner groaned his disapproval just loud enough for Scorpio to hear. "We should have left them back in Maine," he muttered.

"They offered to help find my brother," she reminded him. "I know it was a long flight, but we'll all feel a little better after we settle in and have something to eat."

Scorpio headed for the small office attached to the motel. Rayner reluctantly followed. Maverick and Stone joined them on the porch outside the office door. Ben Stone was a handsome African-American man in his mid to late twenties with a smooth, clean-shaven face, and short black hair. Although not professional wrestler muscular, Stone was about six-foot-four and built solid giving him a moderately intimidating appearance. Despite his height and impressive build, his charming smile indicated he was fun loving rather than serious.

"This place is charming," Stone announced while looking around and offered a playful grin. "Think they'd ever seen a black man before?"

Maverick eyed his taller counterpart with a surprised look. "You're black?"

Stone gave Maverick a playful shove toward the office door. "Seek professional help," he announced.

All four entered the small motel office. What was supposed to be the lobby wasn't much bigger than most public restrooms. The small front desk took up most of the back wall with a door leading to a private office behind it. The tiny lobby had a small table with two chairs near the window, and a small coffee station set up alongside a rack of travel brochures. The area in front of the desk was almost too small to fit all four comfortably. It appeared as if Norman Bates was on his lunch break while 'mother' tended the front desk. The surly looking woman in her mid to late fifties seemed almost bored and possibly bothered that she had to put her magazine aside to tend to potential guests.

"Two rooms?" she questioned without so much as an insincere smile.

Maverick and Stone turned to the coffee station and helped themselves to coffee. They purposely forced Rayner to deal with the less than pleasant woman. Rayner put on his best smile and moved closer to the front desk.

"Yes, we'd like two rooms," Rayner announced.

"How many nights?" the older woman huffed while typing into what had to be the oldest computer still functioning in the civilized world.

"Two nights," Scorpio interjected and moved closer to Rayner and the desk, which was quite a squeeze considering there wasn't much room to move.

"Twenty-five dollars per room per night," the middle-aged woman replied.

Rayner cast a look at Maverick and Stone, who purposely didn't pay attention. He then removed his wallet and handed the woman his credit card. Scorpio smiled sweetly and patted Rayner's arm.

"Don't worry," she informed him. "They're paying for dinner." Scorpio then focused her attention on the unpleasant woman behind the desk. "I'm supposed to meet my brother here. Can you tell me what room Kane Templeton is staying in?"

The cranky woman's eyes suddenly lit up, and she immediately smiled. "Kane?" she asked as if coming to life. "I gave him and his lady friend the end cabin. They're in cabin number ten."

Stone and Maverick finally turned, focused their attention on the clerk, and appeared interested. Scorpio raised her brows in response to the woman's words.

"Lady friend?" Scorpio suddenly asked. "I wasn't aware he was seeing anyone."

"It won't last," the woman announced and waved her hand. "She's not the least bit friendly."

Scorpio couldn't help but wonder what the surly clerk's idea of friendly was since she didn't come across very friendly herself.

"I'll give you cabins eight and nine, so you can be next to one another," the clerk announced then handed them the old-fashioned keys on large, plastic keyrings that had little chance of fitting in anyone's pocket.

"I didn't notice his car out front," Scorpio continued with her charade then considered the comment. "Actually, I didn't notice any cars out front. Did he mention where he was going or when he'd be back?"

"Oh, they left about two hours ago," the clerk informed her and nodded to the road. "They were heading to the abandoned casino."

"Abandoned casino?" Rayner asked with surprise.

"Kane said he was meeting the owner there regarding the demolition," the clerk announced. "The place is being torn down this coming Monday. I assumed he was with the demolition crew. He gave me his business card."

The clerk searched the desk then handed Scorpio a red business card with black writing on it. It read "Midnight Requisition" and contained a phone number. Scorpio flashed the card to Rayner, who only needed to see the phone number briefly to remember it.

"My brother has his hands in everything," Scorpio informed the clerk, which wasn't necessarily a lie. "If it's real estate, he's up to his eyeballs in it."

"Yeah," the clerk announced while grinning. "That's exactly what he said."

Scorpio wasn't too surprised.

"Where is this abandoned casino?" Rayner asked.

"Just follow this road about ten miles then make the first right," the clerk announced. "It's about twenty miles north. You can't miss it."

"Thanks," Rayner announced.

Scorpio collected the two large room keys, and all four left the office. They approached their rental car and paused before it.

"Abandoned casino?" Scorpio remarked with some concern. "What the hell is Kane up to?"

Rayner opened his nylon briefcase, removed his laptop, and set it on the car hood. He typed into the keyboard, waited only a second, and then indicated the screen to Scorpio and the two men.

"There's an old casino north of here," Rayner informed her. "It was built but never completed when the town didn't boom as expected." He scanned the article. "The casino is owned by Sal Romano, a millionaire and suspected mafia kingpin. There was an incident at the casino involving the caretakers and some not-so-friendly mobsters. The clerk was correct. The casino is being demolished next week."

"So now Kane is sniffing around the mob?" Scorpio demanded then groaned and rolled her eyes. "If he's not dead already; I'm going to kill him!"

"We'd better head for this abandoned casino right away," Maverick insisted.

"I'll take the car to the room and unload the bags," Stone announced and held his hand in the air.

Scorpio tossed Stone one of the keys, which he easily caught in his large hand. "Leave our supply bag in the trunk," she announced then frowned. "We may need a few of our *toys*."

Stone jumped inside the SUV and drove to the end of the motel. While they waited for Stone, Rayner returned his laptop to his case and slung it over his shoulder.

"We need a plan when we reach this abandoned casino," Rayner insisted.

"My brother takes off for God-knows-where in search of our not so dead father, fakes his death, and gets involved with the mob," Scorpio remarked then shook her head and cast a stern look at Rayner. "When the hell did he have time to find a girlfriend?"

"Maybe she's with the mafia," Maverick suggested while leaning against the nearby support beam on the porch. "Sort of an undercover thing."

"I wouldn't be surprised," Scorpio huffed while frowning. "He's digging his grave a little deeper every day. What the hell did he get himself into?"

Chapter 3

Kane and Mac crouched behind a large row of slot machines while listening to the men entering the casino through the main doors.

"What the hell did I get us into?" Kane muttered.

"I'm starting to doubt your abilities as a leader," Mac huffed under her breath while attempting to peer between the slot machines.

The newly arrived men called out to their associates. Since the men they sought were bound and had duct tape over their mouths, they wouldn't be responding anytime soon, but it wouldn't be long before they discovered the bound men and realized they weren't alone.

"They're going to find the men we left bound and gagged," Kane whispered to Mac as he shifted looks around the area. "When they do find them, they're going to sweep the casino floor for us."

"Tell me you have a plan," Mac demanded while keeping watch for the approaching men.

"Head to higher ground," he responded.

"There is no higher ground," Mac snapped back while glaring at him. "It's a cathedral ceiling."

"I was speaking metaphorically," Kane remarked.

"Maybe I'll put my foot up your ass," she snapped hotly. "And I mean that literally; not metaphorically."

"There's a side entrance not far from here," he informed her. "We can probably make it to that door while remaining hidden and slip out unnoticed. We just have to hope they don't find the--"

"Over there," one of the men cried out.

"--tied men," Kane reluctantly finished his sentence. He frantically pointed Mac toward the slot machines against the far wall.

They kept low and hurried toward the end of the slot machines then stopped to peer around the corner. They could see the side door just a few yards ahead of them. They made a dash for the door, hoping the new arrivals would be too busy cutting their friends loose to notice them escaping. Kane pushed on the door. It didn't open.

Mac appeared horrified. "What's wrong?"

He grimaced and looked at her. "It's locked."

"So?" she demanded. "Unlock it. Certainly, you know how to pick a lock."

Kane removed a small case from his pocket. "I have the tools," he announced in a hushed tone. "I haven't gotten around to researching how to use them."

Mac groaned, snatched the case from him, and removed the small tools. "Some mastermind," she scoffed in a whisper. "Can't even pick a lock."

"Uh, Mac," Kane announced.

"What?" she snarled softly then looked behind her.

Two men stood before them with their automatic weapons aimed at them. Kane raised his hands in the air.

"This day officially sucks," Mac muttered, dropped the lock pick tools, and placed her hands in the air while following Kane's lead.

§

Twenty minutes later, Kane and Mac were bound with duct tape now back-to-back in two chairs before the slot machines. Since the chairs were bolted to the floor, they weren't going anywhere. The two men they had earlier injured left while their two partners remained in the casino standing guard over them.

"You picked a bad day to be snooping around," the man announced to them. "In case you hadn't heard, this place is scheduled for demolition on Monday."

"The sign out front was sort of a spoiler alert," Kane remarked with little emotion and casually crossed his ankle to his knee.

The man standing over him was smart enough to keep his distance from Kane's feet.

"I have my own spoiler alert for you," the man remarked. "The building is going down now."

They heard the heavy machinery start outside the boarded doors and windows in the back of the casino.

"It'll take the construction cleanup crew months to find the two of you beneath all the rubble," the man continued while grinning.

Kane's phone rang in his pants pocket. He appeared surprised when he heard the familiar ringtone. Mac attempted to look at the man whose back she was tied against.

"You left your ringer on?" Mac suddenly cried out in anger. "What idiot leaves their phone ringer on when they're on a stakeout?"

Mac's cell phone suddenly chimed in and rang as well. She looked at her jacket pocket with some surprise.

"I didn't leave the ringer on," Kane insisted with some annoyance. "I swear I had it on vibrate. And speaking of idiots; what's your excuse?"

Both men standing over them were humored with their bickering.

"It would seem we gave you more credit for intelligence than you deserved," the first man announced.

As the second man laughed with him, both their cell phones rang in their pockets. Each man removed his cell phone and looked at the caller ID. Both showed caller 'unknown'. The first man pressed 'talk' and placed the phone to his ear.

"Who is this?" he demanded into the phone.

"What do you mean?" one of his associates on the other end demanded in response. "You called me, you idiot!"

"I didn't call you," he snapped back. "You called me. What's going on out there?"

"You said you'd call when it's all clear," the man on the other end continued. "Is it clear?"

He was about to shout into the phone when he heard his own voice speaking in response. "Clear."

"Okay," the man from the other end replied and disconnected the call.

They heard the heavy machinery rev and move just outside the back, boarded doors and windows.

"No, it's not clear," the man yelled into the phone and hurried to the end of the aisle without lowering the cell phone. "Damn it, stand down!"

An automated voice was heard over his cell phone. "If you'd like to make a call, please hang up and try redialing your number."

He disconnected the call and pressed the call button for his man outside. As the phone was answered, he heard a loud gasping sound. A thunderous crack echoed throughout the room as the entire building seemed to vibrate. The bulldozer crashed through the outside wall and didn't stop until it hit a support beam just before the mangled remains that was once the table game pit. Both men ran into the open aisle and stared at the bulldozer that still ran despite lacking forward momentum. The man at the wheel was slumped in his seat with blood saturating his debris-covered body. As the dust settled, they saw a woman standing in the massive opening. The sun glimmered off the steel blades of her dual samurai swords.

Both men aimed their assault rifles at her and opened fire, creating more debris. When the debris settled, she was gone. They heard a strange, metallic clunk and swiftly turned toward the bulldozer. Scorpio appeared on top of the bulldozer. As the men fired at her, she somersaulted off the heavy equipment with a sword in each hand, landed gracefully, and immediately sprang up before the two men while slashing crisscross with both swords. Both men dropped their weapons and clutched their bleeding throats. Scorpio watched them fall then twirled her swords and crossed the casino as if she were walking through the park.

Gunfire was heard coming from the interior corridor outside the casino. Once the firing ceased, Maverick and Stone entered with their newly acquired assault rifles. They lovingly caressed their new toys.

"Take out two or more bad guys," Stone announced cheerfully, "win free weapons."

They approached the aisle where Kane was tied facing them. He stared at them with some surprise and near amusement. Mac attempted to look behind her but couldn't turn her head far enough.

"What is it?" Mac demanded. "Who's there?"

Kane suddenly laughed while grinning. "It's my sister!"

Scorpio stood before her brother while Stone and Maverick cut them free from their duct tape binding. Scorpio replaced her swords to the leather sheath holsters strapped across her back then glared at her brother and shook her head. Once he was free, Kane sprang to his feet and happily hugged her. She didn't return the embrace, but it didn't seem to bother him. He then pulled back while grinning.

"You have no idea how happy I am to see you," Kane exclaimed.

Now that she was cut loose, Mac turned to get her first look at Kane's sister. Without emotion, Scorpio punched Kane in the stomach. He groaned and doubled over while clutching his mid-section.

"I call foul. Timeout," Kane gasped and attempted to make a timeout sign. "Unnecessary roughness."

Mac smirked and nodded her approval. "Yeah, I like her."

Chapter 4

Kane and Mac joined Scorpio's team as they left the casino through the large opening left from the bulldozer. Kane placed his arm around his sister's shoulder and attempted to hug her as they walked. She was quick to brush him off her shoulder. Her disinterest in his displays of affection didn't deter him any. Mac, Maverick, and Stone watched the brother and sister duo with great interest.

"How did you find us?" Kane asked while still reeling from the amazing save.

"You mean after you faked your own death?" Scorpio demanded with irritation. "Or how did we find you here in Cripple Creek?"

"Both, actually," Kane announced excitedly while grinning. He then turned serious. "I didn't want you to think I was dead, you know. When I discovered someone ordered a hit on me, I thought it best to stay away from you and home. I didn't want to involve you."

"I was involved, believe me," Scorpio scoffed. "But that's a long story."

Kane stopped her and offered his most sincere, sympathetic look. "I heard about Cal," he announced delicately. "I'm really sorry."

Scorpio frowned and continued walking. "Yeah, me too," she replied. "That's part of the long story."

They headed into the woods and hiked out of view until they reached Kane's car where it had been carefully hidden. Scorpio's rental SUV was parked alongside Kane's car. Rayner had already packed up his laptop and waited for them by the car. Scorpio indicated the handsome computer geek a few yards ahead of them.

"Rayner has been tracking you since before we left Maine," Scorpio informed her brother. "The front desk clerk at the motel pointed us here. Interestingly enough, I told the guys to park here. That's when we discovered your car. Rayner ran the plates on the cars parked in front of the casino, and we realized you'd gotten yourself into something bad." Scorpio leaned against the car and flashed a smile at Rayner. "Rayner was able to hack into every cell phone within the building. When the phones rang, that gave us everyone's location."

Kane chuckled and eyed his sister's three travel companions. "I can't believe you traveled across the entire country for me," he announced and again hugged her.

She pushed him away. "Stop that," Scorpio scolded. "I came halfway across the country to kick your ass for what you put your family through."

"Sure you did," Kane replied with a knowing smile.

Once they exchanged a round of introductions and the standard pleasantries, Scorpio eyed Mac.

"So you're Kane's girlfriend, huh?" she remarked and attempted a polite smile. "Did that happen before or after we were led to think he'd died?"

"He's not my boyfriend," Mac corrected while folding her arms across her chest and seemed offended by the insinuation. "We're business associates. Nothing more."

"It's true," Kane insisted while grinning playfully and indicated Mac. "She hates me."

Mac rolled her eyes and groaned.

"Your business? Midnight Requisition," Scorpio scoffed and shook her head. "I'm not surprised. I've heard enough of that name to last me a lifetime." She then eyed her brother. "What exactly is it your company does?"

"We're sort of like private detectives but not officially," he replied while grinning.

"Don't believe him," Mac announced with less enthusiasm. "We're glorified babysitters. We've had two assignments in the short time we've been working together. Both were bodyguard jobs."

Scorpio nodded then eyed her brother. "Is this what you do now?" she asked then raised her brow. "What about the hotel?"

"I haven't abandoned the hotel," Kane informed her. "I just want to spread my wings a little. You know, see the world."

"Worry your family to death," Scorpio muttered under her breath. "You need to call Grandma and tell her you're okay. She'll want to hear it from you. Probably rip you a new one while she's at it."

"I'll call Grandma and Grandpa," he insisted and waved her off. "As I said, I wanted to make sure I wasn't putting anyone at risk by showing up alive."

Scorpio tensed. She didn't want to tell him the entire sordid story about what happened back home, but she would have to tell him sooner rather than later. Either way, he wouldn't take the news well. Kane seemed unusually tense as well, although she didn't know why.

"Can I have a word with you a moment?" Kane asked but didn't give her time to respond.

He grabbed her arm and pulled her away from the others before she had a chance to protest. He stopped her several yards away and eyed the others, who pretended they weren't attempting to hear the private conversation.

"I was tracking our father, and I came close with this tip." Kane indicated the casino in the distance.

"Yeah, close to dying," she scoffed and gave him a disapproving once-over. "I know everything, Kane. All your research and your conclusions about our father." She hesitated and straightened proudly. "I'd like you to give up your search. If he's alive, he doesn't want to be found."

"I'm sorry, Scorpio," he announced and shook his head. "I need closure. I need to confront him."

"And do what?"

"Talk to him, knock him on his ass, kill him," Kane informed her. "I don't know. I'll figure it out when I finally confront him." He indicated the distant casino. "The guy that owns this place, Sal Romano, knew our father. He let it slip." He then gave a slight nod to Mac. "And Mac had some sort of business dealing with our father and this Sal character. She and Sal had a falling out of some kind. She wouldn't even meet or talk to him. She's been very good at lying about her associations." He stared at his sister with a serious look. "Which brings me to my plea that you don't tell her anything we've learned about our father. I trust her with my life, but not with anything regarding him."

Scorpio stared at him with some surprise. "She doesn't know the man you're looking for is our father?"

"No, and I want to keep it that way," he insisted while shifting looks around them then involuntarily tensed. "I need to know I can trust her first. I think she knows him better than she's leading on. I'm worried she might take off and warn him."

"I won't tell her anything," Scorpio insisted while folding her arms across her chest. "I won't tell her anything, because I won't be around long enough. I'm taking the guys, and we're heading back to Maine. I have a hotel to restore."

"It can wait," he informed her and pleaded with his blue eyes. "Stay here with me a little while. Help me find our father."

"I'm not interested in finding that man," she scoffed in anger. "He means nothing to me. You need to get your ass on that plane and come back with me."

"I'll come back eventually," Kane replied. "I just need a few months to finish what I started here."

"What's that?" Scorpio demanded while glaring at him through narrow eyes. "Your business, Midnight Requisition? That's real cute. Nothing like putting a bloody leg into shark-infested waters."

"What do you mean?"

She groaned and shook her head. "That was the name of the mission our father used to fake his death," Scorpio remarked. "You're purposely throwing that name around in the circles he used to travel. You're trying to bring him to you. There's only one problem with that, Kane."

"What's that?"

"It may work," she launched hotly then threw her hands in the air. "Then what? You don't know this man. You don't know his story. How do you know he won't just kill you without asking any questions first? The fact that you're his own flesh and blood will probably mean very little to him. He's bad news."

"All the more reason for you to stay here with me and watch my back," he insisted while again pleading with his eyes. "Mac is good, but she's not *that* good." He then grinned. "Your new friends are pretty freaking awesome too. We'd make a great team." Kane then raised a curious brow and seemed enthusiastic. "Which one are you doing?"

Scorpio glared at him as the color rose to her cheeks. "That's rude, Kane."

"Come on," he groaned and raised his brows. "If I were doing Mac, I'd tell you. One of them has to be your new main squeeze. I'm guessing the tall black man. He's more your type than the pretty boy over there." Kane indicated Maverick while making a face. "You'd want some tests run on that one before sleeping with him."

Scorpio drew a deep breath, tensed slightly, and then nodded to Rayner. "I'm with Rayner."

Kane stared at her with surprise then cast several looks from her to Rayner. "You're kidding, right?" He then made a face. "He's a desk jockey. A computer nerd." Kane then made a face. "Or worse; a gamer."

"Heaven forbid," Scorpio gasped with fake horror then glared at her brother. "Almost frightening. That sounds an awful lot like you."

"I didn't just describe myself," Kane remarked, taking offense to the comment. "Since when is *that* your type?"

"I know he's nothing like Cal," Scorpio announced, "but it's the differences that I'm most attracted to."

"You're kidding," Kane remarked.

"No, I'm not kidding," she insisted with some hostility then hesitated and collected her emotions. "He treats me like I'm the most important person in the room. Every room. Sure, he may run when I snap my fingers, but I enjoy his company." She then raised her brows. "Besides, he's actually tougher than he looks."

"I hope so," Kane muttered.

"We should get back to the motel," Scorpio insisted, not wanting to continue the conversation further.

Kane frowned and fidgeted. "When do you plan on leaving for Maine?"

"I thought I'd stay a couple of days," she replied.

His smile suddenly returned. "Good. Then that gives me a couple of days to convince you to stay," Kane teased.

Chapter 5

Friday, June 20ᵗʰ. The out-of-the-way motel was quiet and peaceful at three o'clock in the morning. There wasn't a single car on what constituted a main road into the small town. The sound of crickets was almost deafening on the warm, summer night. In addition to the motel's large, brightly lit neon sign, there were two vapor lights on either end of the hotel to keep the parking lot dimly lit in the event they had guests. Currently, only three of the ten rooms were occupied. Scorpio lay on her side facing the closed curtains while Rayner spooned against her from behind. She clung to his arm, which was securely around her abdomen while he slept soundly nestled against her.

Scorpio found herself staring at the small part in the curtains that allowed a sliver of the outside lights into the room. She hadn't been able to sleep, but she didn't want to disturb Rayner by getting up either. At home, she easily managed her insomnia by going downstairs. Stranded in a small motel room didn't give her many options that wouldn't wake her boyfriend. Being the overly devoted boyfriend, Rayner wouldn't mind if she turned on the television or played on his laptop, but she didn't feel like interrupting his sleep just because she, once again, couldn't sleep.

She caught a glimpse of someone walking past the sliver in the curtain and heard them outside on the wooden porch. There was the familiar creak of one of many rocking chairs not far from her room. Someone else couldn't sleep. Scorpio wasn't particular. Anything was better than staring into the darkness of the bland motel room for the next couple of hours. She managed to slip out of Rayner's arm. Despite that he was barely awake; he acknowledged her movement.

"Can't sleep?" he muttered softly.

"No," she replied then leaned down and kissed him on the cheek. "Someone else is up and on the porch. I'm going outside for a while."

"Okay," he replied, rolled over, and immediately returned to sleep.

Scorpio slipped into her discarded pair of jeans on the floor and quietly left the room. She didn't bother with a jacket, since the night was warm, and ventured out in her bare feet. She wasn't going far and didn't require shoes. As she slipped out of the room and onto the porch, she saw Mac sitting on the oversized rocking chair while clutching her knees to her chest. She had been staring out at the open countryside beyond the sorely lacking main road but now focused her attention on Scorpio.

"I didn't wake you, did I?" Mac asked.

Scorpio sat in the vacant rocking chair alongside Mac's chair and casually stretched her legs out, resting her feet on the porch railing.

"No, I have sleep issues," Scorpio replied.

Mac resumed staring across the vacant countryside and sighed deeply. "Yeah, me too." She then frowned. "Your brother talks in his sleep."

"Yeah, awake or asleep; he never shuts up," Scorpio muttered.

Both chuckled at the comment. Scorpio eyed Mac's profile. The woman obviously had a lot on her mind. Despite not knowing much about her, Scorpio could tell she had a lot of layers to her. Her brother chose this woman as a business associate for a reason. He did everything for a reason, but he didn't go too deep into his business angle with her. What little time she'd spent alone with her brother that evening was spent discussing what happened at home and what brought her to Colorado to find him. Kane was emotionally distraught over everything that had happened back home, but it wasn't enough to make him pack his bags and willingly return with her. Despite his decision, he did call their grandmother. He talked with her over an hour, which their grandmother spent most of that time crying because she was so happy he was alive.

"You know your brother isn't normal, right?" Mac finally announced while casting a look at Scorpio and breaking her out of her thoughts.

Scorpio chuckled softly and met the woman's gaze. "I hope you're not asking me to explain him because he's an enigma. I haven't been able to figure him out, and he's been attached to my hip most of our lives."

Her comment made Mac smile. She could tell the woman needed to smile about something. Scorpio didn't know much about Mac, but she could sense she'd had a rough life. Something or someone beat her down and whatever flame had burned inside her was now a dying ember.

"You said the two of you aren't a couple," Scorpio remarked and appeared curious, "yet you're sharing a room. Am I missing something? He's usually a little too open about his relationships." Scorpio frowned. "Immensely open and with graphic detail."

Mac seemed to find the comment humorous, almost as if she already knew that. "No, there's nothing going on between your brother and me," she replied. "We're sharing a room because he's a cheap bastard."

Scorpio laughed knowing the comment to be true. Kane lived and dressed like a pauper. Surprisingly, he owned a ton of real estate and had a few million dollars stashed away. Shortly after they were born, their mother and uncle died in a car accident, which was another story. Their uncle left each of them a sizeable inheritance. With her inheritance, Scorpio bought her uncle's rundown lodge and was struggling to restore it. Up until a few months ago, Scorpio assumed her brother blew his money, since he was living with her rent-free before he took off on his little quest to find their father. She later discovered Kane had made eye-popping investments. Scorpio always knew her brother was something of a genius, despite his outward actions and appearance. She just didn't realize how much of a genius until Rayner hacked her brother's computer and told her what he'd found.

"It's only been a few weeks since he first approached me with this, uh, business venture," Mac informed her and appeared almost humored with whatever had transpired. "In the beginning, he sort of came on like a mutt in heat, but it turned out he was all talk."

"He's only a stud in his own mind," Scorpio replied and smirked at the comment. "I've had the unfortunate displeasure of hearing about his few conquests, and there's little for him to brag about."

Mac grinned and avoided looking at Scorpio. "When the sexual innuendoes and propositions ceased, I'll admit; it gave me a bit of a complex."

"No, that just means he doesn't feel he needs to play games with you anymore," Scorpio replied and eyed Mac. "You must have made an impression on him."

"I don't usually make good first impressions, but it's nice to feel wanted again," Mac informed her then cast a look at her and raised her brow. "In a non-sexual way, I mean. I've made a few mistakes in my life, and it sometimes feels as if the kicks just keep coming." She managed a tiny laugh while sinking into her own, depraved world. "You wouldn't understand. You're too young."

"My mother was murdered when I was a few months old, my father died before I was born, my boyfriend was murdered in front of me, and the man who raised me put a hit out on my brother and tried to kill me," Scorpio announced then raised her brow. "What won't I understand?"

Mac stared at Scorpio a moment then snorted a laugh. "Throw in a few mob bosses and cut-throat mercenaries, and we'd be soul sisters."

"You have mafia ties?"

"Not so much ties as acquaintances," Mac reported then sighed while resting her chin on her knees. "I have a slightly tainted past. I assume that's what drew your brother to me in the first place. Since my options are limited, I accepted his offer."

"You've been around, huh?"

Mac snorted a laugh, humored by the question. "Yeah, I've been around," she replied while grinning deviously. "I've worked for some very questionable men, dated the worst of the worst, and slept with nearly every mercenary I've met." She cast a look at Scorpio and offered a teasing smile. "Bad boys are great in bed."

Scorpio felt herself blush at the thought. "My resume is a little less interesting. Rayner is only the second man I've dated," she announced while grinning. "Though my first boyfriend did have a tattoo."

Mac grinned then chuckled. "You naughty girl," she teased then nodded to Scorpio's motel room. "I see you went a different route with boyfriend number two."

Scorpio sank into thought and smiled at the comment. "Yeah, a little."

"It must be nice."

Scorpio slipped out of her thoughts and eyed Mac. "What's that?"

"Being in love."

Scorpio considered the comment and fidgeted. "I do love Rayner," she remarked, "but I don't know that I'm in love with him."

Mac chuckled in her throat. "You've got it bad for him," she announced. "He's obviously a great guy." She then frowned and ran her fingers through her mussed hair. "I'd like to have that someday." She cast a look at Scorpio. "I always pass up the good ones for the bad ones. Just once, I'd like to be with a guy who actually cares about me."

"You haven't been with anyone who cares about you?" Scorpio asked with surprise.

"Not since I was your age," Mac replied with a defeated sigh. "The one man who loved me, I tore out his heart like he didn't even matter. Since then, it's been a parade of mercenaries and lowlife scumbags. I guess I had my chance and blew it. Now I'm doomed to a loveless existence."

"That's dark," Scorpio announced while shifting uncomfortably in her rocking chair. "Maybe the right guy just hasn't come along."

"It won't matter," Mac informed her. "Because I'll just kick him in the gonads and seek out the worst guy in the room." She stared out across the countryside. "It's who I am."

§

Scorpio and Mac talked until nearly four in the morning. Both were finally tired enough to return to their rooms. Scorpio attempted to enter the room quietly so she wouldn't wake Rayner, who had his back to her side of the bed. She removed her jeans and slipped under the covers. Rayner rolled onto his back, ran his fingers through his mussed hair, and glanced at her.

"Did I hear you talking with Mac?"

"Yeah, I'm sorry if we were talking too loudly," Scorpio replied.

"No, not at all," Rayner replied, although he'd never complain even if something did bother him. At times, he was a little too easy going.

"She has some demons," Scorpio remarked. "I hope Kane rubs off on her and not the other way around."

Scorpio moved against Rayner and clung to him while resting her head on his chest. He affectionately held her against him as if he'd never let go and kissed the top of her head. Scorpio tensed in his arms, which he immediately picked up on it.

"Something wrong?" he asked with concern and attempted to look at her.

She considered the question then pulled away from him and swiftly sat up in bed. Rayner appeared concerned by her hasty departure and was about to sit up as well when Scorpio suddenly climbed on top of him, straddling his hips. She removed her tank top and tossed it to the floor. Rayner grinned his approval to her partial nakedness and caressed her thighs up to her buttocks.

"I guess not," he teased.

She lay on top of him and kissed him affectionately. He barely had time to return the kiss when she pulled away and met his gaze while caressing his bare chest. Her look was serious which seemed to concern him.

"I love you, Rayner," she whispered without taking her eyes off him.

He was slightly surprised by her words, being the first time she'd said them aloud, and groaned. "Oh, Scorpio. I love you too."

Rayner placed his hand to her neck, pulled her mouth closer to his, and kissed her passionately with renewed aggression. He firmly caressed her body before flipping her over and reversing their positions. It was as if she opened the gates of hell and released Rayner's inner demon with those three little words. She was a little startled by his aggression, but she certainly wasn't complaining.

Chapter 6

Friday, June 20th. Colorado Springs. Early evening. The two-story, outdoor mall was spread out over a large area encompassing several city blocks and contained dozens of name brand stores. Within one of the more expensive clothing stores, an attractive young woman in her late teens to early twenties removed blouses from a rack and held them up to her body. Her handsome boyfriend stood attentively by her side and commented on each article of clothes. She handed him another shirt to add to the large stack he already held over his strained arm.

Brandi Hooper was a beauty in her own rights, although it required a lot of work and maintenance to achieve it. Despite that she was a rancher's daughter; Brandi spent more time on her dyed blonde hair and clothes than most women did. She was only a tick over five-foot, making her much shorter than her boyfriend was. Brandi had zero interest in the family cattle ranch, which her brother and sister ran. She was more interested in partying with her friends and having a good time than worrying about tending to daily chores at the farm. Since her father didn't pressure her into working, she let responsibilities of the ranch up to her brother and sister.

"I think you're past the dressing room limit of clothing," her boyfriend, Boyd, teased.

Boyd Flint was a handsome man in his mid to late twenties. He had a head of thick, light brown hair and a sparse beard that gave his youthful face a mildly rugged look. Although he was average height, he was built a bit like a lumberjack with just enough muscle to gain attention.

"It's okay," she announced with a bubbly giggle. "They know me here." Brandi took the pile of clothes from him. "I'll go try these on."

"While you do that, there's something I have to pick up in another store," Boyd announced.

Brandi appeared disappointed and pouted in protest. "How will I know which ones you like best?"

He kissed her quickly on the lips and grinned. "Easy," Boyd announced. "I'll love them all on you. You're going to look hot no matter what you wear."

Brandi managed a smile at the compliment but was still disappointed. "What's so important that you can't wait until I'm done trying on clothes?" she asked.

"I can't tell you," he replied while grinning. "It's a surprise."

Her eyes suddenly lit up. "For me?" she asked now bubbling over.

"Of course it's for you," he announced then laughed. "I'm certainly not buying jewelry for my sister."

"Jewelry?" she announced as her eyes sparkled at the thought of diamonds. Brandi just about pushed him away. "Go. What are you waiting for?"

Boyd laughed and left the store through the front door. Brandi headed toward the back of the store and the dressing rooms. As she rounded a rack of clothes, she nearly collided with a man not much older than she was. Brandi jumped with surprise then immediately frowned when she saw the sturdily built country boy.

"Damn it, Carson," she scolded with irritation. "What the hell are you doing here?" Her eyes narrowed. "Are you following me?"

Carson Reynolds was the stereotypical country boy. His sandy brown hair was kept short, he had some facial stubble that didn't quite constitute a beard, and his skin was bronzed, indicating he'd spent many hours outside. His build was muscular, suggesting a young man who'd spent his entire life doing physical labor.

"Maybe," Carson teased and moved closer to her. "You can't seriously be marrying that guy."

She flaunted her large diamond solitaire ring while raising her brows. "The invitations were sent out last week," Brandi informed him.

"Yeah, I know," Carson replied. "My parents got theirs in the mail yesterday."

"Sorry, you weren't invited," she retorted although her grin indicated she wasn't sorry.

"You broke up with me because you didn't want to marry a wrangler," Carson insisted. "Now you're marrying a wrangler. At least I'll have my father's ranch one day. You're marrying a man with no money."

"He doesn't have a lot, but he has some money," she insisted. "A decent amount from his mother's estate to afford a place for us in the city."

"You're not moving to the city," he scolded.

"I most certainly am," she scoffed while giving him a stern once-over. "You have no say in it."

"Your father would disown you," Carson remarked bluntly. "And we both know you're living off the trust fund your mother left you. Once that dries up, you'll need your father's money."

"It doesn't concern you, Carson," Brandi snapped and turned her nose up at him, snubbing him. "Now if you'll excuse me--"

She pushed past him and entered the changing room. Brandi tried on the first two dresses. She grimaced at the first one but admired the second one. Her cell phone rang in her purse. She removed her phone, glanced at the screen, and saw Boyd on the caller ID. Brandi immediately grinned and answered the phone.

"Hello?"

"Is this Brandi?" the male voice asked.

She again looked at the caller ID then put the phone back to her ear. "Who is this?"

"I'm here with Boyd," the man informed her. "He's had an accident, and he's asking for you."

"Oh, my God," she exclaimed. "Is he okay?"

"He might have a concussion, but he's okay," the man replied.

Brandi grabbed her purse and hurried from the changing room still wearing the dress she'd been trying on. "Yes, I'll be right there," she announced. "Where are you?"

"In the alley between Christy's Fashion and Samson's Jewelers," the man replied.

"I'm on my way," Brandi announced and headed for the back door, which would get her there quicker.

As she disconnected her call, she motioned to the clerk to put the dress on her tab then hurried out the back door into the alley. Brandi looked around the moderately creepy, dimly lit alley then removed her phone from her bag. She redialed Boyd's cell phone. The phone rang from behind her. Brandi was about to turn when she was grabbed from behind, and a hand covered her mouth. She fought against the man holding her captive as he attempted to pull her across the alley. She was suddenly flung forward with tremendous force and struck the concrete. When she looked behind her, she saw a man running away. Carson kneeled alongside her and helped her into a sitting position.

"Are you okay?" Carson gasped and checked her over for injuries. "What were you doing in the alley? You could have been killed."

"Me?" she demanded. "What were you doing in the alley? Did you purposely lure me out here to attack me?"

"What? No," he cried out with surprise. "I saw you leaving the store, so I followed you. It's a good thing I did. There's no telling what might have happened."

Brandi allowed Carson to help her to her feet then pulled away from him.

"You set this whole thing up," she lashed out. "You just wanted to look like a hero or something."

The alley door opened and a mall security officer looked at them.

"Is everything okay?" the security guard asked. "You're not supposed to use this door except for emergencies."

Brandi glared at Carson then looked back at the security guard. "No, everything *isn't* okay," she demanded. "My ex-boyfriend here was pulling some sort of prank on me. My father's office is across the street in the industrial park. Would you escort me there?"

The security guard nodded. "Certainly, Miss Hooper." He extended his hand down the alley then followed her.

§

The mall security guard walked Brandi across the street to a large building that housed many offices of every kind. They took the elevator to the fourth floor and entered her father's real estate office. Brandi's father hurried across the lobby to greet his daughter with a distraught look on his face. Brandi's father, Sig Hooper, was a distinguished looking man in his early fifties with expensive taste in clothes. His hand-tailored suit made him appear more attractive than he actually was. He stood an impressive six-foot-three and had the build of a man who'd spent most of his life farming. His light brown hair was lightly peppered with gray around the sides, giving him a distinguished appeal.

"What happened?" Sig demanded while inspecting his daughter for injuries. "Are you okay?"

"I'm fine, Daddy," she insisted while rolling her eyes. "It was just Carson playing a prank."

"Carson?" Sig demanded then eyed the mall security guard. "What sort of prank?"

"We found her in the alley with the man in question," the guard remarked. "She said he lured her out there and pretended to rescue her."

"How did he lure you into the alley?" her father suddenly demanded.

"I got a phone call from someone using Boyd's phone," Brandi informed her father. "He told me Boyd had been hurt and asked me to meet him." She folded her arms across her chest. "Only it wasn't Boyd."

"But it was Boyd's phone?" Sig asked with some confusion about what happened.

Boyd hurried into the office, saw Brandi, and appeared relieved. "Thank God you're here," he gasped and pulled her into his arms. He drew back and met her gaze. "Someone stole my cell phone. When I went back to the store, they said you'd left. I couldn't even call you to find out where you'd gone."

"Someone stole your cell phone?" Sig demanded then cast a look at the security officer.

The guard shrugged in response. "Looks like the ex *was* playing a prank on her," the mall guard remarked. "I'd keep an eye out for that one. That's stalker level behavior."

"Yeah, I'll do that," Sig muttered then walked the guard to the door. He slipped him a folded bill while shaking his hand. "Thanks for seeing my daughter safely here."

"Anytime, Mr. Hooper," the guard replied, politely tipped his hat, and then left.

Sig returned to Boyd and his daughter. He gave Boyd a curious look. "Did you see who stole your phone?"

"No," Boyd replied. "Someone bumped into me on my way to the jewelry store. A few minutes later, I went to use my phone and realized it was gone. Whoever bumped into me must have boosted it."

"There are a lot of people around this area Friday evenings," Sig reported. He glanced at his watch and sighed. "I have a meeting with a client this evening and an early morning appointment tomorrow. I'll be staying in the city tonight." He gave Boyd a stern look. "Don't let my daughter out of your sight. We don't need any more incidents with Carson. I'll talk to his father tomorrow afternoon."

"Tell the creep to stay away from me," Brandi scoffed then turned to Boyd and smiled while clinging to his strong arm. "We can stop at the jewelry store on the way back to the clothing store. I left my clothes there."

"I like the new dress," Boyd announced while grinning his approval.

"Then I'll wear it to dinner tonight," she announced then kissed him quickly. She looked back at her father, who seemed to be deep in thought. "We'll see you back at the ranch tomorrow, Daddy."

He nodded then watched them leave. Sig turned and headed for the receptionist's desk. The young, attractive woman immediately perked up.

"Lisa," he announced while seeming distracted.

"Yes, Mr. Hooper?" she replied a little too eagerly and purposely displayed her cleavage while straightening.

"Get me a list of local private detectives," Sig instructed without even noticing her attempt for attention. "I need some answers."

"Actually," Lisa announced and removed a business card from her desk. "One of my girlfriends used this new guy in town last week. He resolved her stalking boyfriend problem in one afternoon." She handed him the card.

Sid eyed the card. "Midnight Requisition," he muttered then tossed the card back to her. "Give him a call. See if I can meet him tomorrow after my lunch meeting." He then hesitated and reconsidered his request. "Not around here though. Somewhere secluded."

"Yes, sir," she announced.

Chapter 7

Saturday, June 21st. The diner was located just a few miles down the road from the remote motel near Cripple Creek. Scorpio and Rayner sat with Kane and Mac at the window booth while they finished their lunch. Stone and Maverick chose to sit at the counter not far from them while facing the television mounted in the corner. The two men were more interested in watching sports highlights than catching up on family gossip, most of which they already knew. When Sig Hooper entered the diner, Rayner zeroed in on him. Although Sig was dressed business casual, his clothes were still stylish and expensive.

"I'm guessing that's your man," Rayner remarked and stood. "No one around here can afford those threads."

Rayner headed to the counter to join Stone and Maverick as Sig approached their booth. Since they were the only customers in the diner at two in the afternoon, it was easy for Sig to spot them. Scorpio attempted to slip out of the booth before Sig reached them.

"I should let you to your work," Scorpio announced to her brother, but she didn't make it out of the booth before Sig stopped at their table.

"Mr. Kane," Sig announced and extended his hand.

Kane stood from his end seat at the booth and shook his hand. "Actually, it's first name Kane," he replied while

39

grinning then nodded to Scorpio. "This is my sister, Scorpio." He then indicated Mac, who was seated in the booth by the window. "And that's my associate, Mac."

Mac managed a smile although her people skills were sorely lacking.

Scorpio again attempted to stand, but Sig was now in her way. "I'll just get out of your way," Scorpio announced.

"Stay," Kane insisted then looked at Sig and grinned. "I'm hoping my sister will join the team. I could use some hellfire to go with my brimstone." He then gave a nod to Mac, who was oddly amused that she was his 'brimstone'.

Sig took in an eyeful of Scorpio and seemed slightly intrigued. "We won't be long," he announced. "Stay."

Scorpio reluctantly slid across the booth to the window so the man could join them. The waitress almost instantly appeared. Sig ordered some coffee then focused his attention on Kane.

"I'll get right to the point," Sig announced. "I think my daughter is in danger, but I can't prove anything. Her ex-boyfriend might be stalking her, and I'm not thrilled about the guy she insists upon marrying either."

"So you're looking for someone to protect your daughter and also dig up dirt on her current boyfriend," Kane remarked with increasing interest.

"Unfortunately, I already had a background check done on her boyfriend," Sig announced with a defeated sigh. "There's nothing there. If you take the job, I'll give you the report for reference. That doesn't mean there isn't something that wouldn't show up on a report. I need someone on the inside watching him." He leaned back in the booth as the waitress brought his coffee. Once she was gone, he again leaned forward. "I own a profitable ranch north of Colorado Springs and a real estate business in the city. My children stand to inherit a small fortune after I'm gone, and their mother left them a sizeable trust fund after she died. My daughter is worth quite a bit, but she's a little on the naïve side. I don't want some man using her for her money, which sadly would be easy to do."

"Where does this boyfriend of hers live and work?" Kane asked.

"He's a wrangler at my ranch," Sig replied then snorted a laugh. "And not a very good one either. He lives in the bunkhouse with the other wranglers."

"So in order to keep tabs on the boyfriend, you need someone on staff as a wrangler," Kane remarked. "That's the only way someone could keep an eye on him."

Sig nodded then appeared curious. "Is that a deal breaker?" he asked.

Kane shifted uncomfortably then glanced at Mac alongside him.

"I can ride horses," Mac replied, answering his silent question.

Scorpio found it interesting that Mac was easily able to read Kane after only knowing him a short while. Mac's perception was highly tuned. Kane then looked back at Sig, who now seemed uncomfortable.

"My oldest daughter is the only female wrangler, and she lives in the main house," Sig announced. "If I would suddenly hire a female wrangler, it would raise suspicion." He again shifted in the booth. "And more than a few eyebrows in the communal bunkhouse, if you get my meaning."

Mac appeared humored and grinned. "Actually, it sounds like fun," she replied.

Kane attempted to hide his smile at Mac's enthusiasm for sharing a bunkhouse with a bunch of strange men.

"No offense, but I'd rather not open Pandora's Box right now," Sig replied while casting a look at Mac.

Kane looked at Scorpio and raised his brows. She instantly became uncomfortable and shifted in the booth.

"Don't drag me into this, Kane," she insisted.

Kane suddenly grinned as if reading her uncomfortable look. "You've got a wrangler sitting at the bar," he announced slyly. "Admit it."

Scorpio groaned and covered her eyes. Kane turned in his seat and looked at the three men seated at the bar with their backs to them.

"Hey," Kane called to them. "Any of you guys have experience riding horses?"

All three turned and looked back at Kane. Rayner laughed with humor by the question. Stone and Maverick raised their hands. Kane turned back to Scorpio and raised his brows while snatching one of her leftover French fries.

"Lend me your muscle, Scorp," he announced while grinning then ate the French fry.

"Whatever it is, I'm in," Maverick announced a little too quickly from the counter.

"Me too," Stone chimed in.

"I rode a horse once and fell off," Rayner remarked while frowning. "Count me out."

Kane stared at Scorpio and grinned slyly as he plucked another French fry from her plate. "Come on, Scorp," he teased. "Two out of three says yea. You and Rayner don't have to come along if you don't want to, but let the muscle come."

Scorpio frowned and sank in her seat. "Fine," she scoffed. "If they want to go with you, take them."

Kane smiled at Sig. "You have two wranglers and two bodyguards for your daughter," he announced.

"Excellent," Sig replied with relief then fiddled with his watch. "I have to stay in the city tonight. I'm showing a mansion in a couple of hours. I also have to find a security company willing to come all the way out to my ranch to install a security system. I'm not taking any more chances."

"Security system?" Rayner announced from the counter and jumped off his chair. "Now I'm interested."

Kane grinned at his sister. "And then there was one," he teased.

Scorpio groaned and straightened in her seat. "Fine, I'm in, but then you're coming home to visit Grandma for a week or longer."

"Deal," Kane replied and snagged another French fry from her plate.

Sig seemed pleased and offered a broad grin. "Splendid. I'd like you to get started right away," he informed them. "I can arrange transportation at the Colorado Springs Airport for tomorrow morning. I have a private transport available, but I'll need to make some calls. Does ten o'clock tomorrow work for you?"

"Yeah, that works," Kane replied.

"There's a private entrance to the smaller airfield at the airport," Sig informed him. "I'll text you with directions and the name of your pilot. I'll work on your job descriptions for your cover. My son will be the only one who'll know who you really are. I want to keep this from my wife and daughters. They, uh, wouldn't approve."

"Understood," Kane replied.

Sig then stood and placed enough money on the table to pay for his coffee and their meal. "You can email me a revised estimate to include the additional men." He then turned to Rayner. "I'll work out the security system estimate with you once you have a chance to evaluate the estate."

Rayner handed him a business card and nodded. "I look forward to it."

Once Sig left the diner, Kane enthusiastically pounded on the booth table. "This is the one," Kane announced while grinning. "If we can deliver, that man could be the key to future jobs."

Kane held his hand in the air to Mac. She eagerly slapped his hand while grinning at the prospect. Kane held his hand up to Scorpio across the table. She glared back at him.

"Don't leave me hanging," Kane announced while indicating his hand.

"Don't get excited, Kane," Scorpio remarked.

He frowned and lowered his hand.

"I have a hotel to renovate," she informed him. "I'm going back to Maine after this little job is over."

"Do you speak for the guys?" Kane asked while raising a brow.

"No, they're free to do whatever they want," Scorpio informed him.

Maverick, Stone, and Rayner approached their table. Rayner slid onto the seat alongside Scorpio and placed his hand on hers.

"I go where you go," Rayner announced without hesitation. "I'm not leaving you."

Kane glanced at Maverick and Stone while resting his jaw on his fist. Both men fidgeted. Scorpio eyed them and offered a tiny smile.

"If you choose to stay with Kane and play detective, I won't hold it against you," Scorpio informed them. "Friends don't hold friends back."

Stone and Maverick exchanged looks then looked back at Scorpio.

"No, we'll go back with you," Maverick replied without missing a beat. "We opted for a stable life."

"We already did the nomad lifestyle," Stone added. "We want a home and a family."

Mac suddenly appeared uncomfortable. "Don't we all," she scoffed and immediately received several looks. She eyed them. "Sorry. Just thinking aloud."

Chapter 8

Sunday, June 22nd. Across the tarmac from the busy Colorado Springs Airport was a smaller building and a separate area for private planes. The bland building contained a waiting room, offices, and restrooms for travelers using private air services. The furniture in the waiting room was old and worn. There was a counter by the wall of windows for guests to check in. Vending machines were located near the corridor that led to the restrooms in the back hall. Kane sat on one of the worn sofas while scanning through an email Sig had sent him late Saturday night.

"Wow, this guy is thorough," Kane announced. "He has job descriptions for each of us and even the names of those we'll be interacting with." He flashed his phone to Scorpio and grinned. "Look. He even has some background on the family and workers for us to look over."

Scorpio had to smile at her brother's childlike fascination. "You're really into this, aren't you?"

He stared at her with surprise. "Well, hell yeah," Kane announced. "It's exciting. Someone actually paying us to play detective. Remember all the fun we had playing in the closed hotel?"

"I remember you getting your ass kicked a lot," Scorpio teased.

"Your memory isn't good," Kane insisted as he glared at her. "I won fifty percent of the time."

"I let you win," she remarked, although that wasn't true. She just wanted to deflate Kane's ego. As his twin sister, it was her job and her birthright.

Rayner sat alongside Scorpio and busily worked on his laptop attempting to get a head start on Sig's security needs. Scorpio glanced at his computer only once where he sat on the other side of her.

"You look like a kid in a candy store," she teased. "What's so interesting?"

"This place is huge," Rayner announced and showed her the photo of the plantation style home. It looked as if it came straight out of "Gone with the Wind".

"Nice."

"A lot of work for me without an installation crew," he replied with noted concern.

"Maybe the guys can help in their spare time," Scorpio suggested. "I'm sure some of the wranglers wouldn't mind some extra pay as well."

"We'll see."

Mac stood before the large windows and paced almost like a caged panther. She seemed particularly off since they arrived at the private airport. A helicopter landed not far from the building.

Kane sprang from his seat and hurried to the window to join Mac. "I can't believe we get to ride in a helicopter," he announced with childlike enthusiasm. "I've always wanted to fly in a helicopter." His eyes then widened. "Wow, is that our pilot? She's gorgeous."

Mac stared out the window and saw two, familiar teenage girls jumping from the back of the craft and hurry past the attractive, young woman pilot. Mac backed up and appeared unusually pale.

"We're flying in that?" Mac suddenly asked and took another step back while shaking her head. "Uh, sorry. No, not happening." She again backed up. "I'll wait for Mr. Hooper and drive back with him."

"You're afraid of flying?" Kane asked with surprise and studied her expression.

"I can handle planes, but you're not getting me in that," she insisted and hurried across the building toward the back hallway without even waiting for Kane to respond. "I'll catch a ride back to Hooper's office in town."

Kane stared after her with a strange look then shook his head. A tall, lanky man in his mid-thirties approached the building and entered. The stranger with light brown hair and a clean-shaven face didn't pay much attention to those within the waiting area. Instead, he headed for the vending machines near the hall where Mac had just headed. Something caught the man's attention forcing him to bypass the vending machines and head down the hall toward the bathroom. Mac was nearly to the exterior door at the end of the corridor when she heard the man call her name. She ignored him and was just about to open the door when he called her name again.

"Mac," he called a little louder.

She hesitated, considered her options, and then turned toward the man. She put on a false look of surprise although she wasn't surprised at all. Mac frowned and demandingly folded her arms across her chest. Her true feelings shined through as she gave him a venomous look.

"I should have known I'd run into one of you here," she snarled with limited patience. "What are you doing here, Monroe?" Her eyes then narrowed. "You weren't following me, were you?"

"What?" Monroe asked with surprise then turned defensive. "No, Jackie needs to provide helicopter taxi service for one of the local ranchers. What are you doing here?"

"Not that it's any of your business," she huffed then shifted uncomfortably. "I was looking for work." Her eyes narrowed. "I was fired from my last bartending job for taking off an entire week without giving advance notice." She thoughtfully tapped her finger to her chin. "Hmm, now why was that?" Mac's glare then turned demanding. "Oh, that's right. I was hiking through alligator-infested swamps saving your ass from hired mercenaries."

"That's not fair," Monroe insisted while glaring demandingly. "As I remember, you insisted on coming along for the ride, and you were paid a substantial sum of money when the mission was over."

They heard the awaiting passengers moving around within the lobby. Mac tensed and ran her fingers through her dark hair.

"I really have to go," she announced. "I have another interview, and I can't afford to be late."

"Please, Mac," Monroe pleaded. "Just give me five minutes of your time."

One of the guys appeared in the corridor and glanced around. Mac avoided being seen by her teammate while using Monroe as a wall.

"Fine," she scoffed then bolted through the doorway to her right.

Monroe followed her into the storage closet. Mac turned on the light that did a poor job at lighting the windowless room. Someone was heard in the corridor possibly approaching the restrooms. Mac flipped the lock on the door, catching Monroe's attention.

"Are you avoiding someone?" Monroe asked and appeared curious.

She frowned and again ran her fingers through her hair. "Yeah, but what else is new."

He stared at her as if awaiting an explanation for her actions.

Mac groaned and shifted uncomfortably. "The man who interviewed me was a bit of a jerk," she announced. "And you know I don't exactly play well with others--"

"And now you're avoiding a confrontation," Monroe remarked.

"More like I'd rather not be escorted out by airport security," she replied then leaned against the door while glaring at him. "What did you want?"

Monroe fumbled slightly over himself. "I'm sorry how things ended at Beck's wedding."

"Oh, you mean when you and your friends threw me under the bus?" she huffed. "And I was officially blacklisted from ever working for Sal or your little boys' club."

"I don't remember it going down quite like that," Monroe insisted.

"I do," she snarled while harboring anger over it as she glared at him. "I was there."

Monroe tensed and held his breath while staring into her angry eyes. "I just wanted to tell you that I'm sorry for how things ended; that's all," he gently replied. "It wasn't my decision, and I hated the way things ended. I defended you. I wanted the guys to give you another chance."

Mac straightened while staring at him with genuine surprise. "You did?"

He nodded and shamefully lowered his head. "I regret not making a better case."

She shifted almost uncomfortably while staring at him. "After all our clashes, you were the last person I expected to hear that from," she remarked.

"If I held a grudge against every woman I've ever clashed with, I'd alienate half the female population," he teased and managed a smile.

Mac stared at him a moment in silence as if attempting to gauge his sincerity. She grabbed his face in her hands, startling him, and kissed him passionately. Despite being taken back by her sexually aggressive reaction, Monroe immediately returned the wild kiss, lost his balance, and knocked her against the door. It was unclear if she knew he'd lost his balance or if she took it as a sexually aggressive maneuver. Regardless, she pawed at his body and just about tore his shirt.

Monroe attempted to keep up with her aggression, but Mac was already opening his belt with a sense of urgency. Before he could even open her pants, she already had her hand down his. Monroe groaned and sank against her despite her somewhat roughness toward his highly sensitive body parts. Monroe was barely able to fondle her breasts over her tank top before she dropped to her knees in front of him. He braced his hand against the door in front of him for support, groaned loudly in response, and subconsciously placed his hand to the back of her head while clutching her ponytail.

His ecstasy only lasted briefly when she pulled away much to his disappointment. As she straightened, her mouth eagerly sought his. During the brief moment she was on her knees, she managed to slip out of her shorts. Mac threw her arms around his neck and leaped against him, wrapping her legs around his hips. Monroe again nearly lost his balance and knocked her into the door to help support her as she straddled him in an upright position. He groaned and thrust his body against her jolting the door with a loud clunk.

§

An attractive woman in her mid-twenties with long, dark hair pulled back in a ponytail entered the building. Their pilot, Jackie Falcone, approached the five within the waiting room and smiled pleasantly. Despite her smile, their pilot seemed slightly distracted.

"Good morning. I'm Jackie, your pilot. The helicopter is refueled and ready to go just as soon as I find my co-pilot," she announced and sounded a little irritated by her co-pilot's mysterious disappearance. "Why don't you grab a seat anywhere in the back; and we'll be along in a minute?"

All five nodded. Kane was the first to rush out the door, eager to start his first helicopter adventure. Scorpio and Rayner followed Maverick and Stone from the building in less of a hurry. All four were moderately humored by Kane's enthusiasm and laughed at his expense. As they headed across the tarmac for the awaiting helicopter, their pilot walked toward the vending machines.

§

Monroe rushed to pull up his pants then fumbled with his belt. The female pilot was heard calling his name not far from the supply closet. Monroe was flushed and out of breath as he cast a peek at Mac who dressed in less of a hurry. Oddly enough, she no longer seemed pressed for time and appeared almost indifferent to their quick but wild moment.

"That's Jackie," he announced. "She's waiting for me."

"Don't mention you saw me," Mac practically threatened while sounding annoyed.

Monroe was surprised by the comment but nodded in agreement. "You're right," he reluctantly replied. "We don't need this getting back to Zack." He finished dressing and moved closer to her while grinning almost boyishly. "How about we meet somewhere this weekend?"

She eyed him while she finished dressing then straightened. "I don't think so."

"Okay," he replied. "What about the following Friday?"

"Once-and-done, Monroe," she firmly insisted. "We both needed that, but it's not happening again."

Before he could protest or question her, Mac opened the closet door and shoved him into the hall, shutting the door behind him. Mac insecurely folded her arms across her chest then flipped the lock on the door for added measure.

Chapter 9

The helicopter flew over the beautiful Colorado countryside heading toward the mountains. The scenery was void of homes, roads, and buildings leaving nothing but nature. The five passengers took in the visual beauty while talking among themselves. The pilot had her headset turned to a private channel, so she could have her own personal conversation with her co-pilot. It seemed as if her co-pilot was sulking over something. Scorpio couldn't really comment on the co-pilot's bad mood since she was dealing with her own brooding man. Rayner kept nudging her every few minutes and indicating something on his laptop.

Scorpio didn't want to hurt Rayner's feelings by ignoring him, but every time she attempted to read something on his laptop, she felt sick to her stomach. Rayner finally switched Scorpio's headset frequency so they could speak privately without her brother or the guys hearing their conversation.

"Sig Hooper wants you to pose as his son's new girlfriend," Rayner informed her. He didn't even bother attempting to hide his jealousy.

"I'll talk to Hooper," Scorpio replied while fighting the urge to throw up.

"I'm very uncomfortable with this," he continued.

"Rayner," she announced while attempting to stare into his eyes even though she wanted to keep her eyes straight ahead to avoid nausea. "If we continue this conversation or any conversation, I'm liable to throw up on you."

He looked at her with some surprise. "You're airsick?" Rayner asked. "You've flown before."

"Not in small crafts," she insisted and closed her eyes. "Let me die in peace."

He affectionately patted her hand then offered her a peppermint. She accepted the candy, placed it in her mouth, and again shut her eyes.

The aerial view of the ranch was breathtaking, not that Scorpio could enjoy much of it. She was just glad they'd be on the ground soon. She didn't know why she was so pissed that Kane was enjoying the flight. He was practically giddy with the entire experience. Why wasn't he experiencing the same airsickness she was? It didn't seem right. The massive plantation style farmhouse had an impressive wraparound porch, large in-ground pool, a bunkhouse for the wranglers just across the paddock, and a huge horse barn. There was a large fenced pasture and smaller paddock for the many grazing horses. The cattle pastures seemed to extend forever. There were large herds of cattle in several areas. The helicopter was high enough that it didn't spook the horses or cattle.

The helicopter lowered into a large clearing far enough away from any animals yet surprisingly close to the house. The pilot shut down the helicopter then got out and opened the back door for her passengers while her co-pilot opened the door on his side as well. Scorpio thanked their pilot but immediately resumed her conversation with Rayner.

"You have nothing to worry about," Scorpio insisted. "I'll talk to Hooper."

"I know I'm overreacting," he insisted then fidgeted. "I just can't help it. I hate that this makes me crazy jealous. It's not like me."

"I think it's cute," Scorpio reassured him while grinning and affectionately patted his arm.

Kane climbed out on the pilot's side and took in a sweeping eyeful of their stunning pilot. The attractive woman looked at him and seemed to be checking him out as well. It was a bit of an ego boost for Kane since she was almost certainly his type, but he resisted playing the over-sexed frat boy. Kane, instead, offered a polite smile and thanked her for a smooth flight. It may have been in Maverick's nature to make a play for the admittedly sexy pilot, but being Kane was raised by his grandparents, being respectful was hammered into him. The five were greeted by Sig Hooper's son, Marlon. Marlon Hooper looked like a younger, more attractive version of his father. The man in his late twenties was roughly six-foot-two and had the build of a construction worker. Marlon met them just on the edge of the patio beyond the in-ground pool as the helicopter lifted off. He greeted Maverick and Stone with a firm handshake.

"I'm Marlon Hooper," Sig's son announced politely.

Stone shook his hand first. "I'm Ben Stone, and this is Blake Maverick."

Marlon shook Maverick's hand then looked at the other three. His smile brightened when he saw Scorpio. "You must be Scorpio Wayland," he announced and warmly shook her hand. "My father wasn't exaggerating. You are quite enchanting."

Scorpio could almost feel Rayner's discomfort at the comment. "That's only because he doesn't know me," she replied and politely shook his hand then indicated Rayner, who quietly stood alongside her. "Did your father mention my boyfriend, Rayner Roderick? He'll be assessing your security needs and setting up cameras and monitors."

Marlon was forced to acknowledge Rayner and shook his hand. "Yes, my father mentioned we'd be getting some security cameras and an alarm system," he announced. "Although I'll warn you, my sister, Jasmine, will protest just about everything you suggest. She likes the rustic appeal, and she tends to get her way."

"I'm sure we can come up with something," Rayner replied and didn't sound concerned.

Marlon then approached Kane. "So you must be Kane Templeton," he announced then grinned as he shook his hand. "You're the new babysitter. I wish you luck. Brandi won't make it easy for you, I promise. She may be my sister, but she's spoiled."

"I've lived with that my entire life," Kane announced while pointing at Scorpio. "The fact that she's still alive is a testament to my patience."

Marlon laughed then appeared curious. "You and your sister have different last names?"

"Yes and no," Kane remarked and cast a look at Scorpio, who raised her brow, interested to hear his explanation. He looked back at Marlon. "When I started my business, I thought it best to use an alias, you know, in case I made some enemies."

Scorpio had to keep from laughing at his response. He couldn't exactly tell Marlon the truth. He didn't want to use his real name while attempting to flush out those involved in faking their father's death. They still didn't know the entire story behind "Midnight Requisition", and it was best no one knew their family's name. It was still unclear whether anyone would come after them, and they didn't need a target painted on their grandmother's back. Well, that and Kane had lost his identification when he was supposedly killed. It would take some time to resurrect her brother from the dead as far as the authorities were concerned. For now, his only identification was his assumed identity, Kane Templeton.

Marlon nodded with understanding then looked around with interest. "Wasn't there a second lady?"

"She had a panic attack when she found out we were arriving in a helicopter," Scorpio replied then gingerly held her stomach. "I understand her hesitance now. She said she'll catch a ride with your father."

"They won't be here until after dinner then," Marlon replied. "The three of you can leave your bags in the kitchen. I'll have the maid, Delia, show you to the study. You can wait for me there."

"Delia Flint," Rayner remarked. "She's Boyd's sister, right?"

Marlon chuckled and nodded. "I see you've done your research," he teased.

"Your father gave us a brief bio on every one of interest," Rayner replied.

"He's just the only one who bothered to read it," Maverick teased.

Marlon laughed and pointed at Maverick. "The guys are going to love you," he announced then indicated Maverick and Stone. "I'll take our two new wranglers to the bunkhouse and introduce you to Jasmine."

Chapter 10

Maverick and Stone followed Marlon to the bunkhouse, which was a little nicer than an Army barracks. It was essentially a large log cabin with ten, twin-size beds, five on either side. There was a small kitchen with the usual refrigerator, stove, microwave, and coffee maker. It also had a large, solid wood table and chairs with enough seating for the guys to have a meal together or play cards in the evening. A small living area had several sofas, a couple of chairs, and a large screen television mounted on the wall for recreation. A communal bathroom contained four toilet stalls, four sinks, and four private shower stalls, making it nicer than most school locker rooms but not nearly as fancy as a country club locker room. Maverick and Stone were each assigned a bunk closer to the bathroom. The prime bunks were closest to the beautiful, functioning stone fireplace that was only used during the colder months.

"You can stow your gear in your footlocker by your beds," Marlon informed the men. "A few of the guys are still in town recovering from whatever trouble they got into Saturday night. Typically, the guys have the weekends off with one wrangler having weekend duties just to keep things running smoothly. When they heard new guys were coming, a few offered to show you the ropes for a few hours, so you're not thrown into a full day tomorrow without any prep work."

"That was nice of them," Stone replied.

"Yeah, they're a pretty good bunch of guys. Once you have your gear stowed, I'll take you to the barn to meet my sister. Jasmine and I tend to most of the day-to-day work around the ranch."

"There's also a ranch foreman, right?" Stone remarked as he placed his entire duffel bag in the locker at the foot end of his bunk.

"Yeah, Teddy," Marlon replied. "You'll mostly take orders from him. He's demanding but not nearly the drill sergeant my sister is."

"She sounds lovely," Maverick teased. "Can't wait to meet her."

"It was my father's wish that none of the others are told who you really are and why you're here," Marlon reminded them. "That includes Jasmine. Since neither of you have been actual wranglers, my sister and Teddy have been told to take it easy on the two of you. We have four lifers and usually four who only stay a year before moving on. It's not unusual to have inexperience wranglers in the field so Jasmine won't be suspicious."

"Why didn't your father include your older sister in our true reason for being here?" Stone asked.

"Jasmine and I have an ongoing rivalry over the operations of the ranch," Marlon admitted as he leaned against the nearby wall. "She'd undoubtedly blow your cover just to piss me off. That and her husband is my father's house manager. She'd confide in him, and it would eventually get back to Brandi. If Brandi knew you were here to spy on her boyfriend, it would defeat the purpose of having you."

"So there are eight wranglers not including you and your sister," Maverick remarked.

"That's correct. The two of you give us a full house of ten," he replied. "Over the winter, we only keep our four full-time wranglers. Boyd started dating my sister last summer and managed to stick around the winter as a fifth full-time wrangler.

My father couldn't cut him loose. Brandi protested heavily." Marlon straightened and shifted uncomfortably. "Over Christmas, Boyd asked her to marry him, which secured his position here. They're getting married at the end of August here at the ranch." He frowned his disapproval. "After they're married, Boyd will move into the main house with Brandi. Teddy has expressed his concerns that he'll be bumped as foreman to make room for a greenhorn wrangler because of his new position as the daughter's husband." Marlon waved his hand. "Don't worry; he'll tell you all about it in a day or two. He's got a gift for gossip, that one. The guys spend a lot of evenings bonding over poker."

"Poker?" Maverick announced while grinning. "I'm looking forward to all this bonding."

Marlon laughed then motioned for them to follow him. "Let's not keep the drill sergeant waiting."

Marlon took them outside and into the large horse barn, which was only a few yards from the bunkhouse. Marlon's sister, Jasmine Hooper-Smith, had already picked out two horses for their new wranglers and seemed eager to get them started with the herd. Jasmine was a tall, slender woman in her late twenties with long, strawberry blonde hair hidden beneath her brown cowboy hat. She wore a tank top under her plaid button shirt. The tank top clung to her large breasts and revealed enough cleavage to attract plenty of male attention even though she was married. Despite her attention-grabbing figure, her big green eyes were what men noticed first.

"Jasmine," Marlon announced and indicated the two men. "This is Ben Stone and Blake Maverick."

Both men greeted her with a firm handshake. Despite what they'd been told about Marlon's sister, she gave them an approving once-over.

"I'm impressed," Jasmine announced. "Our father finally brought men rather than boys for a change."

Maverick and Stone were blindsided by the compliment from the sinfully attractive woman. It was difficult to maintain their professional appearance with the thoughts that must have been exploding in their heads.

"Please don't flirt with the new wranglers," Marlon groaned with some annoyance.

Jasmine glared at her brother and raised a cocky brow. "You've worn out your welcome, Marlon. You can leave now."

"With pleasure," Marlon scoffed. "I have guests waiting in the study."

Jasmine cast a sideways look at Marlon as he left. "Of course you do," she muttered although not loud enough for him to hear her.

Once her brother was gone, Jasmine finally shifted her attention back to the two new wranglers and even offered a pleasant smile.

"I want you to know that whatever mean-spirited things my brother said about me aren't true," she insisted.

"I don't recall anything--" Maverick attempted to keep the peace but was quickly interrupted.

"I'm not a drill sergeant," Jasmine insisted while raising her brows. "I have a very good relationship with the wranglers. My brother is just jealous because I run this place better than he does." She then smiled cheerfully. "That being said, you can call me Jasmine. I don't want to hear any Mrs. Hooper-Smith or ma'am. Got it?"

Both men smiled and laughed. "Got it."

"My brother tells me you're both green," she announced while leaning on the rump of the horse in the crossties. "How green?"

"We can ride horses," Stone informed her. "But, to be honest, we've never worked cows before."

"You'll get the hang of it in a couple of days," she insisted while grinning, which only increased her beauty. "The horses will teach you most of what you need to know. The trick is not falling off." She patted the horse. "The horses know their job, and they do it well. You need to read their body language and anticipate their actions." Jasmine then smiled sweetly. "Rule number one. If and when you fall off, we will all laugh at you. Rule number two. If and when you fall off, please don't break any bones. You'll be shot and put out of your misery."

They stared at her with surprise to the comment. Jasmine eyed their expressions then laughed.

"That was a joke," she remarked and shook her head. "You boys are going to need a sense of humor to survive around here." Jasmine then patted the horse she leaned against. "I feed the horses at five A.M. Wranglers have breakfast in the main house kitchen at six, and you're expected to have your horses saddled and A.I.S. by seven."

"A.I.S?" Stone questioned.

"Ass in saddle," she replied while grinning. Jasmine turned toward the tack room then hesitated and gave both men a quick once-over. "Oh, and fair warning. I'm in the bunkhouse just before six A.M., and I'm not easily embarrassed. If you're not properly dressed, that's your problem."

As she entered the tack room, Maverick and Stone exchanged looks then raised their brows. Both grinned and laughed.

Chapter 11

Kane and Scorpio sat in the chairs before the elegant, expensive desk within the rustic study where western saddles and taxidermy wildlife were the theme. There was plenty of detailed woodwork, framed photos of men on horses, and antique saddles used as decorations. There were also several animal heads mounted on the walls, but the large, stuffed grizzly bear in the corner was the showpiece of the room. The menacing taxidermy bear stood on its hind legs and nearly touched the tall ceiling. While Scorpio and Kane took in the ambiance of the room, Rayner busily worked on his computer where he sat in an elegant chair made of steer and deer horns in the corner of the room.

"I wasn't expecting the internet connection to be this fast out here," Rayner informed them. "Not nearly as fast as in Maine, but faster than I'd expected for the sticks."

Kane leaned closer to Scorpio and spoke softly but made sure he was loud enough for Rayner to hear. "Does he ever stop working?"

"Only when I distract him," Scorpio replied.

Kane chuckled at the comment.

Rayner raised his brow and cast a quick look at the brother and sister duo. "I heard that."

"You were meant to," Scorpio teased.

Marlon entered the study, saw their empty coffee mugs near them, appeared pleased, and then took the seat behind the large desk. "I'm glad Delia at least offered you coffee while you waited for me," Marlon remarked then frowned. "We've had better help around here."

"Do you think the guys will fit in out there?" Kane asked as he leaned forward in his chair.

"They're strong, good looking guys," Marlon remarked while leaning back in his chair. "Jasmine was already drooling over them as I left. As long as they're not easily offended, they'll be fine."

Scorpio gave Marlon a bewildered look. "I thought your sister was married," she remarked.

Marlon snorted a laugh. "That's never stopped her from flirting before," he teased then made a face. "It's probably why the guys listen to her more than me. Before we discuss your new positions and meet the rest of the house, have you learned anything?"

"Your father was right," Kane announced and leaned back in his chair. "Boyd's background check was spotless. He's just your average guy."

Rayner finally looked up from his laptop and shut the lid. "I'm more interested in his sister's past," he announced surprising Marlon.

"Delia?" Marlon asked while raising a curious brow. "Other than being a mediocre maid, what makes you suspicious of her?"

"I didn't say I was suspicious," Rayner replied. "Boyd's background check indicated his mother and sister supposedly died in a boating accident several years ago. Six months later, she was discovered in a hospital in Costa Rica suffering from amnesia after the accident."

"Yes, we're aware of the accident," Marlon responded with a bored sigh. "When Boyd discovered she was alive, he went to Costa Rica to get her. Seeing her brother brought back her memory. End of story."

"With gaps," Rayner replied. "It said to this day she has no memory of the accident itself."

"So I've heard," Marlon remarked and appeared curious. "Do you find that troubling?"

"No, just interesting," Rayner replied while eyeing Marlon. "Boyd was estranged from his mother and sister when he went to live with his father after his parents divorced. Shortly after their divorce, his mother moved to Costa Rica with his sister. After the mother died, Boyd received a sizeable inheritance, which he seemed to share with his sister after it was discovered she survived the accident."

Marlon waved him off with little interest. "That sizeable inheritance was only enough to sustain them for a couple of years," he reported. "Sustain meaning they didn't have to hold down full-time jobs, but it wasn't enough to live comfortably. The way I understand it, they have some money left in savings, but it's nothing substantial. Boyd probably spent most of that impressing my sister with that eye-popping engagement ring." He sat back in his chair and smirked. "Brandi is easily distracted by shiny things."

"That's the only red flag I see regarding Boyd," Rayner informed him.

"I hate to sound cold," Marlon announced and eyed all three. "But if you can dig up something that'll stop this wedding, please, dig away."

"You don't like Boyd?" Scorpio asked.

"He came to work for us the past spring with zero experience. He was and remains the worst wrangler we have," Marlon informed her. "By the end of last summer, he charmed the pants off my spoiled little sister. The whole idea is beyond comprehension. My sister never gave a wrangler a second glance before Boyd came along, yet she somehow managed to fall in love with him over the course of a few months." He frowned with disgust. "At the end of August, they'll be married after only being together for one year." Marlon leaned back in his chair and frowned. "It's not that I don't believe people can fall in love and get married so quickly, but I have a difficult time believing it's possible for Brandi. She's my sister, and I love her, but she's a spoiled, immature flake. I'd be very happy if this wedding didn't happen." His attention then shifted to Kane. "So while playing bodyguard to Brandi, if my little sister shows the slightest interest in you, feel free to act upon any impulses you may have."

Scorpio shifted in her chair and glanced at Kane to gauge his reaction. She had to give him credit for not flinching at the comment.

"I'll keep that in mind," Kane replied without reacting either way.

Marlon smiled and laughed with some embarrassment. "Judging by your reaction, I suppose that was out of line," he remarked.

"Your sister might think so, but as her brother, it's your right to offend and torment her," Kane announced then grinned. "That's what little sisters are for."

Scorpio glared at Kane. "I'm older than you."

Kane groaned and rolled his eyes. "By like ten minutes," he scoffed. "Get some new material." He returned his attention back to Marlon. "So does your sister know I'm her new bodyguard? Because following her around might be awkward otherwise."

"Yes, she's aware my father hired you to protect her," Marlon remarked then gently scratched his temple while making a face. "And, to be honest, she's not particularly happy about it."

"Well, Scorpio never cared for me hanging around her either, but I managed to stay glued to her," Kane remarked while grinning. "I don't see a problem."

"If she throws a tantrum, just ignore her and do what you're paid to do," Marlon informed him. "Here in the house, give her whatever space she requires. I'll introduce you to the little princess on our way out." He then looked at Rayner. "Is there anything you need from me regarding your security assessment?"

"Your father gave me a general idea where he'd like cameras, so I just need to poke around and find the best placement for the equipment," Rayner replied.

"By all means," Marlon announced and extended his hand. "Poke around."

"There's no cell phone reception out here, is there?" Rayner asked.

Marlon laughed and shook his head. "No, you have to make calls the old-fashioned way," he announced. "You'll find landline phones in most of the rooms. My sister and I use walkie-talkies to communicate with the ranch hands."

"We're used to limited cell service," Scorpio remarked. "Where we live is in a dead zone too."

"Then you won't suffer from cell phone withdrawal," Marlon teased.

Rayner was about to stand when Marlon focused his attention on Scorpio.

"My father wasn't sure where to place you," Marlon informed Scorpio. "The best we could come up with was introducing you as my new girlfriend."

Rayner slid back in his seat and made himself comfortable. He opened his laptop and fiddled with it as if he hadn't been paying attention, although he wasn't fooling anyone.

Marlon glanced at Rayner and chuckled. "You have nothing to worry about, Rayner," he announced. "I'm a perfect gentleman. I've invited lady friends to the house to spend a week or two without even sharing a bedroom. I don't move nearly as fast as my sister in that arena."

"I wasn't worried," Rayner casually replied.

Kane made a face that Rayner couldn't see then rubbed his eyes while holding back his groan. Scorpio cast a disapproving glare at her brother. She didn't need Kane feeding into Rayner's insecurities. Rayner already had some concerns that they were a mismatch based solely on the fact that her first and only boyfriend prior to him had been a former soldier. Scorpio blamed Rayner's high IQ for his insecurities regarding their relationship. He thought too much. Scorpio didn't need a man to defend her; she could take care of herself. He was attentive and made her feel important. That's what she loved about him. She only wished she had reinforced those feelings when they first got together, but she was too busy feeling sorry for herself over the loss of her first boyfriend.

"Okay then," Marlon announced and sprang up from his chair. "I'll have Delia show Scorpio to her room while I introduce Kane to the she-devil." He then pointed at Rayner. "And you can go do your thing."

Chapter 12

Kane followed Marlon into the game room, where most of the home's entertainment was located. The game room was roughly the size of a three-car garage with a huge, wooden carved bar, a living section with plush furniture, and a large flat screen television mounted on the stone wall. There was an expensive pool table toward the back wall and more than enough room for entertaining a decent sized party. Brandi lay dramatically across the large, sectional sofa with her feet hanging over the back of the sofa and her head hanging off the seat and just about touching the floor. She talked on the cordless phone and appeared bored while flipping through channels on the big screen television.

Marlon eyed Kane and raised his brows while conveying his disapproval. "Well, there's the princess," he announced and shook his head. "Honestly? Does that look like a girl who's ready to settle down and take on the responsibilities of married life?"

"How old is she?" Kane asked while raising a skeptical brow.

"Twenty-one last month," Marlon scoffed and folded his arms across his chest while watching his sister with a permanent frown on his face. "You'd swear she was just a clueless teenager, huh?"

Kane refrained from commenting, but Marlon could read his expression.

"She's only interested in partying, talking on the phone with her friends, and watching videos on social media." He cast a look at Kane. "At her age, I was already running this ranch. That one was thrown out of college for showing up at her classes drunk." He shook his head. "I swear; the hospital must have switched my real sister for that one."

Kane snickered at the comment.

"You and Scorpio are twins?" Marlon then asked with a curious look.

"Yeah, identical twins," Kane replied while maintaining a serious expression.

Marlon eyed him then laughed. "How old are you? Twenty-five?"

"I don't give out that information," Kane remarked simply. "But if you're asking about Scorpio, she's twenty-two."

Marlon again laughed and slapped Kane on the back. "You're okay." He then frowned. "It's hard to believe you and your sister are only a year older than Brandi. It doesn't seem possible."

"We were raised by our grandparents," Kane informed him. "I'm sure that has something to do with why we are the way we are." He then laughed. "Believe it or not; I'm the good twin."

"Your sister is the evil twin?"

"She's got demons," Kane remarked in a serious tone. "Completely unstable. She gets it from our father."

"What was he like?"

Kane shrugged. "I don't know," he replied. "I've never met him."

"What makes you think she's like him?" Marlon asked. "What was your mother like?"

Kane again shrugged with little emotion. "I don't know. I never knew her."

Marlon stared at Kane's profile while he watched the immature woman gossiping to her friend upside down on the sofa.

Marlon shook his head and gave up. "Let's get this over with," he announced and approached the sofa. Marlon took the remote control from Brandi and shut off the television. "We have company."

Brandi glared at her brother and frowned while sitting up straight. "I have to go, Babs," she announced into the cordless phone. "El Comandante is pitching a fit." Brandi disconnected the call and sprang to her feet to face her brother with an annoyed look. "What?"

Marlon indicated Kane. "I'd like you to meet Kane, your new babysitter."

She sneered at her brother then looked at Kane for the first time. Her brows immediately rose as she took in an eyeful of the handsome man.

"Well, if I must have a babysitter, Daddy certainly picked a good one," she remarked then managed a smile. "Welcome to the asylum, Kane."

"Be nice to him. He has permission to use live ammunition," Marlon threatened then placed his hand on Kane's shoulder. "Good luck." Her brother then turned and left the game room.

"He's just the ray of sunshine, huh?" Brandi scoffed, eyed Kane again, and once more smiled. "I was sort of expecting someone, well, the size of a tank."

"You're saying I don't look like a bodyguard?" Kane asked while cleverly raising his brow.

"No, not really," she remarked. "You look more like the lead guitarist in a rock band."

"Yeah, I get that a lot," Kane replied with a strange grin on his face. "The art of illusion is a powerful thing." He grinned in a mildly psychotic manner. "Never reveal your hand until the betting's done."

Brandi eyed him suspiciously while grinning. "You got a gun?"

"Nope."

She gave him a bewildered look. "You're not big and intimidating, and you don't carry a gun," Brandi remarked while folding her arms across her dainty chest. "How do you intend to protect me from the make-believe bad guys my father seems to think are after me?"

"If they're make-believe, I'll just pretend to shoot them," Kane replied.

Brandi stared at him a moment then smiled and giggled. "And what if they turn out to be real?" she asked while grinning then playfully swatted his forearm. "That wit will probably get your ass kicked."

He leaned closer to her and cleverly raised his brows. "I'm secretly a superhero in disguise," Kane whispered.

She gave him a strange look then laughed. "Okay, you're cool," Brandi announced. "You can stay. Do you like horror movies?"

"The bloodier, the better," he replied. "Give me your worst."

Brandi threw herself onto the sofa and patted the cushion near her. Kane collapsed onto the sofa near her while she started a movie she already had in the DVD player. Just as the movie started, Sig's trophy wife entered the game room. Emily Hooper was a voluptuous woman only a few years older than Sig's oldest daughter. One look at the woman, and it was evident why Sig married her. She had long, auburn hair that touched her large breasts, and she dressed in stylish, revealing clothes despite the casual country life in which she married.

"Taking the day off, Boyd?" Emily remarked and swatted Kane on the shoulder as she paused by the sofa.

Brandi and Kane looked back at Sig's wife.

Emily saw Kane, realized it wasn't Boyd, and appeared embarrassed. "Oh, I'm sorry, I didn't--" she fumbled over herself then managed to cover with a smile. "You must be the, uh, bodyguard Sig hired."

Kane sprang to his feet and simultaneously leaped around the arm of the sofa in one fluid motion almost like a stalking cat. He extended his hand to Emily.

"Kane," he politely introduced himself.

Emily studied him a moment then grinned her approval while accepting his hand. "Emily Hooper."

"My step-mom," Brandi informed him with little emotion and resumed watching the movie.

"Oh," Kane remarked with embarrassment and laughed. "I thought you were Brandi's sister, Jasmine."

Emily immediately blushed at the compliment. "Aren't you charming?"

"Yeah, he oozes charm," Brandi muttered from the sofa. "He's either a really nice guy or the world's greatest con artist."

Kane ignored the comment and maintained his smile at Sig's wife while indicating the young woman on the sofa. "We're still bonding."

"Good luck with that. I look forward to getting to know you, Kane," Emily announced while grinning. "I'll leave the two of you to your movie."

As Emily left the room, Kane returned to the sofa. Brandi kept her eyes glued on the television.

"She likes you," Brandi remarked with little emotion.

"I have that effect on people," Kane replied and smiled slyly. "I'm adorable."

Brandi laughed. "Maybe," she replied then turned her head and stared at him with a serious look. "But I meant she *likes* you."

Kane cast a strange look at the young woman. "Isn't she married to your father?"

Brandi shrugged and didn't bother looking at him. "Hasn't stopped her before," she remarked. "My father is gone more than he's here. She's lonely, I suppose."

"That's a dangerous combination," Kane remarked.

"Yeah, it's Peyton Place around here," Brandi casually announced. "You get used to it after a while."

Kane attempted to watch the movie but was now deep in thought. It was going to be an interesting week.

Chapter 13

Rayner walked through several rooms and checked for the best locations to add cameras according to Sig Hooper's security needs. Most of the cameras would be angled to keep an eye on outside entrances. The sheer number of doors and windows requiring alarms was mind-boggling. Rayner entered the sunroom, which was aptly named. The entire room was wall-to-wall windows and roughly the size of a hotel lobby. There were glass doors leading out to the patio with a poolside view. The room contained a light colored tile floor, several sets of wicker furniture, and a large fireplace off to the left. As Rayner scanned the room to decide where he'd need to place security cameras, he noticed a man in his early thirties enjoying a glass of iced tea. The warm afternoon sun poured into the room while the man watched the ranch activities beyond the wall of windows.

"Sorry," Rayner announced and appeared embarrassed for interrupting the man's peace and quiet. "I don't mean to intrude."

The man turned, cast a look at Rayner, and set his laptop aside. He stood while offering a polite smile and extended his hand.

"You must be Sig's new security guy," the man politely announced. "I'm Conroy Smith; Sig's accountant and house manager."

"Rayner Roderick," he announced and politely shook the man's hand.

Conroy Smith was a moderately handsome man in his mid-thirties with light brown hair cut businessman short. He matched Rayner in size and build. Being Sig's accountant, he was probably also Rayner's intellectual equal. The similarities between the two men were uncanny. Conroy eyed the electronic tablet Rayner was using to take photos of rooms and jot notes on each picture with his stylus pen.

"Is that the new tablet I've been reading about?" Conroy asked with increasing interest in Rayner's newest toy.

"Yes," Rayner replied and handed it to him. "I bought it a few days ago before flying out to Colorado."

Conroy touched a few screens and seemed instantly envious. "Mine is on back order," he remarked and eyed Rayner as he returned the tablet. "It's difficult getting the latest and greatest tech out here this far from civilization."

"I have friends who get me the hard to find toys," Rayner remarked.

"I gave up friends and hard to find toys when I moved up here to no man's land," Conroy remarked while attempting to keep his sense of humor. The man was clearly unhappy with his living arrangements.

"You're married to Sig's oldest daughter, Jasmine, right?" Rayner asked.

"Sig got you up to speed on the family, I see," Conroy teased.

"I'm paid to be nosy," Rayner remarked while grinning. "A little background on the family's security needs and daily operations of the ranch helps fit the right security system to the client."

"Certainly he's not putting cameras inside the house," Conroy remarked with a strange look.

"Just on the first floor with a view of outside entrances," Rayner replied as he fiddled with his tablet. He was good at multi-tasking. "As I understand it, the system won't be manned."

"Does it digitally record then?" Conroy asked seeming interested.

"Yes, so the footage can be viewed later," Rayner informed him. "I suggested motion sensor cameras so they wouldn't be activated unless something triggered it, but Sig opted for continuous streaming. I don't know why he wants hours of back door footage when nothing's happening."

"Sounds like you have your work cut out for you," Conroy announced while seeming interested. "I have a lot of time on my hands throughout the day. If you need assistance, I'd be more than happy to give you a hand."

"I may take you up on that," Rayner replied and flashed a smile. "I'm used to working with a crew, but I certainly couldn't fly them out here."

"You're in luck," Conroy announced while grinning. "If it requires tools, the wranglers love playing fix-it around the house. They also enjoy extra pay for their wild weekends in town."

"What sort of weekend entertainment is there around here?" Rayner asked with some surprise.

"There's a town about an hour from here," Conroy informed him. "It's not a big town, but it has a couple of bars, a club, bowling alley, restaurants, and a movie theater. The guys usually find something or *someone* to entertain them."

"Must get pretty quiet around here on weekends," Rayner teased although his mind was already working on the best use of an empty house.

"Very," Conroy announced with a bored sigh. "If you want to go to town on the weekend, I'm sure you'll find someone willing to give you a ride." He offered a tiny grin and chuckled. "I saw you arrive on Sig's air taxi, so I'm assuming you don't have your own car."

"I heard it's quite a haul from Colorado Springs to the ranch," Rayner remarked.

"A lot of long, winding roads through God's country," Conroy reported. "No easy way to drive here, that's for sure. You arrived with Sig's new ranch hands and that bodyguard he hired for Brandi."

Rayner nodded and continued with his work.

"I'd heard we were getting a new maid to help prepare the house for the wedding in August," Conroy continued and seemed to be skirting around the subject. "Was that the new maid that arrived with you?"

Rayner tensed but continued with his work. "Uh, no, I don't think so," he replied. "We didn't really get the chance to talk. I think she's a friend of Sig's son."

"Really?" Conroy remarked and seemed interested. "It's been a while since Marlon's had a lady friend visit."

"Oh?" Rayner replied while attempting to sound disinterested. "Well, lucky him."

Conroy snorted a laugh. "You aren't kidding," he replied. "He doesn't usually find women that hot willing to travel this far from civilization. The country is beautiful, but you sacrifice a lot living this far from the modern world. Not that you can't find attractive women in these small towns, but they're few and far between."

Rayner seemed uncomfortable with the current topic. "I'd better continue with my work," he insisted. "I'd like to have some numbers together for Sig when he returns later this afternoon."

"Yeah, sure," Conroy replied. "Let me know if you need help with that."

"I certainly will," Rayner announced then headed for the door.

Rayner was obviously preoccupied with Conroy's mention of Marlon's imported lady friends and the scarcity of female companionship.

Chapter 14

Later that afternoon, Sig's Army green Land Rover drove the rarely traveled back road beyond a small town, which was their only source of entertainment outside of ranch life. It had been a three-hour drive from Colorado Springs to the small town and another hour until they reached the ranch. Neither Mac nor Sig was much for small talk, so it was a quiet drive without even the radio to break the unnerving silence. Though neither seemed to mind the quiet ride.

"Sorry for the long drive," Sig announced finally breaking the silence. "I guess I should have mentioned the air taxi was a helicopter."

"It's okay," Mac replied and seemed stranded in her own thoughts. "I don't mind the long drive. It's better than the alternative."

"Jackie's an excellent pilot," Sig informed her. "For her age, I was pleasantly surprised at her skills."

"I don't doubt her skills," Mac remarked with some hidden meaning to her words. "Just *seeing* that helicopter made me nauseous."

"Too bad, really," he replied. "Kane filled you in on your position at the ranch?"

"Yeah, he mentioned it," Mac replied and made a face that Sig couldn't see.

"With the wedding in a few weeks, hiring a new maid made perfect sense," Sig announced with little emotion. "No one will be suspicious of that, and Delia will be delighted for the additional help. She can be a bit of a dictator, but Kane said you're a delightful woman and can tolerate just about anyone."

Mac cast a surprised look at Sig's profile while he drove. When he looked at her, she immediately smiled.

"How sweet of him to say," Mac remarked and found it hard to keep from laughing. "Delia? That's Boyd's sister, right?"

"Yeah," Sig replied then sighed while shaking his head. "Felt sorry for her. They finally reconnected three years ago. They were just kids when their parents divorced. The mother took Delia with her to Costa Rica on some humanitarian effort. A few years later, they were out boating, and their boat sank. Parts of the boat washed to shore, so the authorities were convinced both had died. Six months later, Boyd receives word that his sister is alive. She'd survived the wreck, but she suffered from amnesia. He ran off to Costa Rica and brought her home."

"That's interesting," Mac replied almost mechanically since she wasn't the least bit interested.

"Most of us go our entire lives without living through something so traumatic," Sig remarked and shook his head. "Nothing quite so exciting has ever happened in these parts." He eyed her. "How about you? In your line of work, you must have seen some exciting things."

Mac's mind seemed to reel a moment at everything she'd survived. She looked back at Sig, raised a brow, and offered a tiny smile.

"I've met some interesting people in my time," she commented with little emotion. "A few even survived the experience."

Sig looked at her with surprise. Mac grinned in response. He suddenly smiled and laughed at the comment. She laughed along with him because it was funny that he thought she was just kidding.

§

*O*nce they reached the ranch, Mac was introduced to the housemaid, Delia, who showed her to her room within the staff wing just off the kitchen. Mac entered the bland room behind the young maid. Delia Flint was a slender, attractive woman in her mid to late twenties with long, silky amber colored hair. Despite living on a ranch in the middle of nowhere, the casually dressed maid wore carefully applied makeup and seemed to find time to do her nails. Delia turned to face Mac and offered a slightly humored smile.

"Considering the grandeur of the rest of the house, our rooms aren't exactly four-star," the maid announced. "At least they're clean and comfortable."

Mac shrugged with little care as she placed her duffel bag on the bed and sat alongside it. "The mattress is comfortable," Mac replied then looked around. "The private bathroom is a nice touch." She looked at Delia and smirked. "It's nicer than my last apartment in Colorado Springs."

"Like I said," Delia replied and grinned. "It's comfortable. Mr. Hooper said I should show you the ropes first thing tomorrow morning. We have breakfast in the kitchen with the wranglers at six in the morning. We start work at seven. If you miss breakfast, lunch isn't until noon."

Mac nodded then eyed the young woman. "Is the dress code casual?"

"Yeah, come as you are," Delia replied and gave a general wave. "We don't have a dress code or uniforms. It's pretty casual. You can wear jeans if you'd like. I like to dress in layers. It's cooler in the morning then gets pretty warm in the afternoon."

"Thanks," Mac replied and maintained her pleasant smile until Delia left the room.

Mac immediately sneered and collapsed on the bed while clasping her hands over her abdomen. "Housemaid," she muttered. "Fucking fantastic."

There was a soft knock on her bedroom door. Mac sprang from the bed to continue the charade for Delia's benefit.

"It's open," Mac replied.

Kane slipped into the room and quickly shut the door behind him. Mac saw him, groaned, and again collapsed onto the bed.

"Oh, it's just you," she replied then raised an arrogant brow. "Not the most glamorous job. All things being equal; I'd rather be in the bunkhouse with the wranglers."

"It was Sig's suggestion," Kane informed her as he moved her duffel bag and collapsed onto the bed next to her. "Work is work for now."

"I know," Mac replied with a sigh then fell back onto the bed and stared at the ceiling. She let a loud sigh escape. "I'm trying to stay positive. I'll be thinking of you when I scrub my first toilet."

Kane lay back on the bed alongside her and folded his hands across his abdomen. He joined her in staring at the ceiling. "Scorpio's mad at me too," he remarked.

"I'm not mad at you," Mac insisted then hesitated and eyed him where he lay not far from her. "Why is Scorpio mad? She has the glamorous job."

Kane eyed her and raised his brow. "She'd rather play the maid," he replied.

"Tell her she can have it," Mac announced. "I'll gladly trade with her."

"It's too late to switch things up," Kane insisted then groaned. "I think Sig did this on purpose." He shot a look at Mac. "Keep this between us."

"Why?" she asked and propped herself up on her elbows. "What's going on?"

"I think Sig is hoping to pimp out my sister to his son," Kane remarked while frowning. "You should have seen the way Marlon was checking out Scorpio while giving his 'gentleman' speech." He rolled his eyes while groaning. "Rayner is seething with jealousy. I just hope Marlon isn't stupid enough to make a play for Scorpio."

Mac chuckled in her throat and grinned. "She'll rip his head off and hand it to him, huh?"

"I don't have to tell you that the success of this assignment is important," Kane announced then looked at her and raised his brows. "You have no idea how much of a powder keg my sister is."

"She can certainly fight," Mac remarked.

"This has nothing to do with her fighting ability," Kane insisted. "Scorpio can be the calmest most rational person you'll ever meet, but there's a point where she snaps and turns into a raging beast."

"Like at the casino?"

Kane snorted a slightly nervous laugh. "No, that's Scorpio when she's in control," he informed her. "This is something completely off the rails. I've only witnessed it once while we were growing up, but it happened again the night her boyfriend was killed and again when some men attacked her hotel. I don't need her turning into some raging monster because Sig's trying to get his son laid."

Mac sat up and sighed while looking back at Kane. "Anything I can do?"

Kane sat up as well and shrugged. "I'm not sure there is," he replied. "Just keep an eye on Scorpio when I'm not around. If things seem to be getting tense with her cover, we may have to step in."

"You can count on me," Mac replied.

Kane captured Mac's hand and affectionately kissed it. "Do your best," he announced. "If you have any problems, come see me. If you're uncomfortable with your cover, we'll figure something else out."

Mac stared at him a moment then offered a tiny, reassuring smile. "I'll be fine," she replied and raised a cocky brow. "Don't worry about me. I heard I'm a delightful woman who can tolerate just about anyone."

Kane suddenly grinned and laughed. "It sounds even funnier when you say it," he teased then heaved himself from the bed. "Do me one more favor."

Mac raised her brows in question.

"If I look like I'm losing my shit, remind me to keep it together."

"I'll gladly bitch slap you back into reality," she teased while grinning.

"You're my rock," he announced then pointed at her. "Remember that."

"Yeah, fuck off."

"That's my badger." Kane laughed, blew her a kiss, and left the room.

Chapter 15

Monday, June 23rd. Six o'clock the following morning, Mac ventured into the kitchen dressed casually for her first day as Delia's assistant maid. The cook, Alma, already had a hearty breakfast prepared for the ten wranglers and both maids. Alma was a robust, older woman in her early to mid-sixties with a full head of silver hair. Despite her age; country living agreed with Alma. Her makeup-free face had a youthful appearance with few wrinkles, and, like everyone else on the ranch, her skin was bronze from spending her fair share of time in the sun working for pleasure in her own garden. All the fresh vegetables and spices came from her garden as well as the fresh flowers in many of the rooms.

The wranglers were already filtering into the kitchen and seemed to have their usual seats at the large, heavy wooden table. Alma worked her way around the sturdy table filling coffee mugs for the wranglers as they found their seats. Stone and Maverick were last to enter the kitchen since they were just learning the daily routine and this would be their first breakfast. Stone saw Mac, who had been keeping her distance since she wasn't sure where she should sit, and offered her a charming smile as he pulled a vacant chair out for her. Mac smiled in return and felt a little more comfortable about taking a seat at the table filled with unfamiliar men. Stone then took the vacant seat next to her. Maverick found one of two empty seats across the table from them and appeared reluctant to sit. He gingerly sat on the wooden chair and made a face. The other wranglers immediately burst out laughing.

Maverick smirked in response. "Yes, I'm saddle sore," he announced. "Have your laughs. I know the drill. It's been a while since I've been on horseback that long."

"You'll get used to it," the foreman, Teddy, announced.

Teddy was the head wrangler, third in charge after Jasmine and Marlon. He'd been working the ranch since he was seventeen, which made him the senior employee with fifteen years of service. Teddy had sandy brown hair and heavily bronzed skin from all his time outside tending to the herd. He was average height and build, although most of the wranglers were built athletic from all their hard work. Despite that he wasn't the most handsome man; he was friendly and approachable, which was necessary considering the high turnover of wranglers each season.

Delia took the remaining vacant seat as Alma finished pouring everyone coffee. Mac, Stone, and Maverick attempted to gauge the others when none partook in the family style breakfast laid out before them. All three were slightly taken back when the men folded their hands in prayer and bowed their heads. Mac was possibly the most shocked with the prayer before meals idea but followed suit.

"Bless this meal which now we take; to do us good for Jesus' sake," Alma announced while standing over the men and two women at the table. "Watch over and keep everyone safe while they work. We thank you for the new additions to our family. Amen."

"Amen," the men and Delia replied in unison.

Maverick and Mac watched Stone make the symbol of the cross on his chest and join them with "Amen". Both seemed slightly surprised by Stone's participation. Alma smiled and gave Stone's shoulder a gentle squeeze as she passed him, obviously pleased with his participation. The men eagerly dug into the feast before them and politely passed the serving platters around the table. Stone seemed to fit in perfectly while Mac and Maverick worked on a learning curve. Each time Maverick had to move within his chair, he'd do so with discomfort, gaining grins from his tormentors.

Teddy cast a look at Stone. "You said you hadn't ridden in a few years," he remarked. "Why aren't you suffering along with your friend there?"

"My momma tanned my hide growing up," Stone announced while grinning then chuckled. "I have a tough backside."

The men laughed at the comment.

"When do we get to try our hand at roping?" Stone eagerly asked.

Maverick rolled his eyes at the comment. Mac was the only one who noticed the action.

"Are you ready to start roping?" Teddy asked.

"Hell yeah," Stone replied with enthusiasm.

"Language," Alma announced from the counter.

Stone glanced back at her and offered his most sincere apologetic smile. "Sorry, ma'am," he announced. "Won't happen again."

Mac and Maverick exchanged looks from across the table. Maverick mouthed 'hell' to her with a puzzled look. Mac grimaced and shrugged in response. Being in Alma's presence was going to be rough on Mac. Her discomfort indicated her manners were sorely in need of polishing.

"I'll try to get you a little practice time roping this afternoon," Teddy announced then cast a look at Maverick. "If you don't fall off today, we'll see about teaching you to rope later in the week."

Maverick smirked in response.

"You fell off?" Mac asked although she didn't mean to ask it aloud.

Maverick frowned and held up two fingers. There was a round of laughter as the men all held up three fingers in response.

"That last time didn't count," Maverick insisted. "I was already dismounting."

"I'll admit," Teddy announced while grinning. "You do fall with a certain, what's that fancy term?"

"Finesse," Stone teased.

Teddy snapped his fingers at Stone and grinned. "Yeah, that's the word."

There was another round of laughter at Maverick's expense. Mac offered Maverick a sympathetic look since she must have felt almost as out of place as he had.

"Seriously though," Stone announced. "He's a far better card player than he is at wrangling, so you may want to go easy on him."

"You're pretty good with cards?" one of the other men asked.

"I'm a master at gin," Maverick announced while offering a sly smile.

"What about poker?" Teddy asked while raising a brow. "Are you any good at poker?"

"I haven't played in a while," Maverick remarked. "I'm sure it'll come back to me."

There was a round of snickers, including Stone, who cast a sly glance at his friend. Mac hid her grin because she knew a hustle when she saw one. Once the men finished their breakfast and a few cups of coffee, each man took his plate to the sink for Alma. She obviously had them trained. Mac and Delia would help Alma clean up after breakfast so the cook could start on breakfast for the family. The men thanked Alma for their meal then headed back outside for their full day of work. After cleaning up the kitchen, Mac helped Delia set the table in the dining room for the family breakfast. She would also assist in serving breakfast before making beds and cleaning the guestrooms. Despite that Boyd was Brandi's fiancé, he ate breakfast and lunch with the wranglers. He would then have dinner with the family after his workday was finished. Until he married Brandi and moved into the main house, it was the only fair solution Sig could negotiate.

Chapter 16

A few minutes before eight o'clock that morning, Scorpio left her bedroom and saw Rayner waiting across the hallway just outside his room. He smiled when he saw her and approached without hesitation.

"Did you get any sleep last night?" he asked with a curious look.

She managed a timid smile and shrugged. "Not really," Scorpio replied.

"I couldn't sleep either," Rayner remarked and shifted uncomfortably. "It's going to be a long week."

"Or two," Scorpio muttered.

Rayner groaned and rubbed his tired eyes. "At least I have a lot of work to keep me busy," he remarked.

"Walk me downstairs?" she asked with a sympathetic smile and caressed his arm.

"I saw Conroy head down the back stairs a few minutes ago," he replied uncomfortably. "I think it'd be better for appearance' sake if I went that way by myself."

Scorpio felt bad and nodded. "I suppose you're right," she replied timidly. "See you at breakfast."

She blew him a kiss, which made him smile, then headed for the main stairs. Scorpio headed down the grand stairs where she was greeted by Marlon at the bottom. It seemed a little too convenient. He must have been waiting for her.

"Good morning," he announced cheerfully and escorted her to the dining room. "How did you sleep?"

Scorpio didn't want to get into her bouts of insomnia with Marlon and told him what he wanted to hear. "I slept well," she replied.

Scorpio couldn't remember the last time she'd slept through an entire night. To make matters worse, last night was the first time in weeks she'd slept without Rayner alongside her. If she slept an hour, she was lucky. At one point during the night, she considered sneaking into Rayner's room, but she couldn't afford to blow her cover. If Kane's assignment failed, she didn't want it to be because of her lack of commitment. Scorpio and Marlon joined Kane, Rayner, and the rest of the family for breakfast. The family breakfast was more of a formal affair than the wrangler's breakfast in the kitchen had been. When Rayner saw Marlon pulling out Scorpio's chair for her, his look conveyed his disdain for the entire fabricated situation. Naturally, Sig sat at the head of the table while Marlon was honored with the second head of the table.

Although Jasmine sat to her father's left, it was obvious she was bothered that her brother was given the coveted, dominant position at the opposite end. Jasmine's husband naturally sat alongside her. Sig's wife, Emily, sat to his right. Rayner was seated alongside Conroy, where he could watch Scorpio almost directly across the table from him. Kane was seated alongside Brandi, who seemed to enjoy his company since their introduction yesterday. The seating arrangement put Kane alongside his sister. Despite enjoying his sister's company, it was slightly uncomfortable since they had to pretend they barely knew each other in front of the rest of the family. Kane put on a good show, in Scorpio's opinion, but she could tell he didn't like the idea of Mac serving him coffee.

"If I put a call in this morning," Sig announced to Rayner, "the equipment you need to install the security system should be here by this evening."

"That would be fantastic," Rayner replied then indicated Marlon at the opposite end of the table. "Your son tells me some of the wranglers would gladly help with the physical installation."

"Fine men and hard workers," Sig informed Rayner. "Extremely handy with tools and minimal instruction. Marlon will get a few of the guys together after dinner to help you with your project." Sig then looked at his son at the opposite end of the table. "How are the new men working out?"

Jasmine appeared mildly disgusted, possibly that she'd been passed over regarding the new men considering she was the one who did most of the actual work with them yesterday.

"Jasmine hasn't complained," Marlon teased while egging his sister on.

Kane cast a secret glance at Scorpio. The tension between Marlon and Jasmine wasn't playful banter as it was with Kane and Scorpio. Scorpio often complained about Kane, but she knew he appreciated her and would never consider her anything less than his equal. The fact that she could kick his ass may or may not have had anything to do with his respect for her. Jasmine avoided looking at her father and brother while silently seething.

Completely oblivious to his daughter's rising tension, Sig turned his attention to Scorpio, and he offered a pleasant smile. "How are you enjoying the ranch so far, Scorpio?"

"Marlon offered to give me the guided tour on horseback after breakfast," Scorpio announced. She could just about feel Rayner squirm in his chair.

"That sounds like fun," Kane boldly announced and glanced at Brandi. "Want to tag along?"

Brandi made a face at the suggestion then groaned. "Yeah, sure," she reluctantly muttered. "At least I can stop by and say hey to Boyd."

Kane offered a slightly sly and cheap grin across the table to Rayner. "Sounds like you have plenty of time until this evening," he announced. "Want to come along?"

Although Rayner had already made his position clear on horses, he jumped on the offer. "I wouldn't mind giving it a try," he announced. "I've never had the opportunity to ride horses. Who knows? Maybe I'll enjoy it."

Scorpio hid her smile and cast a quick look at Kane. Judging by his grin, he knew she was pleased with his effort to include Rayner. Sometimes her brother was okay. It almost made up for him dragging her into the entire sorted affair in the first place. Almost.

Marlon seemed uncomfortable including his pretend girlfriend's boyfriend but managed a weak smile. "I guess we have a riding party together," he announced.

"I'm just thrilled Brandi is tagging along for once," Sig teased. "Maybe she'll enjoy it and want to help run the ranch one day."

Marlon and Jasmine didn't seem to approve. Whatever power struggle was happening between the oldest siblings, it was obvious they didn't want an interested thirdparty getting involved in it.

Brandi just rolled her eyes. "Doubtful."

Scorpio's mind reeled as she listened to the conversation among the family at the breakfast table. Marlon and Jasmine refused to look at each other. The tension between them was obvious, at least to Scorpio. Scorpio cast subtle glances at her brother. After several months of being separated from him, she'd almost forgotten their unusual 'twin' connection. Kane often boasted that they were the same person just split into two people. He was smart enough to know fraternal twins weren't two halves of one whole, but she couldn't deny that they somehow always knew what the other was thinking. As she caught a look at his profile, she could almost feel his eyes on Emily. She subconsciously glanced at Emily and saw the woman's eyes upon Conroy across the table from her. The look was almost lustful.

Kane casually turned his head and met Scorpio's gaze. He raised his brows in silent conversation as if secretly telling her something. Scorpio scratched her brow while returning the look. A tiny smirk crossed Kane's face. Did Kane actually believe Sig's trophy wife had eyes for her son-in-law? They were only a few years apart in age. Scorpio returned her attention back to her breakfast. She needed to get out of Kane's head and wanted him out of hers. If she intended to get through what promised to be a long day, she was going to need more coffee. Kane leaned back in his chair and caught Mac's attention while offering a pleasant smile.

"Could we have more coffee, Miss?"

Mac grabbed the coffee carafe and approached them. As Mac filled both their cups, Scorpio eyed her brother. Was it learned behavior or was he actually reading her mind? Kane passed her the sugar without looking at her as if silently answering her question. It was quite possible her brother creeped her out.

Chapter 17

After the family breakfast, Sig was getting ready to leave for the city and wouldn't be back until late Saturday or possibly Sunday. Saturdays were big in his real estate office, and he liked to be on hand to help make some sales himself. Brandi returned to her room to change for their ride. Scorpio convinced Rayner to do the same. He was a little overdressed for horseback riding. Kane and Scorpio headed for the game room to play a little pool while they waited for Brandi and Rayner. Although Marlon was supposed to be heading into the barn to start saddling horses, Scorpio and Kane heard his voice within the hallway. They postponed their game and eavesdropped on the siblings talking loud and angry outside the game room.

"Must be nice to take the morning off to joyride with your new girlfriend," Jasmine scoffed at her brother. "Some of us have work to do, you know."

"Give it a break," Marlon snapped back. "Sitting on your horse lording over the men is not exactly work."

"I work harder than you ever had," Jasmine lashed out in a hostile tone. "I care more about the ranch's success than you ever could."

"Don't start that again," Marlon snarled at his sister. "You're just pissed because Dad put me in charge, and your say isn't nearly as equal to mine."

"Damned right," she shouted back at her brother. "Don't think I haven't heard you trying to get me in trouble with Daddy. I've got news for you, Marlon. I'm not going anywhere."

"When you and Conroy start a family, you won't want to be out working the ranch," Marlon insisted. "It's only natural that I'm in charge."

"Oh, you'd love that," she snapped back. "Me barefoot and pregnant in the kitchen with Alma. Forget it, brother dear. That isn't happening. You won't push me aside, and I intend to discuss my future here as an equal partner with Daddy. I won't be second fiddle to you."

"Fine, you talk to Dad when he gets back on Sunday," Marlon scoffed. "I have things to do."

Scorpio and Kane exchanged looks then approached the pool table.

"Did we ever fight like that?" Kane asked while eyeing his sister.

He snatched a pool stick and tossed it to her from several feet across the room. She caught the pool stick and twirled it as if it were a karate bow. Kane watched her with the pool stick and grinned.

"No, our fights were more physical in nature," Scorpio teased and aimed the fat end of the pool stick at her brother. Kane removed a pool stick for himself.

"That was just play fighting," Kane reminded her.

Kane twirled his pool stick fast and aggressive before taking a step toward her and meeting her stick with his.

"Mostly," she replied while smirking.

Kane eyed her with surprise and straightened while lowering his stick. "You purposely tried to hurt me?" he asked with a hurt look on his face.

"A few times," she replied while shrugging and lowering her stick as well. "I remember kicking you in the nuts on a few occasions."

He considered the comment and shrugged it off. "I'll give you that one," Kane replied. "I did steal your bra so I could use it for a slingshot across my minibike handlebars."

Kane propped his pool stick against the table and collected the pool balls in the triangle. Scorpio twirled the pool stick above her head and made an aggressive move for Kane's turned back. Kane snatched his pool stick, spun to face her, and clashed his stick against hers. Both smiled and laughed.

"There'll be none of that," Kane teased. "This isn't some old abandoned hotel. We can't afford to break some of this shit."

Scorpio laughed and moved away from her brother. "You're right about that."

"We can play when we're back home in Maine," Kane remarked.

"You're on."

§

Scorpio and Kane had just finished their first game of pool and started their second game when they heard Sig's car horn toot, signaling he was leaving. Both looked out the window to the front of the house and watched Sig's Land Rover head down the long, dirt driveway. They could see Emily standing in the driveway waving to him as he left. Scorpio and Kane witnessed Emily giving him the middle finger when he was far enough down the driveway that he couldn't see it. They again exchanged looks and raised their brows.

"This family is seriously dysfunctional," Kane remarked and shook his head. "They seem to hate one another with a passion." He then eyed her and grinned. "Admit it; you're happy to have been stuck with me as a brother."

Scorpio hid her smile. "You're not without your charm," she replied.

Kane suddenly grinned and opened his arms to hug her. "You love me!"

Scorpio casually pushed him away, twirled the pool stick in her hand, and approached the pool table to make her shot. "It's a love-hate relationship."

He chuckled in his throat. "You hate that you love me?" Kane teased.

She hid her smile and made her shot. In the distance, they heard what sounded like a gunshot. Scorpio and Kane looked at each other with concern and set their pool sticks down. They headed for the game room door and nearly collided with Brandi and Rayner, who had both changed into casual, riding clothes. It was difficult to tell who looked more stylish. Rayner couldn't help that he had good taste in clothes, but at least he ditched the tie for their ranch assignment.

"We heard a gunshot," Kane announced with concern.

"We were just discussing that," Rayner remarked.

Brandi rolled her eyes and waved him off. "It's nothing," she announced. "All the guys carry rifles. You'll hear that just about every day. The guys shoot them to scare off coyotes and rid the ranch of rattlesnakes."

Scorpio grimaced. "Rattlesnakes?"

"Don't worry," Brandi announced. "I doubt you'll see any on our ride. It's too cool in the morning. They don't come out until later in the afternoon when it's hot."

"That's reassuring," Rayner muttered.

"The guys trap them in a pit not far from the road," she informed them. "Some creepy snake guy comes and hauls them away once a month."

"I'd like to see that pit," Kane teased.

"I'd like to avoid it," Scorpio muttered.

"There's zero chance of you falling into it," Brandi reassured them. "You'll hear them if you're anywhere near it. Believe me."

Scorpio made a face.

Chapter 18

The four headed outside beyond the bunkhouse and found four horses saddled and tied to the long hitching post in front of the barn. There should have been five horses, but Marlon seemed to be missing. One of the wranglers appeared from the barn and smiled when he saw them.

"Morning," the wrangler announced politely and touched the brim of his cowboy hat.

They exchanged pleasantries with the wrangler then looked around for Marlon. Brandi approached the smaller palomino mare and greeted the horse with enthusiasm.

"Hey, girl," she announced and untied the horse from the hitching post.

The palomino mare was obviously Brandi's personal horse, and despite her distaste for country life, she handled the horse without fear or hesitation. She didn't even wait for the others before skillfully mounting her horse.

"I thought Marlon was meeting us out here," Kane informed the wrangler.

"He asked me to saddle the horses," the wrangler replied. "He had to check on something before your ride. He'll be back in a minute."

"Was he investigating that gunshot?" Scorpio asked.

"Gunshot?" the wrangler questioned then seemed to realize what she was talking about. "That? Oh, that was nothing. Probably one of the guys chasing off a coyote."

"Told you so," Brandi remarked with little interest while patting her horse's neck.

"I'll get you situated on your horses," the wrangler informed them. "I'll probably need to adjust the stirrups for some of you." He then indicated Scorpio. "Marlon said the lady should have Vlad." The wrangler untied the large black horse and backed it away from the hitching post.

"Any particular reason why I should have Vlad?" Scorpio asked with some concern by the horse's name.

The wrangler chuckled at her concern. "Vlad is a babysitter."

"A what?" Scorpio asked.

"He takes good care of his rider," the wrangler informed her while patting the horse. "He doesn't play games, and he'll give you a smooth ride."

It took a few minutes to get them situated on their horses and adjust their stirrups for them. Kane was given a moderately spirited horse, which suited him fine. He didn't have any more riding experience than his sister did, but he enjoyed a challenge, where Scorpio just wanted to finish the ride without any broken bones. Rayner was given a lazy horse that would simply follow the other horses. No riding experience was necessary, which suited Rayner just fine. Marlon still hadn't returned by the time they were ready, which irritated Brandi. She grew bored and rode past the others.

"Tell Marlon we're heading for Preacher's Pass," she informed the wrangler. "He can catch up."

"Shouldn't we wait--?" Rayner began, but Brandi was already riding away.

Kane shrugged, nudged his horse onward, and followed her. Rayner seemed to have no choice but to follow, since his horse followed Kane's horse without prompting. Scorpio laughed at Rayner's surprise by his horse's insistence on following. She gave her horse a slight nudge on the flanks with her heels and followed him. They followed Brandi along the pasture for several minutes without any sign of Marlon. As they rode, they could see the main road through the woods. Kane became interested at something he saw.

"Is that a car?" Kane remarked.

"Yeah, that's the road," Brandi informed him. "It's just beyond the woods."

"No, I mean in the ditch," Kane announced and pointed. "It looks like there's a car in the ditch."

Brandi stopped her horse and looked through the woods. All four saw the green Land Rover in the ditch. Brandi appeared concerned.

"Oh, my God," Brandi cried out in alarm. "That's Daddy's car."

She sent her horse into a lope and rode toward the woods. The others followed her through the woods and to the main road. Marlon's untied horse stood in the middle of the road minus its rider and watched the approaching horses. As the group got closer to the Land Rover in the ditch, they saw Marlon talking to Sig, who held a handkerchief to his bleeding temple.

"Are you sure you're okay?" Marlon asked and attempted to look at the bump on his father's head.

"I'm fine," Sig insisted with some irritation. "Just get the guys so we can pull this out of the ditch. I have to be in the city for a lunch meeting."

"Maybe you should see the doctor," Marlon pressed while doting over his father.

"No, no doctors," Sig insisted and became irritated. "I'm fine. It was just a blown tire. Let's get it out of the ditch and change the tire so I can be on my way."

What they thought was a gunshot could have easily been the sound of Sig's tire blowing.

"God, you're stubborn," Marlon scoffed then noticed Brandi as she approached on her palomino horse.

"Daddy, are you okay?" she asked with concern and jumped off her palomino mare. She let the horse roam free without being tied the same as her brother's horse.

"I'm fine," he insisted.

"If you still have the chain in the back of your truck, we can use the ropes and pull it out with the horses," Marlon informed him then indicated the others. "We have enough horses to pull it out easily."

Sig nodded in agreement. Everyone dismounted their horses while Sig and Marlon attached the thick chain just under the front bumper of his Land Rover. Marlon then tied ropes to four of the horse's saddle horns and attached the ropes to the chain. They left Rayner on his lazy horse since his horse wouldn't offer much to the tow job. Marlon then took the reins to all four horses and led them down the road while Sig gave the vehicle gas. Between the horses and the truck in drive, they easily pulled his vehicle out of the ditch. Marlon then helped his father change the tire. As Marlon and Sig placed the spare tire on the car, Kane rolled the blown tire to the back of the vehicle. He carefully inspected the tire before placing it in the back. Kane shut the hatch and approached Scorpio. He paused near her while casually looking into the woods as the men tightened the lug nuts on the new tire.

"That's one badly blown tire," Kane muttered to his sister while folding his arms across his chest.

"Do you think we did hear a gunshot?" Scorpio asked while looking toward the woods.

Kane frowned and shook his head. "I don't know," he replied. "The tire was pretty mangled, but I didn't see anything to indicate it was actually shot out. Maybe I'm just paranoid."

"And maybe you're not," she replied.

"Front driver's side," Kane informed her. "That would mean the sniper would have been in the woods near where we came out."

"From the ranch?" Scorpio asked while casting a quick, concerned look at him.

Kane nodded. As Marlon rolled up the rope and returned it to his father's truck, Kane approached Sig and pulled him aside.

"Have the tire inspected," Kane insisted surprising Sig with his comment.

"Inspected? For what?"

"We thought we heard a gunshot," Kane informed him relaying his concern.

"The tire blew," Sig insisted.

"Humor me, okay."

Sig stared at the serious look in Kane's eyes then reluctantly nodded. "I'll drop the tire off at a garage in the city later today," Sig replied. "I'll ask them to inspect it before they dispose of it."

Marlon brought Scorpio her horse and held it while she mounted. Despite that she didn't have any issue mounting; Marlon gave her an added boost with his hand on her backside. Scorpio was almost certain he knew exactly what he was doing, but she wasn't going to make waves. As far as Brandi knew, Marlon was her boyfriend, so she couldn't exactly protest. Unfortunately, Rayner saw it and wasn't pleased. When Marlon brought Kane his horse, Kane snatched the reins from him and gave him a stern, annoyed look. Rayner was suddenly the least of Scorpio's worries.

"Don't," Kane snarled just loud enough for Marlon to hear.

"Don't what?" Marlon asked almost innocently.

Kane raised his brows while glaring at Marlon. When Marlon saw the look in Kane's eyes, he took a step back and tensed slightly. Kane swiftly mounted the horse and gave Marlon a second glare for added effect.

Chapter 19

Mac and Delia helped Alma clean the kitchen after the family breakfast. Once they were finished in the kitchen, Alma then retired to her room to take a break before starting lunch at eleven. Delia took Mac onto the back patio and indicated the elegant, homey building as large as a three-car garage near the in-ground pool.

"That's the pool house," Delia informed her as they headed toward the building.

"That's a pool house?" Mac asked while raising her brows.

"Yeah, we clean that once a week," Delia replied and opened the door, allowing Mac to enter first.

Mac stepped into what resembled a large, studio apartment. The walls and cathedral ceiling were cedar, and it contained hardwood flooring throughout. There was a living area with a faux leather sofa before the stone fireplace and a large, flat screen television above it, which could be viewed from the living area or the nearby, king-sized bed. It contained a small kitchen with an island counter and counter seating. There was a large bathroom off to the one side, a laundry room, and a four-person hot tub in the back corner near the wall of windows, which contained vertical blinds. A small flat screen television was mounted on the wall above the hot tub so someone relaxing in the tub could watch television as well. A large, fully stocked bar was located near the kitchenette.

"This is nicer than most hotel rooms I've seen," Mac remarked.

"It's meant to be used for pool parties," Delia informed her. "Mostly, it's used by Mr. Hooper when he comes home late from the city. He doesn't like to disturb his wife, so he'll come out here, have a drink while soaking in the hot tub, and unwind while watching television." She then indicated the large bed. "He'll usually end up sleeping out here. That's why we clean it once a week."

"Mr. Hooper is the only one who uses the pool house?" Mac asked with a slightly surprised look.

Delia snorted a laugh. "Well, not the only one," she teased. "Sometimes, when his back is bothering him, Marlon Hooper comes out here to soak in the hot tub." She managed a laugh. "Although I can't prove it, I think the wranglers sneak out here and raid the bar every now and again too."

Delia approached the closet, opened the door, and indicated the cleaning supplies.

"I'll make the beds in the house, and you can clean out here," she informed her. "Cleaning the pool house should keep you busy until eleven when we help prepare lunch for the family. There are fresh sheets in the bathroom closet." Delia turned to leave then hesitated and looked back at Mac. "I'll warn you. Try not to look at the sheets when you strip the bed."

Mac gave the young woman a strange look and was about to question the comment when Delia beat her to it.

"I don't know specifics, and I'd rather not know," Delia announced and raised her brow. "But considering the stains I've found on the bedsheets, someone's been entertaining out here and with great frequency."

"That's pleasant," Mac muttered.

"And we get the pleasure of cleaning up after them," Delia announced with a smirk on her face.

"Do you think the wranglers are sneaking women out here?" Mac asked.

"The closest women are a mile or more away," Delia informed her. "If they're hooking up with local girls, there are about a million places more convenient than coming all the way back here."

Mac appeared curious while staring at Delia. "But there are only five women on this ranch," she reminded her.

Delia grinned and raised her brows. "Yeah, how about that," she teased. "Eventually, you're going to see something. I've found that you're better off minding your own business and keeping your mouth shut if you want to keep your job." Delia flashed a smile then headed for the pool house door. "See you in the kitchen at eleven."

Mac watched Delia leave then looked around the pool house and frowned. "I hate this job already," she muttered.

§

The herd of steer grazed in a lush pasture just out of view of the main house. The wranglers moved the herd into different areas on a rotating basis so the cattle wouldn't overgraze one pasture. Stone galloped his horse after a steer straying from the herd and brought it back. He was having the time of his life on the large horse that he was assigned. He affectionately patted the horse's neck, praising the horse's quick reflexes. The horses tended to pay attention to the cattle more than the wranglers did and often went after the steer with little to no prompting from its rider. It seemed as if the wrangler's job was to be in sync with their horse and anticipate each other's next move.

When a steer strayed from the herd not far from Maverick, his horse whirled around and chased the cow. Maverick didn't even rein the horse since the horse was operating on autopilot. His only job was to hang on and not fall off. When the steer attempted to bolt past the horse, Maverick's horse did his job by anticipating the steer's directional change and cutting it off. The horse's quick reflexes were like a dance to keep the cow from sneaking past it, but the swift movements were too much for Maverick to anticipate. He again lost his balance and toppled off the horse.

Maverick gracefully landed on the ground and rolled with it to prevent bodily harm except for some bruising to his already sore backside and his equally bruised ego. The horse continued to complete its mission and chased the steer back to the herd, leaving its rider sitting on the ground alongside his deflated ego. Jasmine caught Maverick's horse, and she rode across the pasture with the mare in tow. Maverick stood and brushed the dirt from his legs with his moderately crushed cowboy hat. She stopped her horse alongside him and shook her head, although she did offer a sympathetic smile.

"I'm beginning to think Pixie is a little too much horse for you," Jasmine announced while tossing him the horse's reins.

Maverick frowned and easily mounted the horse then met Jasmine's gaze. "One of her mare friends has been spreading rumors around the paddock about me," he informed Jasmine. "She just needs time to get to know me, and then we'll get along fine."

Jasmine laughed at the remark then shook her head. "I've got some bad news for you, Maverick," she announced. "Pixie is a diva. She knows she can push you around, and she's already lost all respect for you. You and Pixie weren't meant for each other. You should probably dump her and move on. We'll switch her out for an old, seasoned gelding. I'll bring Vlad out of retirement."

"Vlad?" Maverick remarked. "You want to put me on a horse named after Vlad the Impaler?" He shook his head. "That's not a very comforting image."

"He's a good horse and a great babysitter," she insisted.

Maverick gave her a look and raised his brow. "There goes what's left of my ego."

Jasmine laughed while taking in a sweeping eyeful of the handsome man. "It wasn't meant to sound that way," she insisted. "He keeps the young colts company when they're weaned from their mothers, and he's a great guest horse. He looks after his rider. You won't fall off him, I promise. And if you did, he'd wait by your side. He's more interested in protecting his rider than cutting cows."

"Sold," Maverick announced and grinned. "Where is the gentleman? I'd like to meet him."

"My brother lent him to his new girlfriend for their morning ride," Jasmine announced. "He's very popular with the ladies."

"Your brother?" Maverick asked with a curious look.

Jasmine laughed at the question. "No, Vlad," she replied then smirked. "My brother wishes he were as popular with the ladies as Vlad. I give his new girlfriend a week before she dumps him."

Maverick seemed to consider the comment and shifted uncomfortably. Scorpio's role as Marlon's new girlfriend reeked of setup. Sig may have had an ulterior motive regarding Scorpio.

Jasmine glanced at her watch then met Maverick's gaze. "We have about an hour before lunch. How about a change of pace?"

"You're the boss," Maverick replied with little care.

She removed her hand radio and pressed the button. "Teddy," Jasmine announced into the radio.

"Yeah, Jasmine," came the somewhat clear response, since the men weren't that far from them.

"I'm taking Maverick with me to ride some fences beyond the creek," she announced. "If Marlon is looking for either of us, tell him I said he should fuck himself."

Teddy chuckled over the radio. "You've got it, boss lady."

Jasmine replaced her radio to her belt then grinned at Maverick. "A nice leisurely ride should help boost your confidence, even if Pixie is a bitch."

"I'm not complaining," Maverick announced seeming pleased with the change of pace.

§

Maverick rode alongside Jasmine not far from the fence line that surrounded most of their ranch to keep cattle from straying off the property. They were looking for any downed barbed wire. When they reached a secluded area within the woods, Jasmine stopped her horse near the stream and dismounted.

"We'll give the horses a chance to rehydrate," she informed him then removed a flask from her inner jacket pocket. "As well as ourselves."

Maverick subconsciously eyed his watch as he dismounted his horse. It was only a little after eleven o'clock and seemed a little early for a nip. Since Jasmine didn't bother tying her horse and let it roam free to get a drink from the stream, Maverick did the same. Jasmine sat on a grassy spot in the small clearing and rested her back against a large tree. Maverick joined her and watched her take a healthy swallow from the flask. She handed it to him. Although he accepted the flask, he was apprehensive about drinking. He took a small sip while giving the illusion of a large swallow then returned the flask. It was straight up Jack Daniels.

Jasmine replaced the flask to her jacket, which she then proceeded to remove. She wore an unbuttoned plaid shirt overtop her low-cut tank top, which allowed a generous eyeful of her cleavage. Maverick had to look away to keep from staring then shifted uncomfortably.

"You and your brother don't really see eye-to-eye, huh?" he remarked then cast a glance at his boss.

By the time he cast a look at her, Jasmine had already slipped out of her plaid shirt and maneuvered onto her knees alongside him. Her cleavage was now at eye level and only a foot away from him. She smiled seductively.

"I don't want to talk about my brother," she informed him then straddled his legs as she placed her arms around his neck and pressed against him. "We have to be back by lunchtime. So that gives us half an hour for *anything goes.*"

Maverick was stunned by her aggressiveness and didn't even have time to think or respond before she kissed him wildly on the mouth. He immediately returned the kiss and instinctively caressed her back and buttocks as she ran her hands firmly along his body. As she feverishly worked on unbuckling his belt, rational thinking seemed to return to him. He stopped her hands and broke off the kiss surprising her. She met his gaze and saw the befuddled look in his eyes.

"You're married," Maverick informed her as if she needed reminding, but it sounded as if he were actually sending a warning to himself.

She suddenly grinned and giggled. "Yeah, so?" Jasmine aggressively kissed his neck and immediately returned her hand to his pants.

"So?" he gasped. Maverick seemed to have trouble thinking rationally with her body pressing against his while kissing his neck and attempting to open his pants. "I've seen your father's study. He's going to mount my head on his wall alongside his stuffed grizzly bear."

She giggled while kissing his neck. Jasmine couldn't open his belt with one hand without some cooperation from him, so she resorted to tempting him by caressing the bulge in his pants. Maverick groaned, and his hands again sought her backside, aggressively pulling her hips against his. She returned her mouth to his and kissed him, pleased with his compliance. Jasmine pushed him onto his back, placing herself on top of him as they feverishly groped each other while kissing passionately. Rational thinking again returned to him. This time, he broke off the kiss, rolled out from beneath her, and sprang to his feet. He clutched his head a moment with some unsteadiness from the abrupt movement.

"Please, forgive me," he announced while fumbling over his words and nervously closed his partially open belt. "I need to think about what I'm doing. When I make bad decisions that only affect me, that's one thing, but I have to think about my friends and how my actions affect them."

Jasmine groaned and ran her fingers through her slightly mussed hair. "You're concerned if we're caught it might affect your friend's job?"

Maverick considered the comment and seemed to think fast. "Yes," he responded, although he couldn't tell her about his *other* friends and the actual job they were hired to do. "Stone is enjoying the work. If I do something to jeopardize my job, he'll leave too. I can't do that to him." He hesitated and held his breath. "I can't do that to my family."

Jasmine sighed and extended her hand to him. He took her hand and helped her to her feet. She smiled and gently caressed his face.

"Will you at least consider continuing this conversation at a later date?" she asked while staring into his blue eyes.

Maverick groaned at the thought and nodded. "Believe me; I probably won't stop thinking about it for a long time," he insisted.

She kissed him quickly on the lips and managed a smile. "That'll have to be good enough for now," Jasmine replied then indicated their horses. "We should get back."

They headed for the horses where they grazed nearby. Maverick took in an eyeful of the woman and withheld his groan.

"I'm really sorry," he informed her. "You have no idea how sorry."

She smiled and laughed. "Your loyalty to your friend only makes you that much more appealing," Jasmine remarked and cast a look at him. "It's an open invitation. Just let me know when you change your mind."

As she mounted her horse, Maverick eyed her backside and whimpered softly. He cursed at himself under his breath, reclaimed his horse, and mounted with less enthusiasm.

Chapter 20

It was later that night, and almost everyone in the house and the bunkhouse had turned in after a long day. Scorpio sat on the wooden fence surrounding the paddock while the horse she rode that afternoon affectionately rubbed her leg with its forehead. Scorpio scratched the horse behind the ear and laughed at the faces Vlad made while enjoying the scratching. She heard familiar male voices softly arguing near the bunkhouse and getting closer. Scorpio glanced toward the bunkhouse and saw Stone and Maverick in a heated conversation while attempting to keep their voices down.

"Not exactly stealth," she teased as they got closer to her and the paddock.

Maverick climbed onto the fence and sat alongside her. "My boss came on to me this afternoon," he announced then cast a glare at Stone. "And I'm *not* making it up."

"Marlon?" Scorpio gasped with surprise.

Maverick looked at her with his mouth hanging open. "What? No," he gasped then groaned. "Jasmine."

"Women flirt with you all the time," Scorpio remarked. "What's the big deal?"

"She didn't *flirt* with me," Maverick insisted. "She *threw* herself at me."

Stone laughed while shaking his head. "She did not," he announced humored by the entire situation. "You've been reading too many porn articles."

Maverick groaned then looked back at Scorpio. "She tackled me to the ground and pounced on me," he insisted.

Stone laughed.

"She was like an octopus in heat," Maverick insisted while glaring back at Stone, who laughed even harder.

"You're not exaggerating?" Scorpio asked while raising a slightly humored brow. She didn't want to laugh, but it was hard to envision.

"No," he launched with increasing irritation. "What's with you people? Women *have* come on to me in the past. Why do you find it so hard to believe?"

"She'd be taking a big risk ravishing you with a dozen workers roaming around," Stone remarked indicating he still didn't believe his friend's story. "You weren't gone long. You expect me to believe she took you to some secluded location and jumped on you like Lassie in heat?"

Maverick sneered at him. "Yes, that's exactly what happened." He then looked at Scorpio. "I'm not making it up."

Scorpio then realized he must have been serious. "She's a married woman, Maverick," she announced in a scolding tone.

Maverick stared at her with surprise. "I didn't *do* anything," he protested then shook his head. "I do have some self-control, you know." He then glared at Scorpio. "I'm pretty damned proud of the way I handled myself, considering I haven't been in mixed company since we came to work for you."

"I can attest to that," Stone teased while grinning at Scorpio. "Women in nowhere Maine don't find him nearly as charming as city girls."

Scorpio eyed Maverick suspiciously. "A gorgeous woman with cleavage to spare seduces you, and you expect us to believe you turned her down?" she asked with surprise then grinned. "I'm with Stone. I find that difficult to believe."

"She's married," Maverick again huffed with some irritation. "Even if I could get past that, I thought it might jeopardize our assignment if Sig found out I'd slept with his married daughter."

He glared at both and turned defensive. "Should I have accepted her offer? I thought I was doing the right thing."

"All kidding aside," Scorpio announced and gave him a stern stare. "Having an affair with our employer's daughter would probably be unwise."

"So we agree that I made the right call?" Maverick demanded with some irritation. "Because I can easily rectify the situation. She extended an open invitation."

"You made the right call," Scorpio insisted then cast a look at Stone. "And don't encourage his bad behavior. This is important to Kane. The boss's wife and daughters are off limits."

"Does that include the boss's son?" Stone teased while grinning slyly at her.

"Don't go there," Scorpio groaned then turned serious. "And don't either of you tease Rayner about this. He's miserably jealous as it is."

"So no sex and no teasing Maverick or Rayner?" Stone asked then frowned and shook his head. "You just ruined my good time."

Maverick cast a look across the yard then hid his smile. "I think you have a stalker," he teased.

Scorpio glanced into the nearby tree line and saw Rayner leaning against a tree. She looked back at Maverick and Stone and offered a sly grin.

"He's not stalking me," she announced with humor. "I have a date."

"Secret meetings in the middle of the night?" Stone teased then cast a look at Maverick.

"Someone's doing something naughty," Maverick added while grinning. He then gave her a condescending look. "Does your boyfriend know you're cheating on him?"

"I don't need to keep my indiscretions from Marlon," she insisted. "Just the rest of the ranch."

"Have fun," Stone teased.

Scorpio grinned and jumped off the fence. "I intend to," she replied then gave them each a serious look. "Don't let me catch you following us."

"Trust me," Stone announced while making a face. "We don't want to see that."

"Well," Maverick muttered with a tiny shrug. "It's still Scorpio naked, so--"

"True," Stone replied.

"Don't," she snapped while pointing a warning finger at both men.

Stone laughed at Scorpio's expense. She ignored him then headed toward the woods and away from the barn area. Scorpio joined Rayner in the shadows within the woods and threw her arms around his neck. He held her against him then kissed her warmly but passionately. She broke off the kiss, pulled away, and smiled while gently caressing his chest.

"Are you sure you're okay with this?" she asked while grinning almost slyly.

"As long as Abbott and Costello don't spy on us," Rayner remarked. "I'm game."

She took his hand and led him away from the house and deeper into the woods. "Abbott wants no part of seeing that, but Costello's in hormone overload."

"Which one's Costello?" Rayner teased.

Scorpio drew a deep breath and cast a look at Rayner while they walked. "Maverick said Jasmine threw herself at him this afternoon," she informed him.

Rayner groaned with some irritation. "Don't tell me he slept with Sig's married daughter."

"No, he resisted," she insisted but was curious that he didn't doubt Maverick's story. "Have you interacted with her husband?"

"Conroy?" Rayner remarked. "Yeah, I've talked with him a couple of times since we arrived. I've seen him with his wife. Jasmine is cold toward him."

"So there's trouble in paradise, huh?"

"If she threw herself at Maverick, I'm guessing that's an understatement."

"What's your opinion of Emily Hooper?" Scorpio asked while they walked to their distant destination deeper within the woods.

"I think she's lonely," Rayner remarked. "Sig is gone five or six days every week."

"I saw her checking out Conroy at breakfast this morning," Scorpio informed him.

He gave her a surprised look then shook his head with conviction. "I haven't noticed anything between them," Rayner informed her. "In my defense; I've been busy and haven't been watching their every move either."

"I doubt she'd do anything while her husband is at home," Scorpio replied. "He's gone the rest of the week. We should keep tabs on his wife and Conroy."

"They're not exactly the assignment," Rayner reminded her. "Sig didn't hire us to catch his wife having an affair."

"No, but Kane's a little suspicious about that blown tire Sig had this morning that landed him in the ditch," Scorpio reminded him. "He thinks someone may have shot out Sig's front tire to make it look like an accident. Someone may be looking to get him out of the way. There's a lot of money and the ranch at stake if he dies."

"If Sig dies, his wife may stand to inherit a small fortune," Rayner remarked.

"His children too," Scorpio insisted. "Conroy can then divorce Jasmine, and he and Emily have quite the little nest egg."

"Everyone seems to benefit from Sig's death," Rayner deducted.

"Well, not everyone," Scorpio remarked. "Jasmine loses what little power she has as a less than equal co-owner to her brother. I think the ranch is more important to her than the money she'd receive from her father's death."

"Can we account for anyone's whereabouts around the time Sig ended up in the ditch?" Rayner asked while casting a glance at Scorpio as they continued through the woods.

"Just Brandi," Scorpio replied. "She was upstairs in her room changing. Emily had been on the porch as Sig pulled away. She could have easily removed a rifle from the living room cabinet and taken a shortcut through the woods. The area where a shooter may have been waiting isn't that far from the house."

"I can't account for Conroy's whereabouts after breakfast either," Rayner insisted. "He could have left the house before Sig even got in his car."

Scorpio stopped him in a small clearing and turned to face him while grinning. "I think this is far enough," she informed him. "Are you sure you're okay with this?"

Rayner pulled her into his arms without warning. "I'm willing to risk it," he announced.

She kissed him warmly and with some aggression. Rayner groaned and returned the aggressive kiss. He broke off the kiss and appeared curious.

"Should I have brought a blanket or something?" he asked while looking around. "What about poison and snakes?"

Scorpio chuckled in her throat. "We won't need a blanket," she informed him. "You're going to learn some new tricks."

She again kissed him with increased aggression as she backed herself against the nearby tree.

"I like when you teach me new tricks," he teased between kisses.

Chapter 21

Tuesday, June 24th. Late morning. Since his security equipment arrived Monday evening, Rayner solicited Conroy's assistance to begin installing the new security system. He didn't expect to get far with just the two of them working on it, but several of the wranglers had happily agreed to assist after dinner. As Conroy had surmised, most of the men were excited to do additional work to make extra money on the side. Rayner suspected he'd only need them that evening. The rest he could manage on his own or with a little help from Conroy. Rayner was on a stepstool within the sunroom and mounted one of the small cameras in a crevasse among the exposed ceiling beams near the glass doors.

"So we're installing these on all entrances inside and outside the house?" Conroy asked from where he stood below the stepstool and handed tools to Rayner.

"Yes," Rayner replied. "Sig just wants to keep an eye on anyone sneaking into the house. They're not being installed to spy on the family."

"That's sort of surprising," Conroy muttered, catching Rayner's attention.

Rayner glanced at the man near his legs. "Why's that?" he asked.

Conroy made a face and shrugged. "Sig's a bit controlling," he remarked then reconsidered the comment. "Actually, that's an understatement. He's a tyrant, plain and simple. No one is after Brandi. He just wants to know what goes on around here while he's too busy to stick around and find out."

"What does he think is going on around here?" Rayner asked as he continued to work and pretended he wasn't overly interested in the response.

"That we all just sort of slack off while he's away in the city six out of seven days," Conroy remarked then thought about the question. "That his children are plotting against him. That people are talking about him behind his back. I don't really know what goes through his head. Trust me; whatever it is, it's for a selfish reason."

"Jasmine and Marlon seem to handle the day-to-day operations rather well," Rayner remarked then climbed down from his stepstool and eyed Conroy. "Of course, I haven't really been here long enough to make any assumptions."

"That's the interesting part," Conroy informed him. "Marlon comes off as the 'man in charge', but Jasmine is the one actually running things. Marlon has an overinflated ego like his father. He likes to strut around like lord and master while everyone else does the work. Jasmine has some say in what goes on around here, but Marlon always has the final decision. Even if she says something to Sig, her authority is usually overridden."

Rayner studied Conroy a moment and appeared curious. "What do you think about Marlon?"

"I think you already know," Conroy remarked.

"Not what I really meant," Rayner fumbled over himself in an attempt to hide his jealousy. "It's just, well; his new girlfriend seems a little out of his league."

"That?" Conroy waved him off. "She'll dump him the moment he takes her home. That's if she even lasts that long. He's had a few women up here to spend some time on the ranch. Sort of a test run, I suppose. He wants to see how they handle life away from the real world. He comes across as a gentleman, but he's a tyrant."

Rayner saw Emily enter the sunroom with a cup of tea. He secretly attempted to silence Conroy, who hadn't seen Sig's wife enter, but Conroy didn't pick up on his subtle signal.

"Just like his father," Conroy announced.

Rayner grimaced and looked at Emily while attempting a smile. "Good morning, Mrs. Hooper."

Conroy turned and looked behind him where Emily casually leaned in the doorway while sipping her tea. She grinned at the men.

"Please, call me Emily," she announced while smiling. "And you don't need to worry. I already know Sig is a Tyrant."

Rayner and Conroy exchanged looks then grinned at the remark. Rayner folded the stepstool and offered a polite smile to Emily.

"We're finished in here," Rayner announced. "You can enjoy your tea in peace."

"I don't mind the company," Emily remarked with a slight shrug then made a face. "It gets boring around here with just Brandi and me most days. Alma doesn't even let me help with lunch."

"If you know the difference between a Phillips-head screwdriver and a flat-head, you can always help us," Rayner informed her.

"I do," she announced with enthusiasm, "and I'd love to help."

"We're heading into the kitchen," Rayner remarked and nodded to the door.

Emily and Conroy headed for the door.

"I forgot my borrowed tool case," Rayner announced then headed back toward the glass doors.

Rayner grabbed his loaner tool case and turned in time to see Conroy and Emily leave the sunroom. Conroy's hand caressed her backside as they disappeared through the doorway. Rayner hesitated, considered what Scorpio had said, and raised his brows.

"Well, this should be interesting," he remarked then headed out of the sunroom after them.

§

Mac walked down the back stairs with little enthusiasm while carrying two excessively large bundles of sheets. It was a few minutes after eleven that morning, and she'd just finished with the guest bedrooms. She entered the kitchen and headed for the laundry room, which was just to the right. Delia and Alma were at the kitchen counter preparing a lite lunch for the family. Delia saw Mac with her bundles of sheets and approached.

"You're late," Delia informed her with a mildly disgusted huff.

"I wasn't finished with the guestrooms," Mac informed her while hauling her bundles to the laundry room.

Delia followed her while maintaining her look of irritation. "I told you to be back downstairs for eleven to help with lunch."

"You also said the linen in the guestrooms needed to be stripped, and that the rooms should be finished first," Mac insisted then looked at her watch. "They're finished, and I'm only ten minutes late."

Delia placed her hands on her hips and glared demandingly at Mac as if attempting to intimidate her. "There are three extra guests. We needed you down here."

Mac straightened and returned the glare. "How did you manage before I came along?" she scoffed in response.

"I don't like your attitude," Delia snapped back.

Mac folded her arms across her chest to keep from striking the insufferable woman. She seemed to consider her actions before reacting irrationally and drew a deep breath to remain calm.

"I'm doing my best to keep up," Mac finally announced and did her best to keep from escalating the situation. "This is my first housekeeping position."

"Well, you had better learn to multi-task and pick up the pace," Delia snapped. "I don't know what positions you held before, but timing is important around here. There's no putting your feet up and taking it easy in this job."

There was a small explosion behind Mac's stare. Delia knew nothing about the moderately dangerous woman she was pushing around.

"I'll do better," Mac remarked while obviously biting her tongue.

"You'll need to if you want to keep this job," Delia snarled.

Mac's fist tightened beneath her folded arms. She had enough and was just about ready to strike when Alma suddenly appeared behind Delia. Alma folded her arms across her broad chest.

"If you're finished gossiping, Delia," Alma demanded in a condescending tone. "I could use your help with lunch."

Delia looked back at Alma and attempted to explain what had happened. Alma raised her commanding brows and gave a firm nod to the kitchen. Delia frowned and scurried for the kitchen. Alma shook her head and looked back at Mac while allowing her arms to return to her sides.

"Honey, you need to stand up for yourself," Alma insisted. "Don't let that girl push you around. You'll end up doing all your work and half of hers."

Mac relaxed her fists as well as her arms and somehow managed to pull off a bullied schoolgirl look. "I don't want to cause waves," she replied timidly while frowning. "My mouth tends to get me into trouble."

"Yeah, mine too," Alma confessed then indicated the laundry. "Throw one load of linen in the washing machine here, and take the second load into the pool house laundry room. You just stay out there until the washing machine stops. I'll bring you your lunch plate out there."

"What about Delia?" she asked. "I thought you needed my held with lunch."

"We've got that covered. Don't worry about Delia," Alma insisted. "There's a comfy sofa in the pool house. Put on the noon soaps, and we'll have our lunch together out there."

Mac snorted a laugh and managed a sincere smile. "You've got it."

§

Scorpio swung the banister from the grand stairs and walked along the hallway toward the kitchen for lunch when she heard Brandi scream from one of the nearby rooms. Scorpio bolted into the game room, prepared for battle, and slid to a stop within the doorway. Kane and Brandi stood in front of the large television with their game controllers in their hands and pounded on the controls. Brandi continued to scream as Kane's Viking warrior repeatedly struck Brandi's game character with a broadsword. She cried out as her game character died at the hands of her opponent's mighty sword. Brandi let out a shrill shriek and slapped Kane on the arm.

"You killed my guy," she shouted. "I liked that guy. He was cute!"

"It was a fair fight," Kane insisted while laughing at her fluffy rage.

Scorpio shook her head. Kane was having a little too much fun with his newly adopted, little sister. Considering her brother could be mature beyond his years, he sometimes acted like a five-year-old.

"You cheated," Brandi huffed and tossed her game controller over her shoulder and onto the sofa.

"It's pretend fighting," he announced and seemed humored by her tantrum. "How on earth did I cheat?"

"Well, I, uh," she fumbled then raised her brows. "Because you're a guy, and you're bigger than I am."

"It's a game," he insisted while indicating the television. "I'm also taller, smarter, and better looking, but that doesn't change the fact that it's still a fair fight."

Brandi gasped at his remark and again smacked his arm. "You are certainly not better looking!"

Scorpio rolled her eyes after reliving a moment from her childhood then left the room.

Chapter 22

Later that afternoon, near the end of the workday, a large tractor towing a wagon loaded with more than two hundred bales of hay arrived at the ranch. All the wranglers had gathered to help unload the hay and stack it in the hay barn located nearly one hundred yards from the horse barn. Jasmine collected four of the wranglers' horses then called to Maverick. He approached the attractive woman holding the reins to the saddled horses.

"Yes, Jasmine?" he politely asked while the men started stacking hay.

She handed him the reins to the four horses. "Take these horses to the barn and start unsaddling them," Jasmine announced. "I'll get the rest."

Maverick looked from the horses to the men unloading the hay then glanced back at Jasmine. "I don't want to get on Marlon's bad side--"

"Don't worry about Marlon," she announced with some irritation at the mention of her brother. "The horses need to be unsaddled, brushed, and fed. I don't need Marlon's permission to volunteer you to help me. This way we get finished earlier rather than later."

She nodded him to the barn with the horses. Maverick conceded and led the horses to the barn while Jasmine went back for the rest of the tied horses. Stone and Teddy grabbed bales of hay being tossed from the wagon, passed Boyd with his bale of hay, and hauled their bales several feet where they stacked them inside the hay barn. Stone caught a glimpse of Maverick leading the horses to the main barn and gave a slight nod. Teddy glanced in the direction Stone indicated then shook his head.

"Looks like your friend got out of hard labor," Teddy teased.

"To be honest," Stone announced while tossing the bale of hay on top of others then faced Teddy. "I enjoy physical labor. I don't work out nearly as much as I used to. I'm starting to get flabby."

Teddy eyed Stone's muscular shoulders and broad chest then raised his brows. "Yeah, you're totally out of shape," he scoffed then pulled his shirt up to reveal his tiny potbelly. "This is flabby, dude. When you lose your six-pack abs, we'll talk."

Stone grinned and chuckled. They headed back to the hay wagon, again passing Boyd with his bale of hay. Teddy indicated Jasmine leading the remaining horses to the barn several yards behind Maverick and laughed.

"Trust me; your friend will be getting a workout too," Teddy informed him.

"Unsaddling horses?" Stone asked then shook his head. "Somehow not the same."

Teddy eyed Stone and raised his brows. "You know he's getting laid, right?"

Stone stopped at the comment and appeared moderately stunned.

Teddy stopped as well and looked back at Stone while grinning. "He didn't tell you that's why she's been singling him out? I thought he was your friend?"

"He mentioned she came on to him," Stone remarked, "but I thought it was just bullshit. When it comes to women, he's a legend in his own mind."

"Nah," Teddy announced as they continued back to the hay wagon. "I saw her eyes popping out of her head the first day he was here."

"Isn't she afraid her husband will find out?" Stone asked and now seemed curious.

They each grabbed another bale of hay and continued back to the hay barn again passing Boyd.

"Jasmine's overactive sex drive is a well-guarded secret among the wranglers," Teddy remarked. "It doesn't leave the bunkhouse."

They tossed their bales of hay on top of the pile. Stone turned to face Teddy and appeared curious. "Seems like a pretty big secret for so many to keep willingly. Are the guys that devoted to her?"

"Devoted?" Teddy remarked then grinned and laughed. "No. Waiting their *next* turn is more like it."

He turned to leave when Stone caught his arm and stopped him.

"Their turn?" Stone asked with surprise and raised his brow in suggestion. "You mean--?"

"Oh, yeah," Teddy announced while grinning. "She's slept with all the wranglers."

"Boyd?" Stone asked and raised his brows.

"Maybe not Boyd," Teddy remarked as they continued back to the hay wagon. "He started dating Brandi soon after he started here." He chuckled at the thought. "All the guys are dying to know, but no one is willing to ask."

"All the wranglers, huh?" Stone again asked and then shook his head as he secretly pouted. "Okay, now I am a little jealous. She hasn't even given me a second glance. She must not like brothers."

Teddy laughed at the comment but didn't bother looking at Stone. "You have nothing to worry about," he replied while grinning. "She's been checking you out."

They each grabbed a bale of hay and headed back for the hay barn.

"Why do you suppose she's passed me over?" Stone asked while eyeing Teddy alongside him.

Teddy shrugged then cast a look at Stone. "Fear of not walking right for a week?" he teased.

Stone caught Teddy's humored grin. Both men smiled and laughed.

"I can live with that," Stone replied.

As they again passed Boyd while toting their bales of hay, Stone appeared curious and looked at Teddy.

"Is he moving that fast or that slow?" Stone finally asked. "Didn't we pass him four times already?"

Teddy rolled his eyes and shook his head. "He does half the work," he insisted. "If he hadn't climbed into Brandi's bed, he would have been permanently relieved last fall. I'm afraid we're stuck with him now that he's marrying Brandi. He's been doing less and less work with each passing day." Teddy frowned. "Can you imagine how little he's going to do once he's a member of the family?"

"Marlon doesn't complain?" Stone asked with surprise and noted how slowly the man seemed to move while carrying his bale of hay. It was possibly still the same bale.

"He's spoken to him several times," Teddy remarked. "Boyd tattles to Brandi, she throws a tantrum, and daddy scolds Marlon. Trust me; no one is looking forward to that slacker marrying daddy's little girl."

§

Maverick patted his new horse, Vlad, while speaking softly to him. The horse scratched his large forehead against Maverick's leg and nearly knocked him off his feet. Maverick laughed, scratched the horse behind its ear, and then unsaddled him. He removed the saddle and carried it into the tack room within the barn. As he turned to leave the tack room, Jasmine entered and shut the door behind her. She smiled almost deviously while seductively leaning against the door.

"I've been waiting to get you alone," Jasmine cooed and took a step closer to him.

Maverick closely watched her without backing away. He raised his brows with a curious look. "I was wondering if you had an ulterior motive."

She aggressively ran her hands along his chest while staring into his eyes with a lustful look. "And you came willingly," Jasmine remarked. "That's encouraging."

"Actually, you're sort of my boss so--"

"Yes, I am your boss," she cooed and allowed her hand to travel down his abdomen while heading for his crotch. "I was thinking about what you said the other day, and I think I have a solution to your dilemma."

He studied her while casting a quick glance at her traveling hand that soon found its intended target. As she caressed the bulge in his pants, Maverick drew a deep breath but refrained from reacting either way.

"And what's the solution?" he asked almost eager to hear her response.

"Just a small taste," she cooed while grinning. "A teaser, if you will."

"Are you suggesting--?"

She giggled and nodded. "Yes, *that*."

Maverick was about to say something when the tack room door suddenly opened. Jasmine jumped with surprise and spun toward the door behind her. Maverick turned for the nearest saddle and adjusted it on its stand. Marlon stood in the tack room doorway and glared at both. Maverick appeared convincing at looking busy without looking back at Jasmine's brother.

Jasmine gave Marlon a disapproving sneer as she folded her arms across her chest. "Ducking out on chores again?" she scoffed.

Marlon smirked at her in response. "Blowing the wranglers again?"

Her look turned angry. "What do you want, Marlon?" she demanded.

"A sister with a shred of self-respect would be nice," he remarked.

"Go away, Marlon," Jasmine huffed.

"With pleasure," Marlon announced then glared at Maverick. "Jasmine has the horses, Maverick. Go help unload the hay wagon."

Maverick tensed slightly, shifted looks between the feuding brother and sister, and then left the tack room without any protest.

"You have no right undermining my authority," Jasmine proclaimed.

"Your authority?" Marlon scoffed then laughed. "You mean undermining your sexual perversion. You honestly wonder why

Dad put me in charge and not you?" He shook his head and left the tack room.

Jasmine stared after her brother. "Wait until Daddy gets home!"

Chapter 23

That evening, Marlon had planned a last-minute, outdoor barbeque for dinner. The family and their guests were treated to an evening pool party. Brandi and Jasmine offered to loan Scorpio swimwear since she hadn't packed her own. When she left Maine to find her brother, poolside attire was furthest from her mind. She reluctantly accepted Brandi's offer and borrowed one of her bikinis, although her selection of modest swimwear was limited. Most of the young woman's bikinis left little to the imagination, and that wasn't happening. Jasmine had more modest swimwear, but Scorpio knew she'd drown in the large breasted woman's tops. Kane had zero issues borrowing a swimsuit from Conroy, who was more his size than Marlon. Rayner, on the other hand, was completely opposed to borrowing another man's swimwear.

As Marlon cooked on the grill, Alma prepared the side dishes while Mac and Delia helped set up a buffet at poolside. Kane ventured into the kitchen from the back stairs in his newly borrowed swim trunks and bright colored, tropical button shirt. Alma seemed to be buzzing around the kitchen looking mildly flustered while Mac and Delia attempted to keep up with the older woman. Kane paused to watch Mac feverishly working to help prepare the picnic menu. He frowned with some disapproval, obviously feeling bad for the shit assignment she'd been given. Mac had been on her way to the patio and paused to take in a sweeping look of Kane in his borrowed, poolside attire. When she saw him looking oddly like a surfer dude rather than his normal steampunk meets transient look, she had a tough time containing her smirk. He grinned when he caught her look.

"What?" he teased. "You didn't know I cleaned up this well?"

Mac eyed his bare feet and held back her laugh. Before she could comment, Delia buzzed past her and shot a demanding look at her.

"Let's go," Delia announced sternly.

Mac rolled her eyes as Delia headed out the kitchen door then followed her. Kane again frowned then approached Alma at the main counter as she bustled to drain diced potatoes for potato salad. Kane opened the refrigerator and removed several items, placing them on the counter near her. She eyed the ingredients needed for her current side dish. Kane then removed some celery and grabbed the cutting board. Alma watched as he diced some celery and onion for her potato salad. She eyed him only a moment before grabbing the jar of mayonnaise.

"That's not your job, you know," Alma informed him.

Kane shrugged without looking at her while he worked. "I know my way around a kitchen," he replied matter-of-factly. "I lived with my sister who couldn't cook a decent meal to save her life."

Alma managed a soft laugh then returned to her work, appearing frazzled for the first time.

Kane cast several looks at the older woman before commenting. "I'd think with Marlon cooking at poolside you'd have a bit of a break for a change," he remarked and eyed the flustered cook. "Why do you seem so stressed over picnic food?"

She frowned and shook her head. "I shouldn't say."

Kane glanced behind him to the empty kitchen and shrugged. "Why not? It's just us."

Alma cast the mayonnaise jar to the counter with a little more force than necessary and turned to face him. "Marlon pulls this stunt every time he has a lady friend over," she boldly announced with annoyance in her tone. "He waits until the last minute to tell me of dinner changes, and then I'm rushing to throw something together. Not only did I already have a large roast in the oven, but I also had to thaw out a dozen steaks at the last minute. My dinner is just sitting in the oven half cooked while I cater to another one of his whims to impress his new lady friend." She threw her hands in the air and returned to her potato salad. "I'm just frustrated, that's all."

"Marlon's not winning any popularity contests around here today, is he?" Kane remarked then skillfully diced the onions with the large butcher knife.

Alma eyed his skills with the knife and actually paused to watch him. He then pushed the cutting board aside and tore lettuce, which he tossed it into a large, wooden bowl.

"I heard he got into it with Jasmine earlier," Kane continued and hid his smile. "For a bunch of manly men; those wranglers certainly like to gossip."

"They give me all the good barn gossip," Alma informed him as her mood lightened slightly. "It's no secret about Marlon and Jasmine. Those two are always at each other's throats. I doubt Sig knows just how bad they are when he's gone. Their fights aren't exclusively kept outdoors, you know. They get into it quite a bit right here in the kitchen. I usually retire to my room until they're finished fighting. Complain all you want about Brandi, but she's the only one who doesn't give me a headache."

"I haven't had any problems with her," Kane insisted while he created the salad by adding sliced mushrooms, cucumber, and some tomato. "It's like a high-paid babysitting gig."

"I guess it does seem that way to you," Alma announced and seemed to relax now.

Kane ate a baby carrot then held one to Alma's mouth. She eyed him suspiciously then allowed him to place the carrot in her mouth. She couldn't help but smile at his charm.

"Must be awkward," she continued while crunching on her carrot. "Being bodyguard to a girl only a few years younger than yourself."

"Actually, we're the same age," Kane informed her as he diced the carrots into the salad.

Alma cast a look at him. "She's twenty-one," the cook insisted. "You're about twenty-five, right?"

Kane grinned and laughed. "No, I'm twenty-two," he replied. "I've had a rough life. I guess it prematurely aged me."

She again eyed him. "I didn't mean you looked old in that way," Alma insisted. "You're certainly mature for your age. That's all."

"My sister and I were raised by our grandparents," he replied. "I think that had something to do with our overabundance of maturity."

"It was rough on you being raised by your grandparents?" she asked.

"You have no idea," he announced dramatically then sighed. "My sister and I weren't even allowed to play inside the house."

"You poor child," Alma announced while staring at his profile. "Children need to play."

"I know, right?" Kane squawked and shook his head. "I mean, who leaves a ten thousand dollar vase just sitting around with a pair of tweeners running amuck?"

Alma eyed him and raised her brow. "Ten thousand dollar vase?" she questioned.

"Yeah," he replied and waved his hands around while holding the sharp knife. "You'd think they'd have learned after we broke the china closet." He shook his head and resumed cutting vegetables. "You don't hire a karate instructor for a pair of impressionable seven-year-olds and assume there won't be any roughhousing."

"Your grandparents were wealthy?" Alma asked with some surprise.

"Yeah," he replied.

Alma continued to stare at him. "I'm sorry; what made your life so rough?"

"Obviously, you've never met my sister," he casually replied.

Alma shook her head and hid her smile. "You're the strangest young man, Kane."

"I have flawed DNA," he replied while smirking. "It's possible my father was an assassin. I never met him so we may never know."

She cast a strange look at him but let the comment go. "What about your mother?"

"Died a few months after we were born," Kane informed her.

"That's awful," Alma remarked. "Does that mean you and your sister are twins?"

"Yes," he replied. "She was bullying me since before we were born."

The cook grinned and laughed at the comment. "You have a girlfriend?" Alma asked while resuming her work.

"Is that an offer?" he teased and cast a quick look at the older woman.

Alma glanced at him with some surprise then managed a smile. "Oh, Kane," she announced with a sigh. "If I were forty years younger--"

Alma took a moment to scan the kitchen to ensure they were still alone then leaned closer to Kane, who eagerly listened to what she had to say.

"Marlon's new lady friend is a nice, young lady," Alma informed him. "I've seen you talking to her a few times. You'd make a cute couple."

Kane suddenly grinned and laughed. "Although I'll admit we have a lot in common, she's really not my type."

Alma frowned and shook her head. "If she's not; she should be," she huffed. "You may want to reevaluate your life choices. You're going to miss out on the good ones."

Scorpio came down the back stairs and saw Kane at the counter with Alma. Scorpio didn't comment but gave him a slightly humored look. Kane looked back; saw Scorpio in the bikini top and sarong skirt cover-up. He rolled his eyes and shook his head with obvious disapproval.

"Can I take anything out with me, Alma?" Scorpio asked.

Alma looked back, saw Scorpio pool ready, and grinned. "No, we have it just about covered now," she announced and gave her a quick once-over. "You look lovely in Brandi's bikini." Alma then nudged Kane and raised her brows. "Doesn't she look lovely?"

"If the goal is to catch Marlon's attention, she's achieved it," Kane remarked while raising his brow at his sister.

Scorpio sneered at Kane. Alma caught the exchange and stared a moment at each with bewilderment.

"I'll be outside," Scorpio announced then left the kitchen.

Kane returned to his salad prep without acknowledging his sister's comment. Alma continued to stare at Kane as if attempting to read his profile. Her eyes suddenly widened.

"Oh my God," she exclaimed while staring at him then indicated Scorpio. "She's your sister!"

Kane looked back at Alma with some surprise, but it was already too late to deny it. "Why would you say that?" he asked.

"I've seen you gawking at Mac's backside, but you didn't even give that girl a second glance," Alma remarked while shaking her head. "She's not your type because she's your sister!"

Kane tensed and jerked slightly. "Okay, not so loud," he announced and looked around, although there was no one in the kitchen. "Yes, she's my sister, but it needs to stay between us. She's my partner in the business. Sig came up with the girlfriend cover story."

"So Marlon knows?"

"Of course he knows," Kane replied.

Alma suddenly snorted a laugh. "No wonder he's going out of his way to impress her," she remarked and laughed long and hard. "I should have known he couldn't land a girl that nice on his own."

Chapter 24

Despite the fiasco within the kitchen, the poolside dinner picnic seemed to come together flawlessly. Apart from Kane, no one else was aware of what happened in the kitchen. The outdoor, self-serve bar was open along with the buffet. Boyd and Brandi enjoyed swimming in the pool and goofing around together. Jasmine only stuck her feet in the pool once then spent the rest of the time working on her tan alongside Emily, who looked just as good in her own bikini. Rayner relaxed on one of the poolside lounge chairs and spent most of his time sneaking peeks at Scorpio in her borrowed bikini. He sat alongside Conroy, who didn't seem interested in swimming either.

At first glance, it appeared as if Conroy was ogling his wife across the patio, but he was actually taking in sweeping eyefuls of Emily on the lounge chair next to his wife. Whether Jasmine knew her husband was watching the woman alongside her or not, she cast an almost loathing look at the man she married from across the pool. Rayner and Conroy each had a few drinks while talking shop, but Rayner was having a tough time ignoring Marlon's attentiveness toward Scorpio within the pool. Although he couldn't hear their conversation, it was evident Marlon was turning on the charm, and it wasn't just for show either. Since Kane didn't have to babysit Brandi while Boyd was around, he made it his mission to interrupt Marlon's romantic interlude with Scorpio. Kane's presence definitely put a damper on whatever he had in mind for his pretend girlfriend.

Kane relaxed in the pool alongside Marlon and Scorpio. He noticed Marlon watching Brandi and her boyfriend on the opposite end of the pool. Marlon couldn't hide his disapproving look. Brandi had Boyd backed into the corner of the pool and clung to him while they talked and laughed. When she thought no one was looking, she'd steal a kiss. Kane glanced across the pool several times to witness the affectionate couple. Their overly affectionate behavior was getting uncomfortable to watch. Kane finally looked away and glanced at the house. He could see someone watching the pool party from the kitchen. It was quite possibly Mac, who once again wasn't part of the fun. When the peeper from inside the house was spotted, she moved away from the window.

"Do you ever invite the staff to swim in the pool?" Kane asked Marlon while giving him a curious look.

Scorpio knew why he was asking but didn't let on that she knew why.

"They can come out and use the pool whenever they're not on the clock," Marlon informed him. "Alma wouldn't dream of it. Claims no one wants to see her in a bathing suit. Delia comes out now and again. She's probably hesitant because of the guests."

"So I can invite Mac?" Kane asked.

Marlon shrugged. "She's more than welcome," he replied. "Just don't expect me to ask Jasmine if she can borrow one of her bikinis. I'm on Jasmine's shit list today." He then considered the comment. "Well, I'm on her shit list every day, but today she's a little extra bitchy."

"Why's that?" Kane asked.

"I caught her coming on to your man in the barn this afternoon," Marlon remarked. "I'm tired of her playing fast and loose with the wranglers."

"So you know about that, huh?" Kane replied.

"Worst kept secret on the ranch," Marlon remarked while casting a hateful look at his sister.

"I told him to keep his distance from her," Kane informed him.

"No one really cares," Marlon insisted and waved off Kane. "I just don't want her messing around with the guys when they're supposed to be working."

"She doesn't know Maverick and Stone are part of my team, does she?" Kane then asked.

"No, I certainly didn't tell her," Marlon insisted. "Just tell your guys to keep their hands off her during work hours. What they do on their own time is their own business."

"Yeah, I'll tell them that," Kane remarked with a soft chuckle. "I'm sure Maverick will jump at the offer if he's given the green light."

"Don't be so sure," Scorpio finally chimed in; reminding them she was still there.

Both men looked at her.

"Maverick actively avoids women with boyfriends. He's respectful of boundaries," she remarked and secretly cast a look at Marlon as if making a point. "I can't imagine him getting involved with a married woman."

"I'm glad to hear he has some morals," Kane remarked in an attempt to drive home Scorpio's point for Marlon's benefit. Kane then appeared enthusiastic. "I'm going to invite Mac to join us."

Kane left the pool, dried off as best he could, wrapped the towel around his waist, and headed barefoot into the kitchen.

Marlon seemed pleased once Kane had left and turned to face Scorpio in the pool. "Did you know there's a hot tub in the pool house?" he asked.

"Yes," she replied. "I took the self-guided tour the other day."

"We could use the hot tub if you'd like," he announced while grinning. He obviously hadn't heard a word she said moments earlier. "There's a television and a fully stocked bar in there."

Scorpio considered giving Marlon the benefit of the doubt, but she needed to end his attempt to get her alone. "Are you purposely trying to piss off Rayner?" she asked while glaring at him.

"No," Marlon replied innocently. "I'm just keeping your cover. Hanging out in the hot tub is something I would do with my lady friends. Rayner knows it's just an act. I'm sure he'd be fine."

"Thanks," Scorpio replied and didn't push the issue, "but I'm good."

Kane returned only a few minutes later with a strange look on his face as he climbed back into the pool near Scorpio and Marlon.

"There wasn't anyone in the kitchen," Kane announced and shook his head. "I swore someone was peering out the window just a minute ago."

"Did you try her room?" Scorpio asked.

"Of course," he announced. "She wasn't there either." Kane shook his head. "I don't know where she wandered off." He seemed to be deep in thought then brushed it aside and looked at Scorpio while grinning. "Race you to the end of the pool."

Scorpio laughed. "You're on."

Before Marlon could even comment, the brother and sister duo swam across the pool for the opposite side. Kane beat Scorpio by nearly a foot. He reached the edge of the pool first, pushed his wet hair back, and laughed at her. She pulled the wet hair from her face and frowned.

"You cheat," she insisted.

They were now closer to Brandi and Boyd and could hear the romantic couple's conversation. Brandi kept Boyd pressed against the pool wall while clinging to his neck.

"I've been thinking a lot about our wedding," Brandi informed him.

"Oh?" he asked. "Did you want to make some sort of change to the menu? There's still plenty of time."

"No, silly," she announced and playfully smacked his wet chest. "I meant about the wedding night."

Boyd grinned and chuckled in his throat. "I already told you," he announced. "You don't have to wear white on our wedding night. I'm fine with any color nightgown as long as it's sexy. You won't be in it all that long anyway."

"That's what I wanted to discuss," Brandi lightly teased and warmly kissed his lips then met his gaze. "I don't know that I want to wait."

Boyd stared at her with surprise. "Brandi, we're almost to the finish line," he insisted. "We survived this long. We may as well wait now. It's what you wanted, remember?"

"It just doesn't seem as important now," she remarked while grinning. "I want to make love to you now."

He groaned while grinning. "I love hearing you say that," Boyd announced then turned serious. "But we should wait. It'll make our wedding night all the more special. I don't want you to have any regrets."

She reluctantly frowned. "Yeah, you're probably right," she pouted.

Scorpio and Kane exchanged surprised looks. "Well, I didn't see that coming," Scorpio remarked.

"I commend her for it," Kane replied without hesitation. "But at the same time, I find it difficult to believe."

"Yeah, no kidding," Scorpio scoffed.

Chapter 25

Wednesday, June 25th. Later that morning, Mac had finished making the beds and cleaning the guest bathrooms in record time. She consulted her watch. It was only ten o'clock, which gave her an hour before she needed to help with lunch. Adhering to Delia's schedule was easier when Mac simply skimped on cleaning. She'd taken numerous shortcuts to keep herself on schedule, which essentially allowed Delia to live since Mac was seriously considering killing the little dictator. Noting that Alma frequently took a break between breakfast and lunch, Mac knew the kitchen would be empty. She headed down the back stairs and entered the empty kitchen.

Voices were heard beyond the staff wing doorway, which had to be Delia and Alma. Although, it was unclear what Delia would be doing in the staff wing when she was supposed to be cleaning the common areas. Mac didn't feel like suffering Delia's wrath if she discovered she had finished with the upstairs rooms faster than anticipated, so she ducked into the laundry room to keep from being seen. There had been a load of linen waiting to be washed anyway. Mac partially shut the door behind her to remain unseen. She had just placed the set of sheets into the large washing machine when she heard the staff wing door open.

Mac heard faint voices then realized one sounded like a man. She hesitated, approached the mostly closed laundry room door, and attempted to peek out. Her view was limited, but she caught a glimpse of a man crossing the kitchen. Unfortunately, all the wranglers dressed similar in jeans and plaid shirts, so she couldn't make out whom she'd seen. Mac cursed softly under her breath. It was odd that one of the guys had been in the staff wing or even in the kitchen for that matter at that hour. Her curiosity got the better of her, and she decided she'd risk Delia's wrath just to catch of glimpse of the unauthorized male visitor.

Mac left the laundry room and entered the kitchen just in time to see Delia shutting the outer kitchen door. Her opportunity to catch the man had passed. Delia turned and saw Mac within the kitchen. The young maid first appeared startled then quickly turned angry.

"You're supposed to be upstairs cleaning the guestrooms," Delia scoffed.

"And you're supposed to be cleaning the common areas," Mac snapped back in response.

Delia became flustered and further enraged. "You're not in a position to challenge my authority."

"No, maybe not," Mac scoffed. "But I could question why there was a man in the staff wing. You know the rules."

"Not that it's any of your business," Delia lashed back while folding her arms across her chest, "but I don't need permission to speak privately to my brother."

Mac withheld her frown. She had her there. What could have been a pivotal piece of evidence to shake Delia from her back had gone up in smoke. A visit from Boyd wasn't nearly as damaging and couldn't be used to hold over Delia. Although, Mac couldn't be certain it was actually Boyd she'd seen leaving the house. It was still possible Delia was entertaining one of the other wranglers. There was insufficient evidence and nothing that would help at the moment.

"I don't need this," Mac huffed. "I still have another room to clean."

Mac swiftly spun on her heels and headed up the back stairs to the second floor. Despite that she had already finished upstairs, Delia didn't know that. She'd hide out in Kane's room until closer to eleven. It was the only way she could avoid punching Delia in the face.

§

After lunch, the wranglers returned to their duties. Stone had purposely tied his horse at the long hitching post alongside Maverick's horse so they could talk privately for a few minutes. Both men tightened their horse's girths while pretending they weren't secretly speaking.

"I notice Boyd is late again returning from lunch," Stone remarked to his friend with his back to him and his horse. "He spends a lot of time in the bathroom."

Maverick eyed Stone overtop of his horse, Vlad, and leaned on the saddle. "Always the first one in the bunkhouse and the last one to leave," he remarked then looked around and swiftly changed the subject. "Marlon's miserable today."

Stone grinned as he turned and faced his friend overtop of the horse between them. "Yeah, I hear his girlfriend isn't putting out," he teased.

Both men chuckled at Scorpio's expense. Maverick glanced around and watched as the other men were already mounting their horses. Boyd still hadn't returned from the bunkhouse, which wasn't unusual. Maverick then caught a glimpse of Jasmine mounting her horse. She spun her horse and rode away with purpose.

"Jasmine's kind of pissy too," Maverick informed his friend while watching Jasmine's backside slapping against the leather saddle as she rode away.

"Probably because she isn't getting any either," Stone remarked while grinning slyly.

Maverick took his eyes from Jasmine and glared a disapproving look at his friend. "Don't start again," he muttered and untied his horse.

"You've gotten the green light from Kane," Stone remarked while maintaining his grin. "What's the problem?"

Maverick mounted his horse then looked back at Stone. "Who said there was a problem?"

Stone shrugged then mounted his horse as well. "I just think if you'd have made your move, she'd be in a better mood, that's all." He cast a glance at his friend. "Since she's not; I'm guessing there's a problem."

They were about to join the others when they heard loud, angry voices. To their surprise, it was Teddy and Marlon, who were now engaged in a shouting match.

"That's not good," Stone remarked.

They rode from the barn area and to the nearby corral where Marlon and Teddy had just dismounted their horses for their face-off. As Maverick and Stone got closer, they could hear the angry conversation.

"I don't know what your problem is, Marlon," Teddy launched in anger, "but you need to back off my men."

"*Your* men?" Marlon shot back in response then indicated the ranch. "This is *my* ranch, and those are *my* men; not yours. I'm in charge here."

"You're never around," Teddy lashed back. "Jasmine already gave us our assignments for this afternoon, and I happen to agree with her. Her way is more efficient and a better use of our time."

"I'm the boss; not Jasmine," Marlon snarled back and seemed irate that his sister was even brought into their quarrel. "I give the orders around here."

"In your absence, Jasmine is in charge," Teddy reminded him. "Since you invited your little friend to the ranch, you've been absent. That means we take orders from Jasmine. If you have a problem, you need to take it up with her." Teddy mounted his horse and looked at the men now surrounding them. He motioned to the men. "You have your assignments. Get to work."

"Now wait just one damned minute," Marlon launched and looked at the men, who seemed uncertain what to do. "I'm in charge here."

Jasmine raced her horse up to them and slid to a sliding stop not far from her brother. The horse jumped around excitedly. Jasmine's look was angry and hateful.

"We have it covered, Marlon," Jasmine informed him. "The men have their assignments." She then looked at the men surrounding them and motioned with anger. "Everyone back to work."

The men all turned their horses and did what she said, which left Marlon stunned and enraged. Stone and Maverick remained where they were; interested to see how it played out. Marlon turned to his sister, who remained on her horse and hovered over him.

"You will not undermine my authority," he launched back in a threatening tone.

Jasmine stared down at him and sneered. "And you will not undermine *my* authority." She looked back and saw Stone and Maverick still on their horses near them. Her look was angry. "Show's over. Back to work."

Stone and Maverick turned their horses and did as they were told. They exchanged looks while listening to the brother and sister continue their heated exchange.

"Daddy's going to get an earful when he returns," Maverick teased.

"Oh, I don't know," Stone remarked while taking time to look around the beautiful, sunny day. "One of them may be dead before Sig gets back."

"My money's on Jasmine. She'd easily kill Marlon," Maverick responded while casting a quick look at his friend. "She can be downright vicious. I don't think Marlon has the balls to back up his ego."

"Probably because he had everything handed to him," Stone replied. "Jasmine had to scratch and claw to keep what little authority she'd been granted. It made her a lot tougher than her brother."

They saw Boyd finally meander from the bunkhouse and head for his sole horse at the hitching post.

"Well," Stone scoffed and shook his head. "Look finally decided to show up for work after his executive bathroom break."

"Banging the boss's daughter has its perks," Maverick teased.

"Yeah?" Stone asked while raising his brows then grinned. "Let me know how that goes for you."

Maverick sneered at his friend. Stone laughed and sent his horse into a gallop. Maverick shook his head, nudged Vlad, and galloped after Stone.

Chapter 26

That evening at dinner, everyone took their usual places at the table. Jasmine was the last to enter the dining room and approached her seat alongside the vacant head of the table. Instead of taking her usual seat, she pulled out the end chair and sat in her father's empty seat. The tension from those within the dining room could almost be felt. Scorpio and Kane exchanged quick glances then cast looks at Marlon from the corner of their eyes. Marlon stared at his sister occupying their father's seat in his absence and appeared ready to kill her with his eyes.

"What do you think you're doing?" Marlon demanded of his sister.

Everyone at the table immediately shifted and minded their empty plates.

"Daddy isn't here," Jasmine announced boldly while glaring at her brother at the opposite end of the table and folded the napkin over her lap. "I have just as much right to the head of the table as you do. Therefore, in Daddy's absence, I'll be sitting at the head of the table."

"Like hell you will," Marlon lashed out and threw his linen napkin to the table.

Everyone, including Alma and Delia, stared in silent horror at the war that was about to erupt in front of the entire family at the dinner table.

"You want me to move?" Jasmine demanded while leaning back in the chair. She then raised a cocky brow. "Come here and remove me."

Marlon sprang up from his chair and stormed across the dining room. Kane slid his chair backward and into Marlon's path, successfully stopping him. Kane casually looked up at the irate man from where he remained comfortably seated. There was something unsettling about the way Kane stared at Marlon, despite that the larger man hovered over him.

"Take it up with your father," Kane announced firmly, "but you won't lay a hand on her."

"This doesn't concern you," Marlon snarled while attempting to stare down the man still in his chair.

"If you lay a hand on your sister, it does," Kane reassured him while eerily void of emotion.

Marlon was about to lash out when a harsh voice stopped him.

"Sit down, Marlon," Alma shouted in anger.

All eyes were suddenly on Alma. She had a wildly unpredictable look in her eyes while her hand gripped the water pitcher so tightly her knuckles were white.

"It's not your place--" Marlon began but was immediately cut off.

"Don't you talk back to me, young man," Alma scoffed while glaring at him. "Now you sit down and be still. I will not have you disrupting the family dinner!"

Marlon attempted to stare down Alma, but her glare cut through him forcing him to look away. He returned to his chair, flopped in it, and stared at his empty plate while silently seething. Kane casually pulled himself and his chair back to the table. Once everyone was seated, Alma nodded to Delia and Mac to uncover the serving dishes. Jasmine was possibly too smug for her own good, but she'd made her point. The victory would probably be short-lived after their father returned on the weekend, but she wasn't going to let that spoil her current good mood.

§

After dinner, everyone retired to the game room, where the family usually spent most of their evenings. Boyd and Brandi snuggled together on the sofa and watched a romantic comedy. Since Kane was no longer on the clock while Boyd was with Brandi, he challenged Scorpio to a game of pool. Scorpio was supposed to keep her relationship with Rayner a secret, so she accepted Kane's challenge. The other alternative was socializing with Marlon, who was currently seething over the altercation in the dining room and was hitting an expensive bottle of scotch with a vengeance. Emily had her usual glass of wine and sat in her favorite corner chair with her book. She seemed to do a lot of reading in Sig's absence. While Kane and Scorpio played their game of pool, they assessed those within the game room.

"I see your boyfriend is hitting the sauce a little hard tonight," Kane teased.

Scorpio straightened before making her shot and glanced across the room at Rayner where he enthusiastically moved his chess piece across the elegant board.

"He's still working on his first glass of brandy," Scorpio remarked. "I doubt he'll have a second. I don't know what you're talking about."

Kane grinned and cast a look at the bar where Marlon refilled his scotch glass. "I meant your *other* boyfriend."

Scorpio rolled her eyes. "Don't even tease," she scoffed. "He's seriously losing his shit."

"Probably because his hot girlfriend isn't satisfying his needs," Kane again teased while adding a devious grin.

"Seriously," she snarled while glaring at him. "Stop that."

"Face it," Kane continued and leaned on his pool stick. "Sig only gave you that cover story to get his son laid. I don't think his plan is quite working the way either Hooper had hoped."

"Marlon has delusions of grandeur," Scorpio informed her brother. "Abetted by his father, who doesn't see Jasmine as his son's equal."

"Yeah, Sig has this whole "True Grit" thing going on," Kane joked while hiding his smirk. "Can I assume even if

Rayner weren't in the picture, you wouldn't be jumping 'second to the throne'?"

"I'd consider lesbian sex with Jasmine before I'd think about doing Marlon," Scorpio informed him.

Kane eyed her and frowned. "You managed to ruin lesbian sex for me," he scoffed. "Thanks, Scorp."

"Speaking of the mistress of the ranch," Scorpio announced and again scanned the room. "Where is Jasmine?"

"Brandi said her sister enjoys evening rides just before dusk," Kane remarked then cast a look at Scorpio and grinned. "Personally, I think she's out riding a wrangler."

She eyed her brother and raised a curious brow. "Any particular wrangler?"

"I suppose it just depends upon the day of the week," Kane teased. "Apparently, she works her way through the bunkhouse."

"I think Marlon was exaggerating," Scorpio insisted.

"I'm not referring to what Marlon said in the pool," Kane informed her. "I got this from Stone who heard it from Teddy. If you ask me, I think Stone is anxiously awaiting his turn."

Scorpio rolled her eyes and shook her head. "I love that man to death," she announced, "but he has a real weakness for redheads." She leaned across the table to make her final shot winning the game. Scorpio straightened while grinning proudly. "And that's two out of three. You officially lose."

"One more game," Kane insisted.

"Nope, I'm leaving the winner," she announced and set her pool stick down. "Get Marlon to play with you."

Kane made a face and waved her off. "I'd rather watch the rom-com with the pre-newlyweds." He considered his options then grinned. "Maybe I'll visit Mac."

"Wasn't she planning on soaking in the tub and then going to bed early?" Scorpio questioned.

He gave his sister a stern look. "Unlike you, Mac doesn't mind talking to me while she's relaxing in the tub."

"Please tell me you're joking," Scorpio demanded.

Kane gave her an innocent look. "What do you mean?"

"You don't seriously sit on the bathroom floor and talk to her while she's in the tub, do you?" Scorpio snapped with some irritation. "It's bad enough you did that to me while we were kids." Scorpio considered the comment and frowned. "And when I was in the tub with Cal."

"If he didn't mind, why should you?" Kane snapped back. "I always knocked first."

"Don't," she scolded.

"Don't what?"

"Just don't," she again threatened. "Let Mac have a few minutes of privacy. She's going to get pissed and kill you in your sleep."

"Mac adores me," he insisted then raised his brows. "She's a far cooler sister than you are."

"Seriously, Kane," Scorpio scoffed while shaking her head. "You're not as charming as you think you are."

"Of course I am," he announced then grinned. "You're just jealous."

"This conversation is over," she huffed. "I'm going to the library and find a book. I'll be in my room reading." Her eyes burned through his. "Don't even think about bothering me any more tonight."

"So Rayner is slipping into your room, huh?"

"No, we're behaving," she insisted. "He's not coming into my room, and neither are you, so deal with it."

"My God, you're cranky," Kane muttered.

Chapter 27

Scorpio entered the library, which wasn't a very large room, but it seemed to have a large assortment of fiction books as well as a large section on real estate. She scanned through several titles and attempted to find the section containing the romantic thriller type books Emily had been reading. The books didn't seem to be arranged in any particular manner making it difficult to find something of interest. She certainly didn't want to spend the entire evening attempting to find a book. If she had asked, Emily probably would have shown her where to find books of interest. Marlon entered the library. Despite having had a few glasses of scotch, he didn't give any indication that he was even buzzed let alone drunk.

"Here you are," he announced and managed a smile. "You were gone a while. I had hoped you hadn't turned in without saying goodnight."

She glanced briefly at him and again returned her attention to the shelves of books. "I was trying to find a book similar to the ones Emily's been reading, but I can't seem to find them," Scorpio remarked.

"That's because you're in the wrong section," he informed her then approached the bookcase near the window. He indicated several shelves in the middle. "This is Emily's section."

Scorpio approached and glanced at the shelves of books. She saw a lot with the same author among the rows. "Thanks," she replied and scanned the titles for something interesting.

Marlon leaned against the desk behind her and watched her. Scorpio could feel his eyes on her and attempted to ignore his uncomfortable stare.

"I was thinking maybe you and I could go horseback riding tomorrow afternoon," Marlon finally spoke up. "Just the two of us."

She glanced back briefly at him and showed little reaction either way. "I suppose we could do that," Scorpio replied.

"Maybe have Alma fix us a picnic lunch," he continued then fidgeted. "Jasmine is taking great pride in pointing out how little time you and I spend together. The girlfriend cover is starting to unravel."

Scorpio glanced back at him then removed a book from the shelf and read the back cover. "Despite what Kane might say, I'm not his partner in his business venture. I'm actually only helping out," she informed him. "I won't put any added stress on Rayner just to keep the girlfriend story alive. We haven't dated long enough for him to feel secure in our relationship yet."

"So you two weren't dating that long?"

"About a month," she replied but wasn't surprised that was the part of the conversation he focused on.

"Probably not my place," Marlon announced from where he leaned against the desk, "but the two of you have about as much in common as Jasmine and Conroy."

"You're right," Scorpio announced with a sigh of defeat then cast a cold glare at him. "It's *not* your place."

Scorpio returned the first book and removed a second. As she read the back cover, Marlon straightened and moved closer to her.

"You're young," Marlon announced from behind her. "I get it. You're looking for a mature man with an established career behind him. All things considered, though; wouldn't you rather be with someone who has more to offer than some guy in home security?"

Scorpio lifted her head and cast a look back at Marlon. "Is that what you think?" she asked then laughed. "That Rayner is just some home security guy?" She shook her head and returned to the book she held. "He's much more than that."

Marlon placed his arms around her waist from behind and rubbed against her while placing his lips close to her ear. She tensed the moment he touched her.

"Between the ranch and the real estate business, my share of my father's estate will be millions," he announced proudly.

Scorpio could smell the stench of alcohol on his breath with how close his face was to hers. Against her better judgement, she resisted the urge to react with physical violence.

"Get your hands off me," she instead snarled in response.

Marlon didn't take the warning seriously. "What does your boyfriend have that I don't?" he remarked and drove his pelvis against her backside.

She could feel his enthusiasm firmly pressing against her causing her hostility to rise in time with his arousal. "For one thing," Scorpio snarled. "He's a genius."

Scorpio then grabbed his thumb and easily applied enough pressure to pull his arm from around her waist. He cried out in anguish as she spun around to face him without releasing his thumb or dropping her book. She glared at him with a hardened look in her eyes.

"And he has a nasty, kickass girlfriend," she snarled while releasing his thumb only seconds before she thrust her palm upward into his crotch.

Marlon clutched himself and just about fell to his knees with crippling pain.

"That was a warning shot," Scorpio informed him while raising her brows and seemed unusually calm. "Touch me again, and you won't walk right for a week."

Without waiting for a response, Scorpio took her book and left the library. She bypassed the game room and headed for the grand stairs. As she rounded the banister, she heard a sound coming from the front sitting room. Scorpio set her book on the steps and approached the darkened lounge. She paused before the partially open door, hesitated, and then pushed the door open the rest of the way. She felt the inside wall for the light switch when she was suddenly grabbed around the waist from behind. Scorpio immediately rammed her elbow backward and connected with the man's mid-section then spun around prepared to swing. Rayner held his abdomen and backed up a step.

"Whoa, hey," he gasped while holding up his free hand. "I'm sorry. I didn't mean to startle you."

Scorpio gasped with horror and immediately moved closer to Rayner and touched his face. "I'm so sorry," she gasped. "I didn't mean to--"

"No, totally my fault," Rayner gasped then straightened while gingerly rubbing his abdomen. "I'm just grateful you were holding back."

"You should be grateful I didn't rip your testicles off," she remarked with concern. "I thought you were Marlon."

Rayner's expression suddenly dropped as he straightened while seemingly forgetting about the pain she'd just inflicted upon him.

"Marlon?" he demanded and gave her a strange look. "Why would you think I was Marlon? And why would you want to rip off his testicles?" His eyes suddenly narrowed as he came to his own conclusions. "What happened?"

Scorpio groaned and ran her fingers through her hair. "I ran into him in the library," she replied then fidgeted. "I guess he had a little too much to drink, and he made a pass at me."

Rayner's entire body stiffened. "What sort of pass?" he growled.

"It's fine," she insisted. "I took care of it. There's no reason for you to overreact."

"No, none at all," Rayner snapped in anger. "It's not as if he knows you're already in a relationship." His look turned demanding. "Oh, wait. He does know. I guess he conveniently forgot."

Scorpio moved closer to Rayner and placed her left arm around his neck while touching his face with her right hand, forcing him to meet her gaze.

"It's under control," she again insisted. "I dealt with him. You have a job to finish. Once you're done, if you want to leave, we're gone. Okay?"

Rayner drew a deep breath then captured her hand on his face and warmly kissed it. "I'll let it go," he replied gently. "As long as you sent a stern message."

"The message was sent loud and clear," she informed him. Scorpio gently pulled her hand from his, lovingly caressed his chest, and offered a sly smile. "I have an idea. Why don't we meet in the pool house after everyone has gone to bed? Mac says it has a king-sized bed and a huge shower for two."

His smile slowly returned as he moved closer to her. Rayner placed his arm around her waist and allowed his hand to caress the small of her back and down her backside.

"I like where this is going," he groaned while grinning.

"And I like where your hand is going," she teased back.

"What time?"

"The wranglers are up at five, so we should be out of there by then," she replied. "How about three in the morning?"

"It's a date," Rayner eagerly replied.

She kissed him quickly on the lips then returned the smile. "I'll meet you there then," Scorpio replied then pulled away. "Walk me to my room?"

Rayner hesitated then managed a timid smile. "Actually, I was on my way to the hall bathroom when I saw you heading toward the lounge," he informed her. "I'm three moves away from checkmate."

"Kick his ass," she teased with a grin.

"I intend to," he replied cheerfully.

Scorpio collected her book from the steps and headed upstairs. Rayner watched her until she disappeared at the top of the steps. His smile then faded, and a sneer replaced it.

§

Marlon collapsed onto the library sofa, shut his eyes, and groaned with some discomfort. When he opened his eyes, he saw Rayner casually leaning against the nearby bookcase with a book in his hands as if he'd been standing there reading the entire time. Marlon looked around since he'd only shut his eyes a moment, and possibly wondered how Rayner managed to slip into the library so quickly and quietly. Rayner cast a look at Marlon, shut his book, and casually replaced it to the bookcase.

Marlon groaned, ran his fingers through his hair, and sat forward on the sofa.

"I don't have time for your petty jealousy," Marlon remarked with limited patience.

"I suggest you make time," Rayner scoffed and placed his hands in his pockets.

"Seriously?" Marlon demanded. "*You're* going to threaten *me?*"

"I realize you don't take me seriously because I'm not excessively tall and extraordinarily muscular," Rayner announced. "I also realize you don't respect me or my relationship with Scorpio."

"So you're going to bore me to death?" Marlon demanded while raising a brow.

Rayner offered a moderately psychotic smile. "No, because I'm not nearly as boring as you might think either." He stared at Marlon long enough to make the man uncomfortable. "To a fault, I'm too smart for my own good. I wanted to give you the benefit of the doubt, but I was almost positive you'd eventually make moves on my girlfriend. You have, and she turned you down." Rayner tilted his head and raised his brow. "I'm sure she threatened you into behaving like the gentleman you want everyone to think you are. In case her threats didn't quite sink in, or you have a momentary lapse in judgment regarding *my* girlfriend, I feel compelled to issue my own threat."

Marlon laughed. "This should be good."

"In fact, it is," Rayner announced without taking his eyes off Marlon. "Carson--Brandi and Boyd will be at the mall in Colorado Springs on Friday, June 20th for a day of shopping and a late dinner."

Marlon shifted on the sofa while staring at Rayner, who appeared to be reading from some invisible letter.

"Boyd is planning a surprise for Brandi," Rayner continued, "and he'll probably duck out on her while she's trying on clothes at one of the trendy clothing stores. The rest is up to you." Rayner stared at Marlon and tilted his head. "The rest of what, Marlon? Were you assisting Carson in the abduction of your sister?"

"Where did you get that?" Marlon demanded while attempting to hide his horror.

"You sent an email to Carson from your father's computer," Rayner replied. "That is your email account, isn't it? Lonestranger@compuserve.com?"

"You hacked my email?" Marlon cried out.

Rayner smirked slyly. "Oh, I hacked more than your email," he insisted while maintaining his unpredictable look. "Dear Attorney Rodney Larkin; enclosed is the requested check in the amount of fifty thousand dollars and zero cents payable to Ms. Annette Patton to resolve case number--"

"Enough," Marlon suddenly cried out while staring at Rayner then pointed a warning finger at him. "That is confidential, and I'll have your ass if you ever repeat that to anyone."

"I don't need to repeat it," Rayner casually replied. "I just need to post it on social media." His eyes narrowed while glaring at Marlon. "Don't discount me as a threat, Marlon. I'm not nearly as harmless as you might think. Mind your manners around Scorpio, because if she doesn't take you down; I can and will." He offered a pleasant yet devious smile. "You have a good night."

Rayner turned and left the library.

Chapter 28

The sun had already set, and darkness was falling upon the ranch. The interior barn lights were on as well as the usual vapor light that came on automatically at dusk. Marlon walked across the pasture to his grazing horse. The horse lifted its head and playfully snickered at him. Marlon attached the lead rope to the horse's halter and led it back to the gate. Teddy approached the fence and watched Marlon remove his horse from the pasture then tie it to the hitching post.

"I saw the barn lights on from the bunkhouse," Teddy announced and eyed Marlon and his horse. "You're going riding this time of night?"

"It's still light enough," Marlon insisted then indicated the bright moon. "And there's more than enough moonlight."

Teddy leaned against the hitching post and watched Marlon head into the barn. He returned a moment later with his saddle, blanket, and bridle.

"Women trouble, eh?" Teddy asked.

"Every single one of them in that house," Marlon grumbled with disgust. "I'd love to send them all away on an extended vacation."

Teddy snorted a laugh. "Been there."

Marlon saddled the horse in record time. Within a few minutes, he had already removed the halter and put the horse's bridle on.

"Don't go too far," Teddy announced. "I don't have to remind you of coyote out there."

"I'm not going far," Marlon replied with a defeated sigh. "I'll probably just check out the area near the herd. I won't go as far as the woods."

"That's best," Teddy replied then waved as Marlon mounted his horse. "Happy trails, boss."

As Teddy returned to the bunkhouse, Marlon rode his horse at a leisurely walk toward the large corral containing the cattle. He rode along the first large field where it was still light enough to see the pasture, although the barn and house were now off in the distance. His horse stomped its foot several times while they walked, which almost always indicated flies pestering the animal, but there weren't any flies at night. When he reached a flat, worn path not far from the woods, he sent the horse into a slow gallop. The horse picked up speed and ran along the wide, flat trail. The horse suddenly bolted sideways without warning, snorted loudly, and reared up in the air. Marlon managed to remain on the horse and attempted to calm the animal. The horse no sooner landed when it kicked out and bucked, almost certainly wanting to toss Marlon off its back.

After managing to stay on the horse for nearly thirty seconds, he finally lost his balance and flew from the saddle. Marlon hit the ground harder than expected, rolled twice, and then lay motionless. The horse continued to snort while kicking and bucking as it ran off across the pasture as if some invisible predator had attacked it.

§

It was nine o'clock that night and nearly an hour after Marlon had gone out for his ride. Stone and Maverick left the noisy bunkhouse while hiding their grins. Maverick removed a wad of cash from his pocket and started counting it while the two men laughed and walked toward the barn.

"It was a pleasure taking their money," Maverick announced while grinning.

"You're officially a marked man, my friend," Stone teased while slapping his back.

"I don't care," Maverick replied while raising his brows. "They took great pleasure in laughing at me all those times I fell off. Now it's my turn to laugh at them."

"I can't believe you let them beat you the first night we played," Stone remarked and shook his head. "I even thought you lost your touch."

"No, I was going for the long con," Maverick insisted. "Let them completely drop their defenses then go for the jugular."

"Well, you certainly bled them dry," Stone replied then raised a brow and gave him a stern look. "I think you even took some of my money."

"Yeah?" Maverick asked then grinned slyly. "Well, you laughed at me too."

Stone chuckled at the comment. They saw Marlon's saddled, sweated horse standing outside the barn. Both men appeared bewildered and hurried for the horse. The horse saw them, snorted, and lunged away from them. Stone managed to calm the heavily breathing, skittish horse. He ran his hand along the horse's shoulder then looked at Maverick.

"This horse is drenched in sweat," Stone announced then looked around. "I don't see Marlon anywhere." He then indicated the bunkhouse. "Get the guys. Someone needs to check with the house and see if Marlon's there."

Maverick nodded and ran back to the bunkhouse. Stone led the frightened horse to the hitching post and tied it by its reins. As he unsaddled the horse to help cool it down, the horse panicked and jumped around nervously. Stone again had to calm the horse in order to remove the saddle. He set the saddle and blanket on the hitching post then retrieved a bucket of water and a sponge. He wiped the horse down with the wet sponge, which also helped the horse relax. The men ran from the bunkhouse and stared at the horse a moment. Teddy immediately looked around.

"Where's Marlon?" Teddy asked with concern. "He went out over an hour ago."

"I don't know," Stone replied and concentrated on caring for the overheated horse. "His horse came back spooked and sweated."

"We need to go out there and look for him," another wrangler announced.

"Let's saddle some horses and find him," a second wrangler replied.

The two wranglers hurried into the pasture to fetch the horses. Maverick returned from the house with Jasmine, Boyd, and Kane.

"Marlon's not in the house. What happened?" Jasmine asked while looking over the horse. "His horse came back like this?"

"Some of the guys are going to go out looking for him," Teddy announced.

The men brought two horses to the gate when Kane nodded across the pasture.

"There he is," Kane announced and pointed.

Marlon walked toward the barn looking a little more than beaten and bruised. Everyone ran to check on Marlon. Despite some minor scrapes, he was fine.

Jasmine shook her head while glaring at her brother. "You never should have gone out so close to dark," she insisted with annoyance. "And after drinking like that."

"It wasn't me," Marlon informed her then shook his head. "The damned horse just went insane. I guess he saw something in the woods."

"Let's get you cleaned up," Jasmine announced and motioned him to the house.

Jasmine, Boyd, and Kane escorted Marlon back to the house where Brandi waited on the patio. Maverick shook his head and removed the saddle from the hitching post.

"Don't drink and ride," Maverick scoffed and carried the saddle into the well-lit barn.

Teddy removed the horse's bridle and slipped the halter over its head. "I'd better check his horse for injuries and cool him down," he remarked then handed Stone the bridle. "I'll look after Marlon's horse."

Stone nodded then headed into the barn and entered the tack room. Maverick placed Marlon's saddle on the saddle rack while Stone hung up the bridle. Maverick then picked the discarded saddle pad off the floor and gave it a swift shake to remove excess dirt. Something clattered to the concrete floor catching their attention. Stone reached down and picked up what looked like a bullet casing but was made of plastic.

"What the hell--?" Stone commented while studying the strange object.

Maverick glanced at the object in Stone's hand then looked at the blanket. There was a tear within the saddle pad lining. Maverick's eyes widened as he again looked at the object in Stone's hand.

"What is this?" Stone asked.

Maverick took the object from Stone and gave him a concerned look. He pressed a button on the end, and the smooth, plastic bullet vibrated. Stone eyed Maverick and remained confused.

"It's a vibrator," Maverick informed him.

"Yeah, I can see that," Stone replied, took it from his friend, and shut off the small device. "Where did it come from?"

Maverick groaned and rolled his eyes. "It came from the saddle pad," he announced with concern. "Someone slipped that inside the tear. When enough pressure hit the button, it vibrated against the horse's back." Maverick shook his head. "The poor horse must have gone insane with that vibrating between the saddle and its back."

Stone stared at Maverick with his mouth hanging open in disbelief. "You mean someone put it there in hopes Marlon would be thrown from his horse?"

"Maybe more than just thrown," Maverick insisted.

Stone's eyes widened. "You think someone wanted to kill Marlon?" He then groaned and shook his head. "Jesus. Not Jasmine."

"There's no telling when that was put inside that blanket," Maverick insisted. "Marlon's been very unpopular among all the wranglers and even those within the house I'm told."

"Where would someone even get something like this?" Stone asked while studying the small bullet.

Maverick stared at Stone in disbelief. "You're kidding, right?"

Stone eyed him with surprise. "What do you mean?"

Maverick made a face, squirmed slightly, and gestured a moment. "You know," he attempted to respond.

"No, I don't," Stone remarked and shook his head. "Will you spit it out?"

Maverick groaned. "You find them in vibrating, uh, sex toys."

Stone's eyes widened with understanding. "Oh, *that*."

"Yeah," Maverick replied.

"This sounds like a job for Mac," Stone insisted and handed Maverick the bullet. "Let her search drawers for sex toys missing their vibrating, grrrr, grrrr things."

Maverick shook his head and placed the small device in his pocket. "You're going to make some woman an unhappy wife one day."

Chapter 29

Friday, June 27th. Morning. Kane entered the kitchen and found Mac and Delia helping Alma clean up after the more elegant family breakfast. Mac approached the linen closet with the folded tablecloth and was about to put it away when Kane appeared in the doorway just out of view of those within the kitchen.

"How's it going?" Kane asked while attempting to keep his voice down.

"It's going," Mac replied with little enthusiasm. "Can't say I'm learning anything interesting. Same boring thing day after day."

"Yeah, same here," Kane replied with a sigh. "I'm bored out of my mind."

"It's been almost a week," Mac remarked with some irritation. "How long are we going to play this game? I can't continue this charade until after Brandi's wedding. I won't last two months."

"Rayner is finishing up the security system sometime today or tomorrow, so his project is almost complete," Kane informed her while keeping his eye on the area outside the closet for either Alma or Delia. "Brandi and Boyd are going to town tomorrow evening, which may expose her to potential danger. If we don't learn anything this weekend, I think it's time to head out."

"Monday?"

"Yeah, we'll leave Monday," he replied then fidgeted. "Have you seen Brandi? She said she was going upstairs, but she didn't return, and she's not in her room."

"She's on the back patio," Mac informed him. "I'm supposed to take her some tea when it's ready."

"Oh, I'll take some tea too," Kane announced a little too enthusiastically.

She glared at him without humor. Kane laughed at the look he received and headed for the patio. Mac finished in the linen closet and joined Alma and Delia in the kitchen. Alma finished making Brandi's tea and passed it off to Mac, who then took the tea and headed for the back patio. As she stepped onto the patio, she saw four horse and riders in the near distance. Mac hesitated a moment and watched the riders with curious interest. Her eyes suddenly widened when she noticed the familiar horses and their teenage riders. They were the same two girls Mac had seen departing the helicopter at the airport in Colorado Springs.

"Shit," Mac gasped under her breath then slipped back into the kitchen and took a moment to peer out the glass door to the patio.

The sole man in the group riding a large black horse veered off and rode in the direction of the herd and Jasmine. The three teenage girls rode their horses toward the house. Mac cursed under her breath, set the tea mug down on the counter, and bolted up the back stairs. She paused on the second floor and crept onto the terrace, where she could watch the familiar girls from her past as they approached Brandi on the patio. She couldn't afford to be seen by either girl.

Back on the patio. The three teenage girls rode up to the porch and stopped their horses before Brandi. The youngest of the three girls, Selena, was a slender, thirteen-year-old girl with sandy brown hair beneath her cowboy hat. She rode a spirited gray gelding. Brandi seemed excited to see the younger teenager.

"Hey, Brandi," Selena announced cheerfully.

"Selena, hey," Brandi cried out excitedly then eyed the other girls. "Who are your friends?"

"This is Monique and Colleen," she announced. "They're visiting for a few weeks."

Monique and Colleen were the ultimate tomboys in their blue jeans, cowboy boots, and plaid shirts. The only thing girly about either was their shoulder-length hair and even that they wore in ponytails beneath their cowboy hats. Colleen Cooper was a lean, dark-haired, fifteen-year-old girl riding a large black horse. Monique Harris was the same age as Colleen except she had long, blonde hair. Monique sat on her brown and white paint stallion and gawked at Kane where he stood on the porch a few feet away from Brandi.

Selena then grinned and indicated Kane. "Who's your *new* friend?" she asked. "Did you trade in Boyd?"

"No," Brandi squawked. "Absolutely not." She then eyed Kane and shrugged. "Not a bad trade though." She offered a tiny giggle. "This is Kane. He works for Daddy."

There were some brief pleasantries. The young, blonde girl was almost giddy around the handsome young man. Her brunette friend gave her several strange looks.

"We were hoping to wrangle a few cows," Selena remarked. "Think your sister will mind?"

"Well, she's in one of her moods," Brandi replied then grinned. "But I'm sure she'll say yes if you ask nicely. She likes you more than she likes me."

Selena glanced across the pasture at Jasmine, who was talking to the man from their small riding party. Selena then looked back at Brandi and grinned. "I think we have that covered," she replied then laughed. "See you later."

Just upstairs, Mac stood on the second floor balcony and watched the three teenage girls ride across the yard and toward the herd where the man, who was all too familiar to Mac, sat on his horse and talked with Jasmine. Mac nervously ran her fingers through her hair and frowned while watching the man from her past.

"Son-of-a-bitch," she muttered.

"Mac?" Delia was heard calling.

Mac hurried back inside through the second floor balcony door and nearly ran into Delia.

"What are you doing up here?" Delia asked and looked back at the balcony door.

"I didn't feel good and needed some fresh air," Mac informed her and gingerly rubbed her stomach for a convincing touch.

Delia frowned her disapproval. "Brandi didn't get her tea," she announced with some irritation. "Didn't you take it to her?"

"No, I never made it to the patio," Mac again insisted. "I thought I might puke. I didn't think I had time to say anything. The fresh air helped."

"If you're feeling better, why don't you start straightening the guestrooms," Delia announced while glaring at Mac with limited patience. "I'll take Brandi her tea and then start on the family's rooms."

As Delia spun and walked away, Mac sneered at her turned back. "Yes, ma'am," Mac scoffed and gave her the middle finger once she was out of view. It was possible Mac was going to kill Delia yet.

Chapter 30

Saturday, June 28th. It was a little after sunrise. Mac stood in the shower beneath the hot stream of water and cursed under her breath. It had been a long week. After the family was served their breakfast, she and Delia would make the beds, and then they'd have off until Monday morning. Mac just needed to get through the next few hours without killing anyone and it would all be over. Mac was ready to pack it in. There were too many ghosts from her past staying somewhere nearby, and the boring life of a maid wasn't for her. She needed a job that required a vigorous workout. She'd spent most of her evenings doing pushups and sit-ups just to burn off excess energy. If she didn't hit someone soon, she was going to punch Delia just to make life interesting. Perhaps she'd take a long run that afternoon and burn off some energy that way.

Mac got out of the shower, dried off, and wrapped the large towel around her body. She used a second towel to dry her hair as she left the bathroom. Mac walked across her bedroom, tensed slightly, and turned toward her bed. Kane sat on the freshly made bed with his legs stretched out and crossed at the ankles while reading the book she'd left on her bedside table. Mac barely flinched when she saw him. Sadly, it hadn't been the first time he'd made unannounced and silent appearances. He was good at it. For a guy who claimed he didn't know how to use a lock pick, he seemed to have little trouble entering her bedroom despite the locked door.

"Damn it, Kane," she scoffed under her breath knowing she had to keep her voice down. "What are you doing in my room at this ungodly hour?"

He shut the book and looked up. Kane took in an eyeful of her in the towel, raised an approving brow, and tossed the book aside.

"It would appear as if I'm a peeping tom," he remarked with little emotion then grinned. "The wet look on you works, by the way."

"Kane," she scoffed with increasing irritation.

"Catching you alone to talk isn't easy," he informed her. "I looked for you a few times yesterday afternoon and evening, but you were nowhere to be found. Where have you been hiding?"

Mac huffed and folded her arms across her towel-covered chest. "I've been hiding out in my room after dinner to avoid Alma."

"Alma?" Kane remarked with surprise. "That sweet, old woman?"

"She mothers me," Mac informed him. "I wasn't all that fond of my own mother. I certainly don't need someone else scolding me for my foul mouth."

"Personally, I'm suffering from f-bomb withdrawal myself," he remarked. "No one around here curses much."

"That's because Alma will give them the stink eye," Mac muttered.

"Ironically, you haven't been in your room the last few times I've looked for you," Kane remarked and appeared curious. "Where do you go?"

Mac tensed slightly then frowned while running her fingers through her damp hair. "I don't want to say," she remarked while avoiding looking at him.

"Why?"

"You'll think I'm strange," she muttered.

"I already do," he replied without hesitation and immediately received a glare from her. He chuckled with amusement. "It's okay. I'm strange too. That's why I like you."

Mac drew a deep breath then reluctantly sighed. "I slip out to the hay barn and beat the living crap out of bales of hay," she informed him while frowning.

Kane eyed her a moment then chuckled. "I wish I'd thought of that."

Mac seemed somewhat relieved and managed a tiny smile. "Better the hay than Delia's face."

"That's the spirit. Have you learned anything to warrant us sticking around?" Kane asked while resting against the headboard, making himself comfortable on her bed.

"Nothing that suggests anyone is out to get Sig's daughter," Mac replied as she approached her dresser.

She tossed a pair of black underwear and matching bra across the small room and onto the bed. Kane eyed the undergarments not far from him and appeared mildly interested. He then looked at her turned back as she removed clothes from the dresser drawer.

"Have you come up with anything of interest on that vibrator someone planted in Marlon's saddle blanket?" Kane asked.

"No, but Delia handles cleaning the family's bedrooms," Mac informed him. "I have the three guest bedrooms and Brandi's room. If Brandi has any toys in her room, I haven't found them. Delia keeps me on a short leash during the day, and there's too much activity in the house in the evening to sneak into the family's room to search for something personal like that."

"We have to find a way to search Jasmine's room," Kane insisted. "If it came from a woman's toy, she's our prime suspect." He again eyed Mac as she brushed her damp hair with her back turned to him. "Anything in Brandi's room that raises red flags on Boyd?" he asked.

Mac set her hairbrush down then turned to face him and approached the bed. Kane lazily twirled her lacy, black underwear around on his finger while maintaining his professional demeanor. Mac sneered and snatched her underwear from him.

"No, but he's not supposed to be spending overnights in her room either," Mac informed him then smirked. "Daddy's rules."

"The guys reported him sneaking from the bunkhouse a few times after lights out. They saw him come into the house, but I haven't found any evidence that he's been sneaking into Brandi's room. I've patrolled the upstairs hallway periodically throughout the night since we've been here," Kane informed her then frowned. "I have to assume he was raiding the family frig for a midnight snack."

"According to Delia, Sig is a bit of a prude and won't allow Boyd to share Brandi's bed until after they're married. That rule applies to guys sneaking into the staff rooms too," Mac informed Kane and raised a cocky brow.

"Doesn't apply to me," Kane remarked with little interest in Sig's rules. "We're working a case."

Mac had to smirk at the comment then appeared humored. "Supposedly, Brandi is still a virgin, and they're waiting until their wedding night."

"Yeah, so I've heard," he muttered but didn't seem convinced. "I overheard them discussing their wedding night. I just assumed they knew I was listening and said it for my benefit." Kane grinned and chuckled in his throat. "Either way; that's not what Boyd's been spreading around the bunkhouse."

"It makes sense. If he's not having sex with Brandi, he wouldn't want the guys to know that little tidbit," Mac informed him. "He's certainly not going to admit he's not having sex. Guys don't do that."

"I'm not having sex," Kane informed her without hesitation. "I have no problem admitting it."

Mac eyed him and raised a clever brow. "Yeah, but you're not normal," she insisted.

"I am so normal," he protested.

"Yeah, sure you are," she remarked then casually removed her towel and let it fall to the floor.

Kane immediately turned his head and looked away. Despite that he didn't look, he wasn't even remotely uncomfortable. Mac snorted a laugh, obviously proving her point, and slipped into her undergarments. When she reached for her shirt, Kane resumed looking at her. Oddly enough, he didn't seem to mind sneaking a peek of her in her matching undergarments. Mac's athletic body was beyond impressive, and there was no denying she looked good in her black, lacy unmentionables. However, several glaring scars were difficult to ignore and quite possibly what Kane was actually studying. Mac had a conspicuous gunshot scar on her left shoulder. There were several knife scars on both her upper and lower arms as well as on her thighs and calves. She had another bullet wound scar on her right thigh, a large, jagged scar across her left ribcage, and a bullet wound scar on her abdomen. There was no denying that the old injury to her abdomen had been life-threatening at the time.

"That right there," Mac announced while indicating her and Kane. "You wouldn't even look at me while I was completely naked. That's not normal."

"Why? Because I'm a gentleman?"

"Gentleman?" Mac scoffed. "You weren't exactly a gentleman when you invaded my apartment the night you asked me to be the dynamic in your duo."

"That was different," he insisted and smirked. "I was just playing with you."

"And if I'd taken you up on the offer?" she questioned while raising a curious brow.

"You didn't," he casually replied. "So I guess we'll never know."

"Like I said," Mac remarked making her point, "you're not normal. I'm 99.9% convinced you're into women, so what's the deal?"

"I'm not aware I have a deal. My sister and I were inseparable since birth," he informed her. "If someone disrespects her; they disrespect me." He studied Mac and raised his brows. "If I treat you with less respect than I treat my sister, essentially, I'm disrespecting myself."

"With that attitude, it's a wonder you ever get laid," Mac remarked as she slipped into her shirt. She then eyed him suspiciously. "You have, haven't you?"

Kane grinned at the comment and laughed. "I manage just fine, but I appreciate your concern," he teased.

Mac groaned and slipped into her jeans. She looked at him and shook her head. "You make my head hurt," she informed him then sat on the bed to put on her socks and shoes. "I need to get out of this place. I'm bored out of my mind. I'm considering punching Delia in the mouth just to spice things up."

"I'm going to ask nicely that you don't do that," Kane announced with little reaction.

He then slid across the bed closer to where she sat and massaged her shoulders from behind. She was apprehensive at first then reluctantly allowed him to work his magic fingers on her tense shoulders.

"You really are tense," he announced and dug a little deeper into her tight muscles with his fingers.

Mac groaned at how good it felt.

"Brandi and Boyd want to go to some club in town tonight," Kane informed her. "It's some little dive of a town about an hour from here."

Despite his massaging hands, Mac tensed at his words. He didn't seem to notice.

"Did you want to come along?" he asked while concentrating on massaging her shoulders. "I don't know if Stone and Maverick are going, but I'll arrange something if you need to get out and unwind."

"Dive town, huh?" she remarked then snorted a soft laugh. "Thanks, but I think I'll pass."

"You could use a night on the town," he insisted while casting a look at her profile. "They have a club with entertainment and some local bars. Have a little fun; cause a little trouble." He then grinned slyly. "Make some badass cry. I don't want you losing your shit here. Go to town and make a mess."

She stopped his hands from massaging her shoulders and partially turned on the bed to face him. Her look was serious. "I have to be honest with you, Kane," Mac reluctantly announced then held her breath before continuing. "Sig drove through that little town on our way here. I was there once a while back. There are some people there I don't care to run into again. If they saw me, they'd question my reason for being out this far. That could eventually get back to the ranch and blow our cover."

He stared into her eyes at the comment then shifted slightly. "I keep forgetting that you've been around," Kane remarked then offered a sympathetic smile. "I feel bad for domesticating you like this. I should have insisted Sig make you a wrangler and not backed down. You got the shitty end of the stick on this one, but I'll make it up to you."

"Oh?" she asked while raising her brow then chuckled. "And how do you intend to do that?"

"Paintball battles?"

Mac laughed.

Kane raised his brows in suggestion. "Alligator hunting in Louisiana?"

She continued to laugh.

"Cliff diving in Maui."

Mac patted his arm while laughing. "Okay, stop," she insisted and hid her smile as she stood. "It's almost time for breakfast, and I don't want to be late."

Kane sprang to his feet, smiled warmly, and gently touched Mac's face, surprising her. She tensed from his touch and stared into his blue eyes as he grinned.

"I like making you smile," he announced then turned serious and brushed the stray lock of hair from her face. "I don't know who broke you, but I'm glad you trust me enough to help put you back together again."

Mac drew a sharp breath as she stared at him and resisted pushing him away. It was almost as if she wanted to believe him, but something kept her from it.

"I have your back, Mac," Kane announced as if reading her expression then kissed her warmly on the forehead.

He offered a sincere smile then crossed the room toward the window, exiting dramatically like a plundering pirate jumping ship. Mac watched him leave as a tear rolled down her cheek. She sniffed, harshly wiped the tear away, and attempted to collect herself.

Chapter 31

Evening. Most of the wranglers and only six of those within the house had planned on visiting town that evening. Scorpio drove to town with Marlon, who had managed to get her alone for only the second time since she'd arrived. The first time, in the library, didn't end so well for Marlon. The drive was mostly quiet the first half. Marlon finally spoke, breaking the silence.

"I'm really sorry about what happened in the library," Marlon announced in a timid tone. "I'm not myself when I drink."

Although Scorpio would disagree with that statement, she wasn't about to make waves while he was attempting an apology.

"Learning from our mistakes is what matters," she replied without looking at him.

Scorpio couldn't help but think Marlon's 'gentleman' persona was the fake one and the way he acted when he drank was his true personality. His inability to find and keep a girlfriend went beyond living on a ranch in the middle of no man's land. The way he treated his sister was a pretty good indicator of who he really was.

"Your boyfriend has some anger issues," Marlon informed her then shook his head. "Some sort of closet psychopath."

Scorpio cast a look at Marlon with a slightly stunned expression at the comment. She wondered from what sort of bipolar disorder Marlon suffered, but she allowed the words to sink in before calling him on it. It dawned on her that Rayner must have said or done something after she told him what had happened in the library.

"What did he say?" she asked before she could stop herself from speaking.

"I didn't think you knew he'd threatened me," Marlon replied.

Scorpio knew what Marlon was doing. He was attempting to pit her against her boyfriend by making him out to be the bad guy. Although she was a little irritated that Rayner obviously did something after she told him it was handled, she wasn't about to let Marlon manipulate her either.

"I did warn you about him," Scorpio replied. She wasn't playing Marlon's game. By letting him think Rayner was unstable would work in both their favor. "I'll tell him to play nice."

Her comment successfully silenced Marlon, and possibly shut down any further attempts to drive a wedge between her and Rayner.

§

Since there were six people from the house going to the swank lounge in town, Boyd drove Brandi's sports car. Brandi was content to ride shotgun while her boyfriend drove. Kane rode in the back of the sports car with Boyd's sister. Despite Kane's gift for gab, he remained somewhat quiet in the back seat with Delia. Knowing what he knew about her and how poorly she allegedly treated Mac, he didn't have much to say. Mac was his little badger, and he wouldn't stand for anyone mistreating her. Brandi, on the other hand, chirped endlessly the entire car ride. It wasn't much different than when Kane watched movies with her. Once Brandi got started, she didn't stop talking. Boyd had to be in love to listen to her talk nonstop for hours.

Stone drove to town with the other wranglers. They took two pickup trucks with four men in each. Maverick opted to stay behind and snoop a little. The wranglers were eager to blow their pay on booze and women. Some would bowl while others went to one of several bars. The wranglers typically avoided the swank lounge, since there was a cover charge due to the live entertainment, and the drinks were more expensive. Most of the wranglers enjoyed cheap beer and cheaper women at what was considered the seedy bar in town. A majority of the crowd at the dive was wranglers from neighboring ranches with the same goal in mind. Get drunk and seek out overnight company.

Despite its size, the small town had a population of nearly five thousand. It also had its own nightclub, which was something more country and less modern, several restaurants, a movie theater, bowling alley, and at least four bars. There was also a small motel on the way into town, which would gain plenty of business over the weekend. The town was busy on weekends when local ranchers and farmers made the trek for fun and relaxation. Even though there were a lot of rowdy wranglers, most of the younger men were respectful country boys. There was rarely any trouble beyond a few fights, typically over women.

§

Even though it was still light outside, the classy lounge remained dimly lit with mood lighting on small, round tables. There were larger tables and booths off to the sides, and a massive bar lined the back wall of the large room. The club was packed as it was most Saturday nights when the town's most popular singer, Pinto, was performing. Marlon secured a larger, round table for their group of six, although how he managed it remained a mystery. Despite their cover story, Kane was quick to take the seat next to his sister. Scorpio often felt Kane was co-dependent on her, but he functioned fine without her. He'd recently been out of her life for several months, which proved his independence, but since they'd reconnected last week, he latched onto her every chance he had. When they were little, he was practically her shadow, which may have explained his boundary issues.

Delia sat between Kane and her brother, leaving Brandi seated between Boyd and Marlon, who was to Scorpio's right. Kane ordered cranberry juice on the rocks, which essentially looked like a mixed drink. To Scorpio's knowledge, Kane only drank alcohol once. Their grandparents had gone away for the evening, and Kane picked the lock on the liquor cabinet. He and his friends drank an entire bottle of peach schnapps. Kane spent the rest of the night throwing up, and he never touched liquor again. Scorpio learned from his mistakes and didn't drink until she legally could and then only in moderation. Kane leaned in to say something to Scorpio when he thought no one was looking. The filler music in the lounge was loud, so most people had to be close while talking.

"If Boyd and Brandi want to dance later, you may have to help me keep an eye on her," he spoke close to her ear. "This place is packed."

"You mean by dancing with Marlon?" she remarked while raising a cocky brow.

Her brother's eyes were demanding. "It's not going to kill you, Scorp," Kane scoffed. "He knows you're with Rayner. Just play along."

Kane ignored the look his sister shot at him. Had Scorpio told her brother how Marlon humped her in the library, he wouldn't be nearly as understanding.

Delia noticed Kane talking to Scorpio, caught his attention, and leaned closer to speak to him. "If you're interested in Marlon's girlfriend, you'll want to tread lightly," she informed him.

He cast a glance at Delia and hid his surprise at the comment. "Never even crossed my mind," Kane teased and waved off Delia. "She's definitely not my type." He cast a look at Scorpio then leaned closer to Delia. "She's kind of a bitch."

The music changed to a slow song allowing couples to dance before the singer took the stage for her show.

Delia smiled and indicated the dance floor to Kane. "Want to dance?"

Kane was caught off guard, and it possibly just dawned on him that Brandi and Boyd might have been playing matchmaker with him and Delia.

"Uh, yeah," Kane replied then stood and smiled. "I'd love to."

He extended his hand to her, which made her smile. Delia accepted his hand and joined him on the nearby dance floor for the slow song. Scorpio couldn't resist turning sideways in her chair to witness her brother slow dancing with Boyd's attractive and delightfully single sister. Karma really was a bitch. As Kane slow danced with Delia, he caught Scorpio's mocking grin from the table. His eyes narrowed as he sneered at her. Delia seemed interested in dancing a little closer than acceptable for two people who barely knew each other. She seemed to want to talk and needed to be close enough for him to hear her. Even that they danced close, he still had a hard time hearing what she said.

"Did Mr. Hooper actually hire you to be Brandi's bodyguard?" Delia asked.

"That's the rumor," Kane replied.

"Then it's true," she announced with surprise. "You're actually a bodyguard."

Kane managed a tiny grin and a chuckle. "I think my ego just deflated," he teased.

"I'm sorry," she quickly covered. "I didn't mean that as an insult. I always imagined bodyguards being seven feet tall with huge arms and low IQs."

"That sounded a little more like a compliment," Kane remarked and chuckled. "Even though I'm pretty sure you called me short."

"I'm not making a very good impression, am I?" Delia announced while hiding her embarrassed smile.

"No, you're fine. I'm the problem," he insisted then grinned in jest. "I'm a bit of a surly prick. I'm pretty sure I get it from my father."

"I didn't really know my father," Delia remarked.

"I thought your parents didn't get divorced until you were nearly thirteen," Kane remarked.

"How did--?" Delia smiled then nodded. "Oh, you must have been talking to Brandi."

"She tends to talk throughout the movies," Kane informed her while smirking.

"She probably told you Boyd's entire life story," Delia teased. "Which means you know a lot more about me than I know about you."

"I wouldn't say a lot," he confessed. "You lived with your mother after the divorce, and he lived with your father." Kane squinted a moment while sinking into thought. "She mentioned something about you and your mother moving to Costa Rica for several years doing humanitarian work or something to that effect."

"Yes," she replied. "As if being a teenager wasn't hard enough. Boyd and I lost touch with each other for a few years there."

"You had some sort of boating accident?"

Delia tensed then nodded. "Yeah, that's how our mother died," she reported and sank into his arms almost insecurely. "I somehow survived and stayed afloat in the life raft for a couple of days. I had a concussion. It was months before I could even remember my own name." She then offered a smile. "Once they had my name, they tracked down Boyd, and he came for me."

"Your memory returned then?" he asked with a curious look.

She made a face and shrugged while they slow danced. "I remember a lot about my life in Costa Rica, but I don't have a firm grip on my childhood."

"That's why you don't remember your father," he deducted and smiled.

"I remember little things," she informed him. "Not many details though. I didn't even know Boyd when he came for me. After a while, I got some pieces back. He filled in a lot of the blanks for me."

"I have a little sister too," he informed her. "I'm always looking after her."

"That's sweet," Delia announced cheerfully.

"Yeah, that's me," he remarked and grinned. "Thoughtful and caring." Kane's smile faded as he caught several men staring at their table from the bar. "Who are those men at the bar?"

Delia glanced behind her and strained to see. Kane spun her around as they danced so she could take a better look at the group by the bar.

"I'm not entirely sure," she replied. "I think I recognize the one from the ranch near ours."

"The one owned by Brandi's ex-boyfriend."

"Yeah, that's the one," Delia replied and eyed him with concern. "Why? Is there a problem?"

"No, they're just staring. No law against that," Kane remarked and offered a reassuring smile. "I'll just keep an eye on them for now."

Chapter 32

Scorpio politely listened to Marlon as he leaned close to her and attempted to talk above the music. She had to admit, she was more interested in her brother slow dancing with Delia than she was in Marlon's conversation. Once the song ended, Kane took Delia's hand and led her back to the table. When he pulled her chair out for her, she immediately blushed and thanked him. Despite his age, Kane was quite the gentleman and made lasting impressions on most women. Scorpio noticed the glare Kane received from Delia's brother. Was Boyd the type of brother who didn't think any man was good enough for his little sister?

Scorpio never had that problem with her brother. Kane was quick to make friends with her first boyfriend, Cal. Perhaps he was a little too comfortable invading their relationship, but Kane never judged Cal despite his somewhat tainted past. In the brief time her brother knew Rayner, Kane seemed eager to be his friend as well. Not all brothers were happy when their sister's dated, and Kane was definitely the overly protective brother type. Thankfully, he seemed to approve of Scorpio's choice in men. She was happy about that. As Kane took his seat alongside Scorpio, he tapped her shoulder and spoke as he sat.

"Bar three o'clock," he announced then took his seat and avoided further conversation with her.

Scorpio casually glanced at the bar and immediately noticed the men who seemed to be watching their table. Scorpio then leaned closer to Marlon.

"Who are those men at the bar that keep staring this way?" she asked.

Marlon glanced at the bar, frowned, and leaned toward Scorpio. "They're wranglers at Reynolds' ranch."

"Your sister's ex-boyfriend?" Scorpio asked.

"His father's men, yes," Marlon replied although he didn't seem concerned. "I doubt they'll bother with us. They wouldn't dare give my sister a hard time in front of me. Carson's father would give his wranglers hell. Our fathers have a good relationship."

Scorpio was about to respond when she saw Brandi lean closer to Boyd and say something to him. Brandi then got up and headed across the lounge for the bathroom. Boyd nudged his sister and indicated Brandi. Delia got up and followed Brandi across the crowded room. Kane immediately shot looks around the lounge then eyed Scorpio. Delia was going with Brandi, so at least she wasn't wandering off on her own. The three women at the bar with Carson Reynolds' men seemed a little too eager to head across the lounge for the bathroom as well. Scorpio and Kane exchanged looks. Was it just a coincidence? Scorpio waited for the women to pass and followed them from a safe distance.

§

The women's restroom was empty since it was nearly time for the live entertainment to start. Brandi stood before the mirror and applied more lipstick while talking to Delia, who occupied the end stall.

"So you like Kane, huh?" Brandi teased.

"He's, uh, pretty, well--" Delia fumbled.

"Sexy?"

Delia laughed from the end stall. "Yeah, he's definitely that," she teased. There was a moment's pause. "Are you sure he's a bona fide bodyguard? He doesn't look the part. He's kind of small."

"I think Daddy liked that about him," Brandi remarked then giggled. "Like a concealed weapon."

"He's not very intimidating," Delia remarked from the end stall. "I think you're better off letting Boyd protect you."

"I think Kane's just backup," Brandi insisted while making kissy faces at herself in the mirror. "Like when Boyd's not around and stuff." Brandi again giggled. "The guy doesn't even carry a gun."

"Really?" Delia gasped from the end stall. "Not much of a bodyguard, I'm afraid."

"He says he's secretly a superhero," Brandi teased while grinning at herself in the mirror. "Sadly, I think he actually believes it."

"Is he actually that charming?" Delia asked. "Or was he just playing it up?"

"Oh, no," Brandi announced with a serious look. "He's definitely that charming."

The bathroom door opened, and the three women from the bar entered. One leaned against the door while the other two approached Brandi at the sink. Brandi saw them through the mirror and rolled her eyes.

"What do you want?" Brandi demanded without turning to face them.

"Who's there?" Delia cried out with concern from her bathroom stall.

One of the remaining two women approached the stall door and held it closed so Delia couldn't leave the stall. The door rattled.

"Carson's wranglers' skanky girlfriends," Brandi informed Delia while appearing almost bored. She turned to face the woman standing behind her.

"That wasn't nice," the woman announced then suddenly grabbed Brandi by her hair and pulled her head back. "You've been spreading rumors around about Carson." She glared into Brandi's eyes. "Saying he was the one who jumped you in the alley."

Brandi cried out while attempting to pull her hair free but was unsuccessful.

Delia again attempted to open the stall door with a thump but couldn't open it. "Let me out," she shouted in anger. "Get away from her!"

The woman offered a creepy smile while staring into Brandi's concerned eyes. "You don't talk about our friends that way," she announced.

The main bathroom door thumped as someone attempted to get inside.

"Make it quick," the woman blocking the main door announced. "Someone is outside the door."

The woman holding Brandi's hair made a fist and pulled her arm back. There was a thunderous crack against the bathroom door and the woman blocking it was thrown across the bathroom. All eyes were on the restroom door as Scorpio stepped inside.

"What's going on?" Scorpio demanded and allowed the door to fall back into place.

The woman holding Brandi by the hair pointed a warning finger at Scorpio. "Walk out that door and keep your mouth shut or you're next."

Scorpio eyed them with a strange look then turned toward the bathroom door behind her.

The woman looked back at Brandi and laughed. "So much for your friends."

When they heard the deadbolt lock, the women fell silent. All three looked back at the bathroom door as Scorpio turned toward them with little to no expression. The woman closest to Scorpio lunged for her. Scorpio scaled back her aggression while kicking the woman in the abdomen. As the woman doubled over, Scorpio swept her legs out from beneath her, allowing her to crash to the floor. Scorpio casually crossed the bathroom toward the woman holding Brandi by her hair. The woman holding the bathroom door closed on Delia released it, lunged for Scorpio, and attempted to grab her hair. Scorpio blocked her arm, caught her by the wrist, and twisted her arm back. The woman screamed. Scorpio then jabbed her in the gut with just enough force to make her gasp. She then drove her to her knees with the pressure she held on her wrist.

While keeping the woman to her knees, Scorpio casually looked at the woman holding Brandi by her hair. The woman from the main door recovered and lunged for Scorpio, who already seemed to have her hands full. Scorpio backhanded the lunging woman across the face with her free hand, sending her into the stall partition. Scorpio then grabbed her by the wrist, twisted her arm behind her back, and drove her to her knees on the opposite side of the first woman she held. Scorpio now had both women on their knees while holding their wrists. Scorpio looked back at the third woman, who now released Brandi's hair.

"Make wise choices," Scorpio announced with little emotion.

The woman saw that both of Scorpio's hands were busy holding her two friends, giving her the perfect opportunity to take Scorpio down. She lunged for Scorpio while throwing a punch. Scorpio snap kicked the woman in the abdomen. When she doubled over, Scorpio swept her legs out from beneath her causing her to strike the floor. Scorpio then placed her booted foot to the back of the woman's neck and held her face to the bathroom floor, which was about as pleasant as it sounded. Delia stood in the open stall door and stared with shock at the sight before her. Brandi stared with her mouth hanging open as Scorpio held all three women immobile.

Scorpio eyed Delia and raised her brow. "Are you going to wash your hands?" she just about demanded.

Delia hurried to the sink and washed her hands while Scorpio continued to hold the three women immobile. Scorpio then nodded Delia and Brandi to the door. They practically ran for the door. Scorpio drew a deep breath and looked at the woman just about paralyzed beneath her boot.

"Consider this your first and only warning," Scorpio informed them. "If I wanted to hurt any of you, you'd be in the hospital. I won't be nearly as nice if you bother Brandi and her friends again. Understood?"

All three women screamed in response, particularly the woman with her face pressed against the dirty bathroom floor. Scorpio released them, casually turned, and left the bathroom with Delia and Brandi, who couldn't seem to take their eyes off their dangerous travel companion.

"I'm beginning to think you really aren't Marlon's new girlfriend," Brandi remarked.

"Nope," Scorpio replied as they crossed the lounge and headed for their table. Her cover had obviously been blown, so it was no longer necessary to lie about it.

Chapter 33

Scorpio, Brandi, and Delia joined the guys at the table. Kane glanced at the three local women as they walked past looking sore and defeated. The three women returned to their male friends at the bar. Kane eyed the three country girls who looked a little worse for wear then glanced at his sister as he leaned closer to speak privately to her.

"Can I assume the six of you weren't gossiping about boys?" he teased.

"I'd like to believe those young ladies learned a valuable lesson, but I suspect they'd rather sick their boyfriends on us," Scorpio remarked while studying her brother. "My cover has officially been blown with Brandi and Delia, so I don't need to sit it out. How would you like to play this?"

From the corner of his eye, Kane watched the women sobbing to their boyfriends at the bar. "Three on one? I've got this," he remarked while focusing his attention back on his sister. "You just keep their girlfriends from interfering. I'd never hit a woman."

"Except me, huh?" Scorpio replied.

He eyed her then smirked. "That's different," Kane remarked. "You don't count."

Scorpio rolled her eyes with disgust. "It's all you," she replied. "Tag me in if you need me."

Kane eyed his sister and grinned almost slyly. "I always do."

One of the men approached their table and stood over Scorpio with hostility in his eyes.

"Did you attack my girlfriend in the bathroom?" he demanded in anger.

Scorpio casually leaned back in her chair and eyed the man attempting to intimidate her.

"I'm pretty sure she attacked me," Scorpio replied while showing little emotion.

Marlon was already lost in the conversation. "What's the problem?" he suddenly demanded.

"Stay out of this Marlon," the man remarked while looking past Scorpio at him. "This doesn't concern you."

"If you're accusing my girlfriend of something, it damned well does concern me," Marlon announced.

"She's your girlfriend?"

Marlon nodded.

Brandi glared at the man standing over Scorpio. "I don't know which of those three skanks is your girlfriend--" she boldly announced from across the table.

Kane lowered his head and rubbed his eyes as he groaned. Brandi wasn't helping deescalate the situation.

"But they attacked Delia and me in the bathroom," Brandi continued. "When Scorpio showed up, they threatened her too." Brandi folded her arms across her chest and glared at the man. Her eyes narrowed in anger. "They deserved having their asses handed to them."

"They attacked you?" Boyd asked Brandi with surprise as he stared at her.

"I was trying to tell you before we were interrupted," Brandi informed her boyfriend.

The man ignored Brandi and Boyd then pointed a warning finger at Marlon. "You'd better keep your girlfriend in line," he snarled. "Or I'll do it for you."

The man spun to leave and came face-to-face with Kane, who now stood. Despite being a good four inches shorter than the man he confronted, Kane's steely gaze was unnerving. The man glared back at Kane and seemed almost humored at the much smaller man attempting to intimidate him.

"Kane, let it go," Scorpio announced.

Kane offered a creepy, unsettling smirk and politely indicated for the man to pass. The man suddenly seemed untrusting but maintained his superior grin and returned to the bar. Kane gracefully collapsed into his chair.

"I wouldn't worry about them," Marlon informed Kane with little interest. "Even though Brandi's no longer dating Carson, his father will deal with any of his men who get out of line."

"Probably why they sent their girlfriends to rough up Brandi in the bathroom," Scorpio remarked and gave Marlon something to consider.

The announcer took the stage and introduced Pinto, the singer most people came to see. There was a huge applause from the audience as the beautiful woman walked onto stage. The singer wore a form-fitting evening dress that revealed plenty of leg and cleavage. Her long, copper-colored hair was worn in an elegant, French twist. Although a man in the front row just off to the side cheered and clapped excitedly, she seemed hesitant to acknowledge the mildly distracting man's attention. It was fair to assume that the man was in love with the beautiful singer. The room fell silent as Pinto sang her first song of the evening.

§

Evening at the ranch. Apart from Brandi and Marlon, just about everyone else within the house stayed home for the weekend. Sig had returned on Thursday but left again on Friday and wouldn't be home until Sunday afternoon. Mac had plans of her own. She planned on poking around in Delia's room after Alma retired for the evening. Being Delia was Boyd's sister, if he was up to something, there was a chance Delia either knew about it or was in on it. Alma always turned in early with her television blasting leaving Mac free to poke around in Delia's room without worry of being caught.

The house was unusually quiet with the others gone for the evening. Rayner and Conroy faced off over the elegant, expensive chessboard while Emily sat in a comfortable chair not far from them with a book and a glass of wine. She'd been reading her book since after dinner, which was nearly as long as Rayner and Conroy had been engaged in several chess matches. Jasmine entered the game room and appeared bored. She eyed her husband, who was enjoying his game with Rayner. She didn't seem pleased, although it was unclear why.

"I'm going to take a quick ride around the ranch before turning in," Jasmine informed her husband.

Conroy barely glanced up and gave a disinterested wave. Jasmine frowned at the response and left the game room. Rayner instantly picked up on the woman's mood and eyed Conroy.

"If you want to go with her, our game can wait," Rayner insisted.

"Go with her?" Conroy asked then chuckled with humor. "I don't care for horseback riding in the daylight. I certainly wouldn't want to go for a ride in the dark. You don't want to know what sort of creatures are out and about this time of night in these parts."

"You don't really care for ranch life, do you?" Rayner remarked and finally made his move. Ironically, after speaking of horses, he moved his knight.

Conroy studied the board and didn't even look up at the comment. "When I met and fell in love with Jasmine at her father's real estate office, I thought I could adjust to life on a ranch," he replied with little emotion. "I didn't know the ranch was all she cared about. She's in constant competition with her brother over how to best run the place. Competition." He snorted a laugh. "It's an all-out war between them."

"You didn't know you'd be living at the ranch?" Rayner asked.

"Her father initially placed her in charge of the real estate company," Conroy informed him. "She was living in Colorado Springs when we met. Once we were married, she wanted to return to the ranch." Conroy shrugged. "Sig gladly gave me the job as house manager in order to make his daughter happy. I just wanted Jasmine to be happy even if being out here made me miserable." He made his move then leaned back in the chair and sighed. "Competing with her brother has done nothing but make her miserable, but she won't move back to Colorado Springs."

Emily eyed them from overtop of her book as if overhearing part of their conversation. She then pretended to mind her own business.

"Jasmine and I are very different people," Conroy insisted with a depressed sigh. "When you're young and in love, those differences are fun and exciting. After a while, they become a dividing force. She used to love my intellect, but she seems to resent it now."

Rayner looked up from the chessboard, stared at Conroy a moment, and shifted uncomfortably. "Do you think she's bored with you?"

Conroy snorted a laugh. "Absolutely," he remarked without a moment's hesitation. "I've got a few years on her as well. That didn't matter in the beginning, but it certainly has taken its toll on our relationship in recent years. I suppose I'm not nearly exciting enough for her anymore. Honestly, we have nothing in common."

Rayner sank into thought and no longer seemed interested in their game. Conroy's relationship with his wife resembled his own relationship with Scorpio, and it was a little uncomfortable to consider.

Conroy eyed him and appeared curious. "Did I say something?"

Rayner tensed a moment and shifted uncomfortably in his chair. "No, well, maybe," he fumbled. "I'm in a relationship with an amazing woman." He drew a deep breath and sank back into thought. "She's a few years younger than me." He laughed nervously. "Quite a few years younger." Rayner met Conroy's gaze. "I'm not her usual type. Pretty far from it. I'm grateful every day that she's with me, but I'm worried that she'll eventually grow bored with me and find someone more her type."

"That's tough, Rayner," Conroy remarked and shook his head. "I suggest you enjoy it while it lasts. You don't know that she'll break your heart." He studied Rayner while seemingly lost in his thoughts then finally spoke. "It's true, you know."

"What's that?"

"Better to have love and lost," Conroy informed him and offered a tiny smile. "It's not the destination but the journey. Enjoy the journey."

"I want the destination," Rayner firmly remarked while frowning.

"Maybe so," Conroy announced. "But you don't always get what you want."

Emily shut her book and stood. "You boys enjoy pondering life," she announced, indicating she'd been listening to their conversation. "I'm taking a long bubble bath and then turning in."

Conroy chuckled and gave a casual wave. "Goodnight, Emily," he announced. "Enjoy your bubble bath and your chardonnay."

She snorted a laugh then left the room with her book. Conroy waited until she was gone before casting a look at Rayner.

"I may be unhappy in my relationship," Conroy informed him then nodded after Emily, "but I've got nothing on that one. Sig's gone more than he's here. I wish I knew her secret to making it work."

"I'm guessing bubble baths and chardonnay," Rayner teased while grinning.

Both men laughed.

Chapter 34

Within the nightclub lounge, the lovely and talented singer was on the second song of her first set, and the audience loved her. Scorpio and Kane took turns keeping an eye on the men at the bar. There was no doubt in either's mind that the men were going to cause trouble. It was just a matter of when. Before the woman on stage finished her second song, two of the three men approached their table. The third man was already working his way across the room to take them by surprise with a rear assault. Scorpio sat up straight and cast a look past Kane, who remained casually reclined in his chair.

"Two at three o'clock," Kane muttered while showing little reaction.

"One at nine," Scorpio added.

"Ah, a sneak attack, eh?" Kane teased while hiding his sly grin. "I do love a challenge."

Boyd and Brandi seemed to realize something was about to happen by the way Scorpio and Kane were shifting secret looks while pretending they weren't watching. Marlon was happily clueless while attempting to flirt with Scorpio once the singer finished her second song. Scorpio wasn't even paying attention to Marlon, although her occasional nod seemed to indicate to him that she was clinging to his every word. The first of the two men paused before Kane, where he remained comfortably relaxed in his chair. The man then gave him a firm poke to the shoulder.

"You've got a problem?" the man demanded.

Kane cast a look at the man standing over him, showed little reaction, and shook his head. "Not a problem in the world."

"I think you have a problem with me," the man pressed and again poked Kane in the shoulder.

Kane eyed the way the man poked him with his finger then met his gaze. "Seriously? He raised a demanding brow. "You're poking me?"

"Want to take it outside?" the man demanded. "Want to poke me back?"

"I'm not really into guys," Kane replied and raised his brows. "But I don't judge."

The man sneered and grabbed Kane by the shirt. Kane broke his hold on his shirt and swatted his hands fast and hard without taking his eyes off the man.

"Watch your hands," Kane snapped.

"Let's settle this like men," the man snarled back.

Scorpio shifted her stare behind Kane then briefly met his gaze sending him some private signal.

"Are you challenging me to a duel?" Kane teased and dramatically pushed his chair away from the table while moving to his feet.

He was only partway out of his chair when the man who had circled around was now behind him and threw a sucker punch for Kane's back. Without even turning, Kane kicked behind him and struck the man in the abdomen before the man completed his swing. The kick sent him back a couple of feet. The man in front of Kane made his move while his opponent was distracted and swung for Kane's face. Kane blocked the punch with his forearm, grabbed his wrist, and twisted his arm. While holding him immobile, he rammed his knee into the man's ribs as he was bent sideways in pain. As soon as the first man fell to his knees, the second man made his move. Kane already released the first man, leaped onto his chair, and kicked the second man overtop the first man on his knees. The second man was knocked back several feet and crashed into another table causing several women to scream and the angry men to yell.

The man behind Kane recovered from the kick to his abdomen and lunged for him. Kane, who was still standing on the chair, spun into a roundhouse kick. Scorpio casually ducked so she'd be out of the strike zone. Kane kicked the man in the face and gracefully landed on the chair without toppling it. As the first man on the floor straightened, Kane grabbed the back of the chair, using it as leverage, and kicked the man with both feet. When the man flew backward and struck his recovering friend, Kane leaped off the chair without releasing it. He spun the chair around and casually sat, straddling the chair while leaning his arms on the back. Kane relaxed while he waited for the men to recover from their beating. Two very large bouncers approached their table and forced the three men across the lounge toward the door. The three women with them loudly protested, and they were immediately removed as well. Another set of bouncers approached Kane and motioned him to the door.

"No fighting," the first bouncer announced. "You're out of here."

Kane frowned but didn't protest. He politely pushed his chair beneath the table and headed across the crowded lounge without incident.

The second bouncer indicated the others at the table. "All of you," he announced and motioned them to the door. "Let's go."

Marlon groaned in protest as he stood. "Do you know who I am?" he demanded as the large man moved them across the lounge floor.

"Don't care," the large bouncer replied and kept the six moving for the door.

They were escorted out the front door and onto the brightly lit sidewalk of the bustling town. Carson's wranglers and their girlfriends stood several yards away and stared at Kane. It was evident they were contemplating a rematch. Kane stared back at them and raised his brows in silent question. One of the men grabbed a bottle of water from his girlfriend's hand and threw it at Kane's head. Rather than dodge it, Kane caught it directly in front of his face. He eyed the bottle of water then cast a glance at his sister.

"Hey, Scorp," he announced. "Recycle this."

Kane tossed the bottle of water into the air. Scorpio spun into a high roundhouse kick, nailed the bottle of water in mid-air, sending it against the building, and dropped it into the recycle bin. The women gasped with concern, possibly reliving their encounter with Scorpio in the bathroom. They grabbed their men by the arms and pulled them away from the confrontation. The men suddenly seemed a little less certain about picking a fight as well and hurried away. Kane chuckled while turning toward his sister with his hand up high. She smiled back and slapped his hand.

Kane faced the others, grinned, and clapped his hands together. "So who's up for bowling?"

Brandi turned giddy and raised her hand while jumping in place. "Oh, me!"

Boyd grinned and raised his hand as well. Delia and Marlon shared matching frowns at the idea.

Chapter 35

Maverick chose to stay behind and was the only wrangler who didn't go into town. Being alone in the empty bunkhouse gave him an opportunity to poke through Boyd's belongings in his footlocker. He kneeled before Boyd's footlocker and carefully rummaged through it so he wouldn't disturb the contents while searching for anything useful in their investigation. He found a picture of Boyd and his sister when they were younger. The older woman in the picture must have been their mother. Maverick studied the photo. Delia wasn't nearly as attractive when she was a young teenager. The only thing of interest was an old book containing a love letter Boyd possibly had kept hidden from Brandi. According to the postmark, it was sent to him years before he met Brandi, so even that wasn't anything of interest.

Just about everyone had an old flame somewhere in their past. Keeping an old love letter might get him into trouble with Brandi, but, despite what Marlon said, finding an excuse to dissolve the relationship wasn't their job. Maverick looked at his watch and groaned at the time. It was only a little after nine o'clock. Since he had plenty of time on his hands and nothing better to do, he reluctantly gave in and removed the love letter from the envelope. There was a knock on the door, startling him. Maverick attempted to return the letter to the envelope as the door opened. He tossed everything haphazardly into the footlocker, slammed the lid shut, and sprang to his feet while facing the door.

Mac poked her head inside, spotted Maverick, and grinned slyly. "Everyone decent in here?" she teased.

Maverick groaned and nervously raked his fingers through his hair. "Damn it, Mac," he scoffed. "You scared the piss out of me."

"At least someone is having fun," she remarked then looked around the bunkhouse and nodded her approval. "Not half bad for a sausage party."

He shook his head, ignored the comment, and returned to the footlocker. Maverick put everything back exactly how he'd found it and again shut the lid. He straightened as Mac made her way around the bunkhouse as if inspecting it.

"What are you doing out here anyway?" Maverick asked as he searched for the television remote control.

She cast a look at him. "It's nine o'clock on a Saturday night," Mac informed him and raised a cocky brow. "I have tomorrow off, and my big plan is going to bed early. I haven't been this bored since--" She gave the comment serious consideration. "Since I don't even remember." Mac looked around. "At least you guys get to have fun. I'm stuck in a domestic role due to lack of a pecker." She then frowned. "Mine or anyone else's."

Maverick rubbed his eyes, groaned, and shook his head at the comment. "Yet somehow I'm guessing your balls are bigger than mine."

Mac looked back at him and grinned. "And Stone said you were uptight," she teased.

"Stone said I was uptight?" he practically demanded. "When the hell were you talking to Stone?"

"Language," she teased while grinning at him.

"Brace yourself, Mac," he announced with some irritation toward the woman. "I'm about to go off on an expletive-laced rant any minute now."

"You and me both," she scoffed and cast herself onto one of the bunks, resting her head against the headboard.

"You're not supposed to be out here," he informed her while approaching her. "You'll get us both into trouble."

Mac rolled her eyes while stretching out and crossing her ankles. "Who's going to know?" She removed a flask from her pocket. "Besides, we're leaving Monday anyway."

"That's the rumor," Maverick replied while walking toward her then sat on the bunk across from hers.

She tossed him the flask. Maverick caught it, frowned, and eagerly took a swallow. She sat up as he returned it and took another swallow as well then eyed him.

"You don't seem very happy," Mac remarked then offered a teasing smirk. "Fall off your horse again?"

"Not recently," he muttered then eagerly motioned for her to return the flask.

Mac snickered and handed it to him. "Jasmine still backing you into corners and pinching your bum?"

He was about to take a drink when he eyed her with surprise. "Stone told you that too?"

"Yeah, he's quite the gossiping queen," she teased then grinned a little too deviously. "I hear you're playing hard to get."

Maverick took a large swallow from the flask. Mac reached for it when he hesitated, held up a finger for her to wait, and took another swallow before finally returning it.

"She's the boss's married daughter," he informed her. "Despite the popular consensus that no one will care, I don't want to do anything to ruin Kane's business before it's even on its feet."

"That's noble of you," Mac responded, "considering you don't even know Kane."

"No, but Scorpio is my friend," he insisted while shooting a glare at her. "I won't jeopardize that. Despite what she says, she's fond of her brother."

"I see," Mac teased while grinning. "You want to bang Scorpio."

Maverick gave her a disapproving glare. "She dated our friend, Cal," he informed her. "Stone and I took it upon ourselves to look after her after he died. Out of respect for Cal, we agreed neither of us would make a play for her. She has a good thing with Rayner." He inhaled deeply and sighed while sinking into his own thoughts. "Besides, when it comes to relationships, I tend to screw up."

Mac snorted a laugh and raised the flask. "Join the club," she teased.

"You're not the 'settle down get married' type?" he teased while grinning since he obviously knew the answer.

Mac nearly choked on her drink, eyed him, and laughed at the comment. "I'm more of a 'rip out their heart and mount it on a stake as a warning to others' type," she announced a little too proudly.

He eyed her and raised his brows. "Are you really that bad?"

She groaned and collapsed backward onto the bed. "Unfortunately, yes," Mac replied and stared at the ceiling while frowning. "Occasionally, I fuck up and jump a nice one. Then again, I can usually find a reason to hate everyone, so I have no problem getting over it."

"Proudly heartless, huh?" Maverick remarked.

Mac cast a stern glare at him and raised her brows. "You don't get anywhere in this world by being nice," she informed him.

Maverick studied her and appeared curious. "Exactly where has being heartless gotten you?"

Mac eyed him and struggled for a response but couldn't find one. She chuckled then groaned with defeat. "Nowhere, I suppose," she replied. "But I've learned it's better not to feel anything."

"Someone really did a number on you, huh?" Maverick remarked while raising his brows.

She stared at him a long moment then frowned. "I've been betrayed by just about everyone I've ever trusted," Mac informed him. "That being said, I somehow convinced myself to give Kane a shot." She shrugged. "I suppose being used is better than being alone."

"That's sad."

Mac cast a curious look at him. "I'm more observant than I look," she informed him. "I know you and your friend aren't exactly saints yourselves. I'm sure you've used your share of people."

"No, we're far from being saints," Maverick insisted while maintaining his calm demeanor.

"What's your story?"

"Not much to tell really," he replied. "Stone, Cal, and I hung out in the same neighborhood growing up. "Cal and I had horrible home lives, so we'd hang out with Stone and his mother. When she died, we lied about our age, and the three of us enlisted in the Navy together. Once we were discharged, we went into business for ourselves."

Mac offered a tiny, humored grin. "What business was that?"

"Jewel thieves," Maverick replied with little hesitation. "Cal met Scorpio, fell in love, and turned his life around. Stone and I pledged to walk away from our immoral past so we could join Cal in his new life. After he was killed, Stone and I decided to stick with Scorpio and help her renovate her hotel in Maine." Maverick eyed her and offered a tiny smile. "Can I assume your story is somewhat similar?"

Mac shrugged and barely reacted. "Somewhat," she replied. "Just with more mob bosses, hitmen, and mercenaries."

Maverick stared at her and seemed uncertain how to react to the comment.

Chapter 36

Maverick sat on his bunk and drank the last drop from the flask then turned it upside down and frowned. Mac remained casually reclined on the next bunk over while checking out the girly magazine she'd found under the pillow. Maverick tossed the empty flask onto the bunk alongside Mac then eyed her as she flipped through the magazine. Mac grinned and chuckled at something. He raised his brows along with a humored smile.

"Something interesting?" Maverick teased.

"Guys giving guys advice on threesomes," Mac announced while maintaining her humored grin. "I've got some advice for you. Master pleasing one woman before tackling two." She shook her head in disgust. "That's why I don't waste more than five minutes with any guy. Most are only good for a hit-and-run."

Maverick stared at Mac and appeared somewhat offended by the comment. "Five minutes?" he scoffed.

She didn't bother looking at him and flipped the page. "That's all they need," Mac insisted then added a disinterested shrug. "Really all they want. At least with women, we're all on the same page."

Maverick suddenly tensed, stared at her a moment, and gently cleared his throat. "You've, uh, been with women?" he asked while raising a curious brow.

"Not my preference," she casually replied without looking at him, "but I do what needs to be done for a mission." Mac then considered the comment. "Apparently, I make one hell of a lesbian."

Maverick held his breath and avoided looking at Mac. He raked his fingers firmly through his hair as he squirmed on the bunk. There was an unexpected tapping on the bunkhouse door. Both jumped with surprise. Mac shot up on the first bunk as Maverick jumped from the second bunk. He motioned her under the bed.

"They can't find you in here," he announced with concern. "It'll blow our cover."

Mac tossed the magazine aside, dove to the floor, and rolled beneath the bed with ease just before the bunkhouse door opened. Jasmine entered the bunkhouse, saw Maverick and smiled seductively.

"I heard you were the last man standing," Jasmine teased and approached him. "Any special reason you chose to stay behind on your first weekend of freedom?"

Maverick tensed, cast a secret glance at the floor to make sure Mac was hidden, and then managed a smile. "It's been a long week," he informed her. "I thought I'd catch up on my sleep."

Jasmine cast a look at the discarded girly magazine then eyed his crotch and smiled her approval as she moved closer to him.

"Oh, really?" Jasmine placed her arm seductively around his neck and pressed her body against his. "No other reason?" she cooed while running her free hand along his chest and for his crotch.

Maverick tensed, pulled away, and put some space between them. "I'm flattered, Jasmine," he announced while offering a timid smile. "I honestly am, but you're the boss's married daughter. I can't get past that."

"My father doesn't care," Jasmine informed him. "He doesn't even like Conroy. He could walk in and find us going at it like jackrabbits, and he wouldn't even flinch." She again placed her arms around his neck and stared into his eyes. "What's the real problem?"

Mac slid out from beneath the bed, straightened, and insecurely folded her arms across her chest. "It's me," she announced.

Jasmine pulled away from Maverick and looked at Mac with surprise. "What are you doing out here?" she demanded. "You're not supposed to be out here."

"Maverick and I have been dating nearly a year," Mac announced in a rehearsed timid voice. She made a convincing, docile woman when called upon. "Your father knew our situation when he hired us. He didn't care, but he said we should keep quiet about our relationship."

Jasmine eyed Mac then looked at Maverick, who seemed extremely uncomfortable and couldn't look at either woman. "Is that why you've been avoiding me?" she asked him with surprise. "You're in a committed relationship?"

Maverick finally looked at Mac standing alongside him and seemed uncertain how to respond. Mac moved against Maverick, pressed against him, and stared affectionately into his eyes while gently caressing his chest.

"It's okay, babe," Mac insisted with an almost sinister grin. "Mr. Hooper said it was okay. I'm sure he doesn't care that his daughter knows about us."

Maverick eyed Mac's hand as it firmly ran along his chest. He seemed at a loss for words, although his mind was obviously working on something. Mac then looked at Jasmine and appeared almost innocent although there was something more evil lurking behind her eyes.

"I would have assumed you knew," Mac insisted. "*Marlon* knows."

Jasmine's look instantly turned to rage. "Of course he does," she hissed and just about threw a tantrum. "Daddy tells him everything and never tells me anything. I'm always the last to know what's going on around here!"

Jasmine stormed across the bunkhouse then paused by the door and turned to look back. Mac placed her hands on Maverick's face and kissed him passionately and with aggression. He tensed only a moment before pulling her firmly against him and returned the kiss. Jasmine huffed and left the bunkhouse, slamming the door behind her. Mac laughed despite Maverick's lips against hers. She managed to break off the kiss and attempted to pull away, but Maverick was reluctant to release her.

"Acht," he commanded while grinning deviously as he held her firmly against him. "Not so fast."

His mouth eagerly sought hers, and he kissed her warmly but passionately. Mac didn't need much encouragement, obviously feeling his arousal, and returned the kiss with added aggression. Her hands eagerly traveled his body and sought what she desired. Maverick groaned in response. She broke off the kiss and grinned seductively.

"Now that Jasmine thinks we're hooking up, we may as well run with it. I could certainly use the exercise," Mac announced while firmly groping him then met his gaze. "How about you?"

He removed her hand from his crotch and held it affectionately to his chest as he stared into her eyes. "I'm all for that, but no sprinting to the finish line," Maverick insisted in a serious tone then raised his brow. "I don't care for the five-minute quickie."

Mac sneered with annoyance and pushed him away. "Enjoy your cold shower," she scoffed and turned to leave.

Maverick cast himself onto his bed and appeared unaffected by her tantrum. He casually lay on his side and watched her walk away. "Don't you ever miss the passion?" he asked while smirking. "Isn't that what you want, Macbeth? The thrill of feeling alive?"

She hesitated then looked back at him with something resembling hostility. "Don't call me that," Mac snarled.

"Are you afraid you might enjoy having a man make love to you?" he continued while easily ignoring her anger. "Can't handle intense sexual pleasure?" Maverick managed a tiny shrug despite looking very much like a cat on the prowl. "You could go back to your room bored and frustrated, but we both know you want to stay."

Mac turned almost angry and vigorously ran her fingers through her hair. "What's wrong with you?" she demanded with unfounded rage at Maverick's calmness. "Most men would jump at the offer of a hit-and-run."

"And how has that worked out for you?" he asked with a curious look.

"You blew it," she snapped hotly while pointing a demanding finger at him. "You had your chance. It'll be just you and your right hand tonight."

"Why are you getting so upset?" he asked in a calm tone that mocked her.

"Why?" she lashed out irrationally and indicated his come-hither pose. "Because I offered you sex and you want to play Don Juan."

"No, you need to control the situation to ensure you don't become emotionally involved," Maverick informed her while maintaining a level of calm that seemed to infuriate her. He then offered her a playful smile. "It's okay, Macbeth. I won't let you rip out my heart. You don't have anything to be afraid of."

"I'm certainly not afraid," she shot back.

"You fear intimacy," he boldly pointed out and raised an arrogant brow. "You're afraid to feel anything because you may actually *feel* something." He playfully waved her off. "By all means, go back to your room, bored out of your mind and sexually frustrated. You can spend the rest of the night wondering what you gave up."

"You talk too much," she snapped.

"And yet you're still here," he replied while grinning then patted the bed alongside him. "Are you afraid of me? Afraid you might enjoy intense lovemaking?"

Mac frowned and fidgeted as if weighing her options. She groaned with irritation, approached the bed, and sat on the edge near him. Mac glared at him, shook her head, and then cast off her shoes with unfounded anger.

"I'm only doing this because I'm bored," she insisted then cast herself onto the bed alongside him.

Maverick chuckled warmly, gathered her in his arms, and moved against her. "I guarantee you won't be bored for the next two hours," he lightly teased.

Mac attempted to look at him with horror in her eyes. "Two hours?"

Maverick covered her mouth with his and kissed her warmly but passionately. Mac braced her arms against his chest in protest after the two hour comment, but she was soon captivated by his slow, determined kiss. Anything was better than being alone and bored in her room. She attempted to turn up the aggression level, hoping to move things along faster, but he refused to let her pick up the pace. She'd given him too much information, and he was using it against her. Mac reluctantly gave up her quest to speed things up and allowed his hands to travel her body in a sensual manner. He purposely teased her and avoided touching her where she wanted his hands most. When she again attempted to speed things up by groping him, he took her hands in his and pinned them to the mattress on either side of her head, forcing her to accept a slower, erotic pace.

Mac was already writhing beneath him, and neither had removed a stitch of clothing yet. Despite her effort to resist enjoying Maverick's slow attempt at driving her insane, she found herself crying out in pleasure at the way he grinded against her while both remained fully clothed. She begged him several times to do things to her, but he ignored her pleas to pick up the pace. Even after he finally removed some of her clothes, he continued to take his time and let her writhe against him, pleasuring herself to the point of exhaustion. Although he must have seen her scars in the brightly lit room, he didn't seem fazed by them even though his hands thoroughly caressed each one.

By the time Maverick finally made his move, Mac had worn herself out and clung to him while he slowly made love to her. He had her dizzy and disoriented, allowing him to dominate and control every movement. She no longer cared as her head swam with ecstasy to the sensation her body felt against his. He finally collapsed alongside her nearly an hour later while panting heavily. Despite his exhaustion, he pulled her into his arms and held her against him. It was possibly the first time Mac allowed a man to hold her after a sexual encounter, but she was too worn to protest. It was doubtful she would be able to stand until she caught her breath and regained some strength anyway. He affectionately kissed her several times while catching his breath. She didn't resist and allowed her hand to caress his bare chest.

Maverick pulled back just far enough to meet her gaze and smiled while panting. "Was it at least moderately enjoyable?"

Mac laughed and hid her smile. "Mild to moderate," she teased.

He chuckled in his throat but maintained his smile. "You're cruel."

She propped herself up on her elbow while hovering over him and took a sweeping eyeful of his well-toned, naked body. Mac offered a sly grin and caressed his abdomen and hip.

"Considering our paths are bound to cross from time-to-time, I'm willing to ditch my once-and-done rule," she informed him then seemed to tense. "I mean, we both have to scratch our itches and, with you, I know there won't be any misunderstandings."

Maverick stared at her a moment and appeared somewhat surprised. "You have a once-and-done rule?" He shook his head. "Every attempt I've ever made with even a one-night-stand turned into an entire weekend in bed."

Mac eyed him and raised her brow. "I'm not surprised," she muttered under her breath then cast a look at him. "I don't want sex to turn into coffee or lunch. It creates misunderstandings."

"I can promise there won't be any misunderstandings," he announced then considered the comment and smiled slyly. "But if there are, you have my permission to spank me." His grin suddenly broadened. "Actually, I could get into a good spanking."

Mac groaned and rolled her eyes. "I should have known this was a mistake."

She attempted to get up, but he pulled her back down and into his arms. Mac braced her hands against his chest but didn't bother attempting to get away. It seemed pointless.

"You haven't heard my conditions yet," he teased playfully.

Mac eyed him almost demandingly. "*You* have conditions?" she remarked then suddenly appeared almost humored. "What sort of conditions?"

"We keep our 'friends with benefits' between us," he announced and affectionately ran his finger along the scar on her side. "The others aren't told."

"I thought that was implied," she muttered and pushed his hand away from her scar.

He then grinned deviously and met her gaze. "And I'm allowed to call you Macbeth."

Her eyes suddenly narrowed, and she again pushed against his chest with increased hostility. "I don't like being called Macbeth."

"If you want quickies on demand, you'll have to cave on Macbeth," he insisted and moved his hand to the bullet scar on her thigh, gently caressing it with his thumb.

Mac stopped fighting his hold, stared at him a moment, and groaned with irritation. "Fine," she scoffed then cursed him with her eyes as she pulled his hand from the scar on her thigh. "But the moment I get a better offer, you're history."

Maverick chuckled and grinned while warmly kissing her neck. "Deal," he announced then whispered in her ear, "Macbeth."

Chapter 37

Sunday, June 29th. Late morning. A gray Jeep Wrangler drove up the long driveway to the Hooper ranch house. The jeep parked near Brandi's powder blue sports car. The sort of car Brandi owned was unusual for the isolated ranch location. With the first snow, the vehicle would be rendered useless. A woman in her mid-twenties got out of the jeep and eyed the expensive sports car before approaching the house. She carried a large, double-stacked dish containing two fresh baked pies, paused before the door, and rang the bell. Brandi ran to the door, opened it, and saw the young woman, who was considered a neighbor despite that their farms were five miles apart. Brandi squealed with delight.

"Lee," she cried out excitedly. "I'm so happy you stopped by." Brandi stepped out of the doorway and allowed her to enter the massive foyer.

Leeann was an attractive woman with wild, dark hair that she wore pulled back. Stray locks of hair made daring escapes only adding to what most would describe as a country girl appearance. Lee stepped inside while marveling at the grand hallway and the broad, "Gone with the Wind" staircase. There were many breathtaking wildflowers from Alma's garden filling the foyer.

"What brings you here?" Brandi eagerly asked. "Daddy had to run to town if you came to see him."

"No, I actually stopped by to see you," Lee announced then handed her the pies. "I brought you some homemade rhubarb pie."

Brandi accepted the tote container with the pies. "Oh, I love your rhubarb pie," she announced excitedly. "We'll have it after dinner tonight. Did you want some tea? I could make some."

"Tea would be lovely," Lee replied then followed Brandi to the kitchen.

As they entered the bright, white kitchen, Mac caught a glimpse of Lee and bolted into the servant's quarters to avoid being seen by the familiar woman. Lee and Brandi only caught a glimpse of Mac as she vanished from the kitchen.

"Was that Alma?" Lee asked.

"No, that's the new maid," Brandi informed her then rolled her eyes. "She's not working out. Daddy will probably fire her after the wedding."

Brandi filled the kettle and placed it on the burner. She turned to face Lee while grinning.

"What did you want to see me about?" Brandi asked as she bubbled over.

Lee cheerfully handed her the small envelope. "Hand delivering my R.S.V.P. for your wedding," she announced.

"You're coming, right?" Brandi remarked with enthusiasm. "It's here at the ranch, so you can't say no."

Lee laughed and nodded. "Yes, Ross and I will be attending."

"Selena and Liam?"

"Of course," Lee replied. "They wouldn't miss it for the world." They sat at the island counter. "I don't get many opportunities to dress up in these parts. I'm looking forward to it."

"I'm so happy," Brandi announced while giddy at the thought. "It'll be the only exciting thing happening around here this year." She groaned dramatically. "These backwoods are *so* boring."

The kettle whistled. Brandi sprang to her feet, hurried to shut the kettle off, and poured hot water into two mugs. Lee cast a look at the doorway and saw Kane standing within the kitchen. Lee seemed surprised to see him.

"Uh, hello," Lee announced.

Brandi looked up, saw Kane in the doorway, and made a face. "He sneaks around here like a cat," she informed Lee then eyed him. "Kane, this is our neighbor, Lee."

Kane smiled charmingly and approached Lee with his hand extended.

"Kane is helping Daddy around the house," Brandi announced as Lee shook his hand.

"It's a pleasure to meet you, Lee," Kane announced.

"You look familiar," Lee remarked while studying the young man.

"It wasn't me," he announced while grinning. "I've never been there."

Lee stared at him a moment, realized he was joking, and laughed almost nervously. Their visitor's look then turned oddly serious.

"Oh, now I remember," Lee announced. "I saw you at the club in town last night." She gently cleared her throat. "You, uh, were shown the door."

Brandi suddenly bubbled over. "You were there?" She laughed excitedly. "That was amazing, right?" Brandi set Lee's tea mug before her and became animated. "Some guys were giving us a hard time, and Kane whooped their asses."

"It wasn't nearly that dramatic," Kane insisted while hiding his smile. "If something happened to the boss's daughter on my watch, I'd be looking for a new job."

"I'm pretty sure I saw an ass-whooping myself," Lee teased while grinning.

"I got lucky," he replied and easily brushed off the incident. "I'm usually pretty passive."

Lee stared at him a moment then managed a tiny smile and nodded. Kane maintained his smile and his polite demeanor.

"I should get back to work," Kane announced and gave Lee a polite nod. "It was nice meeting you."

As Kane left the kitchen, Lee stared after him a moment then turned back to Brandi, who now sat at the counter with her mug of tea.

"Nice looking man," Lee remarked.

Brandi snorted a laugh. "He's not without his charm," she remarked. "But he's a little strange."

"Oh?"

"Have you ever watched a cat play with a mouse?" Brandi asked.

Lee grimaced. "Yeah, it's a bit disturbing."

"Most of the wranglers around the ranch are pretty much what you see is what you get," she announced then indicated the doorway. "That one--?" Brandi made a face and shook her head. "It's like he's watching and waiting to pounce."

Lee smiled and patted Brandi's arm. "Welcome to my world, Brandi."

§

Later that afternoon, a newer looking pickup truck drove up the long driveway faster than acceptable, leaving a trail of dust behind it. Marlon and Jasmine were somewhere on the property with the rest of the wranglers tending to the cattle, and Sig still hadn't returned from the city. Emily hurried from the front sitting room and rushed into the hallway as Rayner appeared from the study.

"What's that sound?" Rayner asked.

"It's Carson," Emily informed him. "He must be pissed about something."

Rayner hurried down the hall to the game room and found Kane playing video games with Brandi while both sat on the floor with their game controllers.

"Kane," Rayner announced. "Carson's flying down the driveway heading this way."

Kane sprang up from the floor and hurried into the hallway with Rayner.

Scorpio trotted down the stairs. "Who's in the pickup truck?" she asked.

"The ill-mannered ex-boyfriend," Kane replied then motioned Emily to Brandi. "Stay with Brandi in the game room."

Emily nodded and hurried Brandi back inside the game room. Rayner and Scorpio followed Kane down the hallway and toward the front door.

"This doesn't have to be solved with violence," Rayner informed Kane. "Let me talk to him. You don't even know his intention."

Kane peered out the side window as the pickup truck skidded around the last curve. Kane looked back at Rayner while reaching for the doorknob.

"Oh, I have a pretty good idea what he wants," Kane remarked. "When an asshole drives that fast and reckless, violence is exactly what he has on his mind."

"Just let me try it my way," Rayner announced then slipped past Kane and out the front door.

Kane drew a deep breath and eyed Scorpio. "You know; he won't last long in a fight, but at least he's willing to make a stand."

"He's tougher than you think," Scorpio informed him. "Pretty good shot too. Better than me."

Kane eyed her and raised his brow. "Scorp," he announced in all seriousness. "Everyone is a better shot than you."

Scorpio sneered at Kane then joined Rayner on the porch, leaving the front door open. Kane remained inside the foyer and stayed out of sight, allowing Rayner his non-confrontational attempt to deal with Carson. The pickup truck came to a grinding halt in a cloud of dirt not far from the house. Even though he must have been anxious, Rayner didn't flinch. Carson and three men jumped out of the truck and approached the porch with an angry, determined gait.

"May I help you?" Rayner announced.

Carson walked up the first two steps to the porch and paused before Rayner. The look on the young man's face told a chilling story of what he wanted.

"I'd like a word with your new wrangler about what happened in town last night," Carson announced with anger and hostility.

"And you need three friends to have a word with someone?" Rayner asked.

"He beat up three of my men," Carson informed Rayner.

"Carson, is it?" Rayner politely announced. "You are aware that those men sent their girlfriends into the ladies' room to attack Brandi and her friends."

"I don't know anything about that," Carson remarked and suddenly seemed uncomfortable.

"No, I'm sure they conveniently left out that part," Rayner remarked and raised his brow. "What about the part where your three wranglers disrespected--" Rayner hesitated and choked on his next words while indicating Scorpio. "Marlon Hooper's girlfriend?"

Carson shifted and glanced back at the three wranglers behind him. They all shook their heads, indicating they hadn't heard about that either. Carson looked back at Rayner and tensed.

"No one mentioned that either," Carson remarked.

"So you probably also hadn't heard that one of your wranglers attempted to jump the young man from behind while the other two picked a fight with him," Rayner continued. "Is three on one your idea of a fair fight, Carson?"

"Well, no," Carson replied while shifting uncomfortably.

"It sounds more like your wranglers are a bit, uh--"

"Butt-hurt," Scorpio announced from where she leaned against the doorframe in the open doorway.

Rayner indicated Scorpio, agreeing with her term, and tilted his head while looking back at Carson. "Is it possible your wranglers are butt-hurt that one man beat up three of them, particularly when they had every intention to ambush him?"

Carson seemed uncertain how to respond. Brandi stepped onto the porch and folded her arms across her chest while casting an evil glare at Carson.

"That's exactly what happened," Brandi informed him. "Your boys poked a rattlesnake, and they got bit."

Carson stared at Brandi a moment then looked back at Rayner while frowning. "Sorry for the intrusion," he announced while tipping the brim of his cowboy hat then turned and left without incident.

They watched the four men pile back into the pickup truck and drive back down the driveway at a reasonable speed. They heard a thump on the porch roof. Kane dropped down from the roof, landing on the ground, and turned toward the porch steps while grinning. He walked up the steps and patted Rayner on the shoulder.

"You're okay, Rayner," Kane announced cheerfully. "You're right. Violence isn't always the answer. Boring them to death works too."

Kane scooted Brandi back into the house past Scorpio. He poked Scorpio in the ribs with his finger as he passed. She jumped then glared at him as he chuckled. Rayner watched the pickup truck on the driveway until it was out of sight. Scorpio approached him and kissed him on the cheek.

"Nicely handled," she announced proudly.

"Did I sound confident?" Rayner asked without looking at her.

"Of course," she replied while grinning.

Rayner wiped his sweaty palms on his pants legs. "Good," he muttered timidly, "because I thought I was dead for a minute there."

She laughed softly and linked onto his arm, forcing him to look at her. "You had that," she informed him then smiled and shrugged. "And if you didn't, we had your back."

Chapter 38

Tuesday, July 1st. Mac and Delia had just finished cleaning up after the family's breakfast when Sig stopped in the kitchen for his travel thermos of coffee. He was once again leaving for Colorado Springs and needed the additional caffeine for the long trek. The way Mac understood it, Sig would be back for the Fourth of July picnic. It was also a day off for the wranglers and staff who were invited to attend the holiday picnic. Once Sig had left, Alma retired to her room for her usual break before she'd need to start lunch around eleven o'clock. Delia seemed a little less snarly that morning as she turned to Mac.

"I'm going to start some laundry," Delia informed Mac. "Why don't you get started on making the beds?"

Mac nodded then sighed with disgust as she headed up the back stairs. All things being equal, she wished they had left on Monday as they had intended, but Carson's wayward wranglers had to mess up those plans. Mac entered the first room on the left and nearly collided with Kane. She jumped with surprise but refrained from crying out. Mac groaned and shut the door behind her.

"I wish you'd stop doing that," she scoffed.

"It is my room," he teased. "You probably should have knocked. What if I had been indecent?"

"I'd consider it payback for all the times you've invited yourself into my room without knocking," she remarked and moved past him without care.

"If you actually minded, I'd stop doing it," Kane remarked while grinning.

Mac approached Kane's sloppily made bed. At least Kane made an effort to make his own bed. She tended to making the bed more properly.

"Please tell me we're leaving," she muttered.

"Sorry," he replied with a deep sigh. "We're staying at least through the weekend."

Kane flopped onto the bed that she had almost finished making, leaned on his elbow, and crossed his ankles.

She glared at him with disapproval and raised her brows. "Do you mind?"

He didn't move from the bed but instead stared at her with a somewhat serious look. "I saw Maverick chasing after you yesterday," Kane remarked.

Mac straightened and looked at Kane with some surprise then immediately fidgeted.

"Has he been bothering you?" he asked in a serious tone. "I can take care of that."

"No," she replied and attempted to finish making the bed around him. "He's just bored, that's all. He's not bothering me." She considered the comment then shrugged. "Well, no more than anyone else."

"If he does, feel free to pummel his ass," Kane insisted. "I'll back you on it."

Mac chuckled, humored at the comment. "I'll keep that in mind."

They heard voices in the hall but couldn't make them out. Kane slid off the bed and approached the door. He listened a moment then heard a door creak. When Kane slipped into the hallway, Mac felt compelled to follow. Kane approached the door at the end of the hall then looked back at Mac and pointed at the partially open door in question.

"The attic," Mac informed him and appeared slightly curious herself.

"Someone went up there," Kane remarked just loud enough for her to hear.

"Must be stuff stored up there for the holiday picnic," Mac informed him. "Delia said we needed to bring some things up from the basement. Maybe there are things stored in the attic as well."

"Feeling nosy?" Kane teased while grinning.

Mac smirked. "Anything's better than making beds and cleaning toilets," she insisted.

Kane gently pulled the door open a little further while attempting to keep it from creaking. He smiled at Mac and politely extended his hand to the opening. Mac grinned and slipped past him through the attic doorway. Kane silently followed Mac up the broad stairs into the attic. They could hear voices across the partially finished area. Both crept across the large, partitioned area and paused just out of view of whoever was upstairs. They peered across the attic and saw an old day bed set up off to the side. Emily kneeled on the bed and removed her shirt to reveal her bare breasts. As she moved onto all fours on the day bed, Kane and Mac moved a little closer to take a better look. Emily straddled Conroy's hips while eagerly kissing him where he lay naked on the day bed beneath her. He groaned while she giggled. Kane backed away despite that Mac remained to watch a moment. He grabbed her arm and pulled her away with him. They hurried for the attic steps and silently went down them.

"Mrs. Hooper and Jasmine's husband?" Mac gasped as they reached the door at the bottom.

Kane and Mac entered the second floor hallway and eyed each other.

"Now we know what Emily does while her husband is away most of the week," Kane remarked.

"Jasmine spends most of her day outside with the wranglers," Mac informed him. "I guess they figure they won't get caught in the attic."

"I doubt Jasmine cares. She's too busy making moves on the wranglers to really care what her husband does," Kane announced while shifting looks around the hallway. "Brandi was right. It's like Peyton Place around here. Everyone's sleeping with everyone else."

Mac tensed slightly and refrained from fidgeting. "Probably because there's little else to do," she muttered then considered the comment. "When your options are limited, you make bad decisions."

"I hear you. I should find Brandi," Kane remarked and shook his head after what he'd just witnessed. "She should be finished with her shower by now."

Mac glared at him and folded her arms across her chest. "Please tell me you don't wait in her room for her to come out of the shower in her towel."

Kane grinned and held back his chuckle. "That honor is reserved just for you, badger," he teased. "Stay out of trouble. I'll try to get you alone after lunch."

Mac looked at her wrist to check the time and realized her watch was missing. She cursed softly. "I forgot my watch in my room." Mac groaned then looked at Kane and shook her head. "I better go downstairs and get it. Delia has me on a tight schedule. If I'm late again, she'll rag on me, and then I'll have to kill her."

"I'd prefer if you didn't do that," Kane insisted despite showing little emotion.

"I'll take your feelings on the matter into consideration," Mac replied.

"You do that. I'll sneak up on you later," he teased while grinning.

She glared at him with limited humor. "Don't even think about it or you'll be the one I pummel."

Kane laughed at the comment. Mac then turned and headed down the back stairs. Despite the distance, it didn't take her long to reach the quiet kitchen and then head into the staff wing. Unfortunately, her room was near the end of the hallway. As she hurried along the corridor, she heard faint female moans coming from one of the bedrooms. Mac paused near Delia's bedroom door and listened a moment. She again heard female moans. She considered knocking to see if Delia was feeling okay when she realized they were moans of ecstasy. Mac listened a moment longer just to be sure. She could hear the bed creaking and male grunting. Mac stared at the door a moment, pondered who could possibly be in the bedroom with Delia, and then decided to mind her own business.

One of the wranglers must have slipped back into the house for a quickie with the attractive maid. It was quite possible it was the same wrangler from the other day. Mac smirked and shook her head. What Kane said was true. Everyone was sleeping with everyone else. She then continued for her room at the end of the hall.

Chapter 39

Friday, July 4th. The ranch had a holiday picnic on the back patio that afternoon and into the evening for the family, staff, and wranglers. It was a fun afternoon allowing everyone to intermix while everyone drank, socialized, and even hung out in the pool. That evening just after dark, Sig turned off the outside lights while everyone collected on the dark patio and watched the distant sky. Burning tiki torches created a romantic backdrop and allowed just enough light, so no one tripped over anyone. There were several rounds of laughter as everyone sat on the dimly lit patio and waited while watching the dark sky with anticipation.

"Are you sure there'll be fireworks?" Scorpio teased while glancing at Marlon.

"Someone out there has a party every year," Marlon insisted. "They have an amazing fireworks display. We're talking professional quality."

"Usually nine o'clock on the dot," Sig announced and peered at his watch. "Another five minutes."

Brandi and Boyd sat on a picnic table behind the others and stole a few kisses in the dim lighting. When it seemed as if no one was paying attention, Brandi took Boyd's hand and led him to the back door. Kane suddenly appeared alongside them and gave Brandi a stern look.

"Where are you going?" Kane asked and eyed both with disapproval.

"Just inside," she insisted then pleaded with her eyes. "Boyd and I want some time alone, Kane."

"Your father won't like that," Kane reminded her. "If he finds out--"

"Kane, we're engaged," she informed him. "We should be allowed to do certain things." Brandi then smiled sweetly. "Daddy doesn't need to know, and he won't if you don't say anything."

Kane groaned. "Fine," he announced with a sigh. "I never saw you."

Brandi giggled, patted Kane's face, and hurried Boyd inside. Kane shook his head and returned to the others. Mac moved closer to Kane and smirked.

"Is daddy's little virgin not having sex with her boyfriend?" Mac teased.

Kane shook his head. "That's Sig's problem," he muttered under his breath. "I wasn't hired to keep her from having sex with her boyfriend."

Maverick cast a look at them from nearby as he removed a bottle of beer from the cooler.

"Probably a good time for her to slip away," Kane continued and nodded toward the dark sky while staring at nothing. "--while the rest of us are watching darkness for these highly anticipated fireworks."

Maverick seemed to consider what he had overheard, removed a second bottle of beer, and walked behind them. He handed Mac the second bottle, which she gratefully accepted. His hand then caressed her backside as he passed. Mac cast a look behind her and saw Maverick heading for the kitchen door. He looked back at her, raised his brows, and then entered the house.

Mac tensed then glanced at Kane. "I think the fireworks are a no show," she informed him and offered a faux bored sigh. "I'm going to sneak into the kitchen and scrounge up a few more hot wings."

She didn't even wait for Kane to respond and headed for the house. Mac passed through the dimly lit kitchen and hurried into the staff wing while opening her bottle of beer. She took a few healthy swallows before reaching her bedroom and entered the mostly dark room, which seemed to be empty. She closed the door and again looked around. As she was about to head for the bathroom, Maverick appeared from the dark corner near the door and snatched the bottle of beer from her, mildly startling her. He grinned, set the bottle on the dresser, and tackled her against the closed bedroom door. Maverick kissed her with urgency and aggression. Mac returned the wild kiss and firmly ran her hands along his body, easily shedding his shirt. Maverick just about ripped off her tank top, eager to undress her.

Mac threw her legs around his waist without breaking off the kiss and allowed him to carry her two steps to the bed. He took her to the bed with him and aggressively removed her jeans as they kissed. She just about laughed when he realized her shoes needed to come off first. He cast her shoes across the floor and then aggressively removed his own pants while she watched with a sly smile.

"What happened to not sprinting across the finish line?" she teased.

Maverick practically dived on top of her and met her gaze only briefly. "Don't scoff when opportunity presents itself, Macbeth," he announced then aggressively kissed her while his hands eagerly traveled her mostly naked body.

§

Brandi and Boyd hurried along the second floor hallway toward Brandi's bedroom while holding hands and walking close together.

"I can't believe we're doing this," Brandi giggled. "If Daddy found out, he'd kill us."

"We're engaged," Boyd remarked and seemed almost irritated. "We should be allowed to carry on like an engaged couple if we want to. Besides, we're just fooling around a little. No big deal, right."

The fireworks in the distance could be heard, signaling it was nine o'clock. Brandi grinned at Boyd as they paused before her bedroom door.

"I guess it's nine o'clock," she teased. "We're missing the fireworks."

"We'll make our own fireworks," Boyd announced and chuckled as he opened the door for her.

Brandi giggled and hurried into the bedroom, sprinting across the dark room for her bed. She leaped onto the bed as Boyd entered and closed the door behind him. Out of the darkness near the door, a man dressed in black struck Boyd on the back of the head. He gasped and sank to the floor. Brandi let out a scream. A second man was seen standing not far from the bed and lunged for her. She attempted to scramble off the bed, but he knocked her back down. Brandi fought the man on top of her, but he easily subdued her. The man by the door was quick to join him and placed duct tape across her mouth. He then swiftly bound her wrists while the first man held her immobile. As the first man tossed her over his shoulder, the second man duct taped her ankles, making it harder for her to throw the man off balance as he carried her. The men hurried for the door and left the room.

§

Maverick rolled off Mac on the mussed bed and panted while grinning as the fireworks were heard outside in the distance.

"I must be good," he announced while breathing heavily. "I hear fireworks."

As he rolled over and attempted to gather Mac into his arms, she was already leaping to her feet. He just missed her and clutched the comforter.

"Where are you going so fast?" he practically demanded revealing his disappointment.

Mac slipped into her underwear and tank top then cast a look at him while grinning. "There's no obligation to cuddle under the quickie rule."

"When did we decide that?" he remarked with disappointment.

"We didn't," she remarked as her smile mocked him. "It's an unspoken rule."

Maverick frowned, propped himself up on his elbow, and watched her slip into her jeans. She had a little more trouble locating her discarded shoes in the nearly dark room.

"If said quickie takes place in the bedroom then that clearly falls under the 'must cuddle afterward' rule," Maverick insisted while raising his brows and refused to move from the comfort of the bed.

"I disagree," she announced proudly, slipped into her shoes, and then eyed him. "Time's up, lover boy."

Maverick rolled onto his back allowing her full view of his naked body and placed his arms under his head.

"Nope," he announced with little care. "I'm just going to wait here for round two when you return." His sly grin returned. "Have a couple of beers; enjoy yourself, because you're in for a long night."

Mac hid her smile. "If I have a few beers," she announced slyly, "*you* may be in for a long night. You'll be a lot more than saddle sore when I get through with you."

Maverick groaned while grinning with delight. "I accept the challenge."

She laughed while taking in another sweeping eyeful of the naked man, snatched her beer from the dresser, and left the room. Mac nearly finished the bottle of beer by the time she reached the dimly lit kitchen. The fireworks could still be heard outside. Despite their distance from the ranch, they sounded as if they were right next door. Mac set the empty bottle on the island counter and was about to return outside when she heard a faint clunk from within the house. She hesitated, listened a moment, and then headed for the interior kitchen door. Mac walked along the dimly lit hallway and saw movement on the stairs. A man dressed entirely in black hurried for the foyer door while a second man reached the bottom of the stairs with the struggling, young woman over his shoulder.

"Hey," Mac suddenly cried out.

The masked kidnapper in front of the door spun toward her with surprise.

"Go! I've got this," he yelled to his partner then ran for Mac.

Mac charged for the intruder, surprising him. He seemed hesitant and slowed when he saw her aggressive response. Without even slowing, Mac spun into a roundhouse kick and sent the intruder flying across the hallway and into the banister. The man carrying Brandi was nearly to the door when he heard the thunderous crash. He saw his partner fall and then the enraged woman now charging for him. He tossed the bound, struggling Brandi to the floor and spun to face Mac. By the time he turned, it was already too late. Mac kicked him in the chest and sent him backward into the closed door. The door vibrated harshly behind him, rattling the glass. The first intruder on the foyer floor recovered and lunged for Mac while her attention was focused on his partner. He grabbed her from behind and easily lifted her off the floor.

Mac thrust her heel back and into his knee, forcing him to release her as he cried out in pain. With her back still to the man, she rammed her elbow into his abdomen then spun around and punched him in the face, driving him to the floor. The man by the door threw a punch for Mac's face. She blocked his fist with her left arm and punched him in the groin. He clutched himself in agony and fell to his knees. Mac punched him across the face for good measure and drove him to the floor. Mac ran to check on the bound and frightened woman. The first man recovered and stumbled to his feet while pulling a Bowie knife from his belt sheath. He lunged for Mac with the knife.

Seemingly, out of nowhere, a knife struck him in the hand. He cried out and stared at the knife embedded in his hand, forcing him to drop his own knife. Mac spun around and saw the blood pouring from the knife sticking through the man's hand. The man by the door made it to his feet, saw what was happening, and attempted to open the door to flee. A knife flew past Mac and struck the man in the forearm, nailing him to the door with the blade. Mac looked a few feet down the hall and saw Maverick casually approach while playfully twirling a thin dagger.

"Did you know I can nail a cockroach from twenty feet?" he announced while grinning proudly.

"So you *are* useful outside of the bedroom," Mac teased then roughly yanked the knife from the man's arm, freeing him from the door.

The kidnapper clutched his bleeding arm and fell against the door as Mac approached Brandi with the blood-covered knife. She cut the duct tape binding her ankles and wrists then pulled the tape from across her mouth. Brandi gasped then cried out in panic.

"What the hell--?" she screamed and quickly sat up while staring at the bleeding men. Her expression immediately turned concerned. "Boyd!" Brandi sprang to her feet and ran up the stairs.

"You'd better look after her," Maverick announced and approached the first man with the knife stuck through his hand.

Mac headed up the stairs after Brandi.

Maverick eyed the screaming man and shook his head while sighing deeply. "This is going to hurt." Maverick pulled the knife from the man's hand, causing him to cry out and clutch his bleeding puncture wound. "Big baby," he scoffed. "I could have gone for your balls."

Chapter 40

Saturday, July 5th. Late morning. Mac sat on the patio with a cup of tea and watched the wranglers in the distance with a large herd of cattle. As usual, she seemed to be off in her own world. The kitchen door opened and Scorpio stepped onto the patio. She eyed Mac, grinned, and sat on the railing facing her.

"What are your big plans for your weekend off?" Scorpio asked.

"Catch up on my sleep," Mac muttered and finished her hot tea. "The state troopers grilled me like I was the one attempting to make off with the kid."

"Yeah, Maverick said they grilled him too," Scorpio remarked and shook her head. "He's a little too handy with his knives."

"I didn't know that was one of his talents," Mac replied while casting a look at Scorpio. "Honestly, I thought he was just a conman and eye candy."

"He does sort of give that impression," Scorpio teased. "He mentioned his skills with knives once, but he never gave a demonstration." She hesitated and slipped back into a different time not so long ago. "Our altercations were a little more firearm friendly."

"Kane's not firearm friendly," Mac muttered.

Scorpio laughed. "Yeah, Kane and I don't have a lot of experience with firearms," she announced then grinned with some embarrassment. "I'm a *really* bad shot."

Mac smirked and shrugged. "Your body's a weapon," she boldly announced. "Guns are only required when in a gunfight."

"You've seen your share of action?"

Mac groaned and let her head fall back against the rocker. "More than my share; thank you very much."

"Is that why Kane sought you out?" Scorpio asked.

"Actually, he came to me thinking I knew this guy he was looking for," Mac remarked and eyed her. "I couldn't really help him with that, but I guess he heard about my *other* talents and thought he could use someone like me."

"I'm glad he's focused on something else," Scorpio announced. "His little revenge quest would probably have gotten him killed."

"You know about that?"

Scorpio rolled her eyes. "When Kane gets something in his head, he's extremely pig-headed about it."

"What happened?" Mac asked and stared at her with a curious look. "Why does he want revenge on this Zack Kinsley guy? From what little I knew about him, he's not someone you actively seek out." She snorted a laugh. "And he's certainly not someone you seek revenge upon."

Scorpio tensed while studying Mac. "He's a bad man?" she asked.

"As I said, I don't know much about him, but I can tell you that he's incredibly dangerous," Mac insisted and raised her brow. "Kane would end up in a body bag."

"Whatever his reasons for wanting to find this man," Scorpio announced, "I think he's given up on it after your last encounter with those men at the casino."

"I'm glad," Mac muttered and again let her head rest against the back of the rocking chair. "If I'm going to be killed, I'd at least like it to be for something stupid that *I've* done." She stared across the property and seemed to tense involuntarily. Mac shifted uncomfortably, released a sigh, and stood in no particular hurry. "Well, I'm due for a nap. I'll see you later tonight."

Scorpio nodded and watched Mac head inside. She straightened from the porch railing, looked out across the ranch, and leaned against the support beam. She watched five horse and riders off in the distance on the hillside. A large brown and white pinto caught her eye. The riders were far enough away that she couldn't make out who they were, but she was sure she would have recognized the spotted horse if it had been from Hooper's ranch. The man on the spotted horse stopped while the others rode ahead. Out of the five, he was the only one not wearing a cowboy hat, which initially caught her attention. She was almost certain the military jacket he wore was similar to the one her father wore in the only photo she'd ever seen of him. It wasn't a very good photo and contained other men from his Navy SEAL team.

The man on the pinto horse seemed to survey the area. After last night's incident, Scorpio decided to pay closer attention to him and his friends. They didn't appear to be coming from Carson's ranch, which was a plus, but that didn't make them any less of a threat. As Scorpio stared at the man on the spotted horse, he seemed to be staring back at her. Although she could barely make out his features, something about him commanded her attention. The stranger finally looked away and sent the large paint horse into a gallop to catch up with the others. All five riders by-passed the house and headed for the wranglers, who kept watch on their herd.

§

Maverick and Stone sat on their horses not far from the herd and kept a close watch on the five strangers as they approached Jasmine on her horse. Although they couldn't hear the conversation, Jasmine's body language indicated she knew the visitors.

"Are those the kids from the other day?" Stone asked Maverick as neither bothered to hide the fact that they now stared.

"Definitely the same horse from the other day," Maverick remarked and indicated the spotted horse. "No mistaking that horse. Different rider though."

Stone strained to make out the others. "Yeah, it's the same kids and that guy from the other day. The one on the paint is new though." He eyed Maverick and grinned. "Jasmine likes you. Want to keep an eye on those five?"

"Correction," Maverick remarked and cast a look at his friend. "Jasmine *used* to like me."

"Couldn't handle the rejection?" Stone teased.

"She's been unusually cold toward me," Maverick remarked and withheld his chuckle. "I think the flames of lust have extinguished."

"Glad to hear," Stone remarked then grinned. "That means I can make a move on her before we leave."

Maverick cast a look at Stone, but he was already riding away. Maverick frowned and shook his head then continued to watch the strangers with Jasmine. Jasmine finally led the strangers toward the cattle and showed them how to cut cows from the herd. When it seemed as if the newcomers weren't there to cause problems, Maverick lost interest and resumed watching the herd. A little while later, Jasmine rode off with the man on the spotted horse leaving the other four to herd the cattle. When Jasmine and the man disappeared into the woods, Maverick snorted a laugh and shook his head.

"He's in for one hell of a surprise," Maverick muttered aloud.

Chapter 41

Sunday, July 6th. It was a beautiful, sunny morning and Hooper's ranch was alive with activity. A black, luxury sedan pulled up to the ranch, catching Stone's attention where he sat on his horse. Although he had the day off, he was riding that particular morning for pleasure. There was no telling how long it would be before he had the opportunity to ride again after their assignment was over. Stone kept an eye on the fancy car. A wealthy, noble-looking man in his mid-forties got out of the driver's side looking suave and handsome, although very much out of place in his expensive suit. The wealthy man had dark, neatly trimmed hair that was slightly slicked back, giving his regal appeal a slightly intimidating look. He buttoned his expensive suit jacket as he rounded the car to the passenger side. The man opened the door for a raving beauty with dark nearly black hair and perfectly applied makeup.

The man extended his hand to the beautiful woman and helped her from the car. The stunning woman wearing a simple yet sexy dress was enough to catch Stone's attention. Stone pushed up the brim of his hat and watched the couple approach the front door of the house. They didn't get many unannounced visitors and rarely ever any dressed so fashionably. The wealthy, handsome man straightened his suit jacket and rang the bell. There was barely a pause before the door was opened by Delia, who had obviously been watching the strangers through the window. Delia was immediately captivated by the man and smiled.

"Can I help you?" Delia asked and attempted to take a sweeping look of the impressive stranger without acting as if she were checking him out.

"Pardon the intrusion," the man in the suit announced with a little-added charm, seeming aware that he had caught the young woman's attention.

His suave words and sexy voice instantly hooked Delia. That she didn't giggle was actually surprising.

"I'm attending to business around here," he continued. "I'd heard there was some local air taxi service in the area, but the only private airfield never has anyone around. One of the locals in the nearby town said the helicopter may operate from this ranch."

"Oh, no," Delia announced while maintaining her smile. "She doesn't live here. I think she lives on the farm a few miles from here. She seems to go there a lot."

"There's another farm nearby?" the wealthy businessman asked.

"Yes, his daughter rides by here a lot," Delia offered.

"A man and his daughter?" the stranger asked then grinned. "I think they're the ones I'm looking for. What are their names?"

"Liam and Selena," Delia replied.

"No last name?" he asked.

"I haven't worked here that long," she insisted. "I'm sure Miss Hooper knows her name. Would you like to come inside? I could get her for you."

"No, we've taken up enough of your time," the handsome man politely replied then pointed up the road. "Just a few miles that way."

"You can't miss it," Delia replied. "There's not much else on this road."

The wealthy stranger smiled charmingly at Delia, who instantly blushed. "Thank you very much," he announced. "You've been a tremendous help."

The handsome man took his lovely lady's hand and led her back to the awaiting car. Delia remained in the doorway and watched as the suave gentleman opened the car door for the beautiful woman then shut the door for her. Delia smiled dreamily then closed the front door. Mac stood alongside the side window next to the door and eyed Delia.

"Who was that?" she asked with more than a passing interest.

"Just some handsome devil," Delia announced then lustfully raised her brows.

"What did they want?" Mac pressed.

Delia gave her a quick, disapproving once-over. "Aren't you nosy today," she scoffed. "Just directions to one of the neighboring farms."

Mac folded her arms across her chest with her own disapproval and watched Delia walk away. "Bitch," Mac scoffed under her breath.

She eyed the door, appeared deep in thought, and then groaned while running her fingers through her hair.

"Damn it," she cursed softly under her breath.

Mac eyed the keys to Brandi's sports car sitting on the hall table and again looked at the door. She took a step toward the hall table containing the keys when Kane approached from the kitchen.

"Good morning, sunshine," Kane cheerfully announced.

Mac turned to face Kane and attempted a smile. "Hey," she replied and glanced around. "Where's the girl you're supposed to be tailing?"

Kane pointed upstairs. "She wanted to sleep late this morning," he announced.

"Oh?"

"Yeah, I think that's code for 'shacking up with her boyfriend'," Kane teased.

"After she was nearly abducted, I can understand that," Mac remarked then raised her brows. "Don't mention it to Alma though. She's convinced Brandi is a 'good' girl."

Kane chuckled while grinning. "Alma thinks I'm a good boy too," he teased with added humor. "Maverick reported Boyd sneaking out of the bunkhouse the last few nights. Just because I haven't caught him sneaking into her room that doesn't mean he hasn't been." He frowned and looked up the staircase. "I need to wake her majesty. Hopefully, Romeo snuck out already."

"We don't do breakfast on Sundays, but I saw him in the kitchen with the other wranglers grabbing pastries," Mac informed him.

"Good," Kane replied and grinned. "Then it's safe to go up there."

Mac watched Kane hurry up the stairs and again eyed the car keys. She frowned.

"Mind your own business, Mac," she muttered aloud to herself then walked away.

§

Kane roamed the second floor hallway and paused before Brandi's bedroom door. He tapped lightly on the door but wasn't surprised when there wasn't a response. He knocked a little louder, but Brandi didn't answer. It was possible she was already up and in the shower. Kane drew a deep breath and opened the door. He peeked at the mussed bed, but she wasn't there. Kane approached the bathroom and tapped on the partially open door.

"Brandi?"

There was no response, and he didn't hear the shower running. He gently pushed the door open.

"Brandi, it's just me," he announced. "Scream if you're not decent."

Kane opened the door and looked inside the empty bathroom. A strange look crossed his face. He took a quick step to the shower and felt the towel on the rack. It was dry. Kane turned and hurried from the bathroom. He looked around the empty bedroom and eyed Brandi's discarded shoes on the floor. She always wore the same comfortable shoes around the house, but that didn't mean she didn't leave the room barefoot. Kane removed his hand radio from his pocket and pressed the button.

"Has anyone seen Brandi?" he announced with some concern into the radio.

"Did you try her room?" Jasmine asked over the radio. "She sleeps late on Sundays."

"I'm in her room," Kane replied as he nervously looked around. "Anyone?"

"Not since last night," Conroy was heard over the radio. "I'm in the kitchen. I can ask Alma if you'd like. She's in her room."

"Yes, I appreciate that," Kane replied then continued his line of question into the hand radio. "Anyone else?"

"Not out here," Marlon announced. "Her horse is in the pasture. I don't see her on the back patio either. Did she take her car?"

"No, her car was out front," Kane replied.

"Not in the game room," Emily announced over the radio. "I'm heading for the study."

"She's not out front, Kane," Mac informed him over her own radio. "I'll check the lounge, but I didn't see her in the hall."

Kane ran from the room. "Search the house," he announced into his radio. "Look outside. Can someone call her friends?"

"She's not in the study either," Emily replied over the radio. "I can call one of her friends and send an S.O.S."

"Thanks."

Chapter 42

Those within the house joined the wranglers outside the house. Despite that the wranglers were all off for the day; they helped search the area around the barn and pool house. Brandi seemed to have vanished. Boyd looked around then appeared tense as he glared at Kane.

"Wasn't it your job to watch her?" Boyd demanded.

"She wanted to sleep late this morning," Kane informed him and folded his arms across his chest. "When did you see her last?"

Boyd fidgeted and appeared nervous. "Not since last night," he insisted.

Kane raised his brows and glared at Boyd, but he didn't admit to spending the night with Brandi.

"So no one has seen her since last night?" Jasmine demanded then looked at Kane. "Did you search the entire house?"

"The seven of us searched everywhere," Kane insisted as his tension increased over her disappearance. "Is there anywhere outside she might be?"

"Brandi doesn't like the outdoors," Marlon replied while rubbing his sore back then eyed Boyd. "Was she okay when you last saw her? She wasn't upset about anything, was she?" He appeared interested. "Any reason to think she threw a tantrum and stormed off?"

Boyd frowned at the comment. "No, she didn't throw a tantrum and run off," he scoffed with some bitterness to the line of questioning. "Something must've happened to her. She was in a good mood when I last saw her. Her car is still here, and she didn't make plans to leave with anyone."

"None of her friends have seen or heard from her since yesterday," Emily admitted while nervously rubbing her chilled arms.

"Sig didn't come home, did he?" Scorpio asked while eyeing the others. "He wouldn't have shown up and taken her somewhere, would he?"

"No," Jasmine huffed and almost found the question humorous. "Our father isn't the spontaneous type." She then nodded indicating Boyd. "I'm with Boyd. Something happened to her."

Rayner stepped out of the house carrying his laptop. "I reviewed the security footage from last night," he informed them catching their attention. "The cameras were shut down last night around midnight."

"Shut down?" Marlon bellowed with surprise. "How's that possible? What's the point of security cameras if intruders are able to shut them off whenever they feel like it?"

"Intruders can't shut them off," Rayner remarked and raised his brows. "It was done from inside the house."

"Someone in the house shut off the security cameras?" Kane asked and immediately shifted looks at those who were staying within the house.

"Did the cameras catch anyone roaming around inside the house prior to the shutdown?" Scorpio asked.

Rayner shook his head. "The cameras aren't meant to see activity inside the house," he informed them. "The cameras located inside the house are directed at the doors. Anyone inside the house could have slipped into the study and shut off the system."

"Who'd shut off the system?" Marlon demanded with some irritation.

Boyd suddenly tensed and ran his fingers nervously through his hair. "Brandi," he muttered barely loud enough for them to hear.

All eyes were suddenly on Boyd. He fidgeted and avoided looking at the others.

"Since the system has been up and running, Brandi has been turning it off at midnight, so I won't be caught on video entering the house after everyone has gone to bed," Boyd announced then finally looked back at those staring at him. "We weren't doing anything. We just wanted to spend some quiet time together without everyone watching and judging." He shifted uncomfortably at the looks he received. "She always turned it back on after I left the house."

"And what time was that?" Kane demanded.

"I usually leave around five in the morning, so I'm back before the guys get up," Boyd replied sheepishly.

"So she was abducted between five and six," Kane remarked. "That's when the wranglers drop in the kitchen for breakfast."

"Six-thirty on a Sunday," Teddy corrected Kane. "Alma doesn't cook breakfast on Sundays."

"So if someone kept tabs on Boyd," Jasmine remarked, "they could assume the alarm and cameras were disabled anytime he snuck into the house."

"And that doesn't even narrow it down to someone living here," Kane insisted. "If Carson has been stalking her, he could have insider information."

"The police need to pay Carson a visit," Marlon insisted and stretched his back.

Jasmine eyed her brother and the way he held his back. "Did you throw your back out again?" she huffed.

"No, it's just sore from my fall," Marlon snapped. "I'm fine."

Without much prodding, she easily ignored her brother's suffering. "You can forget the police," Jasmine informed those on the patio. "They won't do anything about it until she's missing twenty-four hours, and we have no proof she's at Carson's ranch. No judge will give a warrant to search that place without sufficient evidence."

Maverick and Stone exchanged looks and sighed. Stone frowned while raising his hand. "Maverick and I have some experience getting in and out of places unnoticed."

"That won't do us any good until it's dark," Marlon protested. "You certainly can't slip onto their ranch undetected in broad daylight."

"It would be counterproductive," Stone announced with a frown.

They heard the faint sound of helicopters and instinctively looked up. Jasmine waved it off.

"That's just the woman who flies our father around," she announced.

Two helicopters flew overhead. Everyone looked up and watched them pass.

Mac raised her brows, tensed slightly, and shook her head. "That's not the same helicopter."

"How would you know?" Rayner asked with some surprise and looked back at Mac. "You drove with Hooper."

Mac glared at Rayner and folded her arms across her chest. "I saw the helicopter outside the terminal," she reminded him. "I chose to drive with Mr. Hooper because I saw that it was a helicopter." She then looked at the others and stiffened. "I'd like to be nosy and see what's happening. Can I borrow Brandi's car?"

"Yeah, sure," Marlon replied. "The keys are on the hall table where she always leaves them."

Mac flashed her hand radio. "I'll let you know if I find anything interesting."

"Did you want someone to go with you?" Kane asked while offering a curious look.

Mac looked back at him, managed a tiny smile, and shook her head. "No, I'll be fine," she insisted. "It's probably nothing."

"That man and woman who were here this morning," Delia suddenly gasped and stared at Mac. "Do you suspect they had something to do with Brandi's disappearance?"

"No, I doubt it," Mac replied with conviction. "I just want to poke around and make sure, that's all."

Mac didn't hang around for any further cross-examination and hurried into the house. Once she was out of view of the others, she sprinted across the kitchen and just about ran down the grand hallway.

"Learn your lesson, Mac," she muttered. "You should mind your own business. They can take care of their own problems."

Mac paused before the hall table and stared at the keys only a moment before snatching them. She was about to head for the door when she reconsidered and entered the nearby lounge. Mac approached the gun cabinet and only thought about it a moment before opening the unlocked cabinet. She removed a pump-action shotgun, grabbed a box of shells, and hurried from the room.

Chapter 43

Mac drove Brandi's sports car along the road in the direction of the farm Delia mentioned to the strangers in the luxury sedan. She slowed the car when she saw the same sedan abandoned in a clearing off the side of the road. Mac stopped the sports car and stared at the parked sedan. The man and woman weren't anywhere to be found. Mac sank into thought. She threw the car into drive and sped along the back road for the neighboring farm. She parked the sports car at the end of the driveway, grabbed the shotgun, and hurried into the woods where she followed the driveway to the house. As she neared the house, she heard the two helicopters taking off near the neighbor's barn. The helicopters were heading deeper into the mountains. Mac paused at the edge of the woods and stared at the quiet farmhouse.

"Damn it," she cursed aloud. "Mind your own business. They cast you aside, remember?"

Mac thought about it for only a moment then drew a deep breath, pumped the shotgun, and hurried for the house. When she saw the familiar man who had been riding with the three girls leaving the house, Mac hid alongside the porch. The man from her past leaped onto his large black horse and galloped away from the farm with purpose. That wasn't good. Mac stared at the farmhouse a long moment and carefully debated her next move. She released her breath, summoned her courage, and quickly but quietly headed for the house. The kitchen door remained open and panicked voices were heard from inside. Mac slowly entered the house with her hands firmly gripping the shotgun while aiming it at the floor before her. She passed through the kitchen and entered the living room while raising the shotgun. A man in his forties spun to face Mac with a snub-nosed revolver in his hand aimed at her. The man slowly lowered his gun while staring at her with astonishment.

"Mac?" he gasped.

"Liam," Mac replied with little emotion.

Hooper's neighbor, Lee, sat on the sofa while clutching a towel to her bleeding head. Lee looked up a little faster than she should have, and her eyes widened with surprise or possible horror.

"Mac," Lee gasped with disbelief equaling the man's expression. "How did you--?"

Mac tossed the shotgun onto the breakfast counter with a metallic clatter and hurried to Lee's side. She kneeled before the injured woman and gingerly pulled her bloodied hand and towel from the wound. Mac assessed the injury.

"It's not as bad as it probably feels," Mac insisted then looked back at the man, Liam, hovering over them. "Do you have a first aid kit?"

He nodded.

Mac glared demandingly at him. "Well, go get it," she launched and pointed in anger.

Liam ran for the nearby study and returned with a large field kit resembling the sort of bag an EMT would carry. He placed it on the floor alongside her. Mac rummaged through the kit and removed some cleanser and gauze pads. She tore into the pads with her teeth, soaked them with cleanser, and gently cleaned Lee's head injury.

"What happened?" Mac asked while periodically scanning Lee's face. "Who were the men in the helicopter?"

"They didn't say," Lee scoffed with some irritation. "They were looking for Jackie. It's a long story."

"Yeah, I have a few of those myself," Mac muttered and gently dried the bullet graze. "You're lucky. The bullet only grazed you."

"I don't think it was meant to kill her," Liam informed Mac.

Mac removed some plastic tape strips from a pack and gently applied them to the wound to help keep it closed. The strips essentially mimicked stitches. Liam paced the living room while watching Mac patch up Lee.

"Have you seen Brandi?" Mac asked.

"Brandi?" Lee questioned with surprise. "Why would I have seen Brandi?" She then appeared suspicious. "How do you know Brandi?"

"It's part of my long story. She went missing, and I thought maybe your *visitor* may have had something to do with it," Mac remarked.

"No," Lee replied. "Brandi wasn't with them. I don't know where Brandi is, but this has nothing to do with her, I assure you."

Mac finished placing the last of the strips over the graze on Lee's temple then stared into the woman's eyes.

"I know we've had some differences," Mac announced in a gentle tone then fidgeted nervously, "but do *they* need me?"

Lee tensed while staring back at Mac. "After what happened at Beck's wedding, do you really want to open yourself up to that again?" she asked with a serious look on her face.

Mac frowned and sat back on her feet. "No, not really," she replied while repressing her emotions, "but I don't want to see anything happen to them either."

Lee revealed her bracelet that pulsated a red warning. "I got a warning out. The guys are ready for them," she insisted. "They also have home field advantage. They're probably already on lockdown. If you attempted to intervene, you'd be alone on the outside. I'd sit this one out if I were you."

Mac made a face and sighed. "I'm already alone on the outside," she muttered then met Lee's gaze. "I should get back."

Lee caught Mac's hand and affectionately squeezed it while offering a timid smile. "Thanks, Mac," she announced gently.

Mac stood and managed a tiny smile. "Just repaying my debt," she insisted then hesitated before leaving. "Could you not tell anyone I was here? I have enough problems. I'd rather avoid their wrath."

Lee smiled and nodded. "I won't say anything to the guys," she replied.

Mac managed a tiny smile, grabbed her shotgun, and hurried from the house. Mac no sooner stepped onto the porch when she heard a loud explosion. She looked to the sky and saw Jackie's helicopter in the distance not far from a cloud of smoke. Mac snorted a laugh and shook her head.

"Give them hell, Jackie," she announced then hurried from the farmhouse.

Mac sprinted from the farmhouse, down the long driveway, and finally reached the road where she had abandoned Brandi's expensive sports car. She was about to get into the car when she noticed tire tracks over some tall weeds. With a stretch of the imagination, the small clearing could have been a road at one time. Mac approached the crushed weeds. Although the weeds seemed to be dead, indicating something drove over them more than a week ago; there was fresh dirt over some of the dead weeds. It was obvious something had driven over that area recently. Mac clutched the shotgun as she stared down what almost certainly had been a roadway.

As she took a step closer, she stepped on something metal. Mac brushed her foot across the old, metal sign covered over with dead weeds and dirt. She could make out the words 'packing'. Mac again looked down the overgrown lane. Had there once been a meat packing plant in the area? With all the cattle farms, it was possible. She considered exploring the overgrown lane but changed her mind. On foot, it could take too long, and she'd easily be spotted if she drove Brandi's sports car. She needed backup. Mac removed the hand radio from her back pocket and pressed the button to speak.

"Kane," she announced. "Do you copy?"

"Yeah, Mac," Kane responded back a little too eagerly. "Did you find anything?"

"Secured channel," she replied then switched the walkie-talkie channel without waiting for a response. "Kane, do you copy?"

There was a moment of silence.

"I'm here, Mac," Kane announced over the radio. "Just heading outside for some privacy. What do you have?"

"I don't know," she informed him while looking around. "There's possibly an old meat packing plant a few miles up the road. Someone's been through here recently. If I take Brandi's sports car, I'll risk being seen. If they have her there, I should have some backup."

"You'll have your backup," Kane reported from his end. "We can meet you in five minutes. Hold your position until we get there."

"Roger that," Mac replied then hesitated. She then put the radio back to her mouth. "Kane, this reeks of an inside job, you know that?"

"Yeah, I know that," he replied over her radio. "I won't let anyone else in on it."

Chapter 44

Only a few minutes later, Rayner placed his laptop on the sports car hood and pressed a few buttons while the guys removed several shotguns from the back of the old pickup truck Kane had borrowed. Scorpio and Kane stood behind Rayner and watched him zero in on the maps page, which showed a satellite image of the old meat packing plant.

"I pulled this up before we left the house since I can't get internet outside of the ranch," Rayner informed them. "Here's the road we're on now. The driveway is approximately half a mile from where we are here." He indicated images on the aerial view of the abandoned meat packing plant. "You have the main entrance here, and the loading dock here."

"Doesn't look like much of a loading dock," Stone commented while casually placing the shotgun against his shoulder.

"This particular plant was shut down decades ago," Rayner informed him. "The building is mostly concrete. What few windows you see have been boarded up. The images were updated a few months ago so I couldn't say if the windows are still boarded. More than likely you can enter through the main entrance or the loading dock. If someone took Brandi here, one of those would have been recently opened."

Kane pointed to the image. "It looks like office space in this area over here," he announced. "On the far end from the loading docks." Kane then eyed the others. "If someone brought her here, that's probably where they'll have her stashed."

"Who are 'they' and how organized are they?" Maverick asked.

"Unknown," Kane replied with a defeated sigh. "I think we should split up and enter through both the loading dock and the main entrance." Kane indicated an area within the woods not far from the packing plant. "We'll park the truck around here and hike to either entrance, so no one sees us coming." He glanced at the team. "Mac, Stone, and Maverick will take the loading dock entrance. Scorpio and I will take the main entrance."

"You know I'm not helpless," Rayner informed Kane with a slightly insulted look.

"No, but I've seen your resume," Kane remarked while staring at him. "You can shoot, but you're not a skilled fighter. I'm not sending you into tight quarters without proper training. We'll post you in the woods facing the front of the building. Anyone tries to escape; they're yours to take down."

Rayner nodded with understanding.

Stone offered Rayner a sympathetic smile and handed him a shotgun. "Use it in good health."

§

The abandoned meat packing plant was surrounded by woods in the middle of nowhere. The processing building had a long dirt driveway leading up to it, although it was mostly grown over. Once the pickup truck reached the clearing before the plant, the team staked out the area before implementing their plan. Nothing moved, but there was an indication that someone had used the main entrance at some point in recent months. Fresh tire tracks continued on to the loading dock, which was on ground level.

"Someone has definitely been here," Scorpio informed them while scanning the area.

"No vehicles," Rayner announced and lowered his binoculars. "They could have driven inside the building through the loading dock."

"Okay, let's get in position," Kane announced and grabbed his shotgun.

Scorpio removed her back holster containing both samurai swords and slipped into it. Kane eyed the dual swords then looked at her and raised his brows.

"You do realize one of those is mine," he remarked.

Scorpio grinned, removed one of the swords, and flipped it in her hand. "Finders keepers," she announced.

"It doesn't really work that way, Scorp," Kane remarked while raising a brow.

Scorpio ignored her brother, paused before Rayner, and kissed him quickly on the lips. "Have fun."

Rayner laughed. "Yeah, you too."

All five placed earbuds in their ears so they could communicate with the hand radios and not have others hear their conversation. Mac, Maverick, and Stone headed through the woods to put themselves in position for the loading dock entrance while Scorpio and Kane hurried across the clearing for the main entrance.

§

Stone, Maverick, and Mac paused before the loading dock entrance and discovered the loading bay door was already partially open. Stone eyed the small opening then looked back at Mac and grinned.

"Feel like taking point?" Stone asked. "You're the only one small enough to squeeze through that opening. If we open the door, we lose the element of surprise."

Mac nodded and grinned. "Yeah, it'll be fun," she announced cheerfully.

She lowered herself to the ground and slipped through the small opening. Once inside what looked almost like a large cattle auction house, Mac stared at the Hummer parked between the collapsed and rotting fencing. She scanned the large area.

Nothing moved. She took two steps back for the opening and motioned the guys in while pressing the hand radio attached to her belt.

"There's a Hummer in the loading dock," Mac announced through the radio to Kane and Scorpio. "We've definitely arrived at someone's party."

Stone opened the door a little wider, allowing sunlight to spill into the large, empty area filled with corrals. Both men entered with their shotguns in hand and looked around. A large corridor undoubtedly led the cattle to slaughter. A smaller corridor possibly headed toward the processing area and eventually to the offices. Rather than splitting up, they proceeded together toward the smaller corridor.

"What a delightful odor," Maverick muttered. "Smells like "Texas Chainsaw Massacre" meets "Deliverance"."

Stone lowly hummed "Dueling Banjos".

Mac rolled her eyes. "Oh, I'm never partnering with the two of you again."

"You love it," Stone teased while grinning.

Mac secretly hid her smile.

§

Scorpio walked along the dimly lit corridor with her sword at the ready while Kane brought up the rear, his back turned to hers, keeping an eye behind them with the shotgun in his hand. Scorpio kicked something metallic with her boot then hesitated and looked down. Kane glanced at the floor as well. Scorpio ran the tip of her boot across several 9mm bullet casings. She removed a small flashlight from her pocket and scanned the corridor. There were several bullet holes and chips in the concrete, although she didn't notice any blood. Kane again glanced at what she studied.

"What is it?" he asked.

"Someone's been shooting guns inside here," she informed him.

"Not at all strange," Kane muttered while making a face.

Scorpio took another step. A cutout target of a man with a gun and a male hostage sprang out just ahead of them. Scorpio jumped with surprise. Kane spun with his shotgun aimed but refrained from pulling the trigger. Once their nerves had settled, they uncertainly approached the target, which contained many bullet holes in both the bad guy and the male hostage. Scorpio indicated the male hostage in the cutout target.

"Is it just me or does that look like the guy we saw riding with those girls the other day?" she asked.

Kane studied the images on the cutout a moment and nodded. "It sort of does," he replied then wiped some dirt from the cutout to reveal scribbled writing. "Bogart." Kane eyed Scorpio. "Does that mean anything to you?"

Scorpio shook her head. "This place may belong to that guy we saw with those girls," she remarked. "He could be the one we're looking for."

"Possibly," Kane replied and pressed the button on the radio attached to his belt. "Guys. There's something strange about this place." He looked around. "It looks like someone's sadistic funhouse."

"Copy that," Stone replied. "You should see what we found in the processing room."

§

Maverick walked past several targets hanging up near the back of the large processing room, which contained wood covering the back wall to keep bullets from ricocheting off the concrete. Stone and Mac stood by the small booths set up with pulleys to bring the targets to and from the indoor range. There were piles of empty 9mm bullet casings that had been carefully swept to the sides of each booth. Maverick indicated one of the targets that had glasses made out of bullet holes, a bullet hole smiling face, and its crotch shot out.

"Okay, now I'm a little worried," Maverick informed them while nervously looking around. "I don't want to run into the guy who did that."

Mac tensed while staring at the mangled target. Stone glanced at her and noted her concern.

"You okay?" Stone asked.

She hesitated then nodded. "Yeah," Mac replied then held her breath. "It's just, well, this all seems so organized. Obviously, this stuff has been here a while."

"Like training camp for a militia," Stone muttered.

"Something like that," Mac remarked and remained lost in her own world.

"We need to proceed with caution," Maverick announced as he approached them. "Whoever has been practicing here is good. A little 'out of our league' good."

"Let's just find the girl and get out of here," Mac announced with some concern.

Chapter 45

Kane and Scorpio reached one of many dilapidated offices within the building. Before they even had a chance to look inside, they heard male voices. The men sounded almost panicked.

"Did you hear that explosion? Something's going on out there," one of the men announced with concern in his voice. "We should get the hell out of here before someone investigates that sound."

"We're not going anywhere until we're paid," the second man insisted. "We risked too much to go home empty handed."

Scorpio looked back at Kane for his reaction, but, instead, she saw a large man, who looked like a lumberjack on steroids, standing directly behind her brother. Her eyes suddenly widened as she gasped. Kane looked back and saw the size of the man standing behind him. Kane barely even turned when the man grabbed the barrel of the shotgun and attempted to take it from him. Kane fought to keep control of the weapon and kicked the man in the abdomen. The shotgun flew across the corridor with a clatter. To Kane's surprise, the large man was barely fazed. Scorpio raised her sword as the man lunged for her brother, but she heard the men within the room approaching the doorway. They were alerted to the clatter of the shotgun.

As the first man stepped into the doorway with his gun, Scorpio spun and swung her sword, knocking the gun from his hand. When the large man grabbed Kane's jacket, Kane stylishly slipped out of it while spinning around into a high roundhouse kick, striking the man in the chest. The man stumbled back only a step, surprising Kane.

"Oh, shit," Kane cried out and dodged the large fist that flew for his face.

He caught the man's thick wrist and kicked backward, striking the man in the head. The large man was thrown off balance, but he still didn't go down. Scorpio caught a glimpse of her brother's inability to take down the much larger man. She kicked the man she'd just disarmed with enough force to send him into the second man now in the doorway then spun toward her brother, who had just ducked another flying fist from the large man.

"Kane, footstool," Scorpio shouted then bolted toward him where he remained crouched down.

Kane ducked and rolled his back. Scorpio leaped onto his back with her left foot and used her momentum to spin into a roundhouse kick with her right foot. She struck the man in the head and sent him several feet down the hall before he struck a wall. Scorpio landed a little less than gracefully with her sword still in her hand and sprang back to her feet as Kane straightened. The two men within the doorway were now back on their feet and going for their discarded guns. As Scorpio spun to face the men, Kane pulled the second sword from her back holster. The men abandoned their discarded weapons and ran down the hall with Kane running after them.

Scorpio heard the big man returning to his feet. She spun around with her sword clutched in both hands. The man no sooner made it to his feet when Mac appeared from the nearby corridor, leaped into the air, and kicked him in the chest with both feet. He flew backward only a foot before striking the concrete wall with enough force to knock himself unconscious. Maverick and Stone appeared in the corridor only a moment after she'd taken the big man down. Scorpio pointed down the hall in the direction Kane had chased the two men. Maverick and Stone ran down the corridor with their shotguns in hand. Scorpio entered the nearby room and looked around.

Brandi was tied to a sturdy chair with duct tape over her mouth to keep her quiet. She muffled a relieved scream when she saw Scorpio. Mac entered the room behind her with her switchblade knife already in hand. Scorpio pulled the tape from Brandi's mouth while Mac cut the duct tape binding her wrists to the chair arms.

"Thank God," Brandi cried out while panting in fright. "What the hell is going on around here?"

"What happened?" Scorpio asked.

"I woke up to two men hovering over my bed this morning," Brandi informed them.

"You mean after Boyd left your room?" Kane asked from across the room.

All three looked back at Kane where he stood in the doorway.

"Did you get them?" Scorpio asked her brother.

"No, I wasn't able to catch them," Kane replied. They heard a shotgun firing. Kane then raised his brows and grinned. "But I think Rayner did."

Kane then returned his attention to Brandi as she gingerly rubbed her slightly red wrists and stood up from the chair with some stiffness.

"You turned off the security cameras," Kane scoffed while shaking his head. "Do you have any idea how foolish that was? How am I supposed to protect you if you're doing stupid things behind my back?"

"I didn't want Daddy to know that Boyd was sneaking into my room at night. I swear; we weren't doing anything. We just cuddled," Brandi insisted while offering a pouty face. "Daddy wouldn't care. He'd kill him."

"I'm not your father, Brandi," Kane snapped back. "I'm looking out for your safety. You didn't have to tell your father, but you should have told me. I'm here to protect you; not nark on you to your father."

"I'm sorry," she pouted softly and seemed genuinely upset. "I wasn't thinking." Brandi then looked at Scorpio and Mac while grimacing. "I really have to pee."

Mac rolled her eyes and motioned Brandi to the door. "I doubt it's functioning, but I saw a bathroom down the hall," she announced.

As Mac left the room with Brandi, Scorpio and Kane exchanged looks.

"So Boyd was telling the truth," Scorpio remarked with surprise.

"Yes, so that means someone has been watching the house and keeping tabs on Boyd's nightly visits," Kane remarked while sinking into thought.

"Do you think it's one of the wranglers?" Scorpio asked with concern.

"Stone and Maverick have been staying in the bunkhouse," Kane insisted. "They only noticed Boyd leaving at night. If someone else were keeping tabs on Boyd from the bunkhouse, they would have noticed."

"Back to Carson?" Scorpio asked.

"Carson or someone on his payroll," Kane replied with interest. "No one in the house has a reason to abduct Brandi. Boyd gains more by marrying her. His sister certainly wouldn't want to jeopardize her brother's wedding plans, and the rest are already married into the wealth. A sizeable ransom only takes away from them. The only person in the house who stands to gain anything from Brandi's abduction is Brandi."

"She's the only one who doesn't want anything to do with the ranch," Scorpio concluded then smirked almost humored by the notion. "You don't honestly think she planned this, do you?"

Kane snorted a laugh. "She's not secretly a mastermind criminal," he teased. "I've hacked her laptop. Trust me; it's not an act. She's been clueless for years. She's only interested in partying with her friends."

"So we're stuck here a little while longer?"

"Yeah, I'm afraid so," he replied with a sigh. "Let me break it to Mac." He groaned and ran his fingers through his mussed hair. "She's going to hate me forever."

"She's not the only one," Scorpio informed him while raising her brows. "I can't continue playing Marlon's girlfriend for the benefit of a few. He's getting a little too comfortable in our pretend relationship, and it's not helping Rayner's ego any either. Brandi and Delia already know our relationship is made up."

"Then maybe we need to come clean with the family, if we don't suspect them," Kane replied. "That should ease tension on everyone."

"I think Maverick and Stone are fine playing wranglers," Scorpio informed him. "We don't have to blow their cover just because Mac and I are disenchanted."

"We'll discuss it with them," Kane replied. "We'll talk to Sig when he gets home later today."

Chapter 46

Scorpio, Rayner, and Mac took Brandi home in the sports car and then called the police to meet the guys who remained at the meat packing plant with their prisoners. Kane, Maverick, and Stone kept the three men bound with duct tape in the back of the borrowed pickup truck while they waited for the police. There seemed to be a lot of noise coming from the back road, but the three were surprised that what they heard just seemed to pass them by.

"Do you think they missed the road?" Maverick asked and again looked at his watch. "We've been here nearly two hours."

"Maybe it has something to do with that explosion we heard earlier," Stone remarked.

"We can ask the sheriff or the state troopers when they get here," Kane suggested and seemed to be equally antsy with the amount of time they'd been waiting.

An official-looking, black SUV finally appeared on the long driveway and approached them. Flashing blue and red lights came on within the dash and on the front of the vehicle, indicating it was a police vehicle of some kind. Once the vehicle parked, two men dressed in inexpensive suits got out of the SUV and approached the three men.

"Oh, boy," Stone announced through a false smile. "I smell feds."

"The FBI?" Kane asked with surprise. "Nah, why would they send the FBI?"

"Kidnapping," Stone replied and shrugged seeming uncertain.

"I'm Special Agent Harris with the FBI," the first man announced while flipping his badge open. Agent Harris was a distinguished looking man in his forties. He then indicated the man ten years his junior alongside him. "This is Special Agent Falcone."

His counterpart, Agent Falcone, was a ruggedly handsome man in his mid-thirties with neatly trimmed, nearly black hair. Both men were in excellent shape with athletic builds, lending to their already intimidating appearance.

"You reported a kidnapping?" Agent Harris asked while eyeing the men.

"Uh, yeah," Kane replied and indicated the three bound men in the back of the pickup truck. "These men kidnapped Sig Hooper's daughter early this morning. Our friends took her back to his ranch. Their Hummer is parked in the loading dock around the side of the building."

"And the three of you apprehended the kidnappers yourselves?" Agent Falcone asked with surprise.

"We were looking for Sig's daughter when we stumbled upon this place," Stone announced. "Since there's no cell phone service up this far, we certainly couldn't just leave her there while we waited for the police."

"Good thing too," Maverick remarked and cast a disapproving look at both men. "It took you guys long enough to show up."

Kane shut his eyes at Maverick's insistence on pointing out their tardiness. Apparently, he didn't understand how do deal with men who had the ability to make their lives miserable.

"A helicopter crashed not far from here," Agent Harris informed them with little emotion. "Everyone's been involved with that incident."

"Helicopter?" Kane asked with surprise while staring at the feds. His concern showed. "Not that attractive woman who flies for Sig."

"We're not at liberty to discuss the incident," Agent Falcone remarked with little emotion although he eyed the three with some suspicion. "We'll take your statements and check out the place. The state police are already heading for Hooper's ranch. They'll take statements from anyone else involved including the kidnapped woman."

"You really need to see that place," Stone informed them while gesturing at the meat packing plant behind him. "Someone has quite the little setup in there. Looks like some sort of off-the-grid militia training center. No telling what it's being used for."

"We'll check it out," Agent Falcone replied, although he seemed almost disinterested. Perhaps it was a fed thing. "Any injuries?"

"Apart from a few bruises, no," Kane announced then smirked teasingly. "We asked nicely."

"Any weapons involved?" Agent Harris questioned.

"We had a few shotguns," Stone informed them, "but we only used them to get their attention and stop them from escaping. No one was shot."

"They each had a 9mm Glock," Kane informed them. "They're on the ground alongside the truck. None were fired." He then appeared interested while staring at Agent Falcone. "She wasn't hurt, was she?"

Agent Falcone looked at Kane. "Who?"

"The helicopter pilot," Kane replied with insistence. "Jackie."

The federal agent stared at Kane a moment then shook his head. "No, there weren't any women in the helicopter that crashed."

"Glad to hear," Kane replied.

"Yeah, our pilot was pretty hot," Maverick announced while grinning.

Kane groaned and shook his head. "Show some respect," he muttered.

"Let's start with some names," Agent Falcone announced and eyed Kane. "You first."

"Kane Templeton," he replied and handed Agent Falcone his business card. "My team and I were hired to protect Sig Hooper's daughter. These are my associates, Ben Stone and Blake Maverick."

Agent Falcone accepted the card, eyed it, and then clipped it to his tablet. He focused his attention on Kane. "Tell us what happened starting with the abduction."

Kane retold the story while conveniently leaving his sister, Rayner, and Mac out of it. There didn't seem to be any reason to include them, particularly Mac, who wanted to avoid confrontations with law enforcement. Despite giving their statements, it seemed as if the feds were going to keep them there a while.

Chapter 47

Kane entered the house after returning from the meat processing plant. He barely made it through the door when he was immediately greeted by Scorpio, Rayner, and Mac. He eyed both women, who appeared more concerned than Rayner, and offered a humored smile.

"Were you afraid they were going to arrest us?" Kane teased, although the joke was meant more for his sister and Mac.

"You were gone three hours," Scorpio announced with concern.

"It took the feds two hours just to reach us," Kane remarked.

"The feds?" Mac asked with surprise. "We had the state troopers here. Why did you get feds?"

"Something about a helicopter crashing," he replied. "They didn't say, but I think they wanted to make sure we had nothing to do with whatever happened there."

"Is that what that explosion was?" Rayner asked with surprise.

Mac appeared horrified and stared at him with concern. "Your helicopter pilot?" she gasped with alarm.

"No," Kane replied. "Agent Falcone said it wasn't our pilot."

"Agent Falcone?" Mac asked with some surprise and almost choked on the question.

"Yeah, do you know him?" Kane asked while giving her a curious look.

Mac shifted slightly and managed a tiny smile. "Our paths crossed once," she muttered then eyed him. "You left me out of it, right?"

"Yeah, I didn't mention you or Scorpio," Kane remarked then snorted a slightly humored laugh. "And those guys certainly weren't admitting they were taken down by two women." Kane then appeared curious. "What did you tell the state troopers?"

"What we discussed," Mac replied. "After you and the guys apprehended the kidnappers, you contacted us at the farm, and we came and took Brandi home."

"Brandi went along with that story?" Kane asked.

"If we don't tell her father about Boyd's nightly visits, she's not saying anything about our assignment," Mac replied then raised her brows. "Scorpio said we're going to come clean about that with the family. Does that get me out of the servant's quarters?"

Kane grinned, pulled Mac playfully against him, and laughed as she squirmed to get out of his hold. "Yes, I'll get you out of the servant's quarters."

Before she could get away, he kissed her on the top of her head. Although she made a fuss about it and gave him a playful shot to the ribs, Mac secretly hid her smile.

"Where's Brandi?" Kane asked.

"She's in her room with Boyd," Scorpio replied. "Alma was taking her something to eat after she showered. Boyd's keeping her company."

Emily hurried down the hall successfully ending their conversation. "I just got off the phone with Sig," she announced while waving the cordless phone. "He's not coming home until late tomorrow morning."

"After what happened to Brandi?" Scorpio asked with surprise.

"I, uh, didn't tell him about that," Emily admitted while grimacing. "I didn't want to upset him. He'd only drive back home like a maniac. Since she's okay, I thought it was best to wait until he returned to tell him."

"I suppose that was wise," Kane replied then turned to Rayner. "Can you keep an eye on the security system and make sure there aren't any unauthorized shutdowns between now and tomorrow morning?"

"I have it set to alert me if anyone messes with it or if it goes offline," Rayner replied.

"Until Sig Hooper returns tomorrow morning, we'll just keep doing what we've been doing," Kane announced then winked at Mac.

She sneered her annoyance with him.

"We'll talk to Sig in the morning," Kane informed them. "We can go from there."

§

It was almost ten o'clock that night. Mac stood beneath the hot streams of water within the large standing shower in her private bathroom. It had been a long, boring day with a brief moment of excitement that afternoon at the meat packing plant. Tomorrow would be another full morning of maid detail. With any luck, it would be her last day making beds and scrubbing toilets. There was a good chance she'd be flipping off Delia as well. A sound came from her bedroom, which caused her to tense and listen a moment. It was quite possibly nothing since Kane seemed to take pleasure inviting himself into her room whenever he felt like it. She felt a cool breeze as some of the steam briefly cleared immediately telling her the bathroom door had been opened.

"Kane, if that's you--"

The shower door opened, surprising her. Mac started to turn and nearly collided with Maverick. He caught her from behind and kept her from facing him, pressing his naked body against hers.

"I hope you weren't expecting Kane," Maverick teased while caressing her naked body as he rubbed against her from behind. "Otherwise it might get crowded in here."

"No, I'm not expecting Kane, but he does invite himself into my room when the mood strikes him," Mac informed him with some annoyance.

"Yeah, Scorpio said he has boundary issues," Maverick teased.

"Sounds like someone else I know," she announced and attempted to look back at him.

"Now I know you don't mean me," he remarked while warmly kissing her neck. He moved his mouth closer to her ear and whispered. "I brought some baling twine for you to play with."

Mac tensed slightly then groaned and attempted to hide her smile. "You trust me enough to let me tie you to the bed?" she remarked.

"It's all I could think about since you joked about it," he announced in her ear then continued to kiss her neck while pressing his body against hers.

Mac maintained her grin and caressed his hands as they firmly ran along her wet body. "I love your dirty mind," she groaned in response.

"Hmm, then now might be a good time to tell you that I found a cucumber too," Maverick teased.

Mac cried out with surprise by the comment then squealed as Maverick bit her shoulder. She turned off the shower, spun to face him, and threw her arms around his neck.

"You're going to regret that," she announced and aggressively kissed him on the mouth.

Maverick broke off the kiss without releasing her and laughed with some uneasiness. "Oh, no," he remarked. "I didn't bring that for--"

"You'll be tied," she informed him. "You won't have any say in it."

His expression dropped slightly. "I think we're going to need a safe word," he announced with some concern.

Mac laughed almost devilishly, which didn't seem to ease Maverick's tensions any.

§

Mac and Maverick just about fell through the bathroom doorway and into the bedroom with towels wrapped around their wet bodies. They kissed and aggressively groped each other. Mac tackled Maverick to the bed and was struck by the rolling cucumber. She broke off the kiss, grinned, and picked up the thin green vegetable. Her eyes then strayed to the pillow. Mac's expression dropped as she snatched the note left on her pillow. Maverick eyed her with concern.

"What is it?" he asked.

Mac frowned and read the words scribbled on the piece of paper. "Mac, enjoy your night off. Tell Maverick I said 'hi'. Kane."

She turned the note so Maverick could see it. There was a crudely drawn cucumber at the bottom. Her look turned irritated.

"You said you locked the door," she snapped hotly.

"I did," Maverick protested then muttered, "the bathroom door."

She crumbled the note and threw it across the room. "Great," Mac huffed. "Now Kane knows we're screwing around."

"I'm sorry, Macbeth," Maverick remarked timidly with a defeated sigh and appeared disappointed. "Do you want me to leave?"

She looked at him with some surprise. "What? No, of course not," Mac scoffed and pinned his wrists to the bed while hovering over him. She raised a demanding brow. "You're not going anywhere until I say so."

Maverick could barely control his grin. "Okay then--"

Chapter 48

Scorpio slipped into Rayner's room and shut the door behind her. Rayner was sitting up on the bed with his laptop as part of his nightly ritual. He saw her and grinned with enthusiasm.

"Are we cheating on our boyfriend tonight?" Rayner teased and eagerly set his laptop on the nightstand then gave Scorpio his undivided attention.

Scorpio grinned slyly, flipped the lock on the door, and hurried for the bed. She leaped into the bed with him and pounced on top of him. Rayner groaned and held her against him. She kissed him quickly but passionately then pulled away just far enough to meet his gaze.

"I broke up with him," she teased back. "He just doesn't know it yet."

"I feel so dirty," Rayner remarked then flipped her onto the bed and positioned himself on top.

Scorpio stared into his eyes and affectionately caressed his chest. "I missed you."

"Yeah? I'm going to need you to prove that," he teased and kissed her with passion and aggression.

She broke off the kiss and smiled seductively. "I'm thinking of at least five different places in this room where we can have an adventure," Scorpio informed him. "If you can find them, you can have all five."

Rayner chuckled while kissing her neck. "I know you're eyeing the tub," he remarked.

"One."

"The window seat."

She giggled. "Two."

"The bench seat at the foot of the bed."

"Three."

Rayner had to think a moment and quickly scanned the room. He then offered a sly grin. "That big chair in the corner."

"Four."

He hesitated, seemed baffled, and again scanned the room without moving off her. "I'm stumped."

"Come on," she groaned.

"On the floor in front of the mirror?"

She grinned. "Five."

Rayner groaned and affectionately nuzzled her. "Let's start there."

Scorpio quickly kissed his nose. "Anything you want," she announced.

He kissed her warmly then hesitated and met her gaze with a more serious one. "Have you been sleeping?" Rayner asked with concern.

She affectionately caressed his chest. "Is that really what you want to be discussing right now?"

"Yes," he replied. "I worry when you don't sleep."

"I'll sleep some tonight," she insisted. "I sleep better when I'm with you."

"Let's start with the tub," Rayner suggested while caressing her body. "Maybe then you'll be able to sleep a while after a good soak."

"You're entitled to be a little selfish in this relationship, you know," she remarked.

"Oh, I'm definitely molesting you in the tub," he insisted. "You can sleep after that."

Scorpio laughed and kissed him warmly. As he returned the kiss with added aggression, his laptop softly wailed indicating a nuclear meltdown. Scorpio broke off the kiss and let her head fall back against the pillow.

"What's wrong with that thing now?" she asked.

Rayner groaned and rolled off her. He sat on the edge of the bed and pressed a few keys. "The security system went off," he huffed with irritation.

Scorpio sat up in bed and stared at him. "You mean someone turned it off again?" She looked at the bedside clock. It was just about midnight. "Kane talked to Brandi. She said she wouldn't turn the system off."

"It's not the system," he replied. "A grid is down. Either someone turned it off, or it's a blown fuse."

"Which grid?"

"Looks like the patio area," Rayner informed her and jumped out of bed.

Rayner grabbed his discarded clothes and hastily dressed while casting several looks at her. Scorpio sprang from the bed and awaited instructions.

"See if Kane is in his room," he announced while pulling on his shoes. "I'll head down the back stairs and check the system and the fuse box."

Scorpio nodded and hurried from the room in her bare feet. Rayner followed her from the room and continued down the hall for the back stairs. Scorpio paused before Kane's room and lightly knocked on the door.

"It's open," Kane announced.

She opened the door and stepped into the doorway. Kane sat up on his bed. He hadn't even bothered to undress, although he had taken off his shoes as well.

"Rayner said power went off on the back patio and took out his security feed there," she announced. "He went down to check on it."

Kane sprang from the bed and appeared more angry than concerned. "If she turned off the system again, I'm going to strangle her."

"You and me both," Scorpio remarked.

"I'll check on her," Kane announced. "Arm yourself and meet me in the kitchen."

"Should I wake Mac?"

"No, she's tied up right now," Kane casually remarked. "We can handle this."

Scorpio nodded and ran from Kane's room to her room. She pulled her sword from the sheath then hesitated and removed the second sword. As she headed from her room, Kane was knocking on Brandi's door. Scorpio passed him and tossed him the second sword. He easily caught it and twirled it in his hand.

§

Scorpio entered the empty, dimly lit kitchen and turned on all the back lights with one flip of every switch on the panel. The back patio was flooded with light, which seemed odd since Rayner said the grid was out. That should have included the lights to the patio. The pool was lit giving it an eerie glow, although there wasn't any light on outside the pool house. Scorpio stood in the open doorway and scanned the area attempting to see if anything moved. Despite that he made little noise, Scorpio heard Kane hurrying down the back stairs. She didn't bother looking since she knew it was just her brother. Scorpio stepped onto the back patio with Kane only a step behind her.

"Anything?" he asked.

"No," she replied. "Brandi?"

"Alone in bed watching a movie," Kane replied. "She's definitely alone. It wasn't her."

"Boyd wouldn't have any reason to shut off an entire power grid," Scorpio remarked. "He's already on candid camera by the time he gets inside the house."

Kane motioned her one direction and indicated he'd take the other. Scorpio nodded. They went in opposite directions around the pool. Scorpio headed toward the dark pool house while Kane went in the direction of the bunkhouse. Scorpio paused by the pool house and peered through the window. Despite the darkness, she saw someone lounging within the hot tub. She looked across the patio past the pool toward Kane as he headed for the bunkhouse. She snapped her fingers, immediately catching his attention. She indicated the pool house. Kane nodded and hurried around the back of the pool. He approached the pool house from behind and peered in through one of the windows. He joined Scorpio in the front near the entrance.

"There's someone in there," he remarked just loud enough for her to hear.

"In the hot tub in the dark," Scorpio added while raising a curious brow.

He nodded to the door. Scorpio approached the door and tried the knob. It wasn't locked. She eyed him in silent comment. Kane gripped his sword and nodded. Scorpio opened the door and stood aside, allowing Kane to bolt into the room. She entered only a step behind him. The man in the hot tub didn't move when they entered even though he had to have seen them. Scorpio felt the wall for the lights and flipped them. Nothing happened. The lights suddenly flickered erratically. Rayner must have been doing something from within the house. Although the lights continued to flicker, they provided enough light to see inside the pool house. Both looked at the hot tub that once again bubbled from the jets and saw Conroy lounging within the tub. They found it odd that he didn't acknowledge them or even move. Scorpio and Kane approached the tub while lowering their swords.

"Conroy?" Kane asked.

Both paused several feet away and saw the small television from the wall was now in the tub with him. Conroy's head was tilted back, and his eyes were open. He was dead; quite possibly electrocuted when the television fell into the water. Scorpio and Kane stared at the dead man with horror on their faces.

"What's going on out here?" someone asked from behind them.

Scorpio and Kane turned to see Sig Hooper standing in the pool house doorway. Both were surprised to see him since he wasn't supposed to be home.

"I thought you weren't coming home until tomorrow?" Kane asked.

"The deal fell through," he replied with some irritation. "I came home early. What's with the swords?"

Scorpio and Kane exchanged looks then stood aside allowing Sig full view of the hot tub. He stared at Conroy and gasped with surprise.

"What the hell--?"

"I believe he's been electrocuted," Kane deducted while nervously raking his fingers through his dark hair. "We'll need to call the police."

"Is he--?" Sig asked with horror.

Scorpio and Kane held their breath and nodded in response.

"Jesus," Sig gasped.

Chapter 49

The state troopers arrived a little more than an hour after being called and investigated the chilling scene inside the pool house. The wranglers, as well as the entire house, woke when the state troopers arrived with their lights flashing. Everyone had gathered in the kitchen and added to the already chaotic scene. Maverick managed to blend into the scene without anyone noticing he had actually come from the staff wing. Alma made coffee for the state troopers, which the family drank as well. It seemed as if no one was going back to bed despite the ungodly hour. The entire house was now awake and demanding answers.

Jasmine was clearly distraught over the news about her husband's accidental death, but Emily seemed to take it far worse. Sig noticed his wife's reaction to Conroy's death and didn't appear pleased. He must have suspected his wife was having an affair or he knew without a doubt. Rayner attempted to help the state troopers as much as possible, but he didn't have anything to offer them since the entire grid had shut down when the fuse blew. Despite the police insisting it was an accidental electrocution, it took them two hours to finish their inquiry. It was after three in the morning when the state troopers and the coroner finally left the ranch.

Kane and Scorpio stood over Rayner's shoulder where he worked on his laptop at the island counter even after the troopers had left. The wranglers were already filtering out of the kitchen since there was nothing left for them to do. Marlon took his sisters and Emily to the game room for something stronger to drink while Alma and Delia returned to the staff wing. Once the kitchen had cleared out, Sig and Mac joined Scorpio and Kane by the island counter where Rayner continued to work on his laptop, attempting to find his own answers.

"Do you buy that accidental death crap?" Sig asked them with a demanding look.

"The patio grid went out first, probably when the television hit the water," Rayner informed him. "Only a minute or two later, the kitchen camera went out. I assure you; that camera didn't go off because of the power surge. Someone turned that one off at the main console in the study. If someone turned off the camera to the back door, it means someone was hiding something, and they didn't want us to see it. Whether or not that has anything to do with what happened in the pool house is unknown."

"So the two could be connected?" Kane asked.

"Maybe," Rayner replied. "Maybe not."

"I doubt that television came off the wall by itself," Sig informed them while adamantly shaking his head. "I put that up there myself. It was secured with high-grade brackets. That was no accident."

All eyes were briefly on Sig.

"You think someone murdered Conroy?" Mac asked with surprise. "Who'd want to kill him?"

"I don't think it was him they meant to kill," Sig informed her.

They stared at him with surprise and interest and waited for an explanation.

"It's a known fact when I came home late at night or early in the morning, I hang out in the pool house," Sig informed them. "I don't like to wake Emily, especially since I usually can't sleep right away. I'll fix myself a drink and relax in the hot tub while watching a little television. Since I'm already there, I usually sleep in the pool house."

"But you weren't supposed to come home until tomorrow morning," Kane reminded him. "If that television was rigged to come down when someone used the hot tub next, they couldn't be sure it would be you. The kitchen camera was shut off *after* the television hit the water. We'll have video evidence of someone sneaking out there."

"There's a good chance whoever rigged it knew I'd be the next one in the hot tub," he insisted. "I called and said I'd be home in the morning. That usually means early, which means I'll be in the pool house."

"What was Conroy doing out there in the first place?" Mac then asked and eyed Sig.

"Although they didn't mention it in front of the family," Scorpio announced, "Conroy was naked. Did he often lounge naked in the hot tub?"

"In a private setting like that," Kane announced then shrugged. "I'd probably go commando."

"A lot of people would," Mac muttered.

Sig eyed Scorpio and raised his brows. "He was probably waiting for Emily," he remarked with little emotion.

"Emily?" Scorpio gasped with surprise. "Why would he be waiting for Emily?"

"It was pretty obvious he had a meeting planned," Rayner announced without looking at Sig.

"Mac and I caught them together in the attic," Kane admitted.

"Did everyone know about their affair?" Scorpio asked with surprise, considering she seemed to be the only person who didn't know. Kane had hinted around, and Scorpio noticed some subtle flirting, but she hadn't been let in on what they'd discovered.

Sig stared into Scorpio's eyes and offered a tiny smile. "You have a unique innocence about you," he remarked then drew a deep breath and nodded. "I think the entire house knew."

"And Jasmine didn't kill--" Scorpio held her breath and didn't finish the comment. "Oh."

"Jasmine knew," Sig assured her. "She knew, and she didn't care. They'd lost interest in each other after only a few months into their marriage."

"If it wasn't an accident, you don't suspect she had motive to kill him?" Scorpio asked.

"No," Sig replied as he leaned against the island counter. "She could have divorced him at any time. She doesn't actually have any marital property so he wouldn't get a damned dime. You have to understand Jasmine. She's only interested in the ranch. She stayed married to Conroy because it was convenient."

"If you and Jasmine both knew what your spouses were up to and didn't care," Mac remarked while eyeing Sig, "who else really had motive?"

"To murder Conroy?" Sig asked then shook his head. "No one. Me, on the other hand--"

"Everyone benefits?" Rayner asked.

"Just about," Sig informed him. "Jasmine is probably the only one who'd be worse off if I died."

"Why's that?" Mac asked.

"Even though she gets one-third of the ranch, Marlon would be left in charge," Sig replied then drew a deep breath and reluctantly sighed. "She's not happy about that. As long as I'm alive, she still has some say."

"What does Brandi have to gain?" Kane asked and offered a curious look.

"She could force Marlon and Jasmine to buy her share of the ranch," Sig offered and raised an arrogant brow. "She'd have enough money to live comfortably in a city somewhere. I'd hoped she'd learn to enjoy the ranch like Jasmine and Marlon, but even with Boyd's position as a wrangler, she's still not interested. I think he'd be willing to move to the city with her. She talks about it all the time."

"Does Emily benefit from your death?" Scorpio asked with some discomfort at the question.

"She's better off financially with me alive, but she gets a nice piece of the pie if I die," Sig replied. "She'd also be free to pursue Conroy."

"What about Carson?" Kane asked.

Sig looked at him with some surprise. "Carson? Why would Brandi's ex-boyfriend benefit?"

"If Jasmine and Marlon have to buy out Brandi's third of the property, wouldn't that put a financial strain on the ranch?" Kane asked with some suspicion. "Could it potentially put some of the acreage or all of it on the auction block? If Jasmine and Marlon can't work together, that could put the entire ranch in jeopardy as well."

Sig considered the comment then nodded. "You may have a point," he replied. "I hadn't thought of that. When Carson eventually takes over his father's ranch, I don't doubt he'd be interested in expanding."

"This business with Brandi keeps coming back around," Kane informed him. "I keep wondering if it's not all somehow tied together."

"Three attempts to abduct Brandi," Mac announced with a defeated sigh. "That can't be a coincidence."

"You mean two," Sig demanded and eyed Mac. "One at the mall and one over July fourth holiday."

"No," Kane replied and held his breath a moment while meeting Sig's gaze. "Someone abducted her earlier yesterday morning."

"What?" Sig cried out. "How?"

"It's a long, complicated story," Kane remarked with a sigh. "We found her at the old meat packing plant, and the men were arrested."

"If someone's looking to put the ranch into financial ruin," Rayner announced, "a few million dollars in ransom might help push that along."

"When that doesn't work, move to plan 'B'," Mac announced and eyed Sig.

Sig sank into thought then turned to Rayner. "How smart are you?"

"Smart enough. Why?" Rayner asked. "What do you need?"

"Can you get into my computer and check over my books?" Sig asked while appearing slightly alarmed. "I'd like to know if Conroy was doing anything funny with my finances."

"Yeah, I can do that," Rayner replied. "I'm great with finances. Kane could also help with that."

"Me?" Kane asked with surprise. "What do I know about finances?"

Scorpio rolled her eyes and groaned. "Please, Kane," she scoffed. "We found your locked box in the closet."

Kane shifted slightly and avoided looking at his sister.

"How many corporations and property do you own?" Scorpio demanded. "Living rent-free with me all while sitting on your own fortune."

"Unwilling to spring for two motel rooms," Mac scoffed and folded her arms across her chest. "As if another twenty bucks would kill you."

"I'll admit; I'm good with computers and finances, but it's not something I enjoy," Kane informed his sister. "I prefer getting my hands dirty."

"I wonder where you get that defective gene," Scorpio muttered.

Kane glared at her. "You don't know that I'm anything like him," he remarked. "For all you know, I could be like our mother."

"Yeah, in height," Scorpio remarked.

Mac rolled her eyes. "Fight nice, kids."

Chapter 50

Monday, July 7th. Five o'clock in the morning. Scorpio joined Rayner and Kane in Sig's office where they could view security footage on the main monitor. Scorpio sat on Sig's desk as they watched video leading up until the time the pool house fuse was blown, and the kitchen camera was disabled. Rayner sat in Sig's chair behind the desk and appeared bored. None had been to bed since the state troopers left two hours earlier. Kane sat sideways in the chair in front of the desk closest to the panel of security cameras. He had his left leg casually dangling over the arm of the chair and made himself comfortable for the boring footage. There was a tap on the door. Rayner stopped the playback with the remote control as everyone looked across the room. Mac slipped into the study and shut the door behind her.

"What's up?" she asked.

"We're going over the video from last night," Kane informed her. "Maybe we can piece together what happened to Conroy."

Mac approached Kane's chair and shoved his leg off the chair arm so she could sit on it.

"Did I miss anything?" Mac asked.

"No, not yet," Rayner replied.

Kane attempted to see the monitor around Mac where she sat on the arm of the chair, but she was blocking his view. He groaned, grabbed her around the waist, and pulled her onto his lap. She fought his hold on her, although he was reluctant to let her go.

"Knock it off," Mac snapped hotly.

"Shh," he remarked softly and indicated the monitors. "You're interrupting the movie."

Kane easily ignored her protest, and she eventually gave in without a much of a fight. Scorpio cast a glance at her brother holding Mac on his lap. There was nothing sexual about it, and she was pretty sure Mac knew that. Kane was just overly affectionate and had already claimed Mac as his second sister. That wasn't to say that Kane's friendly disposition didn't cause any misunderstandings in the past. He'd left many girls in high school brokenhearted when they realized he didn't mean anything by his behavior. Mac's initial protests to Kane's affection were from years of hard living and trust issues, but it was evident Kane was slowly breaking down the barriers she'd built around herself. Scorpio could tell by the way that Mac eventually sank back against Kane that she secretly wanted to be held. Rayner took the video off fast forward and played it at normal speed.

"This is about ten o'clock. About two hours before the feed cut out," Rayner announced. "Kane and Mac can watch the two cameras to the left closest to them, and Scorpio and I will concentrate on the two to the right. If you see anything of interest, tell me to pause it."

"Everyone was in bed by this time, right?" Mac remarked while resting against Kane in the chair.

"Pretty much," Rayner informed her. "We shouldn't see anyone moving around outside unless they're up to something we should know about."

"Pause," Scorpio announced while staring at the kitchen door camera. She then pointed at the screen. "Is that Maverick?"

Mac tensed and held her breath since it would seem she'd been caught.

"Yeah," Kane replied with little emotion. "Maverick and I had things to discuss. I can vouch for him."

Mac relaxed and gently patted Kane's arm securely anchored around her abdomen. Rayner resumed the video playback at a slower fast forward to save some time.

"What time did Sig say he arrived?" Mac asked.

"A little before midnight," Kane replied.

"The patio grid went out around midnight," Rayner informed her.

"And you found Conroy around twelve-thirty?" Mac asked then shook her head. "If it wasn't an accident, that's cutting it close, don't you think?"

"No one had reason to suspect I'd be monitoring the security cameras," Rayner informed her.

"Pause," Scorpio again announced and pointed at the back patio video as it paused. "That's Boyd."

"He's clearly sneaking into the house through the kitchen door," Rayner informed them. "This was about eleven o'clock."

"That proves Brandi didn't shut the cameras off for him," Kane announced and shifted beneath Mac on his lap. "She promised she wouldn't."

"But she also said he wasn't in her room," Scorpio reminded him.

"This was eleven," Kane reminded his sister. "The video went out at midnight. He could have been in her room earlier and left around the time the feed cut out. I'm not sure for what reason, but he also could have been the one to cut it himself."

"We'll see as we get closer to the cutoff point," Rayner announced and resumed playback at a slower fast forward so they wouldn't miss any details.

Only a moment passed when Rayner hit the pause button and indicated the screen. "There's Conroy heading into the pool house for his rendezvous," he remarked and appeared curious. "He's alone."

Playback resumed at a slightly faster rate.

"There's light on within the pool house," Scorpio informed them while indicating the screen. "Not a lot. Must be the television over the hot tub."

"He's in there twenty minutes now at this point," Rayner announced. "No sign of anyone else outside the patio or the pool house."

"And no one went in earlier?" Kane asked.

"No," Rayner replied. "There wasn't any movement outside by the pool house."

"Pause," Mac announced and pointed at the left bottom screen at the green Land Rover. "Sig just pulled up to the front of the house."

"It's just about midnight now," Rayner announced. "Right on time."

Rayner resumed playback at normal speed so they could watch it in real time. Kane and Mac watched Sig get out of his vehicle and head into the house.

"Interesting," Kane announced. "He's entering the house close to the time the kitchen camera was cut. That puts him in close proximity to the study."

"You'd think he would have seen someone in the downstairs hallway," Scorpio added.

"Unless he's the one who cut the camera," Mac muttered, expressing what the others were thinking.

"The patio grid is about to go out," Rayner eagerly informed them.

The video feed to the back patio and pool house suddenly went out. A few seconds after that, the kitchen camera went out. They observed the rest of the video, but there was nothing to see.

Rayner shut off playback, drew a deep breath, and eyed the others. "We're downstairs by this time," he announced. "Whatever happened, we missed it."

"So the television was still on in the pool house when the patio grid went out, which has to mean the television caused the blown fuse," Kane deducted then eyed the others. "That means Conroy was electrocuted around midnight."

"So after the grid went out from the television falling into the hot tub, someone then shut off the camera to the kitchen," Scorpio remarked.

"That's strange," Mac insisted while frowning. "For what purpose? We've already established the television fell into the hot tub on its own. It wasn't pushed by someone. No one was anywhere near the pool house leading up until that time, and Conroy was definitely alone in the pool house."

"Two separate incidents?" Kane questioned.

"Possibly. I was downstairs first," Rayner informed them. "I didn't see anyone on my way to the study. Grant it; whoever shut off the kitchen camera had time to move through the house and disappear before I reached the hallway to the study."

"I think Sig is off base on this," Mac announced while shifting on Kane's lap. "I don't think Sig was the intended target."

"No one knew Sig was coming home last night," Scorpio remarked. "That has to mean they intended to kill Conroy. By Sig's own admission, both he and his daughter knew their spouses were cheating. He claims they knew and didn't care, but that could be a lie."

"As he pointed out, if Sig was the intended target, it could have been set with anticipation of him coming home this morning," Kane informed them.

"Why shut off the security system after the fuse blew out the grid?" Rayner remarked. "Who'd do that? It makes no sense."

"Maybe Emily shut it off," Mac replied and attempted to sit up on Kane's lap, although he was reluctant to release her. "Just because Sig knew she was having an affair, that doesn't mean she knew he knew. She could have shut it off so no one would see her sneaking out to the pool house to meet Conroy. I mean, why was he out there in the first place? Just felt like chilling in the hot tub?"

"We don't have the kitchen camera to support what happened after the blown fuse and prior to Scorpio and Kane finding him in the pool house," Rayner announced.

"I doubt Emily ever got that far," Kane deduced. "If she had just shut off the security system in the study, she'd be in the perfect position to see Sig pulling up outside."

"She'd have to abort her rendezvous," Rayner agreed. "Even if Sig walked in on Conroy alone in the pool house, it wouldn't prove he was waiting for Emily."

"Is there any evidence to support Conroy's death wasn't an accident?" Kane asked.

"The brackets were severely bent," Rayner replied. "I peeked through the pool house window this morning. The hot tub is against that wall. The vibration could have caused it to move enough to fall into the tub."

"Not immediately though?" Kane asked.

"It would probably take a several minutes to move it enough to cause it to fall," Rayner agreed.

"So the television probably wouldn't fall the moment someone turned on the hot tub," Kane announced.

"Probably not," Rayner replied. "We saw. He was in there a good twenty minutes before the fuse was blown knocking out the grid."

"But the vibrations alone wouldn't cause the brackets to bend. There's no way that television was heavy enough," Kane insisted. "So if someone intended to murder Sig, the wheels were already in motion earlier that evening, and our killer wouldn't even have to leave the house. Conroy slips out to the pool house to meet Emily, accesses the hot tub, and the trap is sprung."

"That also means that someone entered the pool house after we learned Sig wasn't coming home last night," Scorpio insisted and eyed her brother. "There was a chance anyone could have used that hot tub at any given time, so it had to be carefully planned."

"Not really anyone," Mac informed them. "Brandi and Jasmine have whirlpool tubs in their bathrooms. I've cleaned them. Trust me; they use them regularly. Alma told me I could use the hot tub in the evenings when Sig wasn't home because he was the only one who really used it."

"Not true," Scorpio replied. "That pool house is a bit of a man cave. Marlon tried to get me to go out there a couple of times with him. He said he uses it quite a bit when his father isn't home."

"Probably watching porn," Mac muttered and caught several stares. She glared back at the others. "What?"

"How would you know that?" Kane teased while grinning and casting a peek at her profile.

"I snuck out there and used the hot tub one night," Mac casually replied. "When I turned on the television, porn was playing."

"Hmm," Kane murmured and appeared interested. "Wonder what channel that is on my television?"

"Thirty-two," all three responded.

Kane eyed Mac, Scorpio, and Rayner, who all appeared slightly embarrassed by their quick responses. "At least we know why I'm the only one getting a good night's sleep," he remarked.

"According to Delia," Mac announced to the others. "Someone has been using that pool house as their own personal sex room. Evidence suggests someone has been regularly hooking up out there."

"Evidence?" Rayner asked.

Scorpio shifted uncomfortably since it had to be Rayner who didn't put two and two together.

"Stains on the bed sheets," Mac announced and successfully embarrassed Rayner.

Kane then turned his attention to Rayner. "Anyone entering the pool house from about noon onward?"

"Everyone was in that pool house at some point in time during the day yesterday," Rayner replied. "Including Alma and the wranglers."

"Why would the wranglers be going into the pool house?" Kane asked.

"I'm guessing for the bar," Mac teased while grinning. "I've been cleaning that place every other day since we arrived, and the liquor seems to be disappearing."

"Maybe the guys can verify if the wranglers sneak in there to raid the bar," Scorpio remarked.

"I know I do," Mac muttered.

"Speaking of the guys," Kane announced to the others. "Stone and Maverick are going to continue playing cowboys and keep an eye on Boyd. Sig agreed to keep their cover a secret from everyone but Marlon. He's also agreed to tell those within the house that Scorpio, Mac, Rayner, and I were hired as security to keep his family safe after what happened to Brandi at the mall two weeks ago."

"I'm off the hook?" Mac asked and attempted to look back at Kane from her position on his lap.

"Yes, you're officially security detail and no longer a maid," he replied.

"Fantastic," Mac announced while hiding her grin. "I'm going to the kitchen and tell off Delia."

She attempted to move off his lap, but he refused to release her.

"No, you're going to be professional and suck it up like the rest of us," Kane informed her with little emotion.

"Yeah, we'll see about that," Mac muttered and again attempted to move off his lap.

Kane placed his arm around Mac's neck and easily put her into a headlock. She attempted to wriggle free from him without physically hurting him. He rubbed his fist over the top of her head.

"You'll behave until I say otherwise," Kane announced while Mac attempted to break free.

He finally released her allowing her to spring to her feet. She frowned and fixed her hair. Kane jumped up from his chair. Mac instinctively jumped back a step and seemed suddenly defensive.

"Meeting adjourned," Kane announced.

"So do I get a nicer bedroom upstairs now?" Mac asked while grinning.

"Nope," Kane replied, surprising her.

"Why not?" she demanded as her smile faded.

"You're needed on the first floor," Kane replied. "The guys are in the bunkhouse, and the three of us are on the second floor. With you in the servant's wing, that covers all our bases."

"Oh, let her have my room," Scorpio insisted with disinterest. "Rayner and I will take her room in the servant's wing. More coverage."

"Yeah, what she said," Mac announced while grinning.

"Nope," Kane again replied and eyed Mac's profile. "I'd think you'd prefer being on the first floor with its close proximity to the kitchen." His sly grin then mocked her. "Closer to the *action.*"

Mac eyed him a moment and frowned at the dig. She then realized what he was actually saying and nodded in agreement. "Yeah, you're probably right."

Remaining in the staff wing would allow Maverick to continue sneaking into her room for their nightly rendezvous.

As Kane and Mac left the study, Rayner fiddled with Sig's computer. Scorpio stopped and looked back at him, realizing he didn't follow.

"Are you digging into Hooper's finances before breakfast?" she asked.

"Yes," Rayner replied without looking up. "I'm hoping to find something useful. If Sig was the intended target, he could still be in danger."

"Did you want me to stay?" she asked.

He waved her off and smiled. "You'll only be bored," Rayner replied. "I'll meet you in the dining room for breakfast."

Scorpio leaned down, kissed him quickly on the lips, and smiled warmly. "Have fun."

"I always do," he teased.

Chapter 51

It was six in the morning. The wranglers were having their breakfast in the kitchen while those within the house were attempting to catch up on their missing sleep from the night before. While everyone was either asleep or in the kitchen, Emily rushed around the master bedroom and quickly but silently tossed clothing into a second suitcase. The first suitcase was already packed and waiting by the bedroom door. She reached beneath the bed and removed a leather briefcase bag that had obviously been hidden. She placed the bag on the bed, unzipped it to reveal an expensive laptop computer, and took a moment to stare at it while drawing a deep breath. She zipped the bag shut, placed the briefcase inside the suitcase, and zipped it shut as well. Emily then placed a sealed envelope on the pillow with Sig's name scribbled on it.

Despite the weight of the suitcases, she was forced to carry both bags by the handles. Rolling them behind her would make too much noise even on the carpeted runner within the hallway. She'd wake the whole family. She heaved the heavy bags to the main stairs and paused to look over the banister to the grand hallway below. When she didn't see anyone, she made her slow trek down the broad staircase with both bags. It was then a short trip to the front door. Once she was outside and down the porch steps, she was able to roll the bags behind her for her awaiting car. She placed the bags in the back seat, quietly closed the door, and hurried for the driver's side. She jumped into the car, resisted shutting the door with her usual vigor, and turned the key in the ignition.

Within seconds, Emily was driving slowly down the long, dirt driveway attempting to make as little noise and dust as possible. She reached the end of the driveway and slowed her car when she saw Sig's Land Rover parked at the bottom of the driveway blocking the lane. Emily groaned with disgust while sitting behind the wheel and pondered her next move. When no one got out of the truck, she put the car into park, shut it off, and got out. She approached the back of Sig's truck while shaking her head.

"So now you suddenly care?" Emily demanded as she walked alongside the vehicle toward the driver's side. "I thought this was what you wanted? I get nothing if I divorce you, remember? Give me one good reason to stay."

Emily paused by the driver's side door and looked in through the window. The vehicle was empty with the key in the ignition. She stared at the empty vehicle a long moment while attempting to figure out what was happening. It was entirely possible Sig parked the truck at the bottom of the driveway to deter any visitors after their ordeal last night. Emily finally gave up, got inside the truck, and moved it alongside the driveway. She parked the truck and returned to her car. Emily hopped inside her car, reached for the ignition, and realized the key was missing.

"What the hell--?"

She felt her pockets then saw something move within the rearview mirror. Emily turned her head to look into the back seat. She only saw a blur as something struck her in the face.

§

Emily groaned and attempted to open her eyes. Her face was streaked with blood from the laceration on her temple from whatever had struck her. She looked around with disorientation at the dark area surrounding her within the cramped quarters. She didn't even know where she was at first.

The car's trunk lid opened, flooding the entire trunk with light and nearly blinding her. She squinted while shielding her eyes. A large burlap sack was thrown into the trunk with her. The heavy bag struck her body with enough force to make her gasp from the weight. The familiar yet terrifying rattling sound coming from the bag was almost deafening. The trunk lid slammed shut. Emily screamed as the bag seemed to move on its own against her body. She attempted to shove it away from her while pushing on the trunk lid, but it wouldn't open. She was trapped!

The partially tied bag easily opened on its own, and dozens of rattlesnakes spilled out across her and the trunk. Emily screamed as the venomous creatures angrily struck her with their fangs. The more she screamed and struggled, the more they struck her. The green Land Rover drove away leaving the abandoned car in the middle of the woods where no one would hear Emily's terrified and anguished screams.

§

The family breakfast was served promptly at eight o'clock as usual. This time, Mac was a guest rather than a server, and her wicked smile was concerning. Kane pulled a chair out for Mac alongside his and gave her a commanding look, indicating he intended to watch her closely. Scorpio eyed her watch and looked around the dining room. Rayner still hadn't arrived, and Emily was missing as well. Despite being a potentially sore subject, Brandi was the only one bold enough to question Emily's absence.

"Where's Emily?" Brandi asked her father.

Sig shifted uncomfortably at the head of the table and helped himself to the serving bowl containing scrambled eggs then passed it along.

"Still mourning her loss, I suppose," Sig announced and showed little interest in the topic. "I wouldn't know. I slept in one of the guest bedrooms."

"You didn't check on her?" Brandi pressed seeming surprised.

Sig slammed the meat platter down and glared at his youngest daughter. Several sausage links rolled from the platter and across the table.

"No, I didn't check on her," he lashed out in anger. "Should I comfort her over the loss of her lover? Would you like me to feel sorry for her?"

Brandi sheepishly looked down at her empty plate and shook her head. Rayner finally appeared in the dining room archway and motioned for Scorpio. Scorpio softly excused herself and headed for the hallway to join him.

"What's up?" she asked while keeping her voice down. "Did you find something?"

"Yes, and Sig isn't going to like it," Rayner replied and glanced past her into the dining room. Sig's bad mood was more than evident. Rayner looked back at Scorpio. "Should I wait until after breakfast?"

"Maybe you should," she replied. "He doesn't like his routine disrupted."

Sig tossed his napkin onto the table, stood, and headed for the dining room archway. Scorpio saw him approach and groaned.

"Too late," she muttered.

"What's going on?" Sig demanded with irritation. "Are you two joining us for breakfast?"

"I have some bad news and some really bad news," Rayner delicately informed him. "If you'd rather wait until after breakfast--"

"How bad?" Sig demanded with a chilling look.

"Bad," Rayner replied.

Sig motioned Scorpio and Rayner away from the dining room. All three paused halfway down the hallway and out of earshot of the others.

Sig glared at Rayner with impatience. "What is it?" he demanded.

"Conroy had been skimming money from both of your business accounts," Rayner informed him as delicately as possible. "He covered his tracks very well, but I was able to find the digital trail."

"How much?" Sig asked with concern.

Rayner drew a deep breath while staring at Sig. "Five million dollars," he replied almost timidly.

Sig stared at Rayner with surprise and horror. "Five million?" he gasped. "Son-of-a-bitch!" His look then turned demanding. "Tell me you found it."

Rayner shook his head. "I'm afraid I haven't yet," he replied. "It's possible he took that information to the grave with him."

"Did Emily know about this?" Sig growled in anger.

"I couldn't say," Rayner informed him. "He was smart. Smart men wouldn't share that sort of information. That's not the sort of thing he'd want getting around. I can't imagine he'd have told her until he'd actually gotten away with it."

"Can you find it?"

"I can keep looking," Rayner insisted. "I remember seeing him with a laptop. I'll need to find that. That would be where he'd store that sort of information."

"You can search his room for his laptop," Sig replied while attempting to control his anger.

"I'd better look for it now while Jasmine is at breakfast," Rayner insisted.

"I'll go with him," Scorpio informed Sig.

Sig nodded. "Keep me posted."

§

Scorpio entered Rayner's bedroom an hour later with a tray containing a covered plate and a carafe of coffee. Rayner sat on the bed with an older laptop before him and appeared frustrated while working on it.

"Anything?" she asked and set the tray on the bed.

"No," he replied with noted irritation.

"I brought us some leftover breakfast," Scorpio informed him. "Eat something. You'll think more clearly after you've eaten."

"Eating isn't going to help," he replied and set the laptop aside with disgust. "I'm almost positive this wasn't his laptop.

This one hasn't been accessed in months. I'm sure his was newer than this."

"Do you think it's Jasmine's laptop?" Scorpio asked as she poured him a cup of coffee then sat on the bed alongside him.

"It could be," Rayner announced with defeat. "It wasn't even password protected."

"He may have left it the last place he'd visited," Scorpio remarked. "It could be in Sig's study. You said he frequented the sunroom too. Maybe it's there."

"Maybe Emily hid it," Rayner muttered while casting a look at her.

"If she did, then that would mean she's involved," Scorpio insisted.

Rayner snapped his fingers and pointed at Scorpio. "Didn't Kane say they had a little love nest in the attic?"

"Yes, I think so," she replied and came to the same conclusion. "Maybe it's up there."

"We should check Emily's room and the attic," Rayner announced.

§

Sig sat behind the desk in his study and attempted to do some work on his desktop computer. He ended up angrily striking the keys then leaned back in his chair and stared at the ceiling with disgust. There was a light tapping on his open study door. He sat forward and looked across the room at Rayner and Scorpio where they stood in the doorway. He motioned them in with little emotion.

"Tell me you found the five million," Sig announced as he eagerly straightened.

Rayner frowned and handed Sig the envelope with his name scribbled on it. "We, uh, went to your room to look for Conroy's laptop. We thought maybe your wife had it. Emily wasn't there, but we found this."

As Sig opened the envelope, Scorpio tensed. "Her dresser drawers were open and empty," she added.

Sig read the note, snorted a laugh, and tossed it across the desk. "Good riddance," he scoffed and looked at them. "She gets nothing if she divorces me. I'm finally free from the bitch." Sig then eyed Scorpio and appeared uncomfortable. "Pardon my language."

His language was the least of Scorpio's concerns. Rayner fidgeted and took a step closer to the desk.

"There is the other matter, Sig," Rayner gently announced while skirting around upsetting the man.

Sig stared at him a moment, and his expression slowly dropped as the obvious seemed to dawn on him. "You don't think--?"

"It's possible she knew what Conroy did," Rayner delicately informed him. "I saw Conroy with a laptop when I first arrived, but I can't find it."

Sig suddenly bolted up from his chair. "You think Emily took it with her?"

Rayner tensed and made a face. "It has crossed my mind," he replied.

Sig's face was now a strange reddish color as the veins in his temples appeared ready to explode. "Find Teddy and tell him to take the truck to town to find her," he launched in anger. "I'll contact the authorities and see if we can cut her off between here and the city. There's no telling how much of a head start she has on us."

Chapter 52

It was late afternoon and still a few hours until dinner, which left the kitchen strangely quiet and abandoned. Mac entered the kitchen from the patio with a disgusted and defeated look on her face. Kane hurried down the back stairs and nearly collided with her. He appeared eager to hear the latest on the search party.

"Any word on Emily?" Kane asked.

Mac shook her head. "Teddy is on his way back from town," she announced and drew a deep breath. "She must have gone through town long before he got there. It's in the authorities' hands now."

"They have the car's license plate number," Kane remarked. "I doubt she knows how to disappear without a trace. The state police will cut her off long before she reaches Colorado Springs."

"I'm sure they'll catch her. She didn't have that much of a head start." Mac then eyed Kane and offered a tiny, humored smile. "Not babysitting?" she asked while raising her brows as she approached the refrigerator and poured a glass of iced tea for each of them.

"She's pampering this afternoon," Kane announced and smirked.

"Pampering?"

"Apparently that means taking a bubble bath, shaving her legs, and waxing her houchi," Kane announced then flashed a grin when Mac glared at him.

She shook her head while hiding her smile. "We need to work on improving your vocabulary."

Mac handed him the filled glass and leaned against the main counter. Kane hoisted himself onto the island counter facing Mac and sipped his iced tea.

"What were you up to?" he asked.

"I took another look around the pool house," she replied. "Rayner was right. The wall does vibrate when the jets are on."

"I thought they drained the hot tub when they removed Conroy's body," Kane remarked.

"They did," Mac informed him with a shrug. "But the jets still work."

"And what was your opinion of the brackets?" he pressed with a curious look on his face.

"They're pretty sturdy, relatively new, and seriously bent," she informed him then shook her head. "There's no way the vibrations alone bent them. It was a flat screen television and a small one at that. I can't see the vibrations being strong enough to do that sort of damage."

"What could bend the brackets?" he asked while raising a curious brow.

"A pair of pliers," she replied.

"Pliers," Kane announced and sighed with defeat. "The kind that every single wrangler carries around?"

"Yeah, that kind."

"Did Maverick mention seeing any of the wranglers visiting the pool house?" Kane asked.

She cast a look at him. "I didn't see Maverick," Mac announced. "He's working the herd."

"Ah."

Mac stared at him a moment then frowned and groaned. "You have something to say?" she demanded while folding her arms across her chest. "Say it."

"There's nothing to say. If you and Maverick have a thing, it's none of my business," he replied while shrugging. "If it affects the job, or he mistreats you; then and only then does it become my business."

"We don't have a *thing*," she insisted then avoided looking at him. "It's just, well--"

Kane held his hands innocently in the air while staring at her. "Mac, not the moral police here. You don't need to explain anything to me," he insisted and shook his head. "I should learn to knock, so I don't walk in on another cucumber again."

Mac rolled her eyes and groaned. "I knew that was going to come up," she muttered.

"Imagine how I felt," he announced and gave her a wide-eyed stare. "I'm not sure how I feel about cucumbers anymore."

She shook her head and turned away to avoid looking at him. Kane chuckled lowly in his throat and grinned at her discomfort.

"You're happier now than you were when I first met you," Kane announced. "That's all that matters."

Mac cast a look at him but couldn't meet his gaze. "I wouldn't say I'm happier; just, well, less miserable," she admitted. "Honestly, I prefer my men dark and sinister, but my options are limited. At least I don't need to worry about Maverick getting attached."

"Why do you do that to yourself?" Kane asked while shaking his head.

She cast a look at him. "Do what?"

"Shut yourself off from emotions," Kane replied and jumped off the counter. "It's as if you think you don't deserve to be happy."

"Because it doesn't pay to have emotional attachments," she informed him. "Eventually, everyone turns on you or leaves. It's just the way it is."

"I've got my work cut out," Kane announced while sighing deeply then eyed her. "I know what *will* help."

"No," Mac scoffed as her eyes widened, and she held up her hand defensively.

Kane grinned, opened his arms, and approached her. "My little badger needs a hug."

"I don't want to be hugged," she insisted and attempted to avoid his arms. "And I wish you'd stop calling me your little badger."

He ignored her, placed his arms around her, and gave her a big, affectionate hug. Despite that she didn't resist, she didn't return the embrace either. She groaned with annoyance by his enthusiasm.

"You need professional help," she muttered as he enjoyed the long, one-sided hug.

"Shh," he announced in an almost serious tone while holding her in his arms. "You're counteracting the effects of the hug." He pulled back just far enough to meet her gaze and grinned. "All better?"

Mac groaned and rolled her eyes. "Yeah, I'm all better," she muttered.

Kane affectionately kissed her forehead and released her. He backed up to the island counter and again heaved himself onto it with little effort.

"While Brandi is self-pampering, what can we do to maximize my free time?" he asked while studying Mac. "Let's solve this riddle."

"I'd like to take a peek inside Delia's room again," Mac remarked.

Kane groaned and placed his hand to his eyes. "Come on, Mac," he announced then looked at her. "Let it go with Delia. I hate when you turn into a girl and get all catty."

"It's not being catty," she huffed hotly. "The day we found Conroy and Emily in their attic love nest, I came back downstairs for my watch. When I passed Delia's room, I heard her entertaining someone."

Kane appeared interested. "Late morning?" he asked while raising his brows. "Rayner, Conroy, and I were the only men in the house. Who could she possibly have been entertaining that time of day?"

"That's what I'd like to know," Mac remarked. "Either one of the wranglers snuck back inside, or she had a visitor from somewhere else."

"Okay, that is interesting," Kane announced. "Where is she in her work routine this time of day?"

"She'll be cleaning the downstairs rooms for a few hours," Mac informed him. "There was a messenger bag in her closet. I thought about rummaging through it, but she didn't seem suspicious at the time."

"Well, let's go have a look around her room," Kane announced with enthusiasm. "If we tag team it, we can search her room in under fifteen minutes."

Chapter 53

Kane slipped inside Delia's room with Mac only a step behind him. He shut the door and immediately headed for the closet with Mac on his heels. He opened the closet door, looked around, and found the messenger bag Mac had mentioned. Kane opened the bag then hesitated.

"Is this considered a purse?" he asked.

Mac groaned and snatched the bag from him. "Give it a rest," she snapped. "We both know you're not nearly the gentleman you pretend to be."

"Now that hurt," Kane huffed.

Mac handed him Delia's passport while she continued to route through the bag. Kane opened the passport and appeared curious.

"Nothing before Costa Rica, huh?" Kane remarked.

"She was young when she and her mother moved out of the country," Mac reminded him.

"I wonder how much of a bastard a father has to be to warrant moving to Costa Rica just to get away from the prick," Kane scoffed.

Mac eyed him with some surprise and raised her brows. "Daddy issues?"

"Scorpio and I never knew our parents," he reminded her. "They died shortly after we were born, remember?"

"Yeah, sorry," Mac muttered. "Honestly, though, I would have preferred that to my parents. My father was like a tomcat. Just came around to fulfill his sexual needs and leave my mother with another child she didn't need, want, or love."

Kane stared at Mac a moment and appeared saddened by her words. "She abandoned you?"

"Worse," Mac responded while routing through the bag without looking at him. "She ignored us except when she needed money for booze. Then we'd run drugs for some guy she knew."

Kane couldn't take his eyes off Mac despite that she continued with her mission. "Considering your fighting skills, someone must have trained you. You don't just pick that up on the streets."

"Things got worse at home, so I went to live with my aunt," Mac informed him and shrugged. "She seemed to be living the good life, or so it seemed. Turns out she was dating a hitman for the mob." She snorted a laugh. "Ironically, he treated my aunt better than my father ever treated my mother. I was fifteen when he introduced me to his boss, who gave me a job. One of the guys took a liking to me and taught me everything he knew."

"Everything?" Kane asked and seemed uncomfortable by the question.

She cast a look at him and raised her brows. "Yes, *everything*," Mac insisted, having gathered his meaning. "My morals had been corrupted long before that, I assure you. He was the first man who treated me like I mattered. At the time, that's what I needed most. After he was killed, things just sort of went downhill from there."

Mac returned the passport to the bag then looked up and saw the way Kane was staring at her. It obviously hit him hard. She managed a humored smile and was about to speak when they heard someone in the hallway outside the door. Kane and Mac exchanged concerned looks.

"No," Mac whispered.

They heard the bedroom doorknob rotate. Kane shoved Mac into the closet and darted in behind her. He no sooner shut the closet door when someone entered the bedroom. Mac and Kane moved behind the hanging clothes and hid near the back of the closet. They exchanged looks in the dimly lit closet. Both shook their heads and shrugged. Shoes were heard thumping against the floor. Kane took a step closer to the louvered bi-fold door and peered between the slats. Delia crossed the bedroom in the direction of the closet. Kane leaped behind the hanging clothes with Mac.

"It's Delia," he mouthed to her and pointed frantically at the door.

They heard her approach the closet. Kane pressed Mac tightly into the corner to put them as far out of view as possible and shut his eyes while anticipating the closet door opening. The door never opened. They then heard Delia enter the bathroom. Both sighed with relief.

"Let's get out of here," Mac whispered and took a step for the closet door.

They heard the bedroom door open, surprising them. Mac jumped back, colliding with Kane, and pushed him back a step. She glared demandingly and pointed at the door. Kane moved past her and again peered through the slats. Boyd entered the bedroom.

"Delia?" Boyd called out.

"Be right out," she called back from the bathroom.

Kane again moved closer to Mac and rolled his eyes. "It's Boyd."

"He's supposed to be working," she insisted.

He made a face and motioned with his hands as if commenting 'no kidding'. "Must be something important," Kane whispered.

Both moved to the side of the closet door, kept close to the wall, and listened. With the louvered doors, their conversation would easily be heard. They heard Delia return from the bathroom.

"Anyone see you?" she asked.

"No," he replied. "Did you hear anything about Conroy's death?"

"I don't want to discuss that," Delia huffed with irritation. "I only got two hours sleep, and now I'm working alone again with a houseful of guests."

"What happened to Mac?" Boyd asked.

"Turns out the bitch was one of Sig's spies," Delia snarled in response.

Mac eyed Kane, demandingly raised her brows, and pointed accusingly at the door. Kane frowned, caught her finger, and lowered it with disinterest.

"Catty," he muttered.

They didn't hear any sounds. Kane pulled Mac closer to him and the wall as he stared at the closet door with concern. It was possible one of them heard them in the closet. Kane mouthed 'shh' to her. Both held their breath and remained motionless while listening for someone to approach the closet and find them. When they didn't hear anything, Kane tensed, feeling the need to take a peek. He attempted to peer through the louvers. Mac poked him and gestured in question with her hand. He shrugged in response.

"They're sitting on the bed talking, I think," he whispered to her.

"Must be something good," Mac responded and lowered herself before the door to have a look for herself. She cast a look back at Kane. "I think she's crying."

Mac straightened, unable to see anything, and moved back against Kane alongside the door. They remained quietly within the closet and attempted to listen for any sounds indicating why Delia might be crying. The bed creaked. Both jumped with alarm. It was possible they were leaving the room or even approaching the closet. The bed creaked again. Now they were both off the bed. Kane and Mac listened for the bedroom door, but they didn't hear it. The bed creaked again. False alarm. Kane groaned, moved Mac aside, and peered through the louvers to check on their status. Through the slats, Kane saw Boyd's naked buttocks with a woman's legs wrapped around them. Kane jumped back with horror and stared at the closet door as if unable to move. Mac stared at him with confusion.

"What?" she whispered.

Kane just stared at the closet door a moment then looked through the louvers again. He jumped back, grabbed Mac, and pulled her away from the doors.

"He's screwing his sister," Kane gasped.

Mac stared at him with a strange look then made a face. "Get out," she huffed then pulled away and decided to look for herself.

As she peered through the slates, Mac's eyes suddenly widened. She practically leaped onto Kane and frantically pointed at the closet door.

"Oh, my God," she whispered while gesturing wildly.

They could clearly hear female moans and male grunts through the slats in the closet door.

Kane pinched his eyes shut and placed his hands over his ears while mouthing, "No, no, no!"

Mac cringed as the bed creaked loudly in rhythm with the male and female groans of pleasure. She moved alongside him, pressed her back against the wall, and attempted to block out the sounds that seemed even louder now. She clutched Kane's arm and just about ripped it out of its socket while gesturing wildly at the closet door. Kane attempted to bury his face against Mac's neck.

"Make it stop," he whispered several times. "It's his sister. That's his sister!"

Mac pulled his face into her chest, so his muttered words were inaudible. She gently shushed him while running her fingers through his hair in an attempt to keep him quiet. The headboard slammed against the wall, and the sounds of bodies slapping against each other were clearly heard above the loud groans. Kane gently banged his forehead against Mac's chest to eliminate the sound of the headboard banging against the wall. There was a loud male groan from Boyd. Kane lifted his head and stared at the ceiling.

"Thank God," Kane whispered.

Delia groaned loudly from the bedroom. "I love the way you fuck me."

Kane again buried his head into Mac's chest while softly whimpering. Within a few minutes, they heard Boyd and Delia leaving the room.

"Is it over?" Kane asked without moving away from Mac and kept his face buried in her chest.

She patted his head almost affectionately. "Yes, it's over," Mac gently replied while seemingly mothering him.

Kane pulled away from her, attempted to compose himself, and then cast a look at her. "You go first," he muttered as if unable to find the courage.

Mac opened the closet door and stepped out. Kane peeked out of the closet, made sure the coast was clear, and then joined her.

"His sister," Kane muttered and shook his head while vigorously raking his fingers through his thick hair while just about pulling it out. "I'd cut off my pecker before I'd touch my sister."

"Don't gouge out your eyes just yet," Mac announced and cast a glance at him. "Think about everything we know, and what we don't know about Delia. What if she's not really his sister?"

Kane gingerly rubbed his stomach. "My stomach would be grateful."

"We need to find Rayner," Mac insisted now deep in thought. "He can dig a little deeper into Delia's past."

Mac headed for the door. Kane caught her arm, surprising her, and forced her to face him.

"I'm sorry for calling you catty," he announced and shook his head. "You had every right to be suspicious of Delia. I won't doubt your instincts ever again."

"Well, I guess that fifteen minutes of torture was totally worth it," Mac remarked.

"Not for me," he muttered. "I'm scarred for life."

Chapter 54

Kane entered the sunroom where Scorpio and Rayner hovered over his laptop set up on the coffee table. Kane was still worked up over what he'd seen earlier in Delia's bedroom and had excessive amounts of energy. He appeared ready to burst.

"It's just about dinnertime," Kane announced to them, although neither bothered to look up. "Did you find anything? Please tell me you found something."

"No," Rayner replied and shook his head. "I've been digging around for over an hour. I can't find anything on Delia's boating accident."

"Is that in itself proof that Delia Flint doesn't exist?" Kane asked with a glimmer of hope. "He obviously made up the entire sister story, right?"

"Finding nothing doesn't necessarily mean anything," Rayner insisted without looking up. "The story may not have received much coverage overseas. Boyd's mother may have resumed using her maiden name. There are any number of reasons why I can't find anything on their accident."

"I need to confront him," Kane blurted out while shaking his head. "I need to just throw it out there and deal with whatever happens."

"Just give us a little more time," Scorpio insisted and finally looked at her brother. "If you confront him, he'll have time to cover his tracks. We need evidence of something first. Even if she really is his sister, incest doesn't prove murder. We need proof of murder."

"I know; I know," Kane fired back and nervously paced. "But he'll be at dinner with Brandi. She's going to be all lovey with him, and I'm going to snap." He considered the comment. "Or throw up." Kane shook his head with conviction. "I need to say something to Brandi."

"You can't," Scorpio protested and shot up from her seat. She attempted to stop Kane from pacing and bring him down a notch. "If you say something to her, Boyd goes on the defensive. We need them to continue their usual routine if we're going to get anywhere."

"I can't just let her cozy up to him," Kane insisted while his arms flailed. "She needs to be warned. I need to tell her the truth."

"How about a version of the truth?" Scorpio asked. "Can you reason with her? Does she trust you enough to back off and give you time to investigate this?"

"I don't know," Kane grumbled and again vigorously raked his fingers through his hair. "I'm going to talk to her." He shifted his attention to Rayner, who continued to work. "Find something; anything."

§

Kane stood outside Brandi's bedroom door shortly before dinner, gathered his courage, and then gently tapped on the door. He still remained tense and couldn't seem to figure out what to do with his hands.

"Come in," Brandi called out from the other side.

Kane drew a deep breath and entered Brandi's bedroom. She lay across her bed looking more like a carefree teenager than a woman who intended to get married in a few weeks. Brandi said goodbye to her friend on the computer screen and shut the laptop lid. She saw Kane and quickly sat up with some disappointment.

"Oh, I thought you were Boyd," she announced then managed a smile. "Is dinner ready early?"

"Uh, no," he replied and sat on the bench at the foot end of the bed. "I needed to talk to you about something important."

Her look turned serious. "Okay."

"I--" He hesitated. "The team and I have some concerns about Boyd."

"Concerns?"

"We--" He again hesitated and seemed to choose his words carefully. "I have good reason to believe he has another woman on the side."

Brandi stared at him with surprise. She managed a smile then laughed. Her smile then turned to concern. "What?" She shook her head. "No, you're mistaken."

Kane drew a deep breath and nervously raked his fingers through his hair. "Brandi--" He stared at her through innocent blue eyes. "Can you honestly think of any reason why I'd lie to you?"

She stared back at him and was uncertain what to say. Brandi shifted uncomfortably. It was difficult to tell if she believed him or not.

"Why do you think he's cheating on me?" she finally blurted out while insecurely folding her arms across her chest as she stared at him.

Kane appeared to be racing for an answer that wasn't exactly the truth. "You told me the night Conroy died you didn't meet with Boyd."

"I didn't," she replied.

"We saw him sneaking into the house on the security video around eleven o'clock," Kane admitted, which technically was the truth.

"Maybe he went to see his sister," Brandi quickly responded.

Kane grimaced at the thought and subconsciously placed his hand to his stomach. "Around that same time," he announced and tried to keep from cringing at what he was about to say, "I went to see Mac. She was *entertaining* someone in the shower."

Brandi shifted and became uncomfortable. "It could have been one of the other wranglers," she insisted.

"I don't think so," Kane gently replied. He then shifted on the bench seat. "You told me you and Boyd had never--" He was unable to finish the sentence.

"We agreed to wait until our wedding night," she announced and suddenly seemed concerned. "I told you I've never been with anyone. When he'd sneak into my room, we'd just cuddle."

"Maybe Boyd couldn't wait," Kane delicately informed her while raising his brows.

Brandi managed a nervous smile. "No," she insisted. "I mean; I originally suggested waiting until our wedding night, but I was willing to nix the idea. He convinced me we should wait. If he wanted to scratch an itch, he knows I would have been onboard."

Kane shifted and roughly rubbed his eyes at her words. It somehow even made more sense with what she was telling him. Boyd didn't want to have sex with Brandi, which would explain the kidnapping attempts. Delia and Boyd were after Sig's money. Somehow, Conroy got involved, and they needed to silence him. Brandi tensed and shifted.

"If I were willing, he wouldn't go to someone else, right?" Brandi asked with some insecurity, snapping Kane out of his thoughts. "You must be mistaken."

"There's a lot of information floating around right now," Kane insisted while staring into her eyes with sympathy. "I'll get to the bottom of it, I promise."

"Maybe I should ask him--"

"No, let me handle it," Kane insisted. "After what happened to Conroy, I don't want you anywhere near this until I've straightened it out."

"Conroy's death was an accident," she insisted.

"A very convenient accident," Kane remarked and again pleaded with her. "Please, Brandi. Let me handle this. All I'm asking from you is some distance between you and Boyd for now."

"Distance?" she practically gasped. "You want me to break up with him?"

"No, I want you to develop a headache and just avoid him for a few days," Kane announced and straightened while giving her a serious look. "If he puts his hands on you right now, I'm liable to hurt him."

Brandi stared at him a moment then suddenly smiled and appeared almost giddy. "Oh, I get it," she announced while nodding. "You've developed a little crush on me, and you're trying to come between Boyd and me." Brandi reached out, placed her hand on his leg, and smiled. "I'm flattered, Kane, but I'm marrying Boyd."

Kane groaned with frustration. "I don't have a crush on you," he insisted. "I just--" His eyes pleaded with her. "Just avoid Boyd for a day or two. Come down with the flu, PMS, PTSD. I don't care. Just avoid him until I can figure this out. Do this for me. Please, I'm begging you."

Brandi frowned and groaned. "Fine," she scoffed while rolling her eyes. "I'll avoid him for a day." Her look turned demanding. "One day." She wagged her finger at him in a demanding manner. "You talk to your friend, Mac. Find out what happened and get back to me. If it's true, you can beat him up for me."

Kane stood and grinned. "It will be my pleasure," he announced then kissed her quickly on the forehead. "I appreciate this."

She rolled her eyes and nodded. "Yeah, whatever," she muttered. "You paranoid freak." Brandi opened her laptop lid. "Tell everyone I wasn't feeling well and couldn't come down for dinner." She then glared at him demandingly. "You'd better bring me my dinner. I'm already starving."

"You've got it," Kane announced and headed for the bedroom door.

Chapter 55

Kane's bedroom was dimly lit by the glow of the television that softly played while he slept on top of the covers. He hadn't even bothered undressing except he'd removed his shoes so he'd be somewhat comfortable. His hand radio crackled from the nightstand.

"Kane," came Stone's familiar voice over the radio. "You copy?"

Kane jumped awake and snatched the radio from his nightstand. He flopped onto his back and groaned before responding. "Yeah, Stone," he replied. "I copy."

"Our boy just left the bunkhouse," Stone announced over the radio.

"Roger that," Kane replied in a weary tone. "Rayner? You copy that?"

"I have visual," Rayner replied. "He's heading for the kitchen door now."

"Should I intercept?" Mac asked over the radio.

"No," Kane replied while scratching his mussed hair. "Rayner installed a spy cam in Delia's room."

"Uhg," Mac gasped over the hand radio.

"I need proof before we confront him," Kane insisted. "This is the only way. Rayner, let me know when you have creepy sister sex recorded."

"I don't have to watch, do I?" Rayner groaned over the radio in response.

"Just enough to identify them," Kane insisted. He then heard movement on the second floor and became alerted. "Someone is in the second floor hallway. I need to investigate. Keep me posted."

Kane sprang from his bed and crept to the door. He opened the door just enough to peer into the second floor hallway. Jasmine headed down the hall toward the back kitchen stairs. Kane placed the earbud in his ear and attached the hand radio to his belt. He pressed a button.

"Jasmine is heading downstairs to the kitchen," Kane announced and slipped from the bedroom. "If she intercepts him, this mission is scrubbed."

"Maybe she's meeting him," Stone announced over Kane's earbud.

"Let me know the moment Boyd enters Delia's room," Kane announced softly as he approached the back stairs. "I'm following Jasmine."

Kane waited until he was certain Jasmine had reached the kitchen before creeping down the back stairs.

"Hold up, Kane," Stone announced over his earbud from outside the house. "I have visual on Jasmine. She's heading for the pool house."

"Can you get there and spy?" Kane asked while remaining posted at the top of the stairs. "We need visual on what she's doing in there. It could be important."

"Heading there now," Stone replied.

"I have visual on Jasmine heading inside the pool house," Rayner announced over the radio in Kane's ear. "Stone is a few clicks from there."

"Guys," Maverick suddenly announced over the hand radio. "Teddy has left the bunkhouse and is heading toward the main house."

"Stone, I have a visual on Teddy. He's coming your way," Rayner announced. "Hide."

"Ah, hell--" Stone gasped in a whisper.

Kane was heading down the back stairs then stopped and listened. "Stone?"

"He's hiding in the bushes," Rayner announced over the radio in his ear. "I suspect he's maintaining radio silence. I have visual on Teddy heading for the pool house. It would appear Jasmine has a hot date tonight."

Kane groaned and continued down the back stairs. "Stone, can you play peeping Tom and confirm that the pool house is a hookup hotspot and not the killer returning to the scene of the crime?"

"Yeah, I'm on it," Stone replied.

"Rayner," Kane announced as he reached the bottom of the stairs. "Do you have visual on our friend?"

"Negative," Rayner replied. "Boyd hasn't entered Delia's room yet. She's still asleep."

Kane stepped into the dimly lit kitchen and looked around. There was no sign of Boyd.

"He's not here," Kane whispered while touching his ear containing the earbud. "Anything?"

"No, nothing," Rayner replied.

"There's no one in the staff wing hallway. It's quiet here," Mac informed them from her end. "Are you in the kitchen, Kane?"

"Yeah, I'm here," he replied while looking around then headed for the main door. "I'm going to check the security system in the study. Maybe he went there to kill the video feed."

"Counterproductive," Rayner remarked. "We already have him on video entering the house. Why cut the video now?"

"Where the hell else would he have gone?" Kane muttered and left the kitchen.

The grand hallway was mostly dark except for some moonlight shining in through the windows alongside the main door. Kane approached the study and looked inside. The room was dark and empty. He turned on the light and took a closer look around.

"Launch sequence has begun," Stone announced over the radio and chuckled deviously. "And Teddy is clear for takeoff. Yep, the Uranus mission is a go."

"Thanks for the graphics," Mac snarled from her end in response to Stone.

"Anytime, Mac," Stone teased from his end and laughed. "Anytime."

"Are you sure he's not in Delia's room?" Kane demanded while heading from the study and looked around. "He's not down here."

"No, he's not in her room," Rayner insisted.

"Kane," Scorpio suddenly chimed in over his earbud. "Are you on second?"

"No, I'm on first," he replied casually then raised a cocky brow and grinned. "What's on second."

"I don't know's on third," Mac teased in response.

"That's my badger," Kane announced into the radio with a chuckle.

"Don't encourage him, Mac," Scorpio responded over Kane's ear transmitter. "I hear someone in the hall up here."

Kane hurried for the grand stairs. "I'm on my way up," he announced to his sister through his radio. "Do me a favor and take a peek."

Kane quietly ran up the stairs two at a time, reached the landing, and entered the second floor hallway. Scorpio stood in the hallway, locked eyes with her brother, and shrugged. Kane frowned and hurried along the hall for Brandi's room. He paused before the bedroom door, drew a deep breath, and lightly knocked on the door.

"Brandi, it's Kane," he announced softly through the door. "Can I come in?"

There was no response. Kane cursed under his breath and tapped again.

"Brandi, it's Kane," he boldly announced. "I'm coming in."

Kane opened the door, which wasn't locked, and entered Brandi's dimly lit bedroom. Her bed was rumpled but remained empty. Scorpio approached Kane and peered into the bedroom as he hurried for the open bathroom door. He spun to face his sister.

"She's not here," he announced then pushed the button on his hand radio. "Rayner, keep eyes on Delia's room and visual on the front of the house. Maverick, Stone; keep watch on the back door. Brandi is missing. Anyone have eyes on Brandi or Boyd?"

"Want me to search the first floor?" Mac asked over his radio.

"Yes, you take the first floor." Kane then turned to face his sister. "Take the kitchen stairs. She may have gone that way while I was heading up the front stairs. I'll look around up here."

Scorpio nodded and left the room with Kane. They nearly collided with Sig as he appeared from his bedroom.

"What's going on?" Sig demanded while tightening his robe sash. "Did something happen?"

"Boyd snuck into the house," Kane informed the intimidating man. "While I was looking for him, Brandi went missing from her room."

"Missing?" Sig cried out. "Do you think someone took her?"

"Mac is searching the first floor for her," Kane informed him while listening for any comments through his earbud. "Rayner and the guys have eyes on every entrance. Whether of her own free will or not, she's not getting out of this house without our knowledge."

"Search the empty bedrooms," Sig commanded then hurried down the hall. "I'll wake Marlon."

Kane paused before the partially open attic door and stared at it a moment while Scorpio paused near him. Sig shouted at Marlon from his bedroom doorway.

"Wake up," Sig cried out in anger. "We need to find your sister!"

Scorpio eyed her brother with a curious look. "What is it?"

Kane suddenly groaned and opened the door the rest of the way. "I have a bad feeling--"

He quietly hurried up the steps with Scorpio only a few feet behind him. As they walked along the attic, they heard the familiar sound of the bed creaking. Kane immediately stopped and groaned, allowing his head to fall into his hands. Scorpio hurried past him, stopped, and gasped. Sig and Marlon appeared in the attic and approached Kane. Marlon looked bedraggled and half-asleep.

"What happened?" Marlon asked with concern. "Is she okay?"

"I'm guessing they're getting a jump start on the honeymoon," Kane announced and attempted to herd them back for the steps.

"I'll say," Scorpio muttered and rubbed her eyes after what she'd seen.

"I'm going to kill him," Sig announced in anger.

Kane forced him to turn and head back for the attic steps. "Yeah, you and me both."

Chapter 56

Tuesday, July 8th. Morning. Kane hurried down the grand staircase after Brandi, caught her arm, and forced her into the nearby lounge. She cried out with surprise and spun to face him as he shut the door giving them some privacy.

"What gives?" she demanded.

Kane was clearly annoyed as he glared at her. "What happened to our deal?" he launched hotly. "You were going to keep your distance from Boyd."

Brandi folded her arms across her chest and glared back at him. "I talked to him after dinner," she scoffed.

"You weren't at dinner," Kane insisted.

"He has internet on his tablet," she remarked. "We chatted on facetime." Brandi sneered at Kane. "He denied ever having sex with Mac. He thinks you're in love with me, and you're purposely trying to break us up to have me for yourself."

"No," Kane insisted defensively. "That's not true. You have to believe me, Brandi."

"Considering you and your friends lied to me from the time you got here, I think I'd choose to believe him over you," Brandi snapped then raised an angry brow. "I didn't disregard everything you said though. I tested him. I told him if he loved me and he was telling the truth, he'd have no problem sleeping with me before the wedding. He thought you might try to stop us from sleeping together, so we agreed to meet in the attic bedroom. Looks like he was right. You did try to stop us."

Kane shook his head and appeared at a loss for words. "I tried to stop you from making a mistake," he insisted. "I'm looking out for you."

"If he didn't love me, he wouldn't have agreed to have sex with me," she informed him.

Kane stared at her in disbelief and shook his head. "What the hell sort of talk is that?" he demanded. "Are you hearing yourself?"

"Kindly stay out of my relationship," Brandi huffed and left the lounge.

Kane allowed his head to fall into his hands as he groaned. "Ignorance is bliss."

§

Brandi entered the dining room with her head held high, ignored her father's patronizing glare, and flopped into her chair. Kane entered a moment or two after her while rubbing his temple and took his seat alongside Scorpio, who glanced at him with question in her eyes. Sig glared at his youngest daughter, frowned with annoyance, and shook his head. Jasmine eyed those within the excessively quiet dining room.

"Did I miss something?" Jasmine asked.

"It's nothing," Sig muttered while Alma and Delia placed the serving plates onto the center of the table.

"No, Daddy," Brandi announced displaying her own anger. "I'm practically a married woman now, and I see no shame in what I did." Brandi proudly glanced around the table. "Last night, I gave Boyd my virginity."

There was an uncomfortable silence followed by the shattering of a plate. All eyes were suddenly on Delia, who fumbled to clean up the broken china and bacon scattered along the floor. Kane and Scorpio exchanged curious looks. It was obvious Delia had issues with Boyd and Brandi prematurely consummating their upcoming marriage. Was she jealous? Did that mean Delia didn't anticipate the wedding ever happening? If that were the case, Brandi's abduction suddenly made more sense. Sig tossed his napkin down on the table, abruptly stood, and left the room without a word.

§

A little after eight o'clock that morning, Maverick entered the bunkhouse while Stone paused within the doorway and took a lookout position.

"Make it fast," Stone announced while watching out the door. "The guys are busy, but we don't know how long it'll be before Jasmine or Marlon show up after breakfast."

Maverick hurried to Boyd's footlocker at the end of his bunk near the fireplace. "They're usually not out of the house until eight-thirty or nine o'clock," he insisted and crouched before the trunk.

Maverick opened the footlocker and briefly rummaged through it. He found the book and removed the letter. Despite watching the door, Stone cast several looks at Maverick as he opened the letter and read it.

"What does it say?" Stone asked.

"Give me a minute, will you," Maverick demanded while skimming the letter.

Maverick stood and held up the letter while looking at Stone. "I'm not sure if this is what we're looking for," he informed his friend, "but it certainly looks like Delia's handwriting."

"It's her handwriting?" Stone asked with surprise while raising his brows.

"From the sample we saw, I'd stake my life on it," Maverick replied.

"You have a name?"

"I have a name," he replied then replaced the book and stuffed the letter in his jacket pocket.

Stone stared at him with surprise. "You're taking it?" he demanded.

Maverick shut the footlocker and hurried across the bunkhouse for Stone. "Yeah, I'm taking it," he replied. "If it turns out she's not who she says she is, we'll need this as evidence."

"You better hope so," Stone replied. "Let's get that to Rayner."

"I'll slip it to Mac," Maverick informed him as they left the bunkhouse and headed across the property.

Stone eyed Maverick, shook his head, and followed his friend toward the house. "Just make sure that's all you slip Mac," he scoffed.

Maverick glared at his friend. "Are you suggesting something?" he demanded with some annoyance.

"You've been banging Mac since we got here," Stone snapped back as they headed toward the house. "I know because you're less of a prick when you get laid regularly."

"Not that it's any of your business," Maverick scoffed and avoided looking at his friend.

"No, it's not any of my business," Stone replied while casting a look at him. "I'm just not sure if Mac is the type of woman you want to be messing with."

"We have an understanding," Maverick informed him. "I know what I'm doing."

Stone snorted a laugh, grinned, and shook his head. "I'm not buying that shit," he announced. "Play with fire, man. That's all I'm saying."

"It's just a casual thing," Maverick insisted while shrugging. "We both agreed on that."

"Casual?" Stone remarked and eyed his friend. "Bullshit. If it were casual, you wouldn't be gone for hours. You're burning the midnight oil with that one, and then she's going to burn you."

"Does it matter?" Maverick demanded while eyeing his friend. "Everything goes back to the way it was when we return to Maine with Scorpio."

"And we are returning to Maine," Stone insisted firmly. "We stick together, and we stick with Scorpio. I'm not ruining my chance for a home and a family because you've fallen for another hard luck case."

"I'm not falling for Mac," Maverick insisted and considered the comment. "The sex is great, that's all."

"Good, because you do this all the time," Stone replied with some annoyance. "You fall in love with someone incapable of loving you back, and then I have to listen to you cry in your beer."

"I'm not falling for Mac," Maverick announced with more conviction.

"We stick with our original plan," Stone reminded him.

"The hotel in Maine," Maverick agreed.

"If you have a sudden change of heart though," Stone announced and cast a look at Maverick. "I want you to know the deal is off. I'm making a play for Scorpio."

"As if she's giving up the geek for you," Maverick scoffed and rolled his eyes. "Be real."

"I could win her over in a heartbeat," Stone insisted with conviction then glared at Maverick. "You just stick to our plan, and no one gets their hearts broken."

"I'm not deviating from our plan," Maverick again announced. "Mac and I are finished when this assignment is over."

Chapter 57

Kane stood outside Delia's bedroom within the staff wing corridor while keeping watch. Mac appeared from the maid's bedroom and slapped Delia's passport against Kane's chest. He caught the passport and eyed Mac.

"Big baby," she scoffed and headed across the hall into her room.

Kane hurried into her room after her, shutting the door behind him. Rayner sat on Mac's bed with his laptop and typed frantically on the keyboard. Scorpio handed Kane the letter they'd received from Maverick, allowing him to compare the signatures.

"I'm pretty sure these match," Kane announced.

Rayner stopped typing and held out his hand. Kane handed him the passport and the letter, which contained different names, although the handwriting appeared similar.

"I think they're close enough," Rayner remarked then returned them to Kane. He pressed another button on his keyboard and watched the computer screen with great interest. He threw his hands in the air with enthusiasm. "We have a winner."

Scorpio jumped onto the bed alongside him and peered at the computer screen.

"Casandra and Delia Frommer?" Scorpio remarked and eyed Rayner.

"Apparently, Boyd's mother resumed her maiden name after the divorce and changed her daughter's name as well," Rayner informed them while studying the screen. "That's why I couldn't find anything on Delia Flint."

Kane sat on the edge of the bed to Rayner's right and eyed the screen as well. "Lost at sea," he read from the article. "Missing persons." He eyed Rayner. "Were their bodies ever found?"

"No," Rayner replied then pulled up another screen. "But check out this."

Mac climbed on the bed behind him to see the screen as well. All four stared at the photo of the thirteen-year-old girl then exchanged surprised looks.

"Is that supposed to be Delia as a girl?" Kane asked.

"That's Boyd's sister as a young teenager," Rayner informed him.

"Not much to look at, huh?" Mac muttered and shook her head. "You can't possibly tell me that was her as a girl."

"She's not Boyd's sister," Rayner deducted then removed the letter from Kane.

"Thank God," Kane gasped with relief as his shoulders sagged. "I can wipe those images from my head and not gouge out my eyes."

"Clara," Rayner read the name signed on the love letter. "Delia is Clara. But who is Clara?"

"Think you can figure it out?" Kane asked.

"Just a first name is asking a lot," Rayner insisted while casting a look at Kane. "This letter is dated around the time Delia was miraculously resurrected from the dead. The passport was created around the same time." He indicated the passport. "Boyd helped perpetrate the hoax abroad in Costa Rica, which means Clara needed to get out of Costa Rica."

"If she didn't use her own identity," Mac announced while eyeing the others, "it has to mean her identity is tainted. The woman is wanted for something. Clara has a record."

"You're probably right," Kane replied without looking back at Mac. "Why go through all that trouble otherwise?"

"So she was hiding in Costa Rica, met Boyd, and he introduced her as his missing sister," Scorpio announced.

"Then he secures all the proper identification in his sister's name, and they return to the United States as brother and sister," Rayner added. "She's been living as Delia the last three years. We need to find out her true identity. We need to know Clara's last name."

"If she's wanted, her fingerprints will be all the authorities need," Kane insisted.

"Are we ready to call them?" Mac asked and shifted looks at the others. "We don't have a lot. Even if she and Boyd were behind Conroy's electrocution, it's been ruled an accidental death."

"She's right," Rayner remarked and eyed Kane. "If we call the police out here with little evidence and they can't take her in, she and Boyd are going to take off."

"Can we run fingerprints?" Kane asked Rayner.

"In today's digital world? Of course, we can," Rayner replied. "I can hack into the computer system of a fingerprint registration center somewhere in Colorado Springs, make up a phony business account, and submit Delia's fingerprints for a legal FBI background check. I should get the results in twenty-four hours."

"And how do we get Delia's fingerprints?" Scorpio asked while raising her brow.

"That's a little more tricky," Rayner replied. "I need a full set on a glass surface."

"Both hands?" Mac asked.

Rayner glanced back at her and nodded.

"That's going to be tough," Kane muttered as he sank into thought.

Mac leaned over Kane's shoulder and grinned slyly. "How badly do you want her fingerprints?" she cooed almost seductively.

Kane cast a look back at the devious grin on Mac's face close to his. "Pretty damned bad," he replied and raised his brows with interest and some concern. "Why? Does my little badger have something in mind?"

"Yeah, I have something in mind," Mac replied while grinning. "You're not going to like it though."

Kane stared at the look on Mac's face and groaned. "I know I'm going to regret asking."

Chapter 58

Mac gritted her teeth as she punched Delia in the mouth. Delia was thrown against the French glass doors in the kitchen leading to the patio. Delia pressed her hands against the glass while pushing herself away from the doors. She turned to face Mac with an unpredictable look while dabbing the corner of her bleeding mouth.

"I've been waiting for an opportunity to kick your ass," Delia snarled and swung her fist for Mac's face.

Mac blocked her punch, lightly jabbed her in the abdomen, and jumped back a step. Mac's smirk indicated she was attempting to prolong the fight rather than go for the jugular. Delia sneered with anger and again swung for Mac. Mac ducked the punch, shoved her shoulder into Delia's abdomen, and threw the woman over her shoulder. Delia roughly struck the kitchen floor but was quick to jump to her feet and face Mac, who was prepared to dish out another round. Kane swooped in and caught Mac around the waist from behind. She immediately fought his hold as he attempted to keep the fight from progressing.

"That's enough," Kane lashed out and had to keep from being brutalized himself.

Scorpio stepped in front of Delia and kept her from attacking Mac while she was held immobile.

"What's going on here?" Scorpio demanded while glaring at the two women.

"She knows what she did," Mac cried out while fighting against Kane's grip around her waist.

"I didn't do anything," Delia yelled back. "But I'll gladly kick her ass!"

"No one's kicking anyone's ass," Scorpio launched while keeping Delia away from Mac.

"I've seen the way you've been looking at Kane," Mac lashed out while pointing a demanding, angry finger at Delia. "You aren't going to seduce him the way you've seduced the others."

Delia stared at Mac and appeared almost horrified. "What?" she gasped, clearly unnerved by the accusation.

"I've heard you getting it on with the wranglers when you were supposed to be working," Mac cried out. "I'm not going to let you get your slutty paws on *my* man!"

Kane attempted to hide his smile behind Mac's back, but he couldn't help chuckling in her ear. "Awe, Mac," he whispered. "I didn't know you cared."

Mac lightly jabbed him in the ribs with her elbow. He suppressed his grunt but maintained his grin.

Delia sneered and straightened. "Keep her away from me," she scoffed and stormed into the staff wing.

Scorpio eyed Mac, who attempted to wriggle from Kane's arms as he held her from behind. "Love how you painted that target on your back," Scorpio scoffed.

"It was a nice touch," Mac huffed and fought against Kane's hold. "You can let go now."

"But you love me," Kane teased near her ear. "I thought we were having a moment."

"You're going to have your moment in the emergency room if you don't release me," Mac snarled.

Scorpio rolled her eyes and had to look away. "God, get a room," she scoffed.

Rayner poked his head out from the back stairs. "Is she gone?"

"Yeah," Scorpio replied.

Rayner hurried for the glass doors while pulling scotch tape from a roll. He studied the door and placed tape over the fingerprints left behind. Scorpio hurried to the door to help him. Rayner cast a quick look at Kane, who held the struggling woman then eyed Scorpio.

"What's with them?" Rayner asked.

Scorpio waved her hand. "Nothing," she replied. "They're having a moment. Apparently, Mac loves Kane."

"I do not," Mac snarled back while fighting Kane's playful hold on her.

"Huh?" Rayner announced and continued his work. "Good for her."

"I love you too," Kane announced to Mac and gave her a big kiss on the cheek.

She made a face as he released her then wiped her cheek. Kane grinned and laughed.

§

Mac leaned against the dresser in her room with her arms folded across her chest while watching Rayner install a tiny camera above the doorframe. Her look conveyed hostility, but she was possibly masking concern indicated by the way she fidgeted every so often.

"This is paranoid," Mac announced then glared at Kane, who easily ignored her rant as he casually lay on her bed while playing on Rayner's laptop. "I hit her. She's not going to whack me for hitting her."

"Paranoid is my middle name," Kane announced without looking at Mac.

Scorpio crossed the room and flopped onto the bed alongside her brother. "Actually, it's Winston."

Mac's brows rose. "Kane Winston Templeton?"

"Kane Winston Wayland," Scorpio corrected.

"Even worse," Mac remarked with a chuckle.

Kane smacked Scorpio's thigh. "It's not Winston," he scoffed then eyed Mac. "My grandfather wanted my mother to name me Winston. Thankfully, she nixed it. It sort of became a standing joke."

"Imagine," Scorpio teased. "Just a few minutes sooner, and you could have been Scorpio."

"I'd be an awesome Scorpio," Kane announced then eyed her. "You'd be a creepy Kane."

"Back to the current topic," Mac snarled with annoyance. "I'm not comfortable sleeping with that camera spying on me all night."

"Doesn't matter," Kane replied with little emotion. "You're sleeping in Scorpio's room tonight."

Mac was about to protest.

"Scorpio is sleeping in Rayner's room," Kane added and didn't bother looking up.

"Oh," Mac announced while straightening and managed a smile. "That's not so bad then."

"I'll be your roommate," Kane casually announced without looking at her.

Her mouth fell open in near horror. "Oh, no," Mac protested while vigorously shaking her head. "That's not happening. I can share a hotel room with you when there are two beds, but I'm *not* sharing a bed with you. You'll be trying to cuddle with me all night."

Kane eyed her and raised a curious brow. "Would you prefer Maverick or Stone?" he asked almost demandingly. "I can arrange it."

Mac hid her smile and had to look away. "We'll argue about that later."

§

An hour after dinner, Brandi cuddled with Boyd on the sofa in the game room. The couple seemed rather cozy together since there one-way trip to ecstasy. Kane sat in a chair not far from the door and read a book while keeping an eye on Sig's youngest daughter. Brandi giggled while she and Boyd cuddled like a happy couple. Scorpio entered the game room, eyed the couple on the large sofa, and then approached Kane. She sat on the arm of his chair and eyed the book he read.

"Is she still mad at you?" Scorpio asked.

"Well, when I beat her at 'Alien Assault', she threw her controller at my head," Kane announced. "Damned good thing I have reflexes like a cat or that would have hurt."

Scorpio removed the book from Kane's hand, turned it the right direction, and replaced it to his hands. "What's the plan for tonight?"

"Sig gave Rayner permission to install a camera in the second floor hallway," Kane replied. "He'll be able to monitor anyone coming and going in the hallway after lights out. Unfortunately, we won't be able to see anything happening in Brandi's room."

"What about the *boyfriend?*" Scorpio asked while raising her brows.

"She's trying to convince him to spend the night," Kane announced then eyed his sister. "Against her father's wishes, I might add."

"And Boyd's protesting?"

"Giving every excuse in the book," Kane remarked in a matter-of-factly tone.

"Huh," Scorpio scoffed and found it almost humorous. "Once Rayner got in my bed, it was almost impossible to get him out."

"You'd better believe I'd be in my fiancé's bed if she asked. What man wouldn't?" Kane announced then cast a look at Scorpio and raised his brows. "I'm assuming he already made plans with his *sister*."

"Maybe we should just come out and tell her," Scorpio insisted then shook her head. "It'd make our job a little easier."

"She's not going to believe us," Kane remarked. "She proved that already. Besides, if we press without proof, we risk them fleeing."

"I know," Scorpio replied with a defeated sigh. "Did you get protection for Mac?"

"You don't need to worry about her," Kane offered and casually waved her off. "That girl has a huge box of Trojans. She'll be fine."

Once she caught his play on her words, Scorpio glared at him and smacked his shoulder. He grinned and laughed even if Scorpio didn't get the true inside joke.

Chapter 59

Scorpio cuddled against Rayner on the bed in his room while they watched a movie on the wall mounted television. Both remained fully dressed in the event they'd need to take action in the Delia versus Mac feud. Rayner had his laptop across his legs and periodically checked it. He had eyes on Delia's room, keeping tabs on her through his unauthorized spycam. Despite focusing his attention on Delia's room, he could manually switch it to any of the cameras set up on the property. Rayner glanced at the laptop screen and shook his head. Delia was seen on the screen pacing the length of her small room like a caged panther.

"That girl needs a drink," Scorpio remarked then returned her attention back to the television.

The hand radio alongside Scorpio crackled. "Hey, Scorp," Kane announced. "You guys aren't in the middle of reproducing, are you?"

"Is our sex life going to be the focus of every conversation with him?" Rayner muttered.

"Yeah, so you'll want to get used to it," she huffed. Scorpio groaned, snatched the radio, and pressed the button. "No, Kane," she snapped with noted irritation. "We're just watching a movie." She then hesitated. "And Delia's wearing out the carpet in her room."

"Yeah, that girl's definitely visiting Mac's room tonight. If we're lucky, we'll get footage of her stabbing the pillows on Mac's bed and end this," Kane announced over her hand radio. There was a brief pause. "Can you come to my room? I need some assistance."

"Copy that," Scorpio replied then turned to Rayner and kissed him quickly on the lips. "Such is the life of Kane's sister. I'll be back."

"I'll keep an eye on our caged panther," Rayner announced with little reaction.

Scorpio jumped off the bed and left the room. She headed down the hall a few doors to Kane's room and quietly slipped inside shutting the door behind her. Kane sat reclined on the bed with a permanent frown on his face.

"You're looking awfully pouty tonight," she announced. "Why the sour face?"

"Well, Sig berated me for nearly twenty minutes," Kane informed her with little emotion. "Father of the year just left my room a few minutes ago."

"Why did he berate you?" Scorpio asked and joined him on the bed, sitting alongside him.

"He's pissed that his daughter is having a sleepover with her future husband," Kane remarked then eyed his sister while raising a cocky brow. "Somehow it's my fault that *he* couldn't stop it."

"She's a grown woman," Scorpio announced and shrugged it off. "It's not up to you to tell her she can't have sex. If she doesn't respect her father's wishes, that's his problem. He can't blame you for that."

"His problem is sort of my problem," Kane informed her. "So now I need your help."

"What do you need?"

Kane offered a tiny, devious grin. "I need you to listen through the wall and make sure Boyd is just servicing Brandi and not strangling her."

"Me?" she demanded with surprise as she stared at him. "Why me?"

His eyes widened in near horror. "I can't do that," Kane insisted. "That would violate her privacy and make me seem creepy."

"But it's okay for me?"

"Yeah, sure," he replied. "You're a woman. That makes it okay and not at all creepy."

"You seriously want me to listen through the wall?" she demanded.

"Yes, I seriously want you to listen through the wall," Kane announced while glaring back. "How else will we know if he's murdering her?"

"You're unbelievable," Scorpio scoffed and climbed off the bed. She approached the wall, placed her ear to it, and listened a moment. Scorpio made a face. "Ewe."

Kane shuffled a deck of cards, spread them out on the bed, and played a game of solitaire. "You're doing great," he announced without looking at her, although his sly grin revealed his mood had instantly improved.

"Words of encouragement not required," she hissed back then made a face. "God, she just called him a stud." Scorpio groaned. "Now he's grunting like a pig."

"Play-by-play calls not required either," Kane remarked without looking at her.

"No, but if you're going to make me suffer, I intend to make you suffer along with me." Scorpio listened a moment then eyed Kane on the bed. "They're done."

Kane appeared surprised and looked at his watch. "That's a world's record," he remarked and made a face. "Pity he couldn't have been that quick while servicing his sister."

"She's not his sister," Scorpio remarked then frowned while eyeing her brother. "I hear the tub running. I guess he's not much for cuddling either."

"Yeah, she's got a winner there," Kane muttered then considered the comment and glanced at her. "I'll bet Rayner is a cuddler."

"We're not discussing my sex life, Kane," Scorpio firmly insisted.

"Who's discussing your sex life?" Kane demanded while glaring at her. "And why can't you just admit your boyfriend is into cuddling?" He shook his head shamefully and returned to his game of solitaire. "You certainly have a way of taking something warm and special and making it into something dirty and depraved."

"I do not," she hissed in anger.

He eyed Scorpio and indicated himself. "Personally, I like to cuddle," Kane insisted proudly. "I have no problem admitting it. What's the big deal?"

"Not exactly a news flash there," Scorpio remarked without hesitation. "You're openly affectionate with everyone you meet."

"Am not," he protested and appeared offended.

"After our high school graduation, it took over an hour to leave because you had to do your 'goodbye hug tour'," she remarked while raising a demanding brow. "Was there anyone in our class you didn't hug?"

"I can't help it that I was popular," he announced proudly and grinned. "People like me."

Scorpio glared at him and raised her brow. "You hugged the lunch lady on the last day of school."

"Why shouldn't I have?" he demanded. "She's a person too." Kane then grinned. "And she always gave me extra helpings of dessert."

"You hugged the boy who bullied you our entire senior year," she scoffed and raised her brow while attempting to make her point.

Kane eyed her sharply and pointed his finger at her. "In my defense," he announced, "I only did that in order to pickpocket his wallet."

She stared at him in disbelief. "You stole his wallet?" Scorpio gasped.

"The guy bullied me for three years," Kane informed her and appeared offended. "I may be a nice guy, but I'm also a bit of a prick."

"At least we can agree on that," Scorpio muttered under her breath.

The hand radio on the bed alongside Kane crackled. "Kane," Rayner announced over the radio. "Boyd is leaving Brandi's room."

Scorpio straightened and listened a moment. She heard the bedroom door next to Kane's room softly close. Scorpio eyed Kane with some surprise.

"He's leaving?" she practically gasped. "They've slept together two times. No cuddling *and* he's leaving?"

Kane moved off the bed with his hand radio and eyed his sister. "Not all men are passionate, considerate lovers like me," he announced.

Scorpio rolled her eyes. "Don't say things like that in front of me."

"Mac would have gotten a kick out of it," he teased.

"I'm not Mac," she snapped.

Kane grinned and headed for the bedroom door. "I'm going to see what the *stud* is up to."

"Have fun with that," she muttered.

Scorpio watched Kane leave the room then sat on the bed and played his game of solitaire. A few minutes passed when Scorpio's hand radio crackled in her pocket. She removed her radio to better eavesdrop on the conversation.

"Kane," Rayner announced over the radio. "Boyd just entered Delia's room. Is she ever pissed at him."

"Copy that," Kane was heard replying over the hand radio. "Hey, Rayner. You're a cuddler, right?"

"What?" Rayner asked in response.

Scorpio snatched her hand radio and spoke into it. "Ignore him, Rayner."

"Stone," Kane announced over the hand radio. "What's your six?"

"I'm taking up residence in the pool house," Stone replied over the radio. "This place is nice. I could live here. Did you need me?"

"No," Kane replied. "Just remain accessible. Boyd is in Delia's room. I think they're having a lover's spat. I'm in the kitchen now."

"Roger that," Stone replied. "FYI. I'm a cuddler."

"Of course you are," Kane replied and laughed into the radio.

"Ah crap," Rayner announced over the radio. "Delia found my camera." There was a moment of silence followed by a groan. "Guys, Delia has gone dark."

§

Kane sat on the main counter within the dimly lit kitchen with a bottle of water in his hand. The refrigerator would offer him cover if anyone entered the kitchen through the staff wing door. He placed the earbud in his ear to keep the noise level down and sipped his water. Someone was heard within the staff wing corridor. Kane became alerted, and he pressed the button on the hand radio.

"Rayner, someone is moving around in the staff wing corridor," Kane announced. "Keep an eye on the kitchen door in case it's Boyd leaving."

"Roger that," Rayner replied through the earbud.

The staff wing door to the kitchen opened. Kane remained casually seated on the counter on the off chance he'd be caught. The kitchen light came on, and Alma approached the refrigerator. She saw him and screamed.

Kane smiled with embarrassment. "Hey, Alma," he announced timidly and flashed the bottle of water. "I just came down for a drink."

She glared at him where he sat on the counter. "Off," she ordered. "Everyone has gone insane tonight!"

Kane jumped off the counter and eyed her with a curious look. "What do you mean?"

"You're lurking around in the dark, someone is poking around in the pool house, and Delia is throwing things around inside her room," Alma reported then shook her head. "I have to be up in a few hours to make breakfast, but no one cares if I get any sleep around here."

"What has Delia so upset?" he asked, although he already knew the answer.

"Damned if I know."

"Language," Kane teased while grinning.

Alma glared at him through squinting eyes. "You're lucky you're cute."

"I get that a lot," Kane announced.

"I think that girl has a man in her room," Alma informed him then shook her head. "Well, this is the last time. I'm reporting her to Mr. Hooper tomorrow."

"Want me to intervene and get them to keep it down?" he asked then raised his brows in suggestion. "Remove the young man?"

Alma seemed to consider the question a moment then waved him off. "Nah," she replied. "Don't get involved. They're quiet now."

"I'll bet," Kane muttered and sipped his water while hiding his grin.

She then eyed him suspiciously. "Wait a minute," she announced almost demandingly. "You weren't the one in her room with her, were you? The commotion stopped right before I left my room and found you here."

"Hmm, thanks for the vote of confidence, but it wasn't me," he replied then grinned. "I'm a good boy."

Alma eyed him then smiled and warmly patted his cheek. "I bet you are too."

They heard a crash from outside. Both looked at the kitchen door.

"What now?" Alma huffed, spun on her heels, and headed for the patio door.

She flipped on the set of light switches and opened the door. Kane hurried to join her. Alma stepped out onto the patio and looked around. Her eyes immediately went to the pool house as if she knew there would be trouble there.

"Those boys," she huffed and held up her hand in a slapping motion. "I'm going to give them a piece of my mind and one right upside their heads."

Kane stopped Alma from heading for the pool house and offered a polite smile. "I'll handle it, Alma," he announced then headed across the patio for the small building.

Since it was already known that Stone was in the pool house, there was some reason for concern. There was another crash, forcing Kane to pick up his pace. He entered the pool house with Alma only steps behind him. Alma turned on the lights. Stone and Teddy were in the middle of the pool house. They had each other by the shirt collars and were about to throw punches when the lights came on. The two men stared at each other.

"What the hell?" Teddy cried out.

"Language," Alma scolded.

Teddy and Stone released each other. Teddy sheepishly turned to Alma. "Sorry, ma'am."

"What are you boys doing out here?" Alma demanded and folded her arms across her broad chest.

"Yeah," Kane huffed and folded his arms across his chest in the same manner as Alma. "What are you boys doing out here?"

"I, uh, was just trying to get a good night's sleep," Stone announced then glared at Teddy. "You crawled into bed with me, man. That's not cool."

"I, uh," Teddy fumbled nervously then leaned closer to Stone and whispered. "I didn't know she made plans with someone else tonight."

Stone tensed then eyed Teddy with understanding. "Oh," he replied.

Jasmine appeared in the doorway behind Alma, stared at the scene with surprise, and quietly slipped away before anyone noticed her.

Chapter 60

Rayner sat on his bed and watched the security cameras on his laptop. He grinned while giving a play-by-play analysis of what was happening outside the pool house from the camera's point of view.

"I would have loved to see the look on Stone's face when Teddy crawled into bed with him," Rayner announced into the radio.

"Would have been more entertaining if Jasmine had shown up first," Maverick teased over the radio. "I'll bet she wouldn't have been expecting to find Stone's ass in that bed."

Rayner flipped through his security cameras then noticed video feed of the second floor hallway was out. He pressed the button on his hand radio.

"I just lost the second floor hallway camera," Rayner announced. "I'm going to check the hallway."

"I'll meet you out there," Scorpio announced through his hand radio.

Rayner jumped off the bed and hurried for his bedroom door. He no sooner opened the door when Scorpio entered the hallway from Kane's room. Mac's bedroom door opened as well, revealing Maverick in the doorway, but he didn't leave the room. They had to keep their movements quiet so they wouldn't wake those who may have actually been sleeping. Scorpio and Rayner approached the mostly hidden camera at the end of the hall and studied it. Rayner frowned and indicated the cut wire.

"Someone doesn't want us spying on them tonight," he muttered. "Jasmine was heading back inside. It's possible it was her."

"Whoever did it wasn't in the hallway when we came out of our rooms," Scorpio insisted then indicated the nearby bedroom door. "That's Jasmine's bedroom. She's the only one who could have done it and disappeared in the two seconds it took us to get out here."

Rayner groaned with defeat and gave the severed wires a flick. "I can't fix this tonight," he insisted. "It'll create too much noise and wake everyone."

"We still have the camera in Mac's staff wing bedroom," Scorpio reminded him. "You'd better keep an eye on that. I'll stay in Kane's room and keep ears on Brandi's room in case anyone enters or leaves."

"You should probably notify Kane," Rayner informed her. "He may want to check on the status of Boyd and Delia."

"I'll let him know," she replied.

§

Kane entered the kitchen behind Alma and touched his earbud while listening to Scorpio. Since he had the earbud attached, Alma couldn't hear Scorpio speaking through the hand radio. Rather than respond in front of Alma, he followed the plump cook to the staff wing doorway.

"I'll walk you to your room," Kane informed her. "I want to make sure things are quiet in Delia's room."

"If it'll make you feel better," Alma replied and allowed Kane to follow her along the staff wing corridor.

As Alma entered her room, Kane paused outside of Delia's bedroom and listened a moment. It was unusually quiet. Of course, after having just gotten it on with Brandi, it didn't seem logical that Boyd would be able to hit the reset button so quickly anyway.

"Kane," Scorpio announced over his earbud from the hand radio. "Someone just entered Brandi's room. It could be Boyd."

He pressed the button on his hand radio and spoke softly. "Yeah, it's pretty quiet outside Delia's room," Kane announced with a sigh.

There was a faint clunk from within Delia's room. Kane hesitated and stared at the maid's bedroom door. He seemed to consider his options, frowned by what he had to do, and lightly tapped on the door.

"Delia?" he announced softly through the door. "You okay in there?"

There was no response. Kane considered tapping again then looked at the doorknob. He noticed something on it and touched the knob. When he looked at his fingers, he saw what appeared to be blood. Kane knocked a little louder on the door.

"Delia," he announced. "It's Kane. I need you to answer me." There was no response. He knocked again. "Delia, I'm coming in."

Kane tried the door and found it unlocked. He opened the door and stood just inside the doorway to the dark room. He could see someone on the bed and fumbled over himself with embarrassment.

"Delia," Kane announced uncomfortably. "I'm sorry if I disturbed you, but I needed to check on you."

There was still no response. Kane appeared bewildered and flipped the light switch. The bedroom light came on to reveal a large amount of blood on the bed. Kane's eyes fell across Boyd where he lay on the bed with several stab wounds to his chest and abdomen. He was covered in blood, and his eyes were open and transfixed on the ceiling. Kane held back his stunned gasp while fumbling with the radio on his belt and pressed the button.

"Scorpio, Boyd is dead, and Delia is gone!" he cried out while running from the room.

§

Brandi lounged in the large whirlpool garden tub beneath a layer of gurgling bubbles. She had headphones on and wiggled her body within the water to the music. The bathroom door opened. As someone entered the bathroom, Brandi looked up then gasped with horror. Delia held a dagger in her hand and lunged for Brandi, who had nowhere to go within the tub. Brandi screamed as Delia thrust the dagger downward for her chest. A booted foot kicked Delia in the side and cast her across the bathroom with enough force that she struck the glass shower door. The shower door rattled and cracked from the impact. Delia straightened with some unsteadiness and looked at Scorpio, who was prepared for her second strike.

As Scorpio lunged for Delia, Brandi leaped from the tub and grabbed a nearby towel from the stand. She hastily wrapped the towel around her wet, sudsy body and turned to watch the scene. Delia clutched the dagger in her hand and attempted to impale Scorpio with it. Scorpio dodged the knife, caught Delia's hand, and kicked her in the side twice until she released the weapon. The dagger fell to the floor with a clatter. Delia tackled Scorpio backward with her body. Unable to keep her footing on the now wet floor, Scorpio tumbled backward with Delia into the large, churning, jetted tub. Both splashed into the tub, forcing a tidal wave of water to spill onto the white tile floor.

Mac, Maverick, and Rayner entered the bathroom just in time to witness the two women attempting to drown each other in the tub. Maverick and Rayner ran for the tub in an attempt to pull the women off each other. Delia leaped from the water and knocked Maverick off balance due to the wet tile. Maverick slipped and crashed to the floor. Delia slid across the wet floor and grabbed the discarded, blood-tinged dagger. Scorpio was already out of the tub and only a step behind her. She saw the dagger but was unable to stop on the slippery tile floor as Delia spun and attempted to stab her. Rayner lunged for Scorpio and tackled her to the floor, narrowly avoiding what might have been a fatal blow.

Delia coiled back with the dagger, preparing for another attack on Scorpio and Rayner while they attempted to scramble to their feet on the wet tile. Mac lunged into the dagger's path while catching Delia's arm to prevent her from stabbing either Rayner or Scorpio. Both women were thrown off balance and toppled into the churning, jetted tub. Both women were submerged beneath the water and neither resurface. Blood suddenly filled the tub and swirled around. Maverick cried out and lunged for the tub.

Mac surfaced with a gasp and attempted to get out of the tub while struggling for her footing. Maverick grabbed her under her arm and snatched her from the tub with amazing force. She fell into him, and both crashed to the floor not far from Scorpio and Rayner. Mac scrambled to her knees and off Maverick while he writhed in agony. Unfortunately, she landed on his crotch when he broke her fall. Mac pushed the wet hair from her face and gasped while attempting to catch her breath. Brandi screamed at the sight of the bloodied tub water as Delia surfaced face down with the dagger in her neck. Scorpio sat up on the floor a few feet away from where Mac kneeled and panted.

Scorpio nodded her approval while eyeing Mac. "Nice save," she announced.

Mac managed a smile and collapsed to the floor alongside Maverick, who panted while on his back as he recovered from Mac's unintended groin shot. They heard thundering footfalls enter the bedroom as those within the house appeared in the bathroom doorway.

Chapter 61

Maverick and Stone returned to the bunkhouse with the other wranglers before the coroner and state police arrived to investigate Boyd's murder. The family gathered in the game room while the police questioned them and the coroner conducted his investigation. Despite their differences, Jasmine held her younger sister as she cried over the news of Boyd's murder. Although Kane attempted to explain what they had found on Boyd and Delia, the state police weren't open to the explanation. Once another officer discovered Delia's real name among her belongings while searching her room, they were ready to consider Kane's theory.

After Rayner was given a name, he set up his laptop on the game room bar and went to work. Despite that he wouldn't receive his fingerprint results until sometime tomorrow; now that he had Delia's real name, he easily found everything he needed to know on the woman claiming to be Boyd's sister. The state troopers were suddenly interested in what Rayner had found. Rayner sat at the bar and read aloud what he'd pulled up on the computer screen.

"It would seem that Delia, AKA Clara Rhodes, met Boyd in Costa Rica, where she was wanted for attempted murder," Rayner informed the family and the state troopers. "She not only wasn't his sister but, according to this, it would appear they were married several months before she was resurrected as his sister."

Despite being traumatized by the news of her boyfriend's murder, Brandi suddenly perked up and looked at Rayner at the bar.

"They were married?" Brandi squawked.

"Her being wanted for attempted murder should be the real issue," Mac muttered.

Rayner continued to scan the article. "In order to get her out of the country, he must have obtained the proper documents to convince the authorities she was his missing sister."

One of the state troopers peered over Rayner's shoulder and jotted notes in his notebook. "So they were in on this together from the very beginning," the trooper announced.

"The bastard," Brandi scoffed.

Rayner turned on his chair and eyed those within the game room. "Keeping the sister story alive, they must have lived off Boyd's inheritance for a while. When that ran out, that was probably when they sought employment here at the ranch," Rayner surmised.

"Naturally, they'd want to fly under the radar," the state trooper announced. "Living out here is pretty far under the radar."

"When Brandi took an interest in him," Marlon added, "Boyd saw his opportunity to remain at the ranch so he wouldn't be laid off with the other wranglers."

"And then turned it into a permanent position when he conveniently asked her to marry him," Sig retorted while sneering.

"So it's only logical they were the ones who plotted Brandi's abduction in order to steal millions from Daddy for her safe return," Jasmine deducted and shook her head in disgust then eyed Kane. "Their plan must have taken an ugly turn when you guys got involved."

"Are we assuming Conroy must have stumbled upon their plan, and they killed him to keep him quiet?" Marlon asked while joining them at the bar.

"More like he tried to blackmail them for hush money," Jasmine scoffed while clinging to her emotionally unstable sister.

"I'm sure he needed a bankroll if he intended to run away with Emily."

"Possibly," Rayner replied.

"So why did Delia kill Boyd?" Marlon asked with some confusion.

"After Kane made Brandi suspicious of Boyd, he undoubtedly panicked and somehow needed to gain Brandi's trust," Rayner offered.

"And he felt he had to prove his devotion by sleeping with her," Kane interjected while collapsing into a nearby chair. "Which didn't settle well with Delia, his wife."

"In a fit of jealous rage, Delia murdered Boyd and then went after Brandi," Rayner surmised.

"Sounds plausible to me," the first trooper announced and shut his notebook. "We'll have to see what the medical examiner has to say, but I'm satisfied. Delia was fatally wounded while attempting to kill Brandi in front of several witnesses, and she was secretly married to the man brutally murdered in her bedroom. Finding evidence pointing to her as the killer shouldn't be difficult. If we have any further questions, we'll be in touch."

§

By the time the state police and the coroner left the ranch, it was almost two in the morning. Rayner and Kane seemed troubled by what transpired over the last week, but neither pressed the issue. Sig, Marlon, and Jasmine were satisfied with the evidence provided to the state troopers and easily accepted the entire story. Sig was quick to pass a few pills off to Brandi and send her to bed. Once the family left the game room, Sig turned to Kane and drew a deep breath.

"We'll talk after we all get a few hours' sleep," Sig informed him. "You and your team will be paid for your time, and I'll give you a ride to Colorado Springs sometime after lunch."

After Sig left the game room, Scorpio, Rayner, Kane, and Mac were all that remained. They exchanged looks almost as if coming up with the same concerns.

"I guess I'd feel better about Delia having killed Conroy if there was a tangible motive," Rayner remarked with a defeated sigh. "Something about Conroy's death just doesn't settle right."

"He must have seen something. He could have tried to blackmail them," Mac remarked. "It makes sense when you think about it."

"He skimmed over five million dollars from Sig," Rayner reminded her. "Blackmailing them feels pale in comparison. Almost beneath him. He was about to be a rich man. Why would he risk it for a few extra dollars? How much would he really get from Delia and Boyd in blackmail?"

"He still could have seen or heard something," Mac insisted. "Boyd and Delia certainly didn't know he was getting rich on Sig's dime."

"Or maybe they did," Scorpio countered and eyed the others. "We never found Conroy's laptop."

"Emily's still missing too," Rayner reminded her. "It's possible she took his laptop. If she divorces Sig, she gets nothing, yet she just picked up and left. It's not as if Sig threw her out. She left of her own free will. What would prompt her to do that? I can guess five million reasons."

"Well, it's up to the police and the medical examiner now," Kane replied and wearily rubbed his eyes. "We did the job we were hired to do. It's no longer our problem. We'll catch the first bus out of here after lunch." He scratched his mussed hair. "We should probably get a few hours' sleep before we leave."

Chapter 62

Wednesday, July 9th. Despite being exhausted, Alma was up at five in the morning to start breakfast for the wranglers, who would continue with their usual workday. Alma rushed to put breakfast together since she found herself shorthanded. Mac entered the kitchen at five-fifteen, didn't say a word, and worked alongside the older woman to get breakfast ready on time. Alma glanced at Mac and hid her grateful smile. Since the wranglers were three men short, breakfast took less time than usual. Once the men were served breakfast, Mac made up a tray with two additional plates and a carafe of coffee and took it to the bunkhouse for Stone and Maverick, who were possibly sleeping in late.

The rest of the house didn't get up until closer to noon after only going to bed a few hours earlier. Alma made a light lunch for the family and their houseguests, which Kane showed up early to help her. After lunch, Jasmine and Marlon headed outside to tend to the ranch, and Sig took Kane into his study to discuss payment for the job. After his meeting with Sig, Kane entered the game room where he was supposed to meet the others once they'd finished packing. The rest of his team still hadn't arrived in the game room, but they still had an hour before Sig would drive them back to Colorado Springs. Kane saw Brandi on the sofa watching a movie while hugging her knees to her chest. She once again looked like a little girl rather than a grown woman, except now she looked a little more lost and lonely. Kane approached Brandi and sat alongside her, propping his feet on the coffee table as he stared at her profile.

"Are you okay?" he asked.

She shrugged without looking back at him. "Still a little shocked by it all," Brandi replied in a timid voice then eyed him. "Boyd and Delia were married the whole time?"

Kane frowned and nodded. "Yeah, I'm afraid so."

She stared at him a moment in an awkward silence. "Did you know?" she asked while searching his eyes. "Is that what you were trying to warn me about?"

Kane shifted uncomfortably on the sofa. "I caught them together," he admitted. "I honestly didn't know they were married." Kane made a face. "I actually thought they were brother and sister."

Brandi grimaced. "Freaked you out, huh?"

"A little," he replied.

She gently patted his leg and attempted a smile. "Thanks for trying to protect me from me," Brandi remarked with a tiny spark of enthusiasm.

Kane managed a smile and patted her hand on his leg. "I can't imagine what you're going through," he announced gently. "It'll take some time, but you'll eventually realize you're better off without him."

"Yeah, I'm over him already," she insisted although her smile seemed less convincing. Brandi turned on the sofa, snuggled against Kane, and rested her head on his shoulder. "Do you have to go?"

Kane placed his arm around her shoulder and affectionately hugged her. "Our assignment is over," he replied. "My sister is ready to go home, and I made her a promise."

She laughed while clinging to him. "I can't believe Scorpio is your sister," Brandi remarked and attempted a smile. "What else don't I know around here?"

Kane considered the question. "Rayner is Scorpio's boyfriend," he announced.

Brandi lifted her head and met his gaze with surprise. "No way!"

"Yeah, I'm still shocked about that one too," Kane teased while grinning.

She again snuggled against him and buried her head into his chest. Brandi tensed while clinging to his mid-section. "Please don't leave," she whispered. "I feel so alone."

"You're not alone," Kane gently informed her. "You have your family and Alma. Boyd didn't define who you are. You're going to be just fine without him."

She lifted her head and met his gaze as tears streaked her face. "You don't know my family," Brandi replied and sniffed. "They're cold and unfeeling." She uncertainly placed her hand on his chest and practically pleaded with her eyes. "If you can't stay; take me with you. I won't get in the way, and I'll do anything you want. Just don't leave me here."

Brandi gently touched his face and moved her lips closer to his. Kane avoided her lips and kissed her warmly on the forehead. She sniffed and managed a timid smile.

"I should have seen that coming," she muttered with disappointment and pulled away from him. She again pulled her knees to her chest and appeared insecure.

"You know what the problem is, Brandi?" Kane asked while raising his brows as he stared at her profile.

She frowned and avoided looking at him. "My boyfriend was a two-timing, lowlife con artist?"

"Apart from that," Kane muttered. "You lack direction in your life. What is it you want?"

Brandi cast a look at him and was about to speak when she reconsidered the question. "I just want a family," she replied and managed a smile. "A real family; not this one. I want a loving husband, happy children, and a dog." Brandi stared at him and appeared almost angry as the tears streaked her face. "Is a fucking dog too much to ask for? Everyone here hates everyone else. Maybe if we had a stupid, fucking dog, it wouldn't be unbearable."

"What makes you think a dog would solve everything that's wrong around here?" Kane asked.

"Because," she cried out. "Carson has a dog, and his family is fucking awesome! His father treats his sister like a human being. He actually gets along with his sister; like you and Scorpio. His mother is the greatest. I miss her."

Kane stared at Brandi a moment and raised his brows. "Why did you break up with Carson in the first place?"

She hesitated and considered the question then frowned. "Because I wanted to move to the city, and he wouldn't leave his father's ranch."

"So everything you loved about Carson was what you wanted him to give up?" Kane asked while studying her.

Brandi stared at him a long moment and seemed uncertain how to answer.

"If you lived in the city, you may not be able to have a dog," Kane informed her.

"Maybe moving to the city isn't really what I want," Brandi gently remarked. "Maybe all I really need is a dog."

"Perhaps," Kane replied and offered a tiny smile.

Brandi wiped the tears from her face and snatched the cordless phone from the coffee table. "Could you give me a few minutes?" she asked. "I have to call a man about a dog."

Kane smiled and nodded. "You do that." He kissed her warmly on the forehead, stood, and left the game room.

§

Alma hovered over a cookie tin on the kitchen counter and loaded a plastic bag with cookies while Stone stood alongside her and protested. Maverick leaned on the counter and watched the scene while shaking his head.

"That's plenty, Alma," Stone announced while grinning. "You're going to fatten me up."

"You're a growing boy," she insisted while grinning. "You need to eat more."

"I eat plenty," Stone teased then accepted the bag while Maverick rolled his eyes. "Thank you, Alma."

Stone and the cook happily hugged.

"You take care," Alma announced while patting his broad shoulder as she pulled away. She then glared at Maverick and pointed a scolding finger at him. "And you; you watch your language."

Maverick appeared surprised and defensively held his hands in the air. "What the hell--?"

"Language," she again scolded then left the kitchen.

Maverick groaned and rubbed his eyes. "Get me out of here."

Stone removed a cookie and happily bit into it. Maverick reached for the bag to snatch one. Stone slapped his hand, surprising his friend.

"Those are special for me," Stone announced a little too proudly.

Maverick waved him off and left the kitchen.

Chapter 63

An hour later, the team collected in the foyer with their bags and dropped them by the door. They were waiting for Sig to pull the multi-passenger SUV around in order to accommodate everyone on the excessively long drive back to Colorado Springs. Stone and Maverick were joking around about their stay at the ranch while Mac appeared thrilled to be leaving. Even though they had been handsomely compensated for their services, Kane, Scorpio, and Rayner still had some issues with the solved case.

"I just wish we knew why Conroy was killed," Rayner announced with a defeated sigh.

"They might come up with a motive once they reopen the investigation into his death," Kane informed him.

"Why does it bother you so much?" Scorpio asked while studying him. "He was skimming money off Hooper for years and sleeping with his wife. There's plenty of motive to kill Conroy."

"Not motive for Delia or Boyd," Rayner insisted. "What about Sig's blown tire? If that wasn't an accident, we're back to someone wanting to kill Sig, which would eliminate Delia and Boyd. They have no motive to kill him."

"Not entirely true," Kane remarked. "If Boyd married Brandi, he'd have one-third share of the ranch."

"There was no way Boyd ever intended to marry Brandi," Rayner assured him. "Delia wasn't going to let that happen. That was proven when she killed him for sleeping with Brandi. That was not a woman who was willing to let her man marry another woman. That was never part of their plan, I guarantee it."

There was a strange silence as everyone considered Rayner's comment.

"We also never found Conroy's laptop, which could tell us what he did with the millions he'd skimmed from Sig," Rayner reminded them.

"That's no longer our problem," Kane informed him with a sigh. "I'm sure Conroy's side business had nothing to do with Delia and Boyd's master plan."

Rayner then considered the comment. "That's my point. What if the two aren't related?" he just about demanded. "Conroy's death. Sig's blown tire. Marlon's riding accident. What does any of that have to do with Delia and Boyd? Conroy dies after skimming millions off Sig, and his laptop, which possibly holds the key to finding the money, is missing. Is that all just a coincidence? How can that *not* be part of the master plan?"

"Maybe Delia or Boyd knew Conroy was skimming money. When kidnapping a rich man's daughter fails, finding millions in stolen money is a pretty nice consolation prize," Stone insisted. "No one says they didn't steal the laptop."

"And if they had?" Rayner continued while casting a look at Stone. "Why haven't we found it? The police went through Delia's room and Boyd's personal things. Hiding it in one of the common areas where anyone could find it wouldn't be very smart. If they were involved, we should have found that laptop. That has to mean someone else took the laptop."

"Maybe Emily took it," Mac suggested.

Rayner eyed her and raised his brows. "Okay, let's consider Emily for a moment. She suddenly up and takes off. She had maybe an hour head start, and we're three hours from Colorado Springs. Why haven't the police found her?" he pointed out. "Is Emily some criminal mastermind with the ability to disappear without a trace? No, she was Sig's trophy wife. I don't think the woman was operating on criminal genius level. They should have found her."

Kane tensed and eyed the others in the foyer. "Maybe they haven't found her because she never made it off the ranch," he suggested.

All six exchanged looks.

"Okay," Scorpio announced and gave into the conspiracy theory. "Let's suppose for one moment that Delia and Boyd had nothing to do with everything else that happened around here." She drew a deep breath and raised her brows. "Who had reason to want Sig, Marlon, and Conroy dead?

While the others considered the question, Rayner responded without hesitation. "No one," he replied.

The five looked at Rayner.

"Jasmine hated her brother, and her husband was cheating on her," Maverick remarked.

"She could have divorced Conroy at any time," Kane reminded them. "Sig told us she didn't have any marital property. The ranch and money belong to her father. Apart from a small trust fund, she didn't have anything to lose by divorcing him."

"She'd also be worse off if Sig died," Stone reminded them. "If her father died, Marlon would dominate the ranch, and she'd lose what little say she had."

"What about Marlon?" Mac asked and received strange looks from the others. "We don't actually know that he was thrown from his horse. He could have staged it to make himself look like a victim. With his father gone, he takes control of the ranch and would eventually push his sisters out of the way. If he discovered Conroy stole millions off his father, he'd have enough money to buy off both his sisters. Everything would be his."

There was a strange silence.

"Teddy," Stone announced with a curious look. "He was having an affair with Jasmine and wanted her to run the ranch. If he eliminated Sig and Marlon, she'd have control. Killing Conroy would also conveniently eliminate his lover's husband. He could have learned about the millions Conroy stole, and he also had access to Marlon's saddle pad to plant the vibrator that spooked the horse."

They exchanged looks and considered the comment a moment longer. Kane looked at his watch and fidgeted while considering everything that had been expressed.

"Okay, fine. We'll give this one more shot," Kane announced then turned to Mac and Maverick. "You two search Marlon's room for that laptop."

Maverick and Mac nodded and hurried up the grand staircase for the second floor.

Kane then motioned to his sister, Rayner, and Stone. "The four of us need to search the barn and the bunkhouse," he announced. "We'll grab the hand radios from the kitchen on our way through."

Scorpio bolted for her duffel bag on the floor, unzipped it, and removed the leather holster containing her dual swords. All four ran down the hall toward the kitchen.

Chapter 64

Stone entered the bunkhouse with Scorpio, Kane, and Rayner on his heels. He hurried across the large room and pointed to the bunk near the fireplace.

"His bunk is there," Stone informed them.

Kane hurried for the bunk Stone had indicated, crouched before the footlocker, and opened it. He routed around within the large trunk only a moment before Rayner spotted a burlap sack buried on the bottom.

"That's it," Rayner announced while pointing. "I know that's it."

Kane pulled the brown sack from the footlocker and removed the expensive laptop from the bag. Rayner grabbed the laptop, leaped onto the nearby bunk, and attempted to bypass the password-protected screen. It only took him two tries to gain access.

Kane stared at him and appeared impressed. "How did you guess his password so fast?" he asked.

"I'm a genius," Rayner replied while concentrating on browsing files.

Scorpio frowned and nudged Rayner.

Rayner offered a tiny smile without looking up from the computer. "Conroy used the same password for everything on Sig's computer, so I took a chance he used them on his as well." He chuckled at the irony of it. "He must have given the passwords to Sig at one time, and Sig wrote them all in the back of his day planner."

"I'm starting to think Conroy wasn't nearly as smart as he thought he was," Kane remarked.

"He was great with numbers and figures, and he loved his technology," Rayner replied, "but he wasn't a 'hack the Pentagon' sort of guy."

Kane marveled at the speed in which Rayner manipulated the files. "The trouble I could get into if I could only type that fast," he muttered while rubbing his chin without taking his eyes off Rayner's handy work.

"Ah, lookie here," Rayner announced while grinning. "I found Sig's missing millions." He pressed several buttons and screens popped up and then disappeared. "We'll just put you back where you belong."

"He has Sig's bank account numbers on his laptop?" Stone asked with surprise.

"No, but I remembered the login for the bank and Sig's bank account number," Rayner replied. "Congratulations, Sig. You have your five million back."

"You memorized those numbers?" Kane asked while raising a brow.

"I keep telling you people I'm a genius," Rayner replied without looking away from the computer then shook his head in annoyance. "Why don't you believe me?"

"Anything that will implicate someone in Conroy's death?" Scorpio asked.

"Considering the laptop was removed and hidden in the bunkhouse," Rayner announced without interrupting his work, "I'm guessing there are a few million reasons why Conroy was killed." Rayner opened a file, scanned through it, and stopped. His expression suddenly dropped. "Or this may have something to do with it."

All three peered over his shoulder to view the file and were equally horrified.

§

$\mathcal{S}$tone hurried across the paddock and approached the first wrangler he saw. Kane and Scorpio were only a few feet behind him while Rayner ran back to the house with the newly acquired laptop. Stone paused before the wrangler on his horse and looked up at him.

"Have you seen Marlon?" Stone asked with concern in his tone.

The wrangler stared at him a moment then pointed across the pasture. "He's riding fences in the back forty," he announced. "Is something wrong?"

"I need your horse," Stone insisted.

"What?"

"Just give me your horse," Stone announced more firmly and with conviction.

The wrangler willingly gave up his horse without further question. Stone indicated Kane and Scorpio, who now slipped into her sword harness.

"Saddle two horses for them," Stone instructed. "It's important."

Stone swung onto the horse's back without use of stirrups and sent the horse into a gallop across the field. The countryside whizzed past as Stone ran the horse to the pasture where Marlon was supposedly last seen. When Stone reached the large pasture further away from the ranch, Marlon wasn't anywhere to be found. Stone slowed the horse and rode along the woods' edge, peering into the forest for any sign of the missing horse and rider. There were several trails within the woods, and it was nearly impossible to tell which set of hoof prints were fresh or if there had been multiple riders taking multiple trails already that morning. Stone stopped his horse and cursed. Scorpio and Kane raced across the field on their loaner horses. When they saw Stone, they changed direction and joined him by the woods. Both stopped their excitable horses.

"I thought he said Marlon was out here," Scorpio remarked while scanning the area.

"He could be anywhere by now," Stone informed them as he looked around the vast fields. He then indicated the nearby trails. "Did you take any of these trails when you were out riding?"

Scorpio and Kane looked around then exchanged looks before grimacing and glancing back at Stone.

"I couldn't say. I wasn't really paying that much attention," Scorpio replied.

"They all look the same," Kane insisted while glancing at the different trails. "I'm more familiar with the ones near the house where I jogged."

Stone pointed to the nearby trail. "This takes you to the stream at the far side of the property," he informed Scorpio. "Go as far as the water, turn left, and follow the stream." He then looked at Kane and pointed to the far trail. "If you take that trail over there, you'll come to the stream where it starts on the ranch. Turn right and follow the stream that direction. I'll take the path between the two, and we'll meet in the middle somewhere."

Scorpio and Kane nodded. All three rode onto separate trails and vanished into the woods.

§

Mac and Maverick walked down the grand stairs with matching looks of defeat on their faces. They didn't find anything in Marlon's room that would either prove or disprove his involvement. The front door opened, which was probably Sig, who as wondering where they were for their ride to Colorado Springs. As they reached the bottom of the steps, instead of Sig they saw Brandi. She looked slightly out of breath and moderately perplexed.

"Oh, you're still here," she announced while attempting to catch her breath. "Have you seen my daddy?"

"Isn't he outside with the SUV?" Mac asked with a curious look.

"No, I didn't see him," Brandi remarked. "I thought he'd already left with you guys." She then pointed toward the door. "I was taking a walk in the woods, you know, which I never do, and I saw something strange."

"What's that?" Maverick asked.

"It looked like a car in the woods," she replied then shook her head. "I certainly wasn't going to check it out on my own, you know, since my last abduction."

"We should check it out," Maverick announced then eyed Mac.

Mac snatched Brandi's car keys from the nearby hall table and dangled them. "Let's go."

"It's just beyond--" Brandi began but was interrupted by Mac, who grabbed her arm and forced her back toward the door.

"Don't bother with directions," Mac muttered. "You're coming along."

Before Brandi could protest, Mac forced her out the door. Maverick hurried after them.

§

Brandi's sports car pulled alongside the road not far from an overgrown trail. All three looked into the woods while Brandi pointed.

"It's down there," she announced. "I was in the woods on my walk, but it's definitely down there. It can't be far from the road."

Mac and Maverick got out of the car then both hesitated. Mac turned, glared demandingly at Brandi, and nodded for her to lead the way. Brandi groaned and got out of the car. They walked nearly two hundred yards before spotting the familiar car deep in the woods. Brandi's eyes widened with surprise and near horror.

"It's Emily's car," Brandi cried out and looked at Mac and Maverick. "What's it doing out here?"

Brandi took two steps toward the car before Maverick stopped her.

"I think you should wait here," he announced.

By the time he turned, Mac was already heading for the abandoned car. Maverick hurried to catch up with Mac. They approached the back of the car then cautiously walked alongside it. Both peered inside the car.

"Is she--?" Brandi called with concern but seemed unable to finish the question.

"It's empty," Mac called back then noted the luggage in the back seat.

"So where is she?" Brandi practically demanded while wrenching her fingers together.

Mac and Maverick exchanged looks as Brandi approached the car with some apprehension. Mac opened the driver's side door and popped the trunk while Maverick headed for the back of the car. The trunk sprang open before he even reached the back. The loud rattling sound was almost deafening, forcing Maverick to stop in his tracks. Brandi stared into the trunk no more than ten feet from her and screamed hysterically. Mac bolted for Maverick, who hadn't moved from where he stood alongside the rear tire. He suddenly grabbed Mac and pulled her deeper into the woods, taking a wide birth around the back of the car. Mac then heard the loud rattling sound just about drowning out Brandi's panic-stricken screams. Once they reached Brandi, Maverick pulled her into his arms and hurried her away from the car. Mac was eager to look inside the trunk but was apprehensive about getting any closer. She took a step or two closer and stared with horror. There were more than fifty rattlesnakes in a tight wad within the trunk.

The sight of the rattlesnakes was unnerving by itself, but upon closer inspection, it was even worse. Beneath the ball of snakes was Emily's bloated and discolored body. She was almost unrecognizable due to heat and decay, but even worse, the snakebites had turned most of her body black with venomous rot. Maverick held Brandi in his arms as she sobbed after what she'd witnessed. Mac found a large stick and managed to close the trunk with it. She tossed the stick aside and approached Maverick, who was almost as shaken as the sobbing young woman he held. Mac shook her head while offering little more than an annoyed frown.

"Well, now we know what happened to Emily," she announced and continued past them practically unaffected by the sight.

Maverick continued to hold Brandi while she sobbed and stared after Mac with his mouth hanging open. Her lack of reaction beyond the initial surprise was moderately concerning. It begged the question; what had Mac been through that something so horrible and frightening barely fazed her?

Chapter 65

Kane rode his horse for more than half an hour before finally reaching the stream. He followed the stream to the right in hopes of meeting up with his sister and Stone. If they were lucky, they'd run into Marlon along the way. Kane appeared in a large pasture. In the distance, he saw Marlon's saddled horse grazing in the field. Kane looked around but didn't see Marlon. He rode closer to the grazing horse while cautiously scanning the area. Marlon appeared from the woods while zipping his pants having possibly dismounted for a bathroom break. He saw Kane riding toward him and appeared surprised to see him.

"I thought you and your friends left already," Marlon announced. "Wasn't my father driving you back to Colorado Springs almost an hour ago?"

"Change of plans," Kane announced and nodded to Marlon's grazing horse. "We need to go."

"Go?" Marlon asked. "Go where?"

"I'll tell you on the way."

Marlon shook his head with limited patience and mounted his horse. He'd just situated himself in the saddle when Kane saw the sun reflect off something shiny in the woods.

"Down!" Kane shouted while leaping across his horse and tackled Marlon from his horse.

Both men landed roughly on the ground as a rifle fired, spooking their horses. The horses then took off across the pasture. Kane rolled across the ground and looked toward the woods. Another shot was fired, and the ground near him exploded.

"In the woods," Kane cried out and pointed to the nearby trees that would offer some cover.

Marlon and Kane moved to their feet, kept low, and ran for the woods as the rifle fired several times striking the ground near their heels. They reached the woods and hid behind two trees.

"What's happening?" Marlon demanded as he gasped to catch his breath. "Who's shooting at us?"

"Yeah, about that--"

Jasmine rode her horse from the woods and across the pasture toward them at a slow gallop. She wore a hardened expression as she held her rifle cradled in her free arm. Scorpio raced her horse from the woods at a full run for Jasmine. Jasmine turned without slowing her horse and appeared surprised to see Scorpio. She attempted to aim her rifle at the young woman, who swiftly caught up to her. Without slowing her horse, Scorpio hoisted herself off the saddle, swung her legs to the side, and kicked Jasmine in the chest with both feet. Jasmine toppled off the side while Scorpio caught the saddle horn of Jasmine's running horse and took her seat. Jasmine struck the grassy surface and bounced a few times before rolling to a stop. Scorpio spun Jasmine's horse around and rode back for the fallen woman.

As Scorpio neared Jasmine, she made it to her feet with the rifle in her hand. Scorpio jumped off the horse, threw herself into a forward roll, and sprang up while pulling one of the two swords from her sheath holder. She swung her sword for the rifle. The metal from the sword clashed with the metal on the rifle, forcing Jasmine to drop the weapon. Scorpio held the sword above her head with the tip aimed at Jasmine's face. Jasmine stood immobile while staring at the sword. Scorpio no sooner heard a rifle blast when the bullet ricocheted off her sword blade and knocked it from her hand. The gunfire came from the woods. Before a second shot was fired, Scorpio threw herself to the ground and rolled out of the way. The ground exploded where she had been standing. Jasmine's horse bolted away from the action and headed toward the other running horses. All four saddled horses stopped just short of the woods near Kane and Marlon.

Kane darted from the woods near them and attempted to calm the animals. As soon as he was able to catch the one of the horses, he jumped on its back and rode across the far edge of the woods. The hidden shooter in the woods fired several shots at Kane on Jasmine's horse while the remaining three horses ran after him to keep up with the herd. While Kane had the shooter distracted, Scorpio leaped to her feet and pulled the second sword from her sheath. Jasmine grabbed Scorpio's discarded sword and lunged for her. Scorpio blocked the sword with her own without a second to spare. The swords clashed with a metallic clang. Although the sound startled Jasmine, Scorpio had grown used to the loud clang after years of sword fights with Kane. Scorpio was burdened with keeping Jasmine between her and the shooter, who might easily shift attention from Kane back to her.

The shooter finally emerged from the woods revealing Teddy on horseback. He rode at a gallop for Scorpio and Jasmine in order to get a clean shot. Kane seemed less of a threat at the moment, and Teddy wanted to protect his boss and lover. Stone appeared from the woods, racing his horse across the clearing with his lasso in hand. Teddy looked back when he heard the horse and rider behind him. Before he could even react, Stone threw the lasso, catching Teddy around the shoulders. As the rope tightened, Stone's horse put on the brakes. At the same time, Teddy attempted to slip out of the rope, which instead caught him around the neck. The horse's forward momentum caused Teddy to be plucked from the saddle by the rope around his neck.

Stone attempted to move his horse forward, but the cowpony was determined to pull back and keep the rope tight. Teddy's neck snapped the moment he was pulled off his horse's back. Stone removed the rope from the saddle horn, but it was already too late. He grimaced at the sight of Teddy on the ground not far from him with his head turned in an unnatural position. With the shooter out of the picture, Scorpio concentrated on Jasmine and the sword she held firm in her hand. Scorpio swung her sword with an easy to stop strike. The moment the two swords connected, Scorpio released her sword and spun into a roundhouse kick, striking Jasmine in the chest and dropping her to the ground. Scorpio grabbed both discarded swords, twirled them in her hands, and aimed one at Jasmine's face.

"Be smart," Scorpio announced with a sneer. "Stay down. I won't miss."

Jasmine stared at the tip of the sword in her face while panting heavily and heeded Scorpio's threat.

§

Six horse and riders returned to the barn and quickly caught the attention of the remaining wranglers. Jasmine had her hands tied behind her back as she sat on her horse, which was being led by Marlon. Teddy's body was draped and tied over the saddle while Stone led the dead man's horse. Those within the house, as well as the nearby wranglers, hurried to the barn to see what had happened. Sig approached his son and looked back at his bound daughter.

"What happened?" Sig demanded.

Marlon tossed Sig the reins to his sister's horse. "Jasmine and Teddy tried to kill me," he announced with some anger and hostility.

As Sig stared at Jasmine, she refused to look at her father. "Jasmine," he cried out with surprise.

"We found Conroy's laptop hidden inside Teddy's footlocker," Rayner informed Sig. "She must've figured no one would look for it in the bunkhouse, so Teddy hid it for her. Conroy was collecting evidence that implicated his wife in a plot to kidnap Brandi. Since it seems unlikely he intended to rat them out, he probably intended to blackmail her once she received the ransom."

Brandi stared at her sister with disbelief and gasped. "You?" she cried out. "How could you? What did I ever do to you?"

"Oh, it was necessary," Rayner informed the young woman. "She needed the ransom money in order to buy your share of the ranch from you."

"So she intended to use money she got from kidnapping me to pay me off for my share of the ranch?" Brandi demanded with horror then glared at her sister with hateful eyes. "You sick bitch!"

"Language," Alma scolded Brandi then glared at Jasmine. "But accurate."

"So Conroy was the intended victim all along?" Sig asked with surprise.

"Actually, no," Rayner announced.

"She wanted to kill me?" Sig then asked and glared at his oldest daughter.

"Again, no," Rayner replied. "She wanted to kill her brother." He cast a look at Marlon then returned his gaze to Sig. "Killing you wouldn't do her any good. Marlon would still be in charge of the ranch, and she'd be exactly where she is right now or worse. She wanted to be in charge of the ranch. The only way to do that was to kill her brother. With Marlon out of the way, in the event of your death, everything would then go to Jasmine and Brandi." Rayner offered a slight shrug. "Brandi made it very clear she wanted no part of the ranch. Jasmine would then buy Brandi's share of the ranch with the very money she received as ransom. Unfortunately for her, abducting Brandi fell apart, but she continued with the rest of her plan when opportunity presented itself."

"The hot tub?" Sig asked with a bewildered expression. "But that was meant for me, right?"

"I don't think so," Rayner remarked. "I somehow think it was meant for Marlon, but I still haven't figured out how that's possible."

"I know," Marlon informed him with a demanding glare. "My lower back was hurting that day after my accident. I always soaked in the hot tub in the evening when I had a sore back. Jasmine knew I was having back pain. That has to be when she staged that accident to kill me."

"Obviously, she didn't realize Conroy had already made plans to meet his lover in the pool house," Scorpio remarked then looked back at Sig. "I'm guessing your wife's plans to meet Conroy must have been cut short when you arrived home that evening."

"We have to assume Emily didn't have time to warn Conroy," Kane added. "But it probably didn't matter if you found Conroy soaking in the hot tub."

"But that near miss with my truck," Sig interjected. "Surely that was meant for me."

"That near miss was purposely missed," Kane informed him. "If you had an accident earlier, and it was suspected Marlon's death in the hot tub wasn't an accident, everyone would think you were the intended target. With you as the target, Jasmine was the only one without motive. She gained nothing and actually lost more if you were killed."

"She must have known Conroy had incriminating evidence on her and assumed it was on his laptop," Rayner announced. "I'm guessing she either found his laptop or stopped Emily from taking it. When it was safe to do so, I suspect she handed it off to Teddy for him to hide."

"Emily must have known what was on the laptop," Mac offered. "Maverick, Brandi, and I found Emily dead in her car not far from here in the woods."

There was some surprise to the new information and some concerned chatter.

"If there was all this incriminating evidence on Conroy's laptop," Marlon announced with confusion, "why didn't she just delete it?"

"She couldn't access his laptop," Rayner replied. "She didn't know the password. Later, after she discovered her husband had skimmed money off her father, she knew she couldn't destroy the laptop, or she'd never find the millions."

"With the millions Conroy skimmed, she no longer needed to complete her mission to abduct Brandi," Kane offered. "She just needed to wait until things cooled down, find someone to crack the password for her, and locate the accounts where the money was hidden."

Sig stared at Jasmine who still refused to look at him. "How could you?" he scoffed while shaking his head. "I gave you everything."

She finally looked at him with hateful eyes. "How could I?" Jasmine demanded. "How could you?"

Sig was surprised by her words and hostile tone. He wasn't use to anyone challenging his authority.

"I worked hard to make this ranch a success," Jasmine hissed. "I worked harder and longer hours than Marlon, yet you put him in charge. I had virtually no say *ever*! I was a second-class citizen around here. Why? Because I wasn't your son!"

"You did play favorites," Mac muttered and immediately received looks from everyone including her own teammates. She didn't seem to care that they stared at her and simply folded her arms across her chest as if waiting for someone to prove her wrong.

The wranglers removed the dead foreman from his horse and laid him on the ground. One of the men covered him with his jacket while Alma clutched her cross necklace and whispered a prayer over his body. Stone stood alongside Alma and folded his hands in prayer with her.

Maverick eyed Stone then shook his head and looked at Scorpio. "We need to get out of here," he announced. "Stone is starting to worry me."

Alma made a face and smacked Maverick on the arm. He yelped with surprise more than pain and gave her a startled look.

Chapter 66

Thursday, July 10th. Colorado Springs. Late evening. Scorpio entered the luxury hotel suite and looked around with an approving grin. It was possibly one of the nicest hotel rooms she'd ever seen, and, considering she traveled extensively with her wealthy grandparents, that said a lot. Rayner entered the room behind her with their overnight bags and marveled at the room as well.

"Nice," he announced and nodded his approval.

The suite had a massive, king-sized bed, fireplace, large screen television, and a fully stocked bar. French doors led to the terrace that overlooked the city lights. She glanced back at Rayner.

"It was nice of Sig to put us up in this classy hotel for the night," Scorpio announced. "After what he paid us for the assignment, it wasn't necessary."

Rayner approached the bathroom, poked his head inside, and then looked back at her while grinning. "Luxury garden tub for two," he announced with enthusiasm. "I'm thinking champagne and a bubble bath."

Scorpio nodded her approval then glanced at her watch. "If you want champagne, you'd better hurry before the hotel's gift shop closes."

Rayner kissed her quickly but warmly on the lips and flashed a smile. "I'll be back in twenty minutes," he announced then hurried for the door and nearly collided with Kane, who was entering the suite. Rayner glared at Scorpio's brother. "You have twenty minutes then she's mine the rest of the night."

Kane watched Rayner hurry from the room. He raised his brows then closed the door and turned to face Scorpio. "He's a brassy nerd, I'll give him that much."

Scorpio watched her brother flop on the excessively large, king-sized bed and make himself comfortable. She raised her brows with some annoyance.

"Off."

Kane frowned and sat up on the bed. "I'm starting to think all women eventually turn into Alma."

There was a knock on Scorpio's bedroom door.

"Come in," Kane cheerfully announced from where he remained comfortably seated on the bed and received a loathing sneer from his sister.

Maverick and Stone entered the room leaving the door open behind them.

"We're grabbing a bite to eat in the restaurant downstairs before it closes," Stone announced and pointed to the suite door. "Mac's already downstairs getting us a table. You guys coming?"

"Rayner and I are ordering room service," Scorpio informed them with a sly smile.

Stone chuckled while grinning. "I sort of thought that," he teased.

"Did you book a flight for tomorrow?" Maverick asked with interest.

"Not yet," she replied then eyed Kane, who fiddled with his cell phone. "Will that be four or six for that flight to Maine?"

Kane drew a deep breath, reluctantly sighed, and waved her off. "Yeah, I'll come back home," he replied then eyed her sharply while pointing a warning finger at her. "But I'm not promising I'll stay."

"What about Mac?" Scorpio asked.

Maverick cast a look at Kane while pretending to be disinterested.

"She'll probably come along," Kane replied then grinned playfully. "My little badger can't live without me."

"That's one hell of an ego you've got on you," Stone remarked.

Maverick hid his sly grin at the news that Mac would be traveling back to Maine with them. Stone saw his friend's look and rolled his eyes.

"Either way, we both need a vacation from this last job," Kane announced then pressed a button on his cell phone.

"Why do you call her that?" Maverick asked.

"Call her what?"

"Your little badger," Maverick remarked and appeared curious.

Kane shrugged. "She's cute and cuddly, but she'll rip your throat out when provoked," he remarked then grinned. "Respect the badger." Kane listened to his cell phone and shook his head. "Ten voicemails while we were at the ranch without cell phone service." He listened to the first voicemail and frowned. "Telemarketer." He hit a button then listened to the next message. "Telemarketer." Kane hit another button and again listened. He suddenly became interested in the voicemail.

Maverick and Stone were about to leave when Kane's look caught their attention. Stone hesitated, shut the door, and leaned against it. Kane's expression nearly dropped. He pressed a button on the phone and stared at Scorpio with an indescribable look.

"A man who used to work for Sal Romano called two days ago," Kane informed his sister with a look that concerned her. "He wants to meet to discuss our father."

Scorpio tensed and held her breath. She then shook her head with disapproval. "Let it go, Kane," she insisted. "Nothing good is going to come from looking for him. There's no telling what he's mixed up in."

"I can't, Scorp," Kane announced while staring into her eyes. "I have to settle something with him. I need to bury his memory even if it means burying him."

"I don't like this," she insisted.

"Maybe we should stay another day or two," Stone suggested while straightening. "Provide backup."

Scorpio didn't look away from her brother, who maintained his stare at her.

"Don't you want to know?" Kane asked in a docile tone. "Aren't you the least bit interested?"

"No," she replied firmly then drew a deep breath and held it a moment. "But I'm not going to let you meet this guy alone either. We can stay a few more days. Maine isn't going anywhere."

"Actually," Kane announced. "He wants us to meet him in Virginia tomorrow evening."

Scorpio's expression suddenly dropped. "Oh," she groaned and vigorously shook her head. "I have a bad feeling about this."

"Virginia?" Maverick asked while studying them. "Isn't that where your father was originally from?"

Kane nodded then pleaded with his sister. "This is it, Scorp," he announced. "This is the one."

"Which one?" she demanded. "The one that gets you killed?"

"I'm doing this with or without you," he insisted.

"What about Mac?" Scorpio asked.

Kane immediately shook his head. "No, she can't know," he announced. "I think she knows more about our father than she's willing to tell me. She worked for Sal Romano. I want to trust her, but I can't risk her warning him. This is too important."

"She doesn't even know Zack Kinsley is our father," Scorpio insisted. "What would she possibly be warning him about?"

"Mac stays out of this," Kane announced with noted annoyance. "She can go to Maine with you, and I'll catch up with you after I've met this guy in Virginia."

Stone and Maverick immediately tensed and shot looks at Scorpio.

"Don't do it," Stone announced boldly. "You can't let him meet this guy by himself. We've been down this road before. I'll go with him. He can't go alone."

Scorpio drew a deep breath and stared at her brother. "You're not meeting this guy without a plan," she insisted then groaned. "Discuss the details of this meeting with Rayner. He can check things out. We'll decide how to approach it from there."

Kane managed a smile and hugged his sister. She groaned and reluctantly returned the embrace.

"You're the best, Scorp," he announced then pulled away but remained cheerful.

"What about Mac?" Maverick again asked and shifted uncomfortably. He appeared disappointed. "Are we really keeping this from her?"

"Not a word to Mac," Kane replied with a firm insistence while locking eyes with Maverick. "She's to stay far away from this one. I'll find something for her to do here in Colorado Springs for the next few days. Perhaps have her spy on some poor, unsuspecting person. I'll book her a flight to Maine for later next week."

Chapter 67

Friday, July 11th.   Night.   The abandoned airfield in Virginia was home to a large aircraft boneyard.   Considered an eyesore, the boneyard was located in a secluded area of mostly junk land far from anywhere.   Barely considered an airfield and its seclusion made it the perfect rendezvous or an excellent place to kill a man and hide his body.   Maverick got out of the security of his car and scanned the dark, creepy boneyard where he had been instructed to meet his mysterious contact.

"Perfect," he muttered while frowning.   "This isn't at all creepy."

Maverick walked through the airplane graveyard until he reached an old wrecked four-passenger, prop plane that had the name 'Old Marge' elegantly painted on the side.   The wheels and one wing had been torn off possibly when it wrecked.   The underbelly was severely scraped, and burn marks were visible beyond the seams of the engine compartment.   Maverick studied the wrecked plane a moment.   Despite the moon dimly lighting the area, he could make out an old bloodstain resembling a handprint on the windshield on the passenger side of the craft. The open doorway, missing its door, was level with the ground. Maverick entered the dark plane with his baton flashlight brightening the way. The moment he stepped into the plane wreckage, a large light blinded him and prevented him from seeing the man he was supposed to meet.

"You realize we could have met at some nice, cozy coffee shop," Maverick announced while shielding his eyes from the bright light. "I'm not a fan of all this cloak and dagger business."

"You want Zack Kinsley or not?" the low male voice snarled from the darkness beyond the light.

"Yeah, I want Zack Kinsley," Maverick replied while shielding his eyes from the blinding light. "Where do I find him?"

"Not so fast, pretty boy," the man in the darkness remarked. "I'd like to know why you want him. You have some sort of grudge against him?"

"Me?" Maverick shook his head and appeared almost disinterested. "Never met the guy. My boss is real interested in meeting him though."

"Who's your boss?"

"Midnight Requisition," Maverick replied.

There was a brief moment of silence.

The man in the darkness suddenly chuckled. "What sort of stupid ass name is that?"

"You ask too many questions," Maverick replied without appearing fazed. He cocked his head slightly while squinting at the light. "Where will I find him?"

"I'll arrange a little introduction," the voice in the darkness announced. "I know exactly how to lure him out of his comfort zone and into whatever kill box you want."

"I never mentioned killing him," Maverick remarked without flinching.

The man in the darkness chuckled in an almost sinister manner. "Yeah, but they all want to--" There was a pause. "Eventually."

"How do you intend to lure him onto our playfield?" Maverick asked.

"Now who's asking too many questions?" the voice in the darkness teased with a sinister chuckle. "I intend to lure him to you with the siren's call."

"Siren's call?"

"Yes," the man in the darkness continued. "See, I know his weakness. Every man's weakness, I suppose. Women. In his case, one woman. A *special* woman."

"You won't hurt this woman," Maverick demanded. "There won't be any innocent blood spilled. No *collateral* damage."

"No, I won't hurt her," the voice in the darkness continued. "But he'll show up if he thinks he's there to rescue her. He always does. She's his Achilles heel."

A booted foot appeared from the darkness and slid an envelope across the plane floor to Maverick.

"There's the time and place," the man in the darkness announced. "Don't be late. You'll only get one chance at him. If he suspects a setup, you'll never get another shot." There was a brief pause. "And he'll probably kill you."

Maverick picked up the envelope, placed it in his inner jacket pocket, and again shielded his eyes from the bright light. "Why are you handing him over? What has he done to you to warrant such betrayal?"

"Zack Kinsley is a plague upon this earth and needs to be taken out," the voice in the darkness announced with a vengeful hiss in his tone. "He's poisoned the mind of someone I love and turned her against me." The light went out, and the plane was once again dark. "He claims he loves her, but I know he's not capable of loving anyone or anything. He'll eventually take her from me, and she'll wither and die like everything else he's ever touched."

"Hmm, yeah," Maverick announced and fidgeted. "That's not at all dark and sinister." He gave a half-hearted salute. "Thanks for the rendezvous."

Maverick turned and left the plane. A cell phone lit up the stranger's face to reveal a well-built man in his late twenties. The stranger in the plane, Bogart, was 'hunky actor' handsome with flowing golden-brown hair and sideburns nearly a shade darker. He placed the cell phone to his ear and waited for the call to be answered.

"Is it done?" a male voice from the other end eagerly asked.

"One down; one to go," Bogart replied into the phone with little emotion. "Operation 'Witness Protection: Midnight Requisition' is a go." Bogart disconnected the call, shut his eyes, and rested his head against the interior of the plane. "This is not going to end well."

The End

Coming Soon!
"Witness Protection 8: Midnight Requisition"

A brother and sister duo finds themselves on an explosive collision course with a team of retired Navy SEALS.

Other books by Holly Copella!
Reviews left on Amazon are appreciated!

"The Battle for Andrea Maria"

A cruise ship attack turns six survivors into overnight celebrities after they take credit for the heroic act of a stowaway who died saving them.

The cruise is just what Jess needed--a bit of harmless fun far from her daily grind. But what begins as a relaxing vacation turns into a desperate fight for her life when terrorists take over the ship and start piling up bodies. Teaming up with a mysterious stowaway, Jess attempts to send out a distress call but knows they cannot wait for help to come. If she or the few remaining passengers have any hope for survival, Jess must act now. The papers dub it "The Battle for *Andrea Maria*," but to Jess it is the moment she fought side-by-side with her enigmatic Romeo, saving the ship--and losing him. She thinks the story ends there, but really, the nightmare is just beginning...

"Insanely Deadly"

When the dead return to life, it's up to an admiral's daughter and a mildly insane, former war hero to save their small town.

Jetta Cross, a Navy Admiral's daughter, is tasked with keeping her father's comrade, a former war hero turned town crazy, grounded in the real world. Capt. John Hunter is still fighting the war in his head, where imaginary dead people are part of his world. When a viral outbreak brings about a zombie uprising, Hunter is left to his own devices. He must resume his role as a one-man commando unit in order to destroy the ravenous undead. With Hunter still fighting his own inner demons as well as the undead, the townspeople fear their zombie neighbors may not be the only threat. Stranded at the island's luxurious resort with a handful of workers, Jetta is forced to live up to her father's reputation and take charge of the deteriorating situation at the hotel. She must wage her own war against the infected before the government declares her hometown a total loss.

"Deadly Institution"

A town recluse suspected of killing his wife teams up with a young woman in order to stop a killer.

After being accused of murdering his wife, Konrad Churchill turns his back on the town that once adored him. Ten years later, he still holds his grudge and the title of the most feared man in town. With the reopening of the burned mental institution, where his wife had died, former employees are now murdered one-by-one, throwing suspicion back on Churchill. A young local reporter, Jacey, is forced to reveal her long-time friendship with the infamous recluse in order to clear his name not only in the recent murders but to exonerate him in the death of his wife as well. Will Jacey's relationship with Churchill invite the killer closer to her? Or is the killer already in her life?

"Death Displacement"

A grief-stricken man travels back in time to seek revenge on the woman who murdered his girlfriend but inadvertently falls in love with her.

Kane is about to marry the woman he loves. His life is perfect. A few weeks before the wedding, a vindictive woman from his girlfriend's past mysteriously arrives and kills her. He learns of a traumatic accident that happened five years earlier, which triggers Riley's hatred for his girlfriend. Distraught over his girlfriend's death, Kane uses an antique time machine to travel into the past in order to find and destroy the woman responsible. When he runs into Riley's younger self, he realizes she's not the monster she later becomes, and he can't bring himself to destroy her. With a little help from his oddball friend from the past, they formulate a plan to prevent the accident that sends Riley down her destructive path. Kane's plan backfires when he falls for the younger Riley. His new tortured existence is further complicated when future Riley, his girlfriend's killer, shows up with her own devious agenda that doesn't include him. Will he be able to stop the time ripple, which ultimately ends with his girlfriend's death? Or will future Riley take him out of the timeline forever--

"Dead Village"

After strange happenings isolate a small resort town from the rest of the world, nearly one hundred residents seek refuge at the closed hotel. Only eight survive the night. And that's just the beginning...

One day after the entire population of Fox Ridge Village disappears, a car wreck forces several unsuspecting crash victims to seek help at the closed summer hotel. Within the hotel, they discover the grisly aftermath of a brutal slaughter. Crash victims Vander and Devon, a reluctant clairvoyant, team up to solve the riddle of the "haunted hotel" and the mass hysteria plaguing the remaining survivors. By the time they discover the hotel's secret, they're already drawn into the hysteria. As the body count continues to climb, it's a race to isolate the source and bring everyone back to reality before they kill one another. Will Devon be able to communicate with the traumatized spirits before their fate becomes her own?

"Town Darling"

After surviving a brutal attack that claims the lives of those she loves, a young woman seeks revenge on a corrupt town.

Going back home is never easy, but for Casey, it means returning to her corrupt hometown where she barely survived a brutal attack. Accompanied by two family friends, she seeks justice for the night that destroyed her life. Her physical scars are nothing compared to her emotional ones, forcing the local sheriff to believe that the town darling is back for revenge. As the conspiracy for her revenge appears to be leading up to the coveted town fair, the sheriff is determined to stop her from fulfilling her vengeful scheme...but guilt over his role on that fateful night continues to haunt him. Will his desperate need for Casey's forgiveness be his undoing? Or will Casey's desire for revenge destroy them both?

"Basement Dwellers"

A viral outbreak at a hospital leaves a mortician, sheriff, and coroner fighting for their lives against a horde of undead and the CDC.

After a massive car wreck leaves several survivors in critical condition at the local hospital, a surgeon uses experimental drugs on his critical patients and accidentally causes a zombie outbreak. When local mortician, Lexx, receives an infected corpse as her client, she becomes stranded in the hospital basement during CDC quarantine along with the local sheriff and the coroner. The infamous surgeon struggles to find a cure for his infectious blunder by using the other survivors as test subjects. Meanwhile, Lexx and the sheriff attempt to locate his missing sister, who's stranded somewhere in the battle zone that once was the emergency room. It's a race against time and the ravenous undead. Can they survive the undead before CDC sanitizes the hospital of all infection?

"Misfits, Inc."

A seemingly ordinary, young woman meets four misfits who claim she has given them supernatural powers.

While on a business trip to a remote island paradise, a bored secretary, Hailey, has her world turned upside down when her path collides with a psychic freak, Skyler. He attempts to convince her that they had met in his dreams, and she had chosen him as one of her four mystic warriors. After Skyler foresees a woman's death, they discover an unidentified creature has killed one of the guests. They are joined by a lounge pianist and a rich playboy, who also claim they had met her in their dreams. If Skyler's prophecies are genuine, the evil entity controlling the ravenous creatures needs to destroy Hailey to ensure its survival. Reluctantly accepting her fate, Hailey has to locate the last and most powerful of her chosen warriors, The Guardian. Their fate is in doubt when The Guardian turns out to be a self-absorbed, former cat burglar with a bad attitude. Can Hailey turn her company of misfits into an elite team of mystic warriors? Or will The Guardian's secret agenda destroy them all?

"Deadly Institution 2"

When blackmail turns into murder, a young woman finds herself caught in the killer's crosshairs.

The small town of Stony Ridge is no stranger to scandal and persecution of the innocent. When a brutal killing shakes the town's prestigious country club, Jacey McMurray seeks help from a self-proclaimed vigilante, Konrad Churchill. As her professional and personal worlds collide, Jacey fears the stress of the country club killings have finally taken their toll on Churchill. Can a stressed out vigilante stop the killer before he strikes again?

"Witness Protection"
Also available in audiobook!

After witnessing an execution, a resourceful young woman attempts to disappear while being pursued by a hitman and a handsome federal agent.

A helicopter pilot, Jackie Remus, reluctantly agrees to go on a date with one of her clients, but her date is unexpectedly cut short when she witnesses a man being murdered. After narrowly escaping with her life, she is placed into protective custody. When the safe house is breached, Jackie makes a daring escape from both the hired killers and the handsome FBI agent, who wants to return her to protective custody. With a little help from her sly and crafty friend, Monroe, Jackie is convinced she can disappear until the trial. While on her journey to meet with her friend, she solicits help from a few shady but lovable characters along the way. Although she manages to stay one-step ahead of the hired killers, the federal agent remains in hot pursuit. Will Jackie reach Monroe before she's captured by the FBI and returned to protective custody? Or will the hired killers silence her first?

"Unconditional"

A young woman puts her life on hold to care for an unstable, highly skilled combat soldier, who believes someone is trying to kill him.

A botched military coup leaves a team of elite fighters injured with one clinging to life in a coma. When Harlan wakes from his coma, he's left with no memory of his past life. His commander's daughter, Indy, takes it upon herself to care for the fallen war hero. She's challenged with more than just his physical care as she combats with not only his memory loss but also his newly found desire for her. His infatuation with her becomes the least of her worries when he sinks back into his role of a combat soldier. Believing his life is in danger, his fighting skills surface, turning him into an unpredictable and dangerous man. Will his memory return to him before Indy is forced to commit him? Or will he finally find his nemesis, "the coyote", and possibly claim the life of an innocent person?

"The Pen Pal"

In order to save her friend, she must enter the mind of a serial killer.

When her best friend is abducted, no one believes Jolynn saw it in a psychic vision. With nowhere to turn, Jolynn reluctantly joins Agent Harris Slade and his team on their hunt for a sadistic serial killer known only as "The Pen Pal". Finally confronted with the killer, Jolynn realizes she must enter the mind of the psychopath in order to stop the brutal killings. But when her vision reveals a particularly disturbing death, can Jolynn sacrifice her lover for her friend?

"Witness Protection 2"
The Return of Whiskey Tango Foxtrot

Believing she holds the clue to millions in missing laundered money, a young woman is placed into the protective care of a former Navy SEAL team.

Feeling sorry for her recently separated co-worker, Leeann invites Wiley to join her and her friends on their night out. Little does she know that finding her co-worker murdered is just the beginning of her nightmare. Leeann unknowingly holds the key to fifty million dollars in potentially laundered mob money. With hired killers pursuing her, the FBI places her into a different kind of protective custody. Former Navy SEAL team Whiskey Tango Foxtrot reunites to keep Leeann alive at their secret hideaway. What should be an easy assignment takes an unscheduled turn when secrets, lies, and betrayal threaten to derail their mission. Is the team prepared for a war on their own doorstep? Will Leeann's misguided trust endanger the lives of those sent to protect her?

"Witness Protection 3"
Alpha Mike Foxtrot

A helicopter pilot risks her life to help a team of retired Navy SEALs rescue two girls from a killer.

When former Navy SEAL team Whiskey Tango Foxtrot asks for a simple favor, Jackie reluctantly offers her air taxi services. What could go wrong? What begins as a search and rescue for two girls turns into a fight for survival against a heavily armed drug cartel. Wanted by the law with the cartel in hot pursuit and their home base breached, the team is forced to call in a favor from a questionable ally. Unfortunately, their new safe house isn't what it seems. Without knowing who the real enemy is, can Jackie and the team save their young witnesses from the hands of a killer?

"Already Dead"
Supernatural Collection

From the already dead to the undead. Three supernatural tales of "things that go bump in the night".

"Bloodletting" - A vampire themed resort allows guests to *participate* in their Bloodletting Ritual to celebrate the island's legendary vampires.

"Reaper of Souls" - A young woman must outwit an evil sorcerer in order to save her brother or become one of his minions forever.

"Already Dead" - When Flight 220 crashes, ten passengers make it to an isolated island, but only one man lives to tell the lie.

"Witness Protection 4"
O-Dark-Hundred

A simple assignment turns deadly when a retired Navy SEAL team uncovers a plot to kill a notorious mob boss.

When Whiskey Tango Foxtrot embarks on a simple stalking case, they're not prepared for a trip to a private island paradise owned by an infamous mobster. With one of their own suffering from traumatic head injuries, the team is left scrambling to decide what is real or imagined. The situation escalates even further when they uncover an assassination plot where everyone is a suspect. Now targets themselves, can the team survive their trip to paradise?

"Witness Protection 5"
Outside the Wire

After suffering several casualties on their last assignment, a retired Navy SEAL team discovers their misery is just beginning.

When Whiskey Tango Foxtrot returns home after suffering a devastating loss, they're hit with even more bad news regarding the rest of their team. Their grief is cut short when they discover their names are all on the same hit list. Hunted by relentless assassins, the scattered team must decide whether to remain safely hidden or find the man who put the price on their heads. Against the wishes of her teammates, Jackie strikes out on her own in order to save a friend who wants her dead. In a kill or be killed situation, will Jackie's emotions finally betray her?

"The Murder of Emily Fisher"

After finding their favorite teacher murdered, the lives of two teenage girls are forever changed.

Everyone loved Emily Fisher. While walking home one afternoon, two teenage girls, Sidney and Trisha, stumble upon a gruesome murder scene. The brutal murder of Emily Fisher, a young, attractive schoolteacher, shocks the small town of **Marilina**. After graduation, Sidney moves far away from the memories of the small town while Trisha retreats deeper into denial. Eight years after the murder, Sidney receives a desperate call from her childhood friend, forcing her to return home. Trisha believes Emily's killer was falsely accused and she manages to turn the entire town against her while attempting to prove it. When Trisha receives a death threat, Sidney realizes there may be some credibility to her friend's wild accusations. Is Trisha's mental breakdown a result of childhood trauma? Or is the real killer actually attempting to silence her? In order to save her friend, Sidney must answer the eight-year-old question. Who murdered Emily Fisher?

"Once Upon a Disaster"

A young homicide detective finds herself at the mercy of a hitman in the aftermath of an earthquake

While investigating the murder of a hitman, Detective Jade Wesson pursues a lead connecting the dead man to a break-in at a computer programming company. She's drawn into the world of nightclub owner and front man for the mob, Cody Riley. Her investigation keeps pointing to Cody's right-hand man and possible hitman, Vahn Lott. Despite her efforts to keep her investigation on track, Vahn has plans of his own for the attractive detective. When an unprecedented earthquake rocks their east coast town, Jade must put her life in Vahn's hands if she wants to survive. Can she trust a man who might be the killer she's hunting?

"Awaken the Dead"

A grieving innkeeper struggles to keep her haunted hotel out of foreclosure.

After losing her parents in a suspicious boating accident, Harley Brandon is determined to keep the family hotel out of foreclosure. Unfortunately, the hotel ghosts have other plans. Built with tainted money, the century old Horizon Hotel thrives on a tradition of murder, scandal, and suicide. As the paranormal activity increases to alarming levels, Harley discovers the truth about the hotel and its residents. Can Harley save her friends from the hotel's frightening hidden secrets?

"Castle Bloodshed"
Murder Collection

From a deadly island paradise to haunted castles. Three novella length tales of murder, mystery, and malicious intent.

"Castle Bloodshed" – A tour of Wesley Castle turns into a fight for survival as six stranded tourists discover the haunting secrets within the castle walls. A mystery writer teams up with an uptight butler in order stop a killer who may already be dead. Novella length paranormal murder mystery.

"Fleshies" – Is Uncle Rutger crazy? Five years ago, four business partners died within their newly purchased, fixer-upper castle. Their bodies were never found. The surviving partner, Rutger, claims a demon keeps him as its slave. Rutger's nephew schemes to save his uncle by sacrificing the lives of a group of stranded motorists and a high-profile novelist. Novella length supernatural murder mystery.

"Demon Island" – A group of strangers are invited to a remote island for the reading of a will. The guests soon discover they were brought to the island to be executed one-by-one. It's up to a private detective and a tenacious young woman to solve the murders and find a way to escape paradise. Novella length murder mystery.

"Brighton Island"

When a psychic visits a haunted island mansion, he inadvertently awakens the ghosts' tortured souls.

Something's not right with Simon. When Jacklyn brings her eccentric friend to her uncle's island mansion, she didn't expect him to slip into psychic overload. As Simon attempts to solve a decade-old, double homicide, Jacklyn is confronted with the possibility that she could be next to join the mansion ghosts. When they find themselves stranded on the secluded island, her Uncle Hyland wages his own war to save them from a flesh and blood killer. Will her uncle's "shock and awe" military tactics save them or get them killed? Can Simon bring peace to the tortured souls or unexpectedly join them?

"A.L.F. Resort"

A fantasy vacation turns into a nightmare when the resort's artificial life forms are compromised.

Welcome to A.L.F. Resort where you can live out your fantasies with safe, state-of-the-art artificial life form robots! When a young journalist and a photographer are sent to A.L.F. Resort to do a story for their magazine, Shay and Becka believe they've hit the jackpot of all work-cations. The engineers pull out all the stops to make their fantasies memorable. Unfortunately, the newly designed A.L.F., the Gen X, is smarter than his programming and creates havoc within Shay's fantasy. A computer malfunction removes their safety inhibitors and the A.L.F.s play out their own hostile fantasies. Zombies, bikers, and mobsters run amuck, turning fantasies into nightmares. Shay gets more of a story than she anticipates, but will she survive long enough to write it?

"Jungle Princess"

While stranded on a prison island, a young woman discovers a creature of "unknown" origin.

After their cruise ship sinks, Alex and two of her shipmates are stranded on a deserted, tropical island. Unfortunately, the castaways soon realize they're not alone. They discover an abandoned prison with over two dozen inmates living on the island's south side. While avoiding the prison on the far side of the island, Alex discovers a strange but loveable creature of unknown origin. When one of her fellow castaways is in trouble, Alex reluctantly seeks help from the prisoners. After the brutal murder of several inmates, their questions surrounding the abandoned prison are about to be answered. What really killed over one hundred prisoners? And is it still out there?

"Murder in Wax"

A series of brutal murders plague a quiet farming community when beautiful women audition for the same acting job.

While all the young women in town are fighting over a once-in-a-lifetime acting opportunity, Devon Vincent is excited about her new job at the local wax museum. Although supportive of her friend's acting aspirations, Devon has a hard time understanding the rivalry among the women in town. When the aspiring actresses are brutally murdered one-by-one, Devon fears her friend may be the next victim. Devon finds herself in the middle of a murderous revenge plot that leads back to the wax museum's doorstep and possibly implicates her boss as the killer. Will Devon's newly found feelings for her boss bring a killer closer to her? Or is the killer already in her circle?

"Witness Protection 6"
Alpha Dogs

An easy rescue turns into a wild ride for retired Navy SEAL team Whiskey Tango Foxtrot when everyone wants to kill their client.

It was a simple task. Rescue a young woman from her mob boss father-in-law. Little did Jackie and company realize that rescuing the young woman was the easy part. Keeping her alive would be a massive undertaking, especially when everyone wants a piece of the mafia heiress. The team fights for survival against their toughest adversaries yet. How many innocent people must die in order to save one woman? Can the team survive the ultimate battle between mercenaries and assassins?

"Midnight Requisition"

A series of brutal murders leaves a traumatized young woman on a hunt to find a killer.

When they were just babies, Scorpio and her twin brother, Kane, tragically lost their parents under mysterious circumstances. Refusing to accept his father was dead, Kane set off on a mission to find a man he'd never met. A home invasion gone wrong leaves Scorpio grieving the loss of those she loves. Out of the tragedy of her loss, two fallen heroes are thrust upon her. Scorpio soon realizes someone wants her dead and the killer may already be in her circle. As her entire life unravels in a web of betrayal and lies, can Scorpio trust her new, slightly questionable friends?

"Until Death"

Liars, cheaters, blackmail and murder. It would be a wedding no one would forget.

Despite knowing he's making the biggest mistake of his life, Raina Steele reluctantly attends her father's third wedding. What should have been a boring reception turns into a web of lies, betrayal, and murder. With no one above suspicion, Raina must put aside her feud with the arrogant yet insanely handsome butler in order to catch the killer before he finds his next victim. With a murderer waiting to strike and lives hanging in the balance, the real question remains...the bride is wearing white? Seriously?

"Tainted"

What happens at the Dark Forest Hotel, stays at the Dark Forest Hotel...for all eternity.

What secrets surround Dark Forest Hotel? After her parents die under mysterious circumstances, sixteen-year-old Jeri escapes foster care and seeks refuge at a "closed for the season" hotel. Over the next six years, Jeri graduates from teenage runaway to the hotel's assistant general manager. When she learns a convention is secretly held every year in her absence, she demands answers from her boss, friends, and co-workers. After getting conflicting stories, Jeri sets out to discover the truth. She's suddenly thrown into a horrifying new world where vampires and vicious creatures are craving her virgin blood. After six years of everyone lying to her, is there anyone she can trust?

"Witness Protection 7"
Bravo Foxtrot

An Army deserter on the run brings mayhem to a retired Navy SEAL team when his teenage daughter is caught in a mercenary's cross-hairs.

A weekend of fun turns into a race for survival as Monique and Colleen's surrogate big brother, Bogart, rescues the girls from mercenaries hunting Colleen's Army deserter father. With the girls safely stashed at their Colorado hideaway, trouble brews when the team discovers Colleen's father was framed by his former commander over a stolen, high-tech weapon. In order to clear Colleen's father and bring him home, the team must fight one of their toughest advisories yet...a high-ranking military officer with countless mercenaries and the U.S. military behind him.

Coming Soon!
"Witness Protection 8"
Midnight Requisition

ABOUT THE AUTHOR

Holly Copella has been writing since the age of twelve when her frustration at a book's poor plot drove her to author her own story. Over the last decade, she's written a number of screenplays, some of which she's now adapting into novels. Her fascination with zombies and other darker material lends an edge to her writing, which tends to lean toward horror. As a fan of Agatha Christie, she appreciates the craft of a good plot and the importance of creating significant characters.

Hailing from Pennsylvania, Copella lives in the Endless Mountains on a farm with her rescue horses and other animals. In addition to writing and reading fiction, she enjoys riding horses and traveling to Las Vegas and Disney World.